THE PAPER PALACE

THE
PAPER PALACE

A NOVEL

ROBERT HARLING

If you cun heare a Good Organ at Church, and have the musique of a domestique peace at home, peace in thy walls, peace in thy bosome, never hearken after the musique of sphears, never hunt after the knowledge of higher secrets, than appertaine to thee.

DONNE: Sermons

THE REPRINT SOCIETY LONDON

FIRST PUBLISHED 1951
THIS EDITION PUBLISHED BY THE REPRINT SOCIETY LTD
BY ARRANGEMENT WITH CHATTO AND WINDUS
1952

PRINTED IN ENGLAND BY
HAZELL WATSON AND VINEY LTD
AYLESBURY AND LONDON

THE PAPER PALACE

I

FOR once I need to put down a few thoughts that will not go into a newspaper column, and that is a hard fact to face, especially for a man in this outfit. You get into the habit of seeing the words you write in reassuring linotype inside a week, but this isn't that kind of story. This is an older story, as old as Genesis. Maybe it could even start in the old way, and that, as I remember, was *Once upon a time* . . .

So once upon a time, and that was sometime more than two years ago and that makes it nearly three o'clock on a mid-March Wednesday afternoon, I was sitting in that pigeon coop and the house phone went and I picked up the receiver and the voice said 'Come on in!' and I went on in, down two flights, down to the fifth floor and into the big room and there was the editor, standing by his desk, looking down at a proof, and he waved his hand loosely and forlornly as if he'd already forgotten why he'd rung and perhaps even why he waved his hand, but I'd had all that before and I sat.

I sat watching him and he looked the way I'd always seen him look in ten long years: a tall, fleshy man, not old, not young, in a grey worsted suit from Lesley and Roberts that still couldn't hide a weighty paunch, and there he was, brooding over a proof with his eyes half closed, and, looking at him, you would nod your head in a knowing way and you would say to your inward and complacent soul, *a successful bonehead running to seed*, and all the signs would bear you out and forgive you for this slip, and, still protesting, you could point to the bags under his eyes, the bags under his chins and the bag that was his belly and you would still be wrong, as wrong as you'd been about Hitler, the Russians, or last week's football pool, for here he was, the smoothest editor among a lot of editors and he had been that way for fifteen long unwholesome years and the distant newspaper scene was as bare of rivals as a rabbi is bare of rosaries.

That was the editor and that was David Wensley and I sat watching him as I had watched him ten thousand times before, in this office, in pubs, in clubs, in cars, in trains, and always I watched to see the limp arm grow taut, in anger or in doubt, in resolution or in fear, in sickness or in strength, but never, not in this world. The arm had been born with the man, just that way, and you became part of its limping parabola as the arm waved you into a chair and you flopped into the chair and waited, mute and lackadaisical, and then he looked up from a sprawling page proof just down from the stone or a curling photograph fresh from the hypo, and he began to question, and his words were as limp as his arms, seeming to move from his mouth and hover in the air like insubstantial bubbles, but I always watched, trying to catch the moment when the bubbles became the red-hot cantankerous cinders his words could be, and I watched him again as he said, 'How's *Objects and Subjects?*'

'Today or every day?'

'Today, of course.'

'Not bad. Two pars done. Four to do.'

'Writing one on Waterman?'

'Which Waterman? The pen or the Red?'

'The Red, of course. He's dead. Haven't you been to the Foreign Room yet?'

'Not yet,' I said.

'I've told you before,' he said casually, O, so casually, like a surgeon taking off a wart, 'you ought to go there first, but have it your own way. It's your feature. Here's the cable.' His hand lazily stirred his own copies of the cables in a dark green metal tray and he pushed it across and I read: FLASH BELGRADE GEORGE WESTON WATERMAN KILLED JEEP ACCIDENT NEAR ZAGREB STOP UNDERSTAND WATERMAN INSPECTING POSTWAR HIGHWAY RECONSTRUCTION ON TITO INVITATION STOP UPCHECKING FILING NITELEAD PAXTON.

'Is he really worth a piece?' I asked.

'Not to you maybe, but he is to the Baron.'

'That means to me, then.'

'I'd say so.'

'He was an odd bird,' I said, 'I only saw him about half a dozen times. How'd the Baron come to know him?'

'God knows,' Wensley said. 'Who doesn't that old bastard know? They were about the same age.'

'It's an odder friendship than most, all the same.'

'You know he specializes in 'em. They'd both be about sixty-six or seven. At least one is, one was.'

'Did you know him?' I asked.

'I was a Red myself once,' Wensley said, and he smiled his antediluvian smile. 'I even sat at the feet of Waterman and he was a phoney old prophet if you like. Being a Red's a state of mind young men can't avoid. At least not before they start making some money.'

'Didn't Waterman ever start making any?' I asked.

'He never had to. Mum had her share of the stuff and she saw Georgie never went short. Or maybe he saw.'

'How come he was a Red, then?'

'It's been the romantic thing to be for a century now. It was certainly the romantic thing to be in my young days.'

Wensley was talking like old Father Time himself, and

I remembered he would be forty-three and four years older than myself, but four years can make quite a difference as any woman that much older than an erring spouse would doubtless confirm, but he was going on: 'Some people are made that way, anyway. A young upstanding Tory's the romantic thing to be now, especially with any blue blood in your veins. Thank God my youth had gone by the age of three and my blood was always the colour of Scotch.'

I could vouch for that, I thought, for if Wensley had been gathered to his fathers in that very instant and the relatives, torchbearers and gravediggers had all trooped in and hung around for a sweet and resonant requiem they could have put an empty whisky bottle on the pall, scratched R.I.P. on the coffin and wished him well and justice done; but Wensley was talking and my rich imaginative powers were plainly being wasted on this doleful picture. He was pushing the cable back at me and telling me to take it away. 'I should wander up to the library and dig out a piece on Waterman the late lamented Red,' he said, and his words were as soft and cold as snowflakes. 'It's your feature. Waterman was a pretty colourless bird as I remember him and I don't see how you'll manage to squeeze him into your colourful column,' and he smiled a tired smile and I knew the interview was at an end and I went out and along the corridors, past the frosted glass doors of the cubicles and the plate-glass windows of the newsroom and into the library and called for the Waterman file.

A girl brought me the envelope and I went in through the wicket-gate and sat down at one of the tables set around for seekers after truth like myself. I pulled out the cuttings which made the life of George Weston Waterman as far as this office was concerned and it seemed quite a sheaf that the Lord had reaped.

I began to read and it was odd reading, for it was plain that Waterman had gone through life up to his eyelids in politics, culture and headlines, and yet he had never made a flat-out, two-deck headline for himself. I turned over the cuttings and in one he was tub-thumping somewhere in Dockland in the '26 General Strike, in another he was being hauled off by two coppers good and true, in another he had just published a book. He had made speeches, he had written articles, he had even got himself gaoled twice for having contrariwise opinions, he had been publicly nasty to Churchill in the recent war, he had fallen foul of M.I. 5, and inquisitive Members had asked a lot of questions about him in the House.

George had certainly been quite a handful, but he had never been a household name. No fat skivvy had ever got worked up over his gaoling or his speeches. No buffeting band of Union members had ever marched down Cornmarket pulling George in a handcart. Yet he'd been well enough known in that select and starchy circle of English middle-class revolutionaries. In fact he had been a leader, a bright Red light, as I could see as I went on reading.

There were photographs, too, and the latest was much as I remembered him: a thin-lipped, thin-faced, thin-haired old boy with a close-cropped moustache and big and anxious eyes looming out of horn-rimmed spectacles. He looked more like a Church Army major set to do the Liverpool slums than a revolutionary in London Town, but maybe no revolutionary ever looks like one. Christ probably looked like a tinker and Horner certainly looks like a tailor, but according to my researches, which may not have been strictly academic, no revolutionary ever seems to have looked like a revolutionary, and that must remain my modest contribution to a subject which has occupied the attention of the sages and the soothsayers from the time of the T'angs to the time of Mao himself.

I gave a quarter of an hour to the subject of G. W. Waterman, deceased, and by that time I knew I had enough of him for my paragraph, and I knew, too, that the paragraph would start no Hyde Park riots and bloodshed, for, however I looked at him, I could see only a mild old man with a bonnet full of bees who had got himself mixed up in pink-red politics at a young and impressionable age and had stayed that way until he was sixty-six, and I had just arrived at that charitable view when the phone on the librarian's desk rang out and the assistant answered, and the library was a room in Court House again and not a morgue, and then the girl was standing by the table, and she said, 'The editor says will you go to his room right away, please?'

So I left her with the envelope and the cuttings and went out, back to the editor's room, and there he was, sitting in his swing chair with one of his elegant grey trouser legs on the top of the double mahogany desk, and he was looking at the shining half-brogue that came from Peals and was worth looking at, and he said as lazily as one of those pneumonic crooners, 'It's about Waterman again. I had a suspicion that bastard would haunt us. And I'm right.'

I sat silent, for I didn't like Wensley's use of that word *us* and I wasn't keen that Waterman should haunt me, too, but Wensley was going on: 'Now the Baron's joined in. He wants to give us his thoughts on Waterman. *For what they're worth*, he said, and I said yessir. D'you think I said right?'

'It seems the right sort of soft answer to me,' I said.

'You're smiling too soon,' Wensley said. 'Now it's your turn for soft answers. He wants you up in the house in the park to take over the obit he's done—for what it's worth.'

'Can't we send a reporter?'

'He doesn't want a reporter. He wants it in your column. He's got a few thoughts, he says. You've done it before.'

'Yes, but it was women then. Actresses, cuties, debs. I don't see Waterman under that head.'

'Well, you'll soon find out. You'd better move fast if your feature's not to be late. He may want to talk. You know what he is?'

So I climbed those two flights back to my floor and my room, and plump Miss Arnold was sitting there at her typewriter waiting to type my hack-typed copy and she was red-faced and smiling and that meant she had got her slice of lemon meringue pie at Fuller's in the Strand and I said, 'I'm off to the Baron. He wants to do the column today. Keep the wolves at bay,' and I took my hat and coat and went out and along the corridor to the lifts.

2

DOWN by the lift from the seventh floor, out through the great swing doors and along the courtway towards Fleet Street, and I looked back as I always looked back and there was the building the Baron built: twelve storeys of lavatory brick, vitaglass and tarnished steel.

There it is, Court House, half-shut away up an alley, and maybe the Baron was using his usual common sense in building that way and just there, for all his minions must come in from Fleet Street and walk through the court, and before they have paced out ten tired steps the world is a different world: the gears of the buses might be made of baby wool for all you can hear them, and the stench of oil is lost in the general and genial smell of the world.

And those many minions are doubtless soothed and smoothed by the sight of the miniature fountain and the strip of green garden before them and the three old Georgian houses on the right that the Baron let stay when he built his paper palace. A lexical friend of Doctor Johnson's lived in one, the consulting architect had said, and apparently that made the three of them historical. The Baron was all in favour of history then, for history hadn't quite caught up with him and made a sick man out of him, so he let the houses be and there they are, and meantime, anytime, his minions can view them, for every time they come in from Fleet Street they must spy these rare and historical treasures.

That will be in the first ten steps, but they still have another thirty steps to go before they turn left and in through the great glass doors and across to one of the three lifts and up to one of the twelve floors to the vast-gutted general offices or the eight-by-six pigeon coops. Unless they are editors or advertisement directors, of course, and then they will have rooms to themselves, with one mahogany desk, one Persian rug, one leather armchair, one leather settee, three mahogany chairs and a framed portrait of the Baron, and they can walk to their windows and look down on the court, or, if their luck is the luck of the gods, eastward above the roofs to the dome of St. Paul's or westward across the roofs to the Record Office in Fetter Lane, but they'll still be minions even in rooms of their own.

So there is Court House with twelve full floors of

smooth brick and smoother glass, and the minions are smoothed and soothed and they are back in their offices and they turn to the copy to be typed or the decision to be made and perhaps they are glad to be back in Court House, the palace the Baron built out of pristine Newfoundland newsprint.

Yet not only newsprint, for there was his gift of the gab, and that was a talent lively enough to fill a thousand Albert Halls and cunning enough to keep two million housewives as happy as if they had seen the murder or they had fought the rape the Baron gave them every morning for breakfast, but his gift was not only lively and cunning; his gift was sporting, too. How else could he have got the other million or more, all the sportsmen, all anxious to be reading the back page, the sporting news, all about the football they never played and the horse races they never rode?

There is no other way: only the Baron's way. Unless you want a paper that's stuffed with dust, with a main news page looking like a Lectern Bible, a paper that some stuffed and dusty don at work on a thesis in 1999 will call a brother to *The Thunderer*, but the shekels won't thunder into your coffers today, and that is the sort of thunder the Baron likes or liked, for now he is not so lively or cunning or sporting, but his minions are: they learned the trick and the trick is a sure and certain one. It works.

So there is Court House and the Baron built it.

He built it in the rich and ranting days of the 'thirties when the money came in faster than it went out and that had to be very fast, for the money was going out all the time: we were buying new readers. The new readers were getting wringers and saucepans, life insurance and death insurance, just for reading or promising to read the

Baron's penny newspapers. O, those slaphappy days when you could die in peace in a railway smash, comforted to death as the broken window sliced through your gullet or the hat rack went through your eyes, for there was the Baron, or at least one of the Baron's solicitors, ready and waiting with ten thousand jimmy o' goblins for your widow and your brood, and there were the headlines, too, *Another £10,000 Claim Paid in Tonypandy Rail Crash*, and photographs of the widow and her brood smiling bravely into the camera, and the cheque resting gently on the left knee of the widow's crossed legs if she happened to be under thirty and the brood not too broody or too far gone with rickets.

And all for why?

I suppose someone somewhere had said in a conference, 'We must sell more copies!' and had then sat back as if he'd spoken the formula that would split the atom, and then some other superman had piped up with the notion that anything less than two million was just chicken-feed and advertisers wanted more for their money; look what the *Express* and the *Mirror* were getting away with and why weren't we? and there would be murmurs of approval and looks towards the chairman and then more talk until the conference broke up with a lot of hand-shaking and back-slapping and in no time there would be more free gifts and more bought readers. Thousands of them. Hundreds of thousands.

And down below, down on the first and second floors, those plump pigeons, those wonder boys of advertising, sitting at their leather-topped desks, would soon be phoning their cronies in the agencies up West, saying, 'Just heard, old boy, a new ten-inch double semi-solus on the main news page Bank Holiday. Only two hundred and seventy-five. A real snip. Thought I'd let you in on it!'

and so the chain went on, and because it pays to advertise, and all good goods are advertised goods, the bosses of the lot of them, the bosses of the world, the steel-witted kings of commerce, doubtless sitting in the middle of model garden factories on the Great West Road, the Great North Road or the Greater Road to Erewhon, would press more buttons, ring more phones and off the conveyor belts would come more razor blades, more bars of soap, more bowel-openers, tin-openers and mouse-traps, and for a stamped addressed envelope and fourpence in stamps you could get by return a free sample of custard powder, face powder or flea powder or your first free lesson in the one and only course to get rich quicker or go bald slower.

And everybody was happy: the Baron was happy, the advertisers were happy, the readers were happy, and the editors maybe. Especially on Sundays, for on Sundays there were more papers with more money and you didn't have to die to be amongst the lucky sabbatarians. If death on the railroad hadn't proved too attractive in the week and you were wishful for a modicum of mental exercise on Sundays, you could even live and be a rich man. Or near enough.

There were the crosswords with 2 *across* a word of three letters defining *something indispensable to the happy home* and there it was CAT or COT, and 13 *down* a word of four letters *an element in ancient playacting* and RIME it could be or MIME it could be and the Sunday joint could be getting a cold flat slab before you had put aside your gnawed-down pencil and your dream of two thousand quid in two weeks' time and tottered in to dinner.

Or there was the snaring acrostic, evolved by a staff man with a genius for madness, a citizen who could make the word you first thought of read backwards, forwards

and sideways and still be ten other words you hadn't
thought of in your hunt for an easy thousand.

Or there were the fashion photographs to give you another thousand if you could decide with your unique and
fashionable eye whether Aunt Mabel or Cousin Flo would
look more regal in a mink or sable stole and both looking
like dyed skunk before the rotaries down in the depths
had run off ten thousand copies.

Then came the war that would never come because the
Baron said it mustn't come, and things began to change.
Then came the peace that soon began to taste like ashes.
And the changes still went on.

A paper changes, too, and never faster than the price of
newsprint and the cost of dollars. So the good old high
days and jolly days with twenty-four pages on weekdays
and thirty-two on Sundays are gone with impregnable
sterling, and now we scrape along on a four-pager and
sometimes the six- that will give the advertisers a break
and the reader the smell of the old days when his paper
would take him all the way from Surbiton or Rickmans-
worth to Waterloo or Marylebone and still leave him the
crossword for the evening's return to the little grey home.
And that isn't all that's changed, and the changes didn't
come with the war and the twilight of sterling. They come
every morning with the stillness in the machine-room as
the rotaries run down and the three-millionth copy has
gone away and the final, latest, last and four-starred London edition has gone down the chutes into the vans and
on to the wholesaler, and today's paper is already yesterday's and tomorrow's is today's.

The changes are there all right. I can write of the Baron,
but even he has gone, and there you have it, the Baron

and yesterday's newspapers, they are both in the dustbin, crumpled, smudged and taken away.

But the day the Waterman story broke and I went up to see the Baron, he hadn't gone and maybe he'll never go. In a way he saw to that: he found his minions; he trained them; the minions learned his tricks and the building was built in his image, and now the place reeks of the tricks and the image in the way a doxy reeks of the ruin of her quondam self, and it will never lose its toxic smell until all the minions die or are driven out, and that's not likely, at least not in my time.

3

I HAD been to the Baron's before, as who hadn't? For it had been his lively social habit to give lunch parties, dinner parties, midnight parties, and any other sort of party and mix up his crowds a bit. He seemed to get a kick out of seeing a Minister of Defence ensconced with a so-called spinster with very few defences of any kind, an Anglican bishop hobnobbing with a sleek Latin numero who ran the sort of night club the bishop wouldn't dare preach about. I could see his point there. I had been engrossed myself. There was no other house where you might find yourself involved with a fan dancer on one side and a filibuster of high finance on the other, and that sort of meeting was made for my column.

And I had been solo to the house on those frequent occasions when the Baron was back from examining Ceylon or advising Australia and he had taken a look at the paper and my column in particular and had decided that I needed a refresher course in the mysteries of the craft, to be told again how to seize the attention and hold the interest ('I repeat,' he would rasp, 'you *seize* by many means but you *hold* by interest') and what was to be seized was the attention of those extra million morons who were still outside the magic circle of the paper, and I had listened, as who wouldn't listen to a millionaire giving you the secrets of his millions? And I had gone on listening, as who wouldn't go on listening, to a teacher who paid you nearly enough, plus expenses, just for being taught?

So I got the taxi and gave the address and sat back and wondered what was ahead: a lecture on the art of revolution or some secret dissipation of Waterman's youth, but I gave up wondering and closed my eyes and waited for the lesson to begin, for whatever else it was going to be it would be a lesson.

And then I was at the door and paying off the taximan and turned around to the great fluted pillars that Nash had sponsored over a hundred years before, and I thought that even Nash in his maddest moments couldn't have selected a worthier inhabitant for one of his stucco palaces than the Baron himself, and I stood within the shelter of the vast portico and waited and then the front door opened into a chequered marbled hall and there was the butler and beyond him the great staircase, and it was all like something someone had designed for a Covent Garden ballet, and in a minute Fonteyn would come lilting down the staircase with Helpmann after her, but not this time, for I was trailing up the staircase, after the butler, and I was following him into the library and there was the Baron at a mahogany desk, but his was the size of a squash court and the hand-tooled leather top would have kept a showgirl in handbags for a year. The library was a large and luxurious room with pilastered bookcases up to the ceiling and pile carpets as soft as marshmallows from wall to wall. There was a fire in the marble fireplace, but the room was as chill and still as dawn across the marshes.

The Baron got up from the desk as I was announced, shook me by the hand and gave me an armchair by the fire. At first I was too busy struggling to keep afloat in the oversize chair to give him much of my attention, but finally I thought I had a position I could more or less keep, and I sat up and looked him over to see how he'd changed under the antipodean sun he'd been favouring during the recent English winter.

He was a tall man, something over six feet, with a big, bald head that diminished his height and made him almost top-heavy, yet he always seemed well-balanced, but only in the way a spinning-top is well-balanced about half-way through its act, and sometimes he looked as if he might be beyond the half-way mark and might topple over, but maybe that was because he was wide-shouldered and wore double-breasted dark suits with narrow trousers and that seemed to make him taper off down to his black and shining shoes. He certainly gave no signs of toppling over that day. He looked too full of sun and proteins and vitamins for my state of health, and I sat on that part of the chair I had managed to make my own and tried to look as calm and cool and collected as the average columnist should look in the presence of the average millionaire.

His face was like a mask a native sculptor in a hurry might have hacked out of some African hardwood, and you might spend all day looking for signs of grace and sensitivity in the mask and, finally, around seven o'clock in the evening, you might decide that the long thin line of the lips did sometimes turn up instead of staying down, or maybe it was the coming dusk, but even as you rested in your indecision the long thin line would take a dip and you'd feel the way a Christian in the Colosseum must have felt with the lion padding steadily in his or her direction across the wide arena. It was a hard brown face, like timber that had made a long passage in an antique freighter and had taken a lot of punishment down in the hold. First there was the high chunky forehead tanned to the top of the rounded cranium; then came the brow like a knot above a nose that curved out from the face like a lesser knot and then the lips that were less like lips than a line slit in the wood. Finally, the chin, cleft and jagged and out-thrust over a dewlap the size of a poacher's pocket.

All these homely features were set above a white stiff collar, a wine-red tie and a dark blue suit cut by a master.

And there were still the eyes and I could never tell whether they were blue-grey or grey-blue, but what I did know was that as a colour it was first cousin to stainless Sheffield steel and no colour for Father Christmas or any other legendary character raised to make the world a cosy and familiar crib.

Maybe these details add up to a forbidding and paralysing creature, and it was true I wouldn't have entered him in any *New Statesman* competition on *Millionaires I have Known and Loved*, yet in some odd way, despite these freezing physical qualities, he had an uncanny talent for making anyone talk.

He would sit at the head of a supper table and in less time than it takes to eat an olive he would have an admiral explaining the secrets of a battleship or a bookmaker showing how he couldn't lose. He encouraged argument, he lived for words. He would listen for long minutes to a lisping child and he could prate a politician under the table. Nothing mattered so long as words were in movement and more movement meant more argument and that was what he wanted, and the more pointed and personal the argument the better for the Baron.

He picked up a sheet of paper from his desk and came across to an armchair opposite the one I had. He sat down as if he knew the knack of sitting on these leather balloons and his bulk probably helped. Anyway, he looked comfortable, which was more than I felt.

'I'm glad you were able to come,' he said, in his file-edged voice, and I smiled inwardly at the memory of my speed at being able. 'I knew Waterman. He was a remarkable man in many ways and although he stood for all the things I most detest I thought I'd like to have a note about him in tomorrow's paper. Were you proposing to mention him?'

'Wensley thought it would be a sound idea, sir.'

The Baron nodded. 'Do you know anything about him? Did you ever meet him?'

'I saw him once or twice long ago and I've spent the last half-hour in the library with his file.'

'That would tell you something but not very much. I always think Waterman was remarkable for what he could have been rather than for what he was.'

'Maybe he chose the wrong country for his theories,' I said, and the Baron nodded.

'Possibly,' he said. 'He also chose the wrong class to be born into.'

'But that same class gave him the money and the leisure for his theories.'

'I don't think those things bothered Waterman,' the Baron went on in his harsh, musing voice, 'he had an absolute contempt for money.'

'I've noticed that in many characters who don't have to worry much about the stuff,' I said.

'Perhaps you're right. Do you bother much about the stuff?'

Here comes the personal touch, I thought, *and it's pretty quick today*, but I didn't have to think very long for my answer because I knew the answer twelve times every year, and I said, 'I don't bother overmuch, sir. Now and then it begins to bother me towards the end of the month.'

'Don't I pay you enough, then?'

'You pay me enough, sir, but it seems I don't pay my ex-wife enough, and that's scarcely your responsibility.'

'Can't you find her a job?'

'She doesn't like work.'

'Can't you find her a husband?'

'She was pretty good at that herself, I was number two.'

'Why hasn't she got one now?'

'Word gets around,' I said.

'Why did you marry her?'

'It's an indelicate story, sir.'

He laughed shortly. 'Perhaps that sort of thing helps to make a writer. I don't know. Let's get back to Waterman.'

Let's get back! I thought, *and who the hell took us away?* So we went back to Waterman and we got back by way of an autobiographical fragment, for the Baron said quietly, 'I first saw something of Waterman during the Irish troubles. I was a reporter then and he had gone over to the Irish side. He showed himself a clever soldier and a good leader and a man of some courage. All those things were forgotten later, or rather they never seemed to become known and he never seemed anxious to have them known. Had you heard about them?'

I shook my head.

'Yet you studied history?' he said.

There was nothing wrong with the Baron's memory, I thought. The old vulture studied the lie of the land and then struck when he thought the body was still, but I wasn't quite still and I said that wasn't my sort of history, but he wasn't to be side-tracked. 'You can't divide history up into sections,' he said, 'much as some people would like to.'

'Most students of history can,' I said, 'otherwise not many would be reading for degrees.'

'Perhaps that would be an advantage,' he said grimly. 'The more who read history the fewer make it.'

'Those who think they make it don't seem to have been so very successful, sir, these last few years, do they?' I said amiably, and my *sir* was particularly amiable.

'They've made it: isn't that enough?'

Not quite, I thought, but I wasn't able to compete with that sort of philosophy, and once again we seemed to have come a long way from Waterman, but if the Baron wanted an afternoon of quiet historical hair-splitting, who was I to protest?

But the Baron had decided to get back to Waterman again, and he handed me the sheet of notepaper he had taken from the table. 'I've put down a few thoughts on Waterman, and you might see what use you can make of them. Knock them about as you wish, of course. It's your feature, and I've no wish to interfere.'

So it was my feature. Wensley told me so and now the Baron told me so, and I held in my hand a sheet of paper with a Waterman story that would certainly have had no place in any feature that was mine, and I looked down at the sheet and read the Baron's scrawl. DEATH OF A REVOLU-TIONARY it was headed, and underneath: *Yesterday in Yugoslavia one of England's strangest characters was killed. George Weston Waterman was a dilettante by instinct and revolutionary by conviction. He was the type of revolutionary who can thrive only in Britain: he never seemed to find his wealth and his theories in conflict. In his early days he called himself a man of action and a ruthless enemy of Conservative politics, but after the General Strike of 1926 little was heard of him. He spent much time abroad. During the recent war he was detained for several months in Wandsworth Prison, but after his release he went to live quietly with his mother in Surrey, occasionally travelling abroad. To those who knew him he will remain an enigmatic and controversial figure. He was a man of great integrity and charm. He seemed at one time to be destined to become an outstanding leader of the Left in this country: why his influence faded will always remain a mystery.*

I folded the paper and put it in my pocket.

'Well?' said the Baron. He had got up from the arm-chair. 'He seems to have been an odd bird,' I said. 'He didn't look the ruthless type in the photographs I was looking at in the library.'

'He was the most cold-blooded bastard I ever met,' the Baron said, and the words came through his teeth like an epitaph for a snake and there was a chill in the room like a nip off the ice-cap.

I looked up, and it was plain that the Baron had forgotten me, for he was staring into the fire, and something in the fire wasn't coal but something a long way off in time or space or any other word that Einstein could think of, and then he turned to me. 'You'll gather I didn't like him,' he said. 'I didn't. Anyway, see what you can make of my notes.'

So I struggled up from my chair, had my hand shaken and wandered out and down the great curving staircase, and in the hall was the butler, as big and silent as a turn-key in a tomb, and I took my coat and two minutes later I was out in the park and walking fast towards Clarence Gate, for it was a taxi I was needing to make the edition with six bright pars for *Objects and Subjects*, and one of the subjects would certainly be George Weston Waterman.

And as I walked towards Clarence Gate and Baker Street, and the hope of a taxi, I wondered how Waterman and the Baron had first met and how they had first managed to get across each other and who had won, and it was easy enough to see how they were predestined to get across each other. A lion and a sheep might more easily set up house together in the London Zoo than those two birds ever make their peace. At least, to judge from their published words and manifold deeds.

As I saw it, a chase for power had probably brought them together, but I was wrong in that as it turned out, and, as I saw it again, their chase for power had put them apart and maybe I was not so wrong in that. Even now, with the words beginning to fall into the making of a pattern, no man can be certain, but I was as right as a ready-reckoner about that word POWER.

They might use other words for it, words writ large in flowering script, and their private and particular synonyms and antonyms might have had old H. W. Fowler and his brother guessing for ten short minutes but not much longer, for what other word meant palaces of newsprint for the Baron, a villa in the park, two Rolls in the garage, a valley in Wiltshire, a mountain in Scotland, a vineyard in France, and words that were pap for millions of morons? And for Waterman, what other word was right for the words that were meant for the few, the ice-cold, rock-willed, intellectual few? For him that word meant many words, all pouring out and hate flowing in, and if all went well the chosen few would be masters of the world and mowing down the many, the snob-ridden aristos, the mighty tycoons and their bourgeois friends, and the few, the incorruptible comrades, could run the revolution of the masses by the masses for the masses.

The word as I saw it was just simple old-fashioned POWER.

In between might be quite a herd who could grab their little gobs of it and yet get along. But not those two.

A fat publican sits on a Council in a cold grey town and power for him is signing chits that build a new wash-house, and power for another in the same grey town is running down a touchline and putting in a shot that will bring home the Cup, and power for another is a notebook full of women, all sizes, shapes and colours, and all hanging on the phone for a promise from him, the town's phallic wonder-boy, and no lines get crossed, and the lovers of power, the councillor, the footballer, the treble-crossing womanizer, and a thousand others with a taste for power are all there, in amity, peace and understanding.

But not the Baron and not Waterman.

The world is too narrow for them and the few like them, and life too short. They would get across each other, in life and in death, even though the Baron might sit at his leather-topped desk and dream vast dreams of still bigger empires made of still bigger sheets of still thinner newsprint, and Waterman might lie in his cold Slav grave and his empire had lived and died in his one mind like a floundering bat in a high lone tower.

They would still get across each other in all the world's long life.

4

I HAD my copy in galley and corrected half an hour before my deadline, so I went across to El Vino's and sat with the *Evening Standard* as a superficial companion and looked to see whether they had the Waterman story, and there he was, a news item half-way down the front page under *Socialist Writer Killed* and in the *Londoner's Diary* under the crosshead of *Rich Rebel*, with a few lines about his early days as a tub-thumping Red, his later career as a pamphleteer, and an estimate of his mother's income, and the diarists, true to form, had worked that out as somewhere between fifteen and twenty thousand a year, which doubtless satisfied their love for other people's incomes and suggested to me that anyone could be a revolutionary with mum as well set up as all that.

I wandered slowly back after the beneficent six o'clock Martini, but the mood didn't last, for Miss Arnold said the editor wanted me again. 'Waterman!' I said, and I should have wagered on it. I went down to the big room, and the leader page was down there, too, and Wensley was going through it with his 8B lead and going through the leader-writer with a few unholy words a good deal softer than 8B lead, a good deal blacker, too, and the leader-writer stood there, his usual, shivering, sycophantic self, a round-shouldered scholarly stooge who should have stayed in the schoolroom and not strayed into Fleet Street, but all that scholarship and all that iron in his minuscule soul had helped to make him a good and bitter leader-writer, so he stayed on in Fleet Street, and there he stood, with a dirty grey cardigan hanging from his shoulders like an old woolly bedjacket, and his grey flannel slacks flopping round his knees like grandma's shopping bag, and he was saying, 'Do you think so, sir? Yes, I see what you mean. It's a new slant certainly. I'm afraid I missed that. I'll work it round that way,' and he edged away as if Wensley had been the headmaster telling him he wasn't getting the best out of the Sixth instead of the editor telling him to get some skids under Ernie Bevin's afternoon speech, and then he was gone, the door breathing softly shut behind him, and then Wensley's black pencil was hovering round my feature, *Objects and Subjects*, my very own feature, as he would undoubtedly tell me to my face within a minute, and he was pointing to the Waterman story and saying slowly and disbelievingly, 'Is this the Baron's piece?'

'It is.'

'No help from you?'

'It doesn't read that way, does it? I hope not, anyway.'

'Why didn't you knock it about?'

'I quite like working here.'

'It's like that *Atticus* stuff in the *Sunday Times*,' Wensley said with distaste. 'Gentlemanly stuff. No venom. Just like a pat on the back from a bishop.'

'Well, it's a pat on the back from a baron instead.'

'I know, I know, but a pat on the back from that old so-and-so usually comes with a kick in the fork, and there's no kick here.'

'It's odd,' I said, 'yet he seems to have hated Waterman's guts.'

'Did he say so?'

'He did.'

'It's odd all right,' Wensley said, but he left the Waterman story and turned to my other items, supposedly of general interest. He read through a note on some unknown Edward Lear drawings that one of my bookselling friends had found in the library of a noble household down on its uppers.

'Bit upstage isn't it?' Wensley asked slowly, putting a heavy black line through the paragraph with his 8B pencil.

'Lear upstage! God forbid!' I said.

'How many of our readers have even heard of Lear? He's a middle-class institution. The masses can't make him out. All that Spikky Sparrow stuff makes 'em self-conscious. They don't get it. Maybe fifty thousand readers might be interested and that's putting it high. It's not enough. Unless you can show one of the drawings. There might be something new in that.'

'This is private information. The drawings don't come up at Sotheby's till next week.'

'Then wait till next week and wait till you can show a drawing. We're not a free ad service for booksellers or Sotheby's. Got a filler?'

'Two,' I said grudgingly.

'What are they?'

'One about this windjammer that's coming into London River tomorrow. Another on a tight-rope dwarf due at the Palladium next week. A Czech. Trains on macaroni and spinach.'

'The night editor can deal with the windjammer. You take the dwarf. Why isn't he on the front page, anyway?'

'Ask your reporters. Private information. I didn't want to make the paper a free ad service for dwarfs or the Palladium.'

'*Touché* but childish,' he said. 'Put him in, I like dwarfs.'

He sat back in his swing chair and he was frowning like a man who wonders where he left the keys of the safe.

'What d'you make of this Baron and Waterman business?' he asked and he looked at his brogue as if the answer might reside in the toe-cap.

'A one-day wonder.'

'I don't think so, but we'll see. He hasn't wanted to write an obit since that actress woman of his died last year.'

'Wasn't she a bit of a revolutionary in her way, too?' I asked.

'Not on the stage, she wasn't,' Wensley said, and he sat up and began to doodle his 8B lead absent-mindedly around a proof of a cut-out half-tone of Ernie Bevin's face and I knew it was time for me to be getting back to Miss Arnold and any data that was ready on dwarfs.

My ninety-five words on the subject of the rope-walking dwarf were guaranteed to seize the attention and hold the interest of our reading public and they took ten minutes to write. I took the sheet up to the comps and told Newton, the make-up man on the stone, a filler was coming for *Objects and Subjects* and in less than another ten minutes I had corrected the proof and was free to go where I willed, and I willed to go back to El Vino's before they closed the doors of that seasoned sanctuary.

I whiled away the minutes watching three strong men plying their charms around a young bright blonde and she was sitting pretty, proud to be queening it in that masculine stronghold, and her arms fully occupied with drink and defence. I sat engrossed by this catch-as-catch-can until the peace of my evening was suddenly shattered, for Wensley had taken the chair at my side and he was ordering a double whisky. 'I thought I'd find you here,' he said in his far-away voice, but it was far too near for me, and I said in clear ringing tones that my day was done —at least that had been my fondest hope.

'What's on tonight, then?' he asked.

34

'I'm dining at the House.'

'Who with?'

'Someone who wants me to write for him.'

'Write what?'

'Articles about public men.'

'And can you?'

I sipped my drink, for nobody gets much out of that kind of conversation and Wensley grinned. 'I mean, can you, under your contract with the Baron?'

'I haven't looked at it lately.'

'I look at mine every Friday night. It's not very re-assuring, but it's something. But who's the lucky Member?'

'Elkin.'

'That pink queen.'

'He means well.'

'Most queens do. What does he want to do this time?'

'He wants to start a monthly magazine to tell the Great British Public how Parliament works.'

'And what about those many months of recess? What happens to the magazine then? Does he stop publication? And who's backing him?'

'He thinks he'll get help from the Ministry of Education, the British Council and the C.O.I.'

'A pretty prospect. Well, have a good dinner. I'll be getting back. I've asked for a revise of the leader page just to see your piece on the dwarf.'

'I'm very proud,' I said meekly.

'You put him in?' he asked warily.

'He's in,' I said. 'I'll be back about ten if there's anything fresh.'

'I'll expect you,' he said, and as usual I knew I would be in about ten with a new paragraph or even two new paragraphs, and I knew he would be expecting me, and that was the routine and that would be the routine while the contract held out and the paper was there, for the paper was a drug and Wensley was an addict and so was I and, like most other addicts, we never mentioned our addiction, and he finished his drink as if it was stuff to quench a fire and got up to go, and as he got up, he said, 'I'm puzzled by that Waterman obit from the Baron. I've known him a lot of years now and I've never known him do a thing like that. A puff for some frilly piece in a new revue or a build-up for some strong-arm tough in politics, but not this sort of cock.'

'It's a gesture.'

'Yes, but why? Answer me that!' and he picked up his hat and went, and the quiet insistent words hung in the air as if he had left them there on a peg, and my prospect for a pleasant evening, watching the politicos enjoying their dinners, was already dimmed by Wensley asking the question I had been asking myself all through the afternoon.

No taxpayer worthy of the name would have grudged Elkin and his guest their dinner in the Mother of Parliaments or our coffee and port in the visitors' lounge, and as I drank I busied myself evading the blandishments of Mr Elkin by mentioning my contract with the Baron. He said surely this was a worth-while cause, surely it was just the sort of thing the Baron would approve one hundred per cent? And I said he might, I'd ask him, but wasn't the Baron a Right Wing Press Lord? and Elkin smiled as if he could be big and forgiving and let bygones be bygones, but I was sitting there with a word on my mind.

A word creeps into the mind, and it is the word *Why?* and it begins to nibble in the mind like a maggot with a touch of claustrophobia, and it is why? why? why?

through the endless day and there is no need for the word
to be there, the maggot could have been killed before it
was a grub by someone with a mind not freely given to
maggots, someone with a fondness for having life the easy
way, and I would have included myself as a member of
the group, but apparently not, for the maggot was there,
nibbling away all through dinner, and it was still there,
way in, but trying to get out as I left the House and
walked round into the Yard with Elkin. He thought he
wouldn't stay on for the Division, he said. Instead he
proposed to drive back to his little bachelor snuggery in
Jermyn Street, and I thought again, as I'd thought before,
that if all the Labour M.P.s with private means and flats
in Town and houses in the country could be laid end to
end they'd stretch from Parliament Square to the Bank of
England, a right and proper terminus, but Elkin interrupted this fanciful flow by asking whether I'd care to
drop in at Jermyn Street for a drink, but I said I ought to
be getting back to my editor and could he drop me off at
Trafalgar Square?

'How is Wensley these days?'

'He's still there,' I said.

'One day he'll wake up and find he's been there too
long,' Elkin said, and the words popped out with a prima
donna's pout.

'Don't we all?' I said. I was fast losing interest in Elkin
and all his works and words. Sometimes he talked like
Almighty God's first cousin and I wondered again what
it was that made most of the members of that West-
minster gashouse talk as if they had special access to all
the fruits of the tree of knowledge, but Elkin wasn't perturbed and he didn't agree. 'Some of us have a shake-up
every five years or so, whether we like it or not,' he
said.

'Mainly *not*,' I said, 'who likes losing a thousand-a-year pin money?'

'O, it's not that,' he said quickly.

'No, but it helps,' I said, but by that time we were rounding Trafalgar Square and I said I'd drop off, I wanted to walk back to the office.

'I can take you on.'

'No thanks,' I said, and I meant no thanks. After an evening of Elkin I wanted a breath of the clear nocturnal air of the Strand, but perhaps it was jaundice at meeting a man of merit and ambition, or perhaps Wensley was right and Elkin was just a pink queen and I wasn't in a mood for pink queens.

So I walked slowly down the Strand and the world was sweet again now I was alone in it, although the crowds coming out of the Tivoli were big enough to give me doubts concerning my solitary estate, but by the time I reached Wellington Street I was thinking my own thoughts again, and they were not so very different from the way they'd been all evening, for I was still puzzling over a simple, old-fashioned paragraph the Baron had written in one of the Baron's newspapers and that was certainly a novel experience for me.

5

WENSLEY was in his office and he had a copy of the first edition on his desk and copies of all the other morning papers on the floor and he was sitting there like a man in a trance he's almost enjoying, staring down at the front pages of his competitors. 'Not much fun and games tonight,' he said as I came in. 'Everybody led with the Bevin speech, but we seem to have got away with that Stoke Newington murder. Why a girl killing her brother is less interesting in a newspaper office than a girl killing her boy friend, I can't understand, but they'll follow us in the next, you'll see. Can't understand why the *Mirror* let it pass. That windjammer picture stands up well. I suppose it appeals to the Jack London streak in all of us, but I never had it very strong. I always wanted to be a brewer. How's Elkin?'

'Persistent.'

'He always was. You can't be a successful queen if you're not. Or a good M.P. And in a dreary sort of way I suppose he's that, too.'

I crossed to the desk and picked up *The Times* which didn't come into Wensley's idea of competition. He would get around to that later, after the replating panic had died to a mealy-mouthed whine from the make-up man, so I turned to see how Printing House Square had dealt with Bevin and it wasn't very kindly, and after *Our Political Correspondent* and the First Leader I turned the page and Waterman had made top of the obituary columns with G. W. WATERMAN as title and A POLITICAL JOURNALIST as sub-title.

His only rivals in death that night were a Scottish banker and a Cambridge conchologist, which doubtless meant I should have to write a quick note on conchology in general and that conchologist, deceased, in particular, if Wensley spotted the body. It was a hard life for a columnist, I thought, as I settled down to read the ten-inch notice *The Times* had given Waterman:

Our correspondent in Belgrade now confirms that G. W. Waterman, the political journalist, met his death in a motoring accident in Yugoslavia on March 14*th.*

George Weston Waterman was born in 1883, *the son of a well-to-do Midlands industrialist. He was educated privately and at Balliol College, Oxford, where he took a First Class in Greats in* 1906. *After leaving Oxford he spent much time in reading and travelling, thus equipping himself 'almost by accident' as he once wrote, 'for the peculiar tasks ahead.' Whether the tasks were as peculiar as Waterman imagined is questionable, but that he exerted a considerable if anonymous influence upon Fabian thought, and, later, more violent Left Wing political philosophy, is not open to doubt. As a writer he had a gift for lucid (some have asserted 'too lucid') and forceful expression and the Socialist movement at that time had need for such a vigorous exponent of its more academic Marxist theses. His political writings gradually became strangely and strongly marked by impatience and what Mr Justice Allport once described as 'an almost pathological wish to incite to violence or near-violence'; yet, in his own personality, Waterman was mild-mannered and almost timid, characteristics which were reflected in his physical appearance. He was a scholarly, reticent man, little given to public life of any kind. During the* 1914–1918 *war he was a conscientious objector, forming one of that coterie of Left Wing politicians and political writers, which, headed by George Lansbury, went to prison rather than become belligerents. After the war he began his active career as a political journalist. That career can be said to have begun on the old* Daily Herald. *He was a contemporary of Gerald Gould, Mr Siegfried Sassoon and Mr (now Sir) Francis Meynell. His writings were, however, too violent for the preachers of socialism by gradualism and he quickly left the struggling newspaper and turned his attention to the possibilities of weekly journalism. He*

was a contributor to H. W. Massingham's The Nation
and to Orage's New Age, *but he was too violent in expression for those more tolerant editors and he terminated
his connections with both periodicals after stormy scenes.
'He seemed to have a need for outbursts of an almost
demoniacal intensity at irregular intervals,' one of his
editors has recorded, 'and this compulsion made him an
unpredictable colleague.' In* 1925 *Waterman founded and
edited* Friday, *a short-lived political weekly newsletter.
This periodical never achieved any wide circulation: it
was chiefly remarkable for the violence of its editor's views.
The General Strike in the following year caused him to
cease publication, although it was widely rumoured that
he had been officially advised to close down the periodical
owing to the virulence of his final editorial,* A Call to
Disorder, *addressed to the strikers.*

*After the failure of this venture, Waterman spent more
and more time abroad. He visited Russia four times between* 1928 *and* 1938 *and wrote exclusively and anonymously upon the successive Five Year Plans. He was a
tireless London worker on behalf of the Republican cause
in the Spanish Civil War. During the* 1939–1945 *war he
contributed many articles to Left Wing periodicals. As
early as* 1941 *he was an outspoken protagonist on behalf
of a cross-channel Second Front, and some of his personal
attacks upon Mr Churchill were as vicious as any made
upon the wartime Prime Minister. He was finally confined to Wandsworth under Regulation* 18B *in* 1942.

*After the war he travelled extensively in Europe. He
revisited Russia and the Danubian states, also the Far
East.*

I looked up after reading the obituary to find Wensley
watching me with a smile on his face, and it was the smile

of the old crone watching the innocent do all the things
the crystal foretold. I handed the paper across to him.
'I've read it,' he said. 'I wanted to see what the Baron had
left out.'

'Quite a bit, it seems.'

'I wonder who wrote it,' Wensley said. 'Don't you
know someone down in that outfit?'

I knew I'd had a hint, so I took up the phone and asked
for 'The Times' and then for 'Mr. Mountain of the Home
Room,' and then Mountain was introducing himself and
I asked my question.

'I think it was done here,' he said. 'In fact I know it
was, but I'm busy now. I'll phone you back in five
minutes.'

I gave him Wensley's extension number, and, being a
man of Printing House Square, he did phone back and I
had one phone and Wensley had another and we both
heard Mountain say, 'Sorry about cutting you short before, but there's a bit of a shambles over that Bevin speech.
All clear now. Yes, the Waterman obituary was a staff job.
We had a notice done about eight years ago, just about
the time M.I. 5 popped him into gaol. Gibbings here did
it and he brought it up to date this afternoon. Not that it
needed much. Waterman was a bit of a has-been, wasn't
he? We've cut him for the next edition.'

'Who's Gibbings?'

'One of the subs here in the Home Room. He's at supper now. Like a word with him?'

'Not now,' I said. 'Maybe later. It was a pretty full job,
a lot more than we put in.'

'This is a newspaper,' Mountain said, and after a few
more words of donnish badinage rang off.

'Not much there, then,' Wensley said, sitting back
again.

'Anything in any of the others?' I asked.

'Nothing our own files couldn't have given us.'

'Nothing about Ireland?'

'Not a word.'

'Perhaps there was nothing,' I said, 'yet *he* said so.'

Wensley nodded, and the room was quiet the way his room was often quiet just before eleven, just after the second edition queries had been sorted out, and then it was time for a drink, tea or coffee or something more heartening if something were near to hand, and for Wensley it always was, and he said, as if he were almost asleep, 'Let's go up the road. It seems the Baron's not ringing tonight,' but he was wrong in that.

Even as we were leaving the room the telephone rang and he went back and I heard his 'Yessir,' and that meant the Baron.

So I went on down by the stairs and out through the hall, past the gouty night liftman, past the fat commissionaire, out into the court and I stood waiting and smoking and looking up at the square of night boxed in by the courtway roofs and it could have been a beautiful moment, with the stars thrown in for full measure, but the rotaries were running deep down underground, and by now they would be well into the second million, and that sort of thought can spoil any moment. The imprint of Bevin's face, news of family disunion in Stoke Newington, details of a Czech dwarf's daily diet, pictures of a barque coming up-Channel in the dusk, and sundry other items guaranteed to brighten the British breakfast table, were being plastered along mile after mile of unrolling newsprint, and among those sacred items were my own six *Objects and Subjects* and one of the paragraphs was Waterman, but none of the objects was a mollusc in any form, thank God. I had at least missed that.

Wensley came out. 'He thought we might have shown less of Bevin's face. He says every child in Britain could draw that mug blindfold. I told him it was one of our own and showed how the old boy was ageing, but he wouldn't listen. Maybe he's right. Anyway, I argued the toss a bit and finally he said keep it in.'

'Well, he's shown he's boss.'

Wensley grunted.

We walked round into the garage and hailed one of the editorial cars. 'The Savoy, and take it easy,' Wensley said, and Joe, the driver, took it easy enough to miss a police car moving out of the shadows of Bush House by all of a yard. He was afflicted with the curse that strikes all newspaper drivers, thinking every journey is a trip to a story and carrying on as if life is like something in a film, with a character in the back with a price on his head and the police after him. 'Easy!' Wensley insisted once, but it was no good, speed was part of Joe's bloodstream and by that time we were there.

We went through into the American Bar and there were three others in the room: a man and a woman representative of the world we used to see in *The Tatler* in the carefree days of Baldwin and Company, and a morose long-legged young man who would have been more at home in the Cavalry Club if he could have risen from his supine splendour and reached the doors.

We sat down and Wensley rang and ordered drinks. 'Half an hour,' he said, relaxing.

6

BUT I wasn't so keen that Wensley should relax, for I had a question, and my question was part of the bigger question and it had come to me, better later than never, during dinner with Elkin, and now I said, 'How did you know the Baron would want something on Waterman?'

'Instinct.'

'Ah!' I said. 'I always forget. The editorial instinct.'

Wensley smiled. 'That and memory,' he said. 'I had a couple of chits about Waterman from the Baron during the war. Once I had to play down the M.I. 5 story. You don't forget items like that. So today I just had a hunch he might want a note on Waterman. Instinct.'

'Genius!' I said, and then, 'Now he'll let it drop?'

'Perhaps.'

'Well, Waterman's dead.'

'There's quite a lot of ways of being dead in a newspaper,' Wensley said. 'As a matter of fact, I think you're right. Waterman's way of being dead doesn't stand a chance against that Stoke Newington murder.'

'Sometimes I forget,' I said, 'your job must be very interesting.'

Wensley smiled and rested his fat hand on my knee. 'Don't try to be funny. Stick to *Objects and Subjects*. The really interesting subject is not the dead boy in Stoke Newington or even Waterman or even the newspaper. It's the Baron.'

'Why the Baron especially?'

Wensley sat back and rested his great and flabby substance more slackly into the settee and he looked at the amber drink in his glass and he was staring into a lot more tongue-wagging stuff than two fingers of Scotch, for it was plain he was staring into twelve long years with the Baron as his boss, and it was a subject very near and dear to him. Now and then he liked to open up a bit in the way any fetishist doubtless likes to talk about shoes or mackintoshes or his own particular and personal love, and now he said, 'It's just that the old bastard interests me. I suppose anyone who can make ten or twenty millions out of nothing is a subject for interest. It's different being the second Lord Leverhulme or the second Lord Rothermere. What interests me is how the first one starts. How does he make his first thousand and then his first ten thousand? There's something odd about money and the men it sticks to. The sticking isn't a gift at birth. Some of these giants start quite late. Do they spend the first forty or fifty years learning how the stuff sticks or does it suddenly just start sticking?'

He took a sizeable gulp and looked over the rim of the tumbler at me, but I shook my head. 'Don't ask me,' I said, 'I'm not the sticky type. Ask my ex. She's got the knack.'

But he went on and I was in no mood to stop him. 'Take the Baron. At forty he was still a reporter. He'd come up the hard way. He had a bit of a reputation but not all that. He wasn't a man of ideas. He's no Northcliffe. At least he wasn't. Maybe you can even pick up the trick of being Northcliffe once you start. Then he manages to get dug in, well and truly dug in, in a publishing business. On the money side. In ten years he's got three papers and he's worth two million, and in thirty years, today, at this precise bloody moment, he's got twelve papers and he's worth at least ten million and not even a Labour Govern-

ment can take it away from him. At least, not all of it.' He
finished his drink and rang again.

'My turn,' I said, but he was in no mood for interrup-
tions and he ordered two more and said, 'Expenses. I'll
put it down to staff-instruction. How does it happen? I sit
on my backside in an office and once a month a cheque for
something more than seven hundred quid goes into my
bank, but it'll never be seven thousand or seventy thousand, and he sits up there in that fantastic bloody palace in
the park he calls home-sweet-home and money sticks to
him like flies to a piece of old meat.'

'Honeypot is better,' I said.

'All right. Honeypot it is. And old honeypot can ring
me up any time he bloody well likes and I say yessir, yessir, three bags full sir. What's the difference between us?
What makes him the better man? What made him the
Baron? He was never an editor. He just pokes his nose
right in and says do this or do that and sometimes, if it's
not all that important, I do it, but hell, how did he get
that way?'

Even by that time and on that subject his voice was as
slow and quiet as a deacon's. The young hussar in the
adjacent armchair couldn't have heard a word even if his
had been a listening mood, and *The Tatler* pair were certainly in no listening mood, they were whining away in
tired and bitter tones that boded no joy for their bedtime
ahead. A young couple in evening dress came in and the
prideful male rang for sandwiches, coffee and one large
whisky, and then turned to his young and glowing partner and she began to gabble fast about their evening's
pleasure.

All this was a backstage mumble for Wensley's words,
but he had switched and he was saying, 'If I'd ever had a
son I'd have brought him up in piety and learning. He'd

have won scholarships. And at last he'd have been a Master of Arts of some antique university. D'you know what I'd have done then? I'd have insisted he stayed up to take a Ph.D. And I'd have given him his thesis on a platter. *An Enquiry into the Origins of Man's First Ten Thousand Quid.* It's an enquiry that needs a little subsidy.'

'Maybe the Baron would help,' I said, trying to be funny.

'Maybe he will,' Wensley agreed, drinking again.

By then he was well down the second tumbler and he was beginning to warm up to his subject, but the only signs of warmth were slower words and limper gestures with his free left hand. 'But I've never had a son. My wife breeds corgis. So I've decided to institute a little thesis on my own account. I'm finding out how the Baron made *his* first ten thousand quid.'

'Do you have to go to Oxford or Cambridge?' I asked, for I thought I might as well humour him. Sometimes he had his whims and they were funny; other times he had them and they were not so funny, and this promised to be one of the other times, but he crossed his legs, examined his shoes, then his whisky and settled down for the next stage in the story.

'For twelve long years I've watched that old bastard going and coming about the world, holding Press conferences in Paris and talkie-talks in Timbuctoo, shooting a line about his responsibilities as a British newspaper man, coming back here and ringing me up at midnight and telling me how to run a newspaper. I was an editor before I worked for him. He was never an editor anywhere. I've met a few who knew him in the old days and he was no great shakes then, and now, because the paper I edit sells three million copies and he owns it, he thinks he's King Cophetua and I'm his bloody beggar-maid. I run the paper. I think up new schemes, I build up features like yours, and I get him on the phone telling me to take Ernie Bevin's mug off page one.'

So that was it, I thought, that's the tinder-box tonight, but I was wrong, or part wrong, and I had to keep my thoughts quietly taking their ease, for Wensley was really taking his back hair down. 'For twelve long years I've known him, worked for him, watched him, listened to him. I'd like to know why he ticks, how he got where he is, how he stays there. One day there's going to be a biography of the Baron and I'm collecting material. Right now. That's all. The best biographies usually get written by the boys who hung around at the time. Boswell and Johnson. Caulincourt and Bonaparte. Remember? And now I'm here and so is the Baron and we make a damn fine pair. Don't we?'

'Wonderful,' I said. 'Does he know?'

'Be your age!' Wensley said, driving on, his words like gentle whipflicks. 'I've collected some stuff and there's a lot more to come. I know where he was born, all about his parents, how he grew up. I know how he manages his papers. I know about the wife he married young who died in childbirth. I know about the stillborn son. I know about his lonely life ever since. All that stuff. The tragedy of it all. I've met most of his popsies. I know all that, but there's still a few odd gaps.'

'Such as?'

'One I've told you. I don't know how he got his first ten thousand. All the stuff I've got I picked up as I went along. I've done no research. I'm not the type. For instance, I don't know how he got control of this bloody paper and this was certainly his first. And I don't know how deep the paper was in the doldrums when he got it. And I don't know anything about this Waterman friendship.'

'Were they friends, then? And is it so important?'

'That's for you to find out.'

'Me!' I said, in a voice like a choirboy's falsetto, and I sat there limp, for when the avalanche comes ambling down the mountain the villager is in no mood to dissemble; and when the capsize comes to the mariner he is honest with himself and his shipmates and even with his God; and when you get to the great gate and St Peter is there with the big book with the lies and the peccadilloes, the fears and the flops recorded in simple black-and-white, you, too, are likely to say 'Me!' in just such a falsetto and sit there limp. And this was such an occasion. Wensley had led me straight up a little garden path to such a gate and I was face to face with something I had no wish to see, but there was no compassion in him, and he drank his drink and nodded and said, 'Yes, you. It's all yours. And why not? You're the bright boy who's going to dig it out. You've had that sort of training. Research is your strong point. Isn't it?'

'I'm very flattered,' was all I mumbled.

'No, you're not,' Wensley said, and he had his best bedside manner fitted on tight and he might have been telling the patient it wasn't galloping consumption after all, only trotting or cantering or whatever the medicos call it. 'No, you're not. You're bloody annoyed but you're the bloke. I thought it out this afternoon. At least I thought out this chapter. You were interested enough in Waterman this morning . . .'

He went on, but I wasn't listening any more. An innocent party can protest so much but no more, not even when the old, crabbed judge puts on the black cap and proceeds to a few pointed instructions, and I knew it was no good pointing out that as far as I was concerned Waterman was just another Red with too much money who had been gathered to his fathers a lot too late in life, and, what was more, a citizen who would never have made my column without a push from the Baron and another push from Wensley. But what was the use?

I needed a little moment and a solitary place until my indignation might be overpast, but Lincoln's Inn Fields seemed a long way farther than half a mile away and I knew I was in it up to the last faint curl of my greying locks, and I knew this whim of Wensley's was certainly one that had got out-of-hand and snarled me up on its wayward way.

And as I came back into the sound of words again, Wensley was saying, 'Start with his mother. The *Standard* says she's still alive. She ought to know something about him, although she probably hated the sight of the little runt before he was twenty. Tackle the old duck.'

'Who fixes the introduction?'

'Didn't I say it was all yours from now on? I just want the chapter. You can call it "The Rich Baron and the Rich Red" and you can start from scratch.'

'Any time limit?'

'There's no time limit. I'd just like my little biography finished before the Baron dies, that's all.'

'I didn't hear any death rattle this afternoon,' I said.

Again Wensley let his limp left hand fall plumply and softly on my knee. 'You're still trying to be funny, but I've made special arrangements with Almighty God. The Baron won't die before my little essay is finished. I want to check it over with him.'

'God or the Baron?' I asked, funny to the last, but Wensley pressed the bell.

'We'll have one more and call it a day. Then I'll wander back and see how they've balled up that new front page. I'll drop you off. Same again?'

'Same again,' I said, for it was always the same again with Wensley, for it was always the same when you started.

7

SO Wensley took me back and left me in the square. The stars were still there, pinned overhead like sparklers on a backcloth in a panto, but the stars had dimmed a bit, as indeed the whole of my universe had dimmed a bit, and I took a turn around the Fields and felt about as lively as the skeleton down in the depths of old John Soane's museum in the very same square.

I crossed by the tennis courts under the shadowy planes and climbed to my own top-floor fastness, past the clerical morgues of Doughty, Doughty and Riding, Solicitors and Commissioners for Oaths, and Sutcliffe and Partners, another highly respectable assembly of jurisprudent pedants who would all be there in the morning, man and boy, lifting down their ledgers, digging into deed boxes, making a land fit for lawyers to live in, and as I climbed the stairs it came to me again, as it had come to me before, that there was precious little difference between the Baron and all his works and the Doughtys and the Sutcliffes and all their works. They all battened on divorce, the living and the dead, the meaning of words and the splitting of hairs. But old man Doughty did it all in an office twelve foot square and the Baron needed a twelve-storey block, batteries of rotaries, a set-up in Manchester, another in Glasgow, and several in the Provinces, but they both wore dark suits and they both would die worth a lot of shining shekels.

I let myself in, switched on the lights, took up the vacuum flask and out gurgled the bitter black coffee Mrs Burton had left those hours before, a boon and a blessing to midnight men, and I gulped it down, switched on the fire and sat down for a moment of contemplation, but sitting there, I doubted again whether Pascal had been all that right in his fond belief that the remedy for the world's foremost ills was sitting alone in a small quiet room.

And I thought again of Waterman and my new and additional job, and I thought harsh thoughts of his unreliable jeep.

A man dies and someone somewhere records his birth and his death and the monumental mason chips out the dates and R.I.P. and the tombstone squats in the climbing grass, the flowers moulder in the jam-jars and the mourners come no more. And maybe it is the same among the Slavs.

Yet the dates aren't enough: the digits cannot tell of the nine or the eight or the seven long months the man was a movement in a womb and his mother was a woman in expectation and in fear, already shaping him by thought and motion, food and drink, hope and love. And the digits cannot by any means contain the timeless aftermath, the misery and the happiness the man will leave: his manner in his son, his money with his widow, his frown upon his daughter, his thoughts among his friends, and maybe the digits are wrong by many months at one end and by the rest of time itself at the other.

Waterman was certainly not dead for me. He was already another job.

Born 1883, said the record in *The Times*, but the record was short by the months that were his mother's. 'Tackle the old duck,' Wensley had said. 'There's always two women in a man's life: the first and the last. Mum will tell you all you want to know about him before the world got hold of him, and the last will tell you how the world dusted him up. No matter how many women there were between or how many he got between, the last will know the answers. It seems Waterman's mother was the only woman in his life. That may make it easier. Or maybe it won't. Tackle her first, anyway, and find out. She'll talk. Whether she loved him or hated his red guts she'll talk.'

And I'd thanked him and asked whether that was all and he'd smiled his distant smile, raised his drooping hand, said, 'Till tomorrow!' and then slammed the car door and I was alone in Lincoln's Inn Fields with the stars, the chapel and my own sublunary self.

8

WHEN I woke in the morning the ghost of G. W. Waterman might have been sitting on the bedhead, so quickly did the thought of him come uninvited to my mind, and I groaned and looked at my watch and it was well after nine and it was Mrs Burton who was late this time, and then I knew her key had wakened me, and I lay listening to the opening door, the click of the lock and her size seven shoes shuffling through the living-room and into the kitchen and the wheeze of pleasure in her voice as she realized I was still abed and she could call out, 'Late again, sir!'

'Not the only one, Mrs Burton,' I made playful answer, as I flopped out, put my feet in the sheepskin shoes and shivered in the good fresh air.

'It's the buses, sir. You'd think it was 'orse buses the

time they take. You ought to write something in your paper about them number twenty-four buses, sir. 'Alf an 'our from Pimlico to 'ere! My old man says someone oughter take it up.'

'Maybe I will,' I said from the bathroom, but I was a long way off with an idea in my head and it was growing fast as I went on with the delicate task of shaving a semblance of a civilized mask back on the face in the mirror, and it was still there as I put on a blue flannel shirt, a dark blue tie, a grey tweed suit, grey check socks and black brogue shoes and looked in the wardrobe mirror to see whether civilization had truly claimed me for its own again, and there in the mirror was a citizen all set for the quotidian fray: a thick-set frowning character, just under middle height, just under middle age, dark-haired, dark-browed and ready for breakfast. Then I went out into the living-room, and the time was half-past ten.

And later, as I went slowly down the stairs to Lincoln's Inn Fields again, the plan still seemed a plan worth trying. At eleven o'clock in the morning I was certainly no early bird, but the plan still looked fair enough to catch some sort of worm.

So I walked into the brittle March day, and the pale blue sky with its cotton-wool clouds was the promise of a nobler world than the world of Carey Street, Fleet Street, El Vino's, and then the world of Court House, the world I sometimes dreamed I never left.

I went through the letters, the cards from the galleries, the personal notes from the Government P.R.O.s with someone or something to sell, the books and the invitations. Then I went up to the Foreign Room, but there was little enough there for me, and I left, but with no worries, for Friday's *Objects and Subjects* was already shaping with six bright paragraphs on national frills and furbelows, freaks and frolics, and I knew I had no need that day for any cabled details about Malik's machinations or any P.A. release about another Berlin panic. It would be an Anglican day as far as my modest column was concerned, and, anyway, I had my plan.

Part of the plan was to take the lift down to the second floor, walk along the carpeted corridor and push open the door of another big room.

From one month to another month you couldn't be certain of finding the same citizen at the same mahogany desk, but Johnson had been there as the Sunday paper's London editor for four long months and he seemed to be holding down the job.

He looked up as I pushed open the door and nodded pleasantly enough. I went in and crossed to the green leather armchair and sat demurely down and looked around, for I have always been keen to discover what it is that puts editors apart from mortal men and the answer in Johnson's case was the usual and resounding sweet f.a.

He was a little thin fellow of forty or so with oiled-down hair, a narrow pink head, a pale red face, mud-brown eyes, bloodless lips and a long lean chin, and he was sitting shirt-sleeved at the desk and pummelling a paste-up of a page-to-be. He was hectoring an underling and making it clear how unsure he was of himself and his job, bluffing it out with banging words and sawn-off gestures, but even the underling was unimpressed by the act, and I gave Johnson another two months; but meantime he was the first small piece in my brand-new jigsaw.

He finished with his man with the worn-out words: 'All right, let's see a revise after lunch,' and the underling went, and Johnson turned in his swivel chair and asked why the honour? was I writing him a piece? and to his very great surprise I said, 'Yes.'

'On what, for Christ's sake?'

'On Waterman.'

He was puzzled for a minute and then he said, 'That Red who's just got himself killed?'

I nodded.

'You're kidding.'

'I'm not. The Baron wrote my piece for me this morning. There must have been something in him.'

I'd used the magic word. He leaned across and took up the morning's paper and opened the leader page and scanned my column. 'The Baron wrote that?' he asked, surprised but wary, and I nodded again and he was thoughtful and I could see he was wavering.

'Was he a friend of the Baron's?'

'I don't know. What I do know is that Waterman's made for a Sunday feature.'

'What, in my Tory sheet? God knows I'd like to have you in. The paper's got no personal political stuff, but what has Waterman got for me?'

'I'd say he had a lot. Revolution, prison, unearned increment, sudden death. What more do you want? He's made for a right-wing Sunday newspaper.'

'Why d'you want to do it?'

'The Baron did it for me: I'll do mine for you.'

Johnson understood that language, and he nodded, and then said quickly, 'Why not make it the first of a series?'

Not bad, I thought, and maybe Fred Johnson *will* be here in three months' time, but I disengaged myself from that quick clinch. 'You know Wensley would clamp down,' I said. 'Dailies and Sundays don't mix he says. I just thought this story might be down your alley. If it is, I'll do it. Copy Saturday morning. If it's not, just say no.'

But Johnson wasn't saying *no*.

'Saturday's late for feature stuff,' he said. 'Try tomorrow evening. And try to make it the first of six.'

I said I'd see.

I went back to my room and took down *Who's Who*, and under the Waterman entry was the skeletal form *The Times* had clothed, but there were other oddments the papers had skipped: the maiden name of his mother (Lavinia Adelaide); Club (Savile); hobbies (rambling, travelling); address (Harolde Towers, Near Guildford, Surrey, and 527 Whitehall Mansions).

I read out the details to Miss Arnold. 'Try Whitehall Mansions and then Guildford,' I said, 'Harolde Towers may be mum's house. See if you can find a phone number for it,' and I went out and across to El Vino's, for I needed to be a scribe straightaway if I proposed to set down my paragraphs and travel down to see old Mrs Waterman in that one day.

I ordered gin and with the gin came the words, and my six neat paragraphs, one hundred and twenty words each, were down in black-and-white by half-past twelve. Then I went back.

No messages were being taken for Waterman at Whitehall Mansions, Miss Arnold said, but she had a number for Harolde Towers and in less than three minutes she had the number and she was well ahead with the job of getting past the maid. I closed my eyes and listened. She could deal with maids, footmen, butlers and secretaries as if they were interlopers, keeping their masters and mistresses from secret Derby tips, Irish Sweep tickets or a box at the Opera, and then she handed me the phone and mine was the task of inviting myself to Guildford that very afternoon to talk to Mrs Waterman about her stone-dead son.

Straightaway I knew I'd hit rock and I thought she'd hung up: there were no protests at my honeyed words.

No word. No answer. Nothing. And I said, 'Are you there?' and an aged, arid voice said back, 'Of course I am here. I was listening. That is all. Yes, you may come. The trains are frequent. Harolde Towers is ten minutes from the station by taxi-cab. I shall expect you this afternoon.' And that was that, the phone had clicked and I was there on my own with the receiver in my hand and my mouth wide open with my unvoiced thanks.

'Short work,' Miss Arnold said, and I nodded to agree, but I was slow in coming to, and I said I'd have a sandwich and then come back to see typed copies of my scribbled notes, and I went out and down by the lift, into the court and across to The Falstaff.

And during my snack of smoked salmon and a Guinness I brooded over the farcical nature of the task ahead. *Why was I doing it? Just because Wensley said so?* Well, maybe that was reason enough. I'd once studied Cromwellian history just because someone had told me to, and I hadn't questioned that. I turned to the midday *Standard*. That was one escape.

9

I GOT to Guildford about half-past three, took a taxi from the station out to Harolde Towers and it was all I'd expected it to be: Norman Shaw in a coniferous jungle with a short double-drive within a high brick wall and mock-Georgian wrought-iron gates.

I told the taximan to wait and went up the six stone steps and rang the bell and the door opened at once. Service, I thought, but I had no more bright thoughts, for I nearly staggered backwards at the picture there before me.

The doorway framed a tall, thin, dried-up maid, as old as the Gobi Desert, and she was standing there in a long black dress, a snow-white pinny and a lace mob cap.

I asked for Mrs Waterman and she bowed me in through an outer lobby to an inner hall muffled in rugs and swathed in hangings. A dark staircase with balusters like the dropsical legs of an old, old cook cramped the size of the large inner hall. And the staircase windows that might have lit this lively scene were hung with tapestries worth anybody's guess. It was a place for Christmas, big fires, small children, mince-pies and a jolly old extrovert banker as shining host. It was certainly no place for my particular errand and I was sorry I'd left the thin March sun outside.

Then Gobi returned from an inner room and she nodded me in and I crossed the threshold and the scene had changed.

But not much.

A wizened old woman pushed up from an armchair and offered me another. So we both sat down either side of a cosy stove set firmly on a black-tiled base beneath a high, carved marble mantelpiece. The room was as warm and stale as an old tabby's basket and the furniture stood around like a forest of tallboys, whatnots and breakfront bookcases.

'It was kind of you to come all this way,' the old lady said, in a desiccated voice.

'Kinder still of you to let me come, Mrs Waterman,' I made answer, and wondered as usual who would break from this conversational gambit, but the old lady had no doubts and she went straight on: 'I was glad when you telephoned. There are many things about my son's death I should like cleared up. I've had those people from the *Daily Worker* speaking to me on the telephone, but I can't get any sense out of them. They are all tarred with the same brush, and I told them so. I think my son was killed. I told them so.'

She was going farther and faster than I wanted and she showed no signs of stopping. I shook my head and murmured the usual sort of no, no, no, and I made my contribution with conviction, for why should any foreign character want to put an end to Waterman's career of captious belly-aching when no British Blimp had done so long before?

I wanted to get a full and leisurely all-round glance at Waterman's mother, and it was difficult enough in that smothered light, but at last I began to get things clearer. She was a short, dried-up old thing, with a lined stiff face and small sharp features. I could see all that and I could see her clothes: a long grey dress with a four-deck pearl choker—real enough, I didn't doubt—round her thin scraggy neck. Her eyes were dark, almost black, and deep in their sockets, with shadows below like two black deadly nightshades. Her nose was small and sharp and her chin was cleft like an old crabbed apple someone had nicked with a very sharp knife.

But she was very much alive and not down for keeps the way most of us will be when we're rising eighty-five. She had pulled herself up from the armchair with a quick decisive tug and none of these snatching clutches the half-dead make when the dinner gongs go in the tall old Kensington prisons there in the squares, and I wondered how that sort of vitality lived on in that hot-house room, but there are always queries and I sat on.

'I am glad to have your assurance,' she said, and spoke as if I had come to Guildford hotfoot from Tito. 'The thought had crossed my mind more than once since I heard on Tuesday night.'

'How did you hear, if it isn't too painful a question?' I asked.

'I heard by telephone from Belgrade. An English voice from the Embassy. No, it isn't painful. It was a shock, of course, but I haven't seen eye to eye with my son for over forty years—and that is a long time. It is difficult living with someone with whom you disagree so violently all the time.'

I murmured agreement, but she wasn't out for sympathy and suddenly asked me my own political opinions.

'My trouble is the trouble of too many Englishmen,' I said, 'I'm Left Wing when I read *The Tatler* or the *Bystander*, Right Wing when I read the *Daily Worker*.'

'Sitting on the fence!' she sniffed.

I sat up a bit. I didn't recognize my own historical detachment in these short and cutting words, but she was my hostess and I had come for something and I had to wait, and instead I said mildly that I had been trained long ago as a student of history, and some historians deemed it their task to take no sides on political issues.

'More fools they!' she said with vigour. 'What is the good of living in this day and age if you do not take sides? Where would I have been with George if I had let him trample on my opinions?'

Maybe I should have brought a psychiatrist with me and not a taximan, I told myself, and soon with a little judicious prodding it would all come bursting over the dykes. But I was wrong, dead wrong, as I was wrong in many things that afternoon. I could have brought the psychiatrist, but the dykes were strong enough to stand quite a lot of prodding and I sat looking at old Lavinia, giving her full marks for her lively rancour at her venerable age, but she had switched again, asking whether I was married.

I said no, and that was true enough as far as it went.

'Neither was George,' she said. 'Forty is the best age for a man to marry, but he didn't even marry then.'

I wondered why she got on to that question: maybe she had wanted a few grand children pottering round the house. Well, it was too late now, a lot too late, and all I said was, mightn't forty make for a race of antique parents?

'You will stay for tea?' she asked and decided in one sharp breath and pressed a buzzer on a table at her side. Then she turned to demolish my questions. 'Perhaps, but the children would have more sense. Every study of genius shows that it usually comes from older parents.'

'Do we want a race of geniuses?' I asked. 'Would life be very comfortable?'

'We have never had a race of geniuses to judge, and I scarcely call life as we know it today very comfortable.'

Her tongue was tart enough. There was no endearing old quaver about it, and I could see her ideas of conversation were by no means mine: hers was *dicta* and more *dicta* and dictatorial *dicta* at that, a series of verbal upper-cuts, but tea came in on a wheeled table and Gobi began to hand us tea and scones and it was a far far cry from the Baron's canteen with its bentwood chairs, glass-topped tables and slops of char.

We sat silent until the maid had done her stiff-necked best, but as soon as the door closed I was ready to fire a few questions of my own, and I said, 'As I explained on the phone, Mrs Waterman, I'm hoping to write an article on your son. I believe you could fill in certain gaps in the story, but you may not wish to.'

'I asked you to come here,' she said.

I suffered the rebuke silently, then asked my first

question, but it was not the question I'd intended to ask, some doddering question about his youth. Somewhere, somehow she had riled me and I said instead, 'You didn't get on well with your son?' and as I heard the words bite out I wondered whether I was all the churl they made me out to be, but Lavinia didn't seem to mind.

'No mother ever gets on well with her son after he is twenty,' she said. 'Not if he has an ounce of spirit and calls his soul his own.'

I sipped my china tea. She fought back like old Mendoza himself.

'You didn't agree with his political ideas, then?'

'Of course I didn't. My husband left a fortune of over half a million pounds, all made by his own efforts. He worked like a black from the time he was twelve. He married me when he was twenty-five. He was already well-to-do. I was seventeen. I helped him to grow rich. There is nothing to be ashamed of in wealth. When he died my husband left more than a hundred thousand pounds to charities. How could I agree with my son's ideas?'

'Yet rumour has it you supported him financially.'

'Rumour is right for once. I was his mother!' she said almost with a toss of the old grey head.

'Did you ever suggest he took a regular job?' I asked, and wondered how long this sort of give-and-take could go on: it was certainly not the technique of interviewing as expounded by the old-time Northcliffe men, but it was certainly the way this interview was going.

'He took four *regular* jobs as you call them, but they were not very regular. He was a schoolmaster, a bookseller, a lecturer and a journalist. None of the jobs lasted longer than four months.'

'Some thinkers suggest that he had considerable influence on the political opinions of his day. Were you proud of that?'

'Of course I was. I didn't approve of his ideas but any mother is glad to see that her son's mind and thought are appreciated by men of standing.'

'Did he work here? I mean, write?'

'No. He had various addresses through the years. After this last war, when he came out of prison, he came down here for a time, but not for long, a month or so. Then he moved to a flat we have in Whitehall Mansions. He moved all his books and papers there. That became his home when he was in England, but I have not seen him for several months.'

'It's no good asking to see his study or writing room here, then?' I asked, and sincerest sorrow was in my voice.

'No. I am afraid there is nothing here,' she said, and I knew, too, there was nothing there for me.

That was the first little flaw in my morning plan, but a mind moves on, and even as she was being sorry I knew my next move across the board and into what I hoped was check, so I settled down to routine question and answer, to the job of building up a picture of the youthful Waterman, and what it must be like to be a poor little Red boy, born to wealth and not wanting any of it, only enough to get along on without ever doing a day's solid slogging at the coal face or the Co-op counter. And the picture was mainly old Mrs Waterman's.

Of course it was interesting up to a point but not a very distant point. Anecdotes of a child who became a youth some sixty years ago may have point for mama if she was young then and is now the teller of the tale, but for the average listener the point was blunted long ago by fond and cherished memories of his own wild youth, but she was part of the puzzle—or so Wensley had said. So I listened.

She was trying to sort out a few things about little George. I could see that. Deep down she was striving hard to bring back the skinny youth to this clammy room, to see how it was and why it was and when it was that little George had taken that left-hand turning that took him away from her, and her love, and her ways, and the future she had planned for him: doing all the right things at the right time with the right people.

'He was always strange,' she said, after a break for a toothy bite at a chocolate biscuit. 'As far back as I can remember. Perhaps it was my fault for not sending him to a public school. He was to have gone to Rugby but he was delicate as a child and I was afraid he might find school life too hard. So he stayed in the house—we lived in Warwickshire then—and had a succession of tutors.'

I didn't see how any tutor I'd ever known could have given young Waterman his peculiar line of thought and I said so. She shook her head, agreeing with me. 'I have often puzzled over that myself,' she said, and her voice rasped no more than an old nail-file as she puzzled aloud: 'He read a great deal but not a great deal of history or economics. He read widely, too widely perhaps· for a child, and he was a sound classical scholar. No, all *that* happened whilst he was up at Oxford.'

There was nothing in all this chitter-chat for me, but I listened the way you listen to the buzzing of a blue-bottle in the curtains and carry on half-dozing in the chair, and I said yes and I said no and I knew we were getting along very comfortably. The grating had gone from her voice and although she had not become a sentimental old thing she had certainly become a mother with a memory, and if anyone had pushed a mirror in front of her worn crabbed face she might have seen, for a fine split-second, the features of the dark young mother she had been those years ago.

So I listened and stayed in the chair, and after a civil interval, after my second cup of tea, I waited for the first full stop and then I rose and bowed and smiled my fond farewell, for although she didn't know it, I thought I would be coming back and I wanted *Welcome* on the mat when I came.

IO

I TAPPED out my piece that night, back in my rooms in Lincoln's Inn Fields, six hundred glowing words on THE RICH REVOLUTIONARY, and as I letterspaced the title out in caps and stared at the sheet, I hoped the old lady would recognize and love her stranger-son in the fine resounding phrase. If I didn't use it, a bright sub would. It was too easy, a gift of a title, so I let it be, yet I made a note for Johnson to let it down lightly for I was by no means finished with old Lavinia. Not by many long leagues.

I dipped into the deep bran-tub of the soft and sorry memories she had raked up in Guildford, and the piece wrote itself, but not the way the memories had made him for herself. 'He was such a lonely, sensitive little boy,' a mother says, and maybe the mother is right, and the infant prodigy did go down to the end of the garden and dream great sensitive dreams. But maybe not. Maybe the dreams were nightmares instead, at least for other people, and maybe Sir Galahad was not his fanciful companion but Genghis Khan instead. And mother calls 'Georgie! Where are you, Georgie?' but he is too deep and groggy in his own sweet secret world and he doesn't answer.

And later on, for the other little boys there is school and kicking a ball around and being kicked around, but not for little Georgie. Somehow, somewhere, sometime, George's dreams get mixed up with a lot of other stuff and later still, up at Balliol, George's dreams are dreams no longer but life itself—if only life could be made to fit his measure.

But that was all long ago and now George was dead, and now his mother, with all her love for her money-bags and her hatred of his hateful ways, could smile suddenly in tolerant memory.

I knew. I had seen it that very afternoon.

But all this had no place in my six hundred words. Maybe it had a place, but the place didn't come in the typewritten sheets.

II

THE piece was down in Johnson's room by midday Friday and half an hour later he rang and said good, just what he'd wanted, and would it be the first of six? and what about some living Reds? There were still too many of the bastards still alive and five or six others would make a good series the way I'd dealt with Waterman, so what about it?

And I said, 'They're alive and Waterman's dead: that's

the difference. But ask Wensley, anyway. He's the captain of my soul. Let me see a proof.'

And Johnson said, 'Oke!' in his new crisp editorial style.

12

SO I settled down to my own sweet offering to the Saturday millions, six or seven paragraphs, I remember, one on Tommy Lawton and another on Montgomery's Mill House home, and maybe it is strange I remember those but not the others, but they are there for the record, there in the paper itself, down in *Back Numbers*, and there for me, too, if I like to go back and go down and look them up, but I do not like. For my money they can stay in the big bound volumes that stand on the shelves and for my money, too, they can die in the dust that will surely come at the end.

By the time I came back from being lunched at Rules by a Press agent who moaned long and loud at my neglect of The Theatre in general and his handful of stars in particular, I was ready for the galleys of *Objects and Subjects* and, round about four, up came the piece on Waterman, already in page, and there at the top was a cut-out half-tone of the scholarly Red, and Johnson had certainly done him proud. *The Rich Revolutionary* smashed across the feature, five columns wide, in heavy black sans. I read the piece through, made my corrections and let it go, part of the plan for my very next move. And that afternoon it looked quite a plan, the way most plans look smart to the planner before any other citizen decides to take a hand.

By six I was done, and even Wensley's 8B lead was at

work no more and I was free for my own devices. At least Wensley said so and he usually knew. And my personal devices were simple and innocuous, for the first was a drink and the second was a train, and the train meant Brighton and a quiet hotel and my own undemanding company for two nights and a day.

And two hours later Wensley was no more than a name on a door some fifty miles away, and the Baron was no more than a cheque that paid the bill, and by nine o'clock that night I was in the bar, drinking my drink and listening to the gossip and wondering why the hell I hadn't brought Maureen, but husbands, she'd said, are queer and awkward fish, they like their wives at home, especially at week-ends, so I settled down instead to some long and serious drinking and a little light reading, for what is Friday night without those fierce bombardments from Viscountess Rhondda and Mr Kingsley Martin?

13

THE coastal scene and the food and the drink held me until Sunday morning, but by then the spell had weakened.

It is one thing writing snippets for the presumed delight of the masses and another thing meeting your public face to face on Brighton promenade, and the sight of the Baron's many customers taking their ease in a popular manner in a popular spa on a sunny Saturday afternoon had upset my squeamish taste, and I went back and took the lift four floors up and lay on my bed smoking and watching the smoke rise and curl along the tarnished ceiling.

Perhaps I was soured, but as I saw it the crowds were mine as well as the Baron's, and the thought gave me the pleasure a tasty toadstool might have brought, and I lay and smoked and I watched the smoke and the clouds beyond the window and I did not love my public one small whit.

It wasn't my public, it was the Baron's, I tried to tell myself, it was his every morning, but he handed it to me as he handed it to Wensley, to the sporting boys, to the crime reporters, to the special writers and the make-up men.

And I saw his public, in trains and in pubs, in cafés and in buses, in lifts and in libraries, as I'd seen it that morning in shelters on the prom. I could see it any day, reading the words I had written in yesterday's ink, and that is a rare and strange phenomenon for any writing man as any writer knows. I could see his public and my public any time I damn well pleased. I just popped out and there they were: dried old women with hapless eyes, doomed old men with falling jowls, painted typists and brassy clerks, scrub-faced soldiers and minders of machines. All for a penny could have my words.

And I thought of the words I had written long ago, words of research in fat cheap notebooks, words that I'd hoped would one day make a stir in a world of dons in their grey stone rooms, but those choice words I had left for oblivion in a faraway trunk with some faraway dreams. Now I had a public, and my public was the world, the great, wide, half-wit, net sales world of the Baron and his Board, of Wensley and his chiding 8B lead.

So I left Sunday morning, to write for my public, and in the London Pullman I went through the papers. First, the piece I had written for Johnson and apart from two transposed lines it was as I'd corrected: no cuts, no additions, no twists, even my own black crossheads. And as I read, I wondered whether the words would mean anything to old Mrs Waterman, but I was soon to know the answer to that little question and to one or two other questions I hadn't even asked.

Then I went through the *Sunday Times* and the *Observer* to see how the sober citizens of Gray's Inn Road and Tudor Street had dealt with the news of the day, and I wondered again what it must be like to work for a paper where the death of Stalin will make no more than 36-point caps, and football transfers get less space than ballet notes, and books rate more space than black marketeers, and as I read through *Men and Memories* in the *Sunday Times* I thought how I'd like to put old *Atticus* on to *Objects and Subjects* for a week, just to have Wensley tell him that maybe three out of our three million readers were aspiring gentlemen and might know the Quai d'Orsay was not a French café in Leicester Square, and maybe thirty more might know who had touched down for Scotland versus England in 1883, but not many more, and would he go away and write some stuff a man could read?

The Sunday Press kept me busy to Victoria, and from there I took a taxi to Soho and over lunch I sketched out my first draft for Monday's *Objects and Subjects*. And afterwards I remember I walked slowly along Charing Cross Road, through Covent Garden, down towards Court House.

Fleet Street on Sunday is a dying street in a dying city. Strangers come and stand by Saint Dunstan-in-the-West waiting for the giants to strike the long hours. Others stare forlornly in blank office windows. Others just walk. It is a street as dead as hope.

I hurried through the courtway, through the glass doors and up to my room, and began to type my copy, and I went on tapping for maybe an hour, getting it ready for Miss Arnold who came in on Sundays at half-past three.

But that Sunday things were different.

Soon after three the house phone rang. I answered and it was Wensley and he said 'Come on in. Quick!' So I left my patchwork typescript and went on in, and Wensley was standing by the window with one foot on the radiator, looking down into the courtway. He was wearing dark brown tweeds and looked like a squire in town for the day and as keen as an easterly to get back home to rural life again. He looked round as I went in and said, 'Come over here, it's warmer,' and I walked over and looked down into the courtway to see what kept him there, but it was a dull prospect, even for Sunday London: the spraying fountain and that was all.

'It's the Baron again,' he said.

'Another pal died?'

'Not this time.'

'I thought he spent Sunday deep in Wiltshire with the pedigree herd. What's wrong this time?'

'You'll know soon enough,' Wensley said. 'He wants to see you again.'

'When?'

'Now! Up at that doll's house in the park again.'

'Why me?' I asked, and I noticed the falsetto note was coming back again, but Wensley went on: 'First, he asked me why I let you write for another paper in the group. Said it spoiled your exclusive standing. Then he asked why you'd chosen Waterman. Why did you, as a matter of interest?'

'It was part of a plan.'

'I take it another part of the plan was to go down and see the old girl.'

'I did, but I didn't mention the fact.'

'It's there for anyone who's looking,' Wensley said, and I nodded, for I knew it too. 'Maybe that's what upset him, but take one of the cars and go on up and see what he wants.'

I asked what else I should know. I wanted as sound a briefing as I could get in the short minutes left, but Wensley said, 'It was all along the same lines. Pretty good balls as far as I was concerned. Your Waterman piece rattled him. That's all . . .'

'That's all,' I said.

Wensley laughed. 'Go up to the park, anyway,' he said, 'and see what the old bastard's got to say and then come back here. We can sort things out then if he's tricky.'

14

SO I went on up to the park again, this time in one of the editorial cars, and as we went along Oxford Street at a steady forty-five I told myself I was wondering how I'd upset the Baron, but that sort of self-deception rarely lasts longer than three distended minutes, for I knew well enough how I'd upset the Baron. But I didn't yet know why.

I got out at the house and told the driver to wait, saying I wouldn't be long, and I hoped I was right, and I was right, too. There was very little waiting and it was all very much to the point.

I was taken straight upstairs and into the library. My

heart was dancing like a door-knocker on a spook-ridden house and my legs had the strength of well-warmed candles, but it was all the same in the library, even the old man in his dark blue suit standing by the fire with his back to the warming logs.

I said, 'Good afternoon, sir,' but it seemed he was in no mood for the minor pleasantries of life, and he waved me to the chair and even before I had fought my early battles to settle down he had started, and from his mouth came a sharp and two-edged sword.

'Why did you write that Waterman piece I read this morning?'

I made a frown as if puzzled by his question, but I come of too short a line of actors and my byplay died a still-born death, and I said, 'I've written other Sunday features for the paper from time to time, sir. I did several in Long's time.'

'Well, I've missed them,' he said, 'otherwise I should have stopped it. You have a duty to your paper, to your editor and to myself before you go monkeying about with this sort of extraneous nonsense.'

'I'm sorry, sir. I always think——'

But he cut me short with the curt question: 'Why did you write on Waterman?'

'I found him an interesting study and——'

'There is no "and." Your job is to write for one of my papers and one only. If you find your energies aren't sufficiently absorbed by your present labours write a book.'

'Yessir,' I said.

'Why don't you write a book, anyway?' he barked.

'I haven't the necessary energy,' I said.

He smiled a thin smile that split his face as if an axehead had opened it out, not much, not for longer than it takes to tug out the axe, and then the face was solid hardwood again, and he said, 'Where did you get the material on Waterman's early life?'

'From his mother, sir.'

'When?'

'On Thursday.'

'Where?'

'Where she lives, sir. In Guildford.'

'Why did you go down there?' His voice was louder, hectoring, and I wondered how long this sort of interview went on before the thunderbolt fell and you picked up the pieces and found your way out, but we go on, we always go on until the thunderbolt does fall, and I went on with my plain and factual answers, and I was taking care to keep them short, no explanations, no excuses, no more words than it took to make an answer, so I said in the straightforward voice you keep for Old Bailey, 'I rang her up, sir.'

And then he changed again and he said, 'What did you make of the old lady?' in a quiet and easy voice as if he had been asking what I made of the weather this year. He cast his questions like a criminal lawyer and hit you hard again and again, and then he let up, and that is like a criminal lawyer, too, and now it was a genial and conversational opening, *What did I make of the old lady?*

'I thought she was a remarkable woman, sir.'

'What did you talk about?'

'About Waterman mainly.'

'She was fond of him, I suppose?'

'So it appeared.'

'What else did you discuss?' he said and the crisp note was creeping back.

'There was very little discussion about it, I'm afraid. It was all rather a monologue. She spent most of the time

76

talking about him. By the end of the afternoon I found him rather dreary.'

'He was dreary all right,' the Baron said, musing, and then he was back again, ferreting, 'Why did you let Johnson have the piece?'

'I thought it would suit the paper, sir. I got interested in Waterman after reading the paragraph you wrote and thought I'd try and write one on my own account. Johnson always seems a bit weak on political personalities. He's got nothing to put against Cross-Bencher in the *Express* or Forbes in the *Dispatch*.'

'What did Johnson say?'

'He seemed rather keen on it. At least, he says he wants some more.'

'So he tells me. What did you say?'

'I said he could ask Wensley.'

'Why were you so keen on one subject and then no more?'

'I just got interested in Waterman.'

'Why only in him?'

He was certainly piling it on, but if Sir Patrick Hastings did it to someone he didn't pay, then I suppose it was all right for the Baron to do it to someone he did, so I answered up, like a felon fighting for his freedom, and I answered pat because I was telling the truth, which is sometimes a help, and I said, 'The type has always interested me, sir. The man with money who turns to the Left. Always an interesting psychological study, don't you think?'

'There are others in Parliament. And outside. You ought to tackle some of them.'

I nodded and muttered maybe I should, but the Baron wasn't letting me leave the subject, he was flogging it until he had made it a good dead horse.

'Now you've started you should go on,' he said. 'I'll tell Johnson. He says he asked you for a series. You have my permission to go ahead. There's several: Strauss, Strachey, Stokes, any number of 'em. I'll speak to Wensley. As you say, these people are interesting. Psychologically. It could be important. A book ought to be written on 'em. You ought to write the book.'

By this time his mood had changed. He was as pleased with himself as a Portuguese admiral, and I knew I was out of it with no bones broken and only a few mild bruises, but I could see the pattern, and he had worked it well: I had been put off Waterman; I had been loaded up with work; and if I was on to something concerning the unfortunate George, I had been given a shaking-up plus a warning to lay off. And all without a plain, outright, forthright order. And then, by God, he was talking about the weather, how it had kept him in London away from his Red Polls, and he was giving a dinner on Thursday week and would I care to come? He thought it would be interesting and some useful copy perhaps. Wensley would be coming, a few business men, a lawyer, a couple of actresses, and I was saying, yessir, thank you very much sir, and I was on my way out, back on the doorstep, back in the car, and I sat in the car the way a fighter doubtless sits on the canvas, coming to around the count of eight, and I shook my head to clear away the sludge that comes with the hammer blows.

15

WENSLEY was at work on a proof of the sports page, and the fat, red, solid sports editor with the round bald pate and the stained guardee moustache stood there and took the quiet words and nodded and agreed and then was gone, and Wensley looked up as the door breathed to and said, 'Still alive and kicking, then? What did the old so-and-so want?'

'I got warned off Waterman. That was all.'

'Was he fierce?'

'Here and there.'

'Scared?'

'A bit.'

'Would you like to lay off Waterman for a bit?' he asked. 'Till the bloodhounds go to sleep?'

'I may have to,' I said. 'I've got to write six other features on some of the poor little rich boys of the Left.'

'Maybe it's better that way. How's *Objects and Subjects*?'

'I should think Arnold's got it typed by now.'

'Let's see the galley. What's the picture?'

I told him. I forget what it was. Something in line, I suppose. We tried to keep half-tones out of my column. Line made a bolder, brighter contrast to the news photographs, the art editor said, and Wensley agreed, and three days every week we succeeded, and then along came a photograph of some French actress with a deep dash of cleavage or a Mexican dancer with long uncovered legs; and suddenly the editor, the art editor and everybody else forgot about line, and Wensley would say you couldn't keep that out, not if you had a normal sort of libido, representative of your great and faithful public, and in went the actress or the dancer in ten square inches of half-tone. But as far as I remember there wasn't such a natural that black Sunday for Monday's paper, but it's there in the files for anyone who's interested.

16

WELL, that was the first part of the Waterman story as far as the Baron and Wensley were concerned, and it would have been a soothing, fragrant thought to have known it was the last part, too, but that is too much to hope for in this world. It would have suited me to go my way, write my stint of paragraphs for my old-fashioned public in the new-fashioned way, but I knew that as far as I was concerned the *status quo* had gone for keeps, along with those other remote and enviable states of repose of mind, body and spirit.

Waterman had died and his death had started something, the way all deaths start as well as end something, and maybe Donne was right and the dark Slav night where Waterman lay was part of the Baron, part of Wensley, part of me, part of our mutual grave. We come into life to seek a grave, that old mentor said, but it wasn't a grave I was after: I wasn't even after truth, the great incorruptible, unpalatable truth. I was just after a modicum of peace, but meantime I was also after a few facts for Wensley.

At least, so Wensley said.

17

SO I sent Mrs Waterman a copy of the Sunday paper that she would get by Monday morning's post, and I let Monday go and then Tuesday, midway through the morning, I took the next step and if that step stumbled I could still make another in another direction, but as it turned out the one I took turned out well enough, but that is a personal interpretation of 'well enough.'

That next step was to ring Harolde Towers on Tuesday morning, and by then it seemed my name was known about the house, for I got past the maid and was talking to the old lady herself in less than five minutes. I said good morning and hoped she had read my article and trusted nothing I had written had caused her any pain and she answered briefly, 'Nothing at all. I think you dealt with a delicate task most tactfully, considering your own political views.'

She could win prizes for her own delicate tact, I thought, but my words were a request that I might come down again that afternoon, and, as I'd expected, she bridled a bit and said, 'Why? You are not writing another article?' and she had no need to say the rest: it was plainly *Keep Out*, but the years had trained me in ways round that kind of road-block, and I began to reason with stalling sentences, and I said, 'Not quite an article, Mrs Waterman. It's rather more important than that. I could explain very quickly if I could come down to Guildford. I shouldn't take much of your time . . .' and more besides.

'Very well, then,' she said at last, grudging each word. 'Come tomorrow afternoon as you came before.'

Miss Arnold was watching as I put down the phone, and she spoke up, shaking her head, 'You're not giving that poor old lady much peace, are you? Don't forget she had a son alive this time last week.'

'He's been dead forty years as far as she's concerned,' I said.

'Perhaps she hasn't got around to thinking he's as dead as you keep telling her he is.'

My feminine instinct told me she had, I said, but Miss Arnold sniffed in disbelief.

But did my feminine instinct get me within a million miles of knowing what went on in old Mrs Waterman's mind? I wondered as I travelled down in the train on Wednesday afternoon. And how strong is the maternal instinct at eighty-five or more for a son well into his sixties? I couldn't know and I didn't particularly want to know. I should certainly be no Darby for any Joan of eighty-five who would be able to give me the truth about maternal feelings. By that time my own ex would doubtless be exercising her remarkable talent for maternity on a youngster in his fifties, and I should probably be cringing out my days in an almshouse reserved for indigent newspapermen, with a band of cronies boring each other to the grave with toothless tales of the scoops of their young and carefree days; and this heartening picture of the prospect before me, with some forty years of alimony stretching out ahead, kept me busily computing almost all the way to Guildford.

Now, looking back, and it is not so far to look back, I can see old Mrs Waterman sitting in her chair by the cosy stove and myself sitting opposite, ripening like a vine in the hot-house steam, and I can see old Gobi handing round the tea, and I can remember, too, the conversational skirmishing before old Gobi went out, the old lady asking point-blank the purpose of my visit, almost as the door shut.

It was quite simple, I said. As a one-time historian I'd become interested in her son and his influence upon the world he found.

'He did not change it much,' she said almost bitterly.

'He tried,' I said. 'He pointed out the way to change and sometimes that's important enough.'

'What do you want to do, then?'

'A friend of mine, a literary agent, thinks that a book about your son would be welcomed by the serious reading public.'

'And he wishes you to write the book?'

'Exactly.'

'Would it be a long book?'

'Not very long, I think. In any case, my projected book could only be in the nature of a preliminary study. Someone in his own party will undoubtedly wish to do a longer study later on.'

'Who would publish the book?'

'Several firms would be prepared to, I think. I shall leave that to my agent.'

She nodded. 'When would you wish to start?'

'As soon as possible.'

'That would mean going through his papers?'

I nodded. Here it comes, I thought, this is where she'll kick, this is where the plan falls apart like an old pair of stays, this is where you start again. But no. As simply as she'd ordered tea, she said, 'If my son left any papers they would be at the flat in Whitehall Mansions. I could ask Mrs Macadam—she's the housekeeper there. I shall give up the flat now: there is no point in keeping it on. Perhaps the best arrangement would be to tell Mrs Macadam that you have my permission to look through any papers that are there.'

I mumbled something about her kindness, but I don't think she heard the words: like many old people suddenly given the chance to show their authority and powers of decision she was enjoying the occasion. She asked where I lived. I told her.

'Is that very far from Whitehall Mansions?'

'Not far by taxi,' I said.

'Mrs Macadam has been with us for several years. She was here for some years and then after the war she became housekeeper to my son. I had thought of asking her to come down here after next quarter day. I shall have to give up the flat then. I understand many people want flats these days. I haven't been there myself since before the war. We have had it for thirty years.'

The bite had gone out of her voice and she spoke as if listing things to be done and the burden of affairs the death of her son had brought upon her, and she mused along like an old, old housewife with a shopping list a lot too long, and for me, watching, it was the first time she'd got anywhere near her eighty-odd years. 'There's no point in keeping it on,' she was saying, 'I had thought of asking my solicitors to arrange to go through things, but——'

'Could I help?' I said. I had seen this moment coming my way, as who wouldn't? and I was there, the ready helper, and she said, 'I don't think so, thank you very much. The disposal of the furniture and other things can be dealt with later.' Then suddenly she said, 'Could you do your work within two months?'

'I could select the material I require in a month if I could start very soon,' I said.

'I must think it over first,' she said. 'It is all rather un-

usual of course,' and once again she was the sharp old lady
who had been giving orders in the house, in the village,
on trains, in hotels, at home and abroad for most of her
years, once again she was the rich old lady full of doubts
of others' motives. The habits had got quite a hold, and
she was back in a land she knew, and I wasn't so sure of
my chances as I had been five minutes before. 'How much
time will you wish to spend at Whitehall Mansions each
day?' she asked.

I said it would be difficult to say: I worked during the
day: I should want to be there occasionally in the mornings but mostly in the evenings.

'I shall have to talk it over with Mrs Macadam,' she
said. 'If there seem to be no difficulties you will have to
make your own arrangements with her. I know too well
from experience with my son what erratic hours writers
are apt to keep.'

So we drank our Earl Grey and nibbled our chocolate
biscuits, and I listened to her talking again about her son.
Whatever disappointment he had been in life, he was certainly beginning to make some amends in death, for here
she was, nattering away non-stop about George and
plainly enjoying her voice and words. In some twisted
but understandable way she was getting her well-loved,
long-ago son back into her care through my projected
book, and maybe there are not so many mothers who
would need overmuch selling on a plan for a book about
their own, dead, only sons, and by the time I got up to go
I was mildly hopeful once again, but not too optimistic.
She would soon be alone and doubts would surely come,
suspicions of myself, doubts of the wisdom of her free
and generous gesture. Well, there it was. Certainly the
tart end of Lavinia's tongue would be heard no more by
me: we were like a pair of old busybodies in a Bourne-

mouth boarding-house discussing the merits of two brands of pekinese. Never again a journalist, pestering the life out of the mother of a week-dead son. And as I left she said, 'Perhaps it would be best if you telephoned me here tomorrow. I shall have made my decision by tomorrow morning.'

So I went back to London and to a lot of work, and on my desk was a chit from Johnson saying he'd heard from the Baron, he had seen Wensley and what about the second in his series? and by now it was *his* series and that meant I was going to be busier than I cared to be for a week or so, but I knew the other five portraits in the gallery would take less of my time than Waterman's, for they were alive, the rich boys of the Left I had chosen for my set, and a subject alive is quite a curb upon the imaginative columnist, and I wondered why it is that a painter like John or Gunn can paint a Captain of Industry or a Leader of Men, put him on canvas and there he is, in avarice and gluttony, his red fat face and his bagging eyes, his purpling veins and his thread-thin lips. And all these noble features can tot up to one of Milton's 'ugly headed monsters,' but John and Gunn don't get sued. What they have done is portraiture, not libel. But if I sit down with my old Corona and tap out the portrait in plain black-and-white, with less than half the detail, I should be up before the beak and dipping deep into my pockets. And I knew again that I lived in a world that is harsh indeed for those who live with a pen and not a brush or a sword in their firm right hands.

18

THAT was Wednesday, or part of it. By seven I had corrected *Objects and Subjects* and Wensley had seen and approved. So I left him and went along the corridor and past the cubicles and pigeon coops towards the library, for I had in mind an instructional, biographical hour. I called for the files on the first two citizens I had booked for Johnson and I opened out their envelopes and there they were. Not quite the records they sent to *Who's Who*, not quite enough and by no means all, but as far as they went they made quite a show.

I went through the first and there was his record: his speeches in the Union, his preachings to the poor, his struggles for a seat and his speeches in the House. He had written, too. Two or three books and a couple of pamphlets and there were the cuttings: what he had said and how he had said it, according to the critics. Then came the list of his holdings in the firms that brought him in the shekels. A good, rich, faithful Red.

I took the files away, back to my room. Miss Arnold had gone and I settled down to work. It was good solid reading and I couldn't go wrong. The first two articles wrote themselves.

A politician talks and he talks for the record, it is down in black-and-white: how he changed his mind, how he worked his passage. He has no other life but words, words, words. He loves his voice and he loves his words, and his words are his work, his training and his life.

A writer's life is words, but not that way, confiding them, shouting them, throwing them away by the thousand and the million, and I wondered again as I had wondered before just how a politician starts. When do his words begin to carry him away? How does that first conceit come to his youthful mind? When does he know he's found the answer to the world's besetting doubts? How does he come to think that he alone knows how to run the State, the workers and their lives?

And I looked again at the cuttings and the photographs, and I looked at my first and there he was: black-haired, full-faced, as shiny as new brass, glowing with the brotherhood of man. Nothing could stop him. He had come a long way on the length of his tongue and his father's fat purse. Somewhere a long way back he had learned to talk. He'd listened to his voice and then he'd seen the light, the pure, pink, cosy, left-wing light and now he was in, perhaps a traitor to his dad, but a saviour of the people and ready for the perks the party might provide.

I turned to my typewriter and soon I was tapping, and later, much later, I read the words through and they were tame, as tame as little lap-dogs, a lot of facts and a little innuendo and that was all, but that was enough for Johnson and the Baron and a few million readers, and by then it was ten and I needed a meal, a very long drink and a longer rest from the wheeling words. So I left the Corona and went out from the pigeon coop, down into the courtway, and the edition was running and the edition for the West was shifting down the chutes, words upon words, the countless, meaningless words of tomorrow's penny paper.

But by then I was in Fleet Street and a taxi came as taxis always come in that street, day and night, and I told him The Gargoyle, and there I had a meal and a very long drink and I sat and watched the dancers and listened to the piano and the chitter-chat. Then it was time to sleep, and I went

down by the lift, out into Dean Street and probably home
by way of Leicester Square and Long Acre, but the way
of my way back is mainly conjecture, for the drink had
been very long indeed.

19

THE next day was Thursday and I woke and faced the
fact I had been on my chapter for Wensley one whole
week, and the week would have looked pretty thin if
Wensley had been inclined towards accountancy, but it
was my fond hope that Mrs Macadam might unlock a door
in Whitehall Mansions and thereby unlock more of
Waterman than a housekeeper's memories, but I hadn't
even got as far as Mrs Macadam, and that was another
sobering thought to add to the morning's total.

Meanwhile, Mrs Burton, my own Macadam, was wheez-
ing about the kitchen and then came coffee, a slice of toast
and her morning moan. I forget what it was, doubtless
some slur upon Britain's fair womanhood or the London
Passenger Transport Board, both of which she held in
light repute, but I got up and went about those morning
labours that Job might well have listed.

By the time I got down to Court House I was pessimis-
tic again about my chances of getting near the Waterman
papers, *but why should I worry?* I asked myself; *if the old
girl crabs the idea it lets me out, and what can Wensley say?*
But that kind of thinking fades fast, and I sat and stared at
the spire of the Record Office until impatience won and I
asked Miss Arnold to get the Guildford number. And
when she handed me the phone I started with apologies

to the old lady: would she excuse my impatience and so on and so on. And she said, yes, she quite understood, she had given the matter a good deal of thought after I'd left; somebody would have to do the job and I at least had shown an understanding interest in her son, whatever my political views; she had just spoken to Mrs Macadam and from now on I could make my own arrangements with the housekeeper; she still thought the whole thing somewhat unconventional . . . but I interrupted with a laughing, deprecating reference to writers and their ways, and that seemed to bring her doubts to a trailing end. I couldn't thank her enough, I quickly said. I would phone Mrs Macadam. It would be an interesting task. I would keep her fully informed of my progress and I would certainly try to finish within a month, and thanking her again, I rang off.

Then I phoned Whitehall Mansions and asked for flat 527 and introduced myself, and the answering voice was cockney with no touch of the faraway lochs or northern hills: yes, it was Mrs Macadam speaking, and Mrs Waterman had spoken about me and everything was ready and I could come along when I liked, but best some time before five o'clock.

So just before four o'clock I went down to Whitehall Mansions and it was all as I thought it might be: a great red Edwardian block, with a bent-backed hall porter, a slow, old, cranking lift, and upstairs, on the fifth floor, the seven-roomed flat with all the comforts of Harolde Towers without the turkish bath effects, and I walked through the high-ceilinged rooms and thought how nice to be a revolutionary with that sort of background: paintings by John, Wadsworth, Sickert, two radiators and half a dozen bookcases rising like the fabric of a modest cathedral around the Regency rosewood desk.

I crossed to the desk and saw from the window what
Waterman had doubtless seen ten thousand times before
as he'd looked up from penning a few poisonous paragraphs on the state of society as seen by a faithful member
of the Party: the river, the warehouses, the tugs and the
sluggish lighters. It was certainly a room for a revolutionary with a taste for the minor pleasures of life.

Mrs Macadam was easy. You listen, you give your nodding agreement to all that is said and that is enough, and
what lonely old housekeeper with Master one week dead
can resist asking the visitor to stay on for tea? and by the
time we had finished tea in the old-fashioned kitchen we
were as cosy as a couple of rooks on a haystack. I gave her
a cigarette, lit up for her and added to my knowledge of
her widowed life: her hatreds (being alone in the flat, the
tugs hooting at night and women M.P.s); her ailments
(rheumatism, twinges in the elbow, nerves); her married
daughters (Lil in Camden Town and Rose in Bushey
Heath); her grandchildren (Ron and about four others
whose names I forget); and her habits (shopping first
thing every morning in Strutton Ground, indoors all day
and visits three evenings a week to Lil in Camden Town).
There was more and more than enough, but it was part of
the price, and I sat on and listened and blew smoke rings
until I got my chance, and when it came I said, simply
enough, 'Were you here long with Mr Waterman?'

'I've bin here ten years all told,' she said. 'I was here
just before the war and then when 'e went to Wandsworth—I suppose you know all about that—I stayed on
alone. Not in the worst of the bombing but most of it.
They let 'im out in forty-six and I bin with him ever since.'

'I suppose several people have been enquiring about
him since he died?'

'A lot from the newspapers did, but they got no change

out of me. I keep meself to meself. What they wanted to know they could get from Mrs Waterman.'

'His mother?' I asked. I thought I might as well check on that little item.

'Yes, 'is mother. Mr Waterman wasn't the marrying sort.'

I nodded and was quiet for a second: then I asked whether he always worked in the library.

'I'll say 'e did!' she said. 'Some nights he never got to bed. I used to 'ear 'im walking about all night. Or so it seemed to me. And he was no chicken. 'E was sixty-six. I'm rising sixty-two meself. I know I couldn't keep it up.'

'Did he have a secretary?'

'Yes, Miss Miles, she used to come in most days.'

'Has she been since?'

She shook her head. 'She 'asn't been for a month or more. Not since Mr Waterman went away on this last trip. It's a bit odd I 'aven't 'eard of her since all this, but I suppose she's 'eard through the papers. She was a nice young lady. She'll miss 'im.'

'Won't she have to clear things up?'

'I suppose so. Mrs Waterman was saying Mr Oliphant the solicitor will be needing 'er around, but you're going to help clear things up, aren't you, sir? So Mrs Waterman said.'

I nodded and asked when I could start.

'When you like. It's all one to me now Mrs Waterman says so. It's all them others ringing up I couldn't stick. When would you like to start?'

I said I thought I'd like to come back that evening.

'All you writing people are the same,' she said in understanding of our peculiar ways. 'All alike. Never any reg'lar hours. It was the same with Mr Waterman. Well,

I'll let you 'ave the key. I used to 'ave three nights off a week, but I don't mind telling you, these days every night is my night off. I've bin staying at my daughter Lil's since all this 'appened. I know it 'appened on the Continent, but since the war and the doodlebugs my nerves ain't what they was, and this is a big flat. But if you don't mind being 'ere on your own, sir . . .'

I said I was used to being on my own and probably wouldn't stay very late anyway.

'Mrs Waterman said you was to 'ave the keys and if you did find you was working very late I was to say you could stay 'ere if you wanted, it would be quite all right, but you needn't tell 'er I'm not 'ere every night, if you don't mind.'

I said it wasn't very likely I'd stay, and certainly I wouldn't say a word.

'Well, Mrs Waterman said to do it and I made a bed up. It's in the spare room. I'll show you,' and we went along the hall and into a small spare room with a single bed, wash-basin, light oak bookcase, chest and table, and more heavy rugs, and I nodded and said 'Very nice' again, and Big Ben boomed five and I said I'd have to be getting back to my paper, it had been a very pleasant interlude from Fleet Street, and she apologized for her gossiping, 'You know what it is all day, sir, 'ere on yer own,' and I said I knew, and went, and the keys were in my pocket.

I went back, wrote my paragraphs, went through them with Wensley, ate at The Cock and got back to Whitehall Mansions some time after eight o'clock. Unseasonable fog was moving up from the river and that is easy to remember, for as I let myself into the flat and switched on the light, the fog was stirring in the hall like a mist in a valley, but the library was warm with a fire in the grate, and I blessed the clan of Macadam if there is such an outfit, and

I knew it was just another twenty years of training that Ada Burton needed.

I was glad to be indoors the way you are glad to be by a fire with the fog in your nostrils, volumes of some consequence in the nearby bookshelves and other sundry objects that might hold the unknown words that Wensley wanted for his chapter. I tried the rosewood desk, but the drawers were locked, then the six-drawer filing cabinet and those drawers too were locked, but I wasn't perturbed. Miss Miles could help with those, and I went on wandering and snooping, and there was little enough that wasn't locked, so I turned from those inaccessible furnishings to the bookcase and made my pilgrim's progress around those shelves.

It was a fairly silent progress, for the Oriental rugs were as thick as any Oriental despot could have wished, and I thought again that revolutionary polemics could be a reasonable practice with a domestic background along the lines of Waterman's.

Well, a man's books are a man's life, the pundits have said, but I take leave to differ, for once upon a time my own books had held snippets from the wisdom of the world, and here I am, a minion, and again I take leave to differ, for I have yet to find the character who has no life because he reads no books—the taximen and bookies, pugilists and jockeys, even farmers in the distant shires.

But for Waterman the words held some truth, and I looked along his shelves and there was his record: from the Rt. Hon. Charles Booth's *Condition of the Working Classes* to all Shaw's plays in rust-red Sundour, and the Webbs' solid contributions to the slumbers of mankind in dark blue cloth, and between them were the Fabian pamphlets, rows of Left Book Club issues (and he had written three himself) and enough translations from the

Russians to set him up in a Workers' Bookshop, and it was all the old, old stuff I had seen before in the homes of all the parlour pinks I'd ever known.

There was other bookish addenda too, which was all right and proper and very much in place: all the first editions that only money can buy, but I like books, especially other people's books, and I passed slowly along the shelves, taking down a Golden Cockerel there, a Nonesuch here, persuading myself I was busy on Wensley's chapter.

Then I came to the five large buckram volumes blocked PRESS CUTTINGS on the spine, and I took down Volume I and I knew this was the first item of interest and I crossed to the fire and Waterman's armchair and the fire was glowing redly as I settled down to the collected Press cuttings of George Weston Waterman.

When does man start collecting these cuttings on himself? Why? And what kind does and what kind doesn't? The rich man from the moment he makes his first big killing? The poet when his first slim volume gets pecked at by the week-end critics? The doctor when he sees his paper in *The Lancet* and knows the potent bacillus is his and his alone? The politician when he gets his first one-inch notice in the local rag? God knows, but there was Waterman in five fat volumes, from his early days at Oxford, as carefully listed and accounted for as a bucket-shop balance sheet ready for the suckers.

I turned over the leaves of Volume I, and as I browsed I began to see the bones and the pale pink flesh of the youthful George.

His first speeches in the Union had shown signs of tolerance, strange in youth. He had wanted a world where anyone could live. But not for long. Before he came down, some time in his second year, he was moving Left and moving fast. The Marxist bug had nipped him, that was plain, and in no time at all he was out on the hustings, calling for revolt, and then came the throwaway leaflets announcing his appearance in Spitalfields and Shoreditch, Canning Town and Wandsworth, and there were the leaflets, pasted down. Then came reviews of his first book, *The Fabian Fallacy*, and then came notes on the First World War, his tribunal, prison, a record of his life as a gaoled C.O. written for a weekly, then came peace and his own denunciation of the peace, his attacks upon the British in Russia, his attacks upon the British anywhere, and reading his speeches was like reading Gandhi crossed with de Valera, and that was the end of Volume I. By then he was rising thirty-five and quite grown up, or so he would have said, and I looked to my watch and I had been in the chair for three long hours, an hour for a decade, page after page of a dead man's dirge for his fellows and his times, and maybe he was right in that, but maybe he was not so right in thinking he was the man to put it all right, but that doubt had plainly never struck him, and he still moved on, always fighting, always eloquent, always in trouble, but it was nearly midnight and I had read enough words of one man's misery or maybe grandeur and it was time to go. I put up the fireguard, put back the book, switched off the lights and went out and down in the lift and walked fast against the swirling fog, back up Villiers Street, along the Strand, up Kingsway to my own small flat above the ghostly fields of Lincoln's Inn.

20

SO I started my second week and a new way of life and it was like a movement in a timeless span. I was back twenty years, to rooms in college and midnight reading, snatched between parties and too much drink, but now I was reading, not for a First that would never be mine, not for a thing worth a beggar's coin, but only for a chapter in a book that would never see type.

Once or twice I asked myself why I went on with it. I even asked the question sitting there in Waterman's flat that first night. But half the time you just take the job on because it's a job and you do not question, for if you ask no questions you need not try an answer, and maybe that is really the simple way you wanted it all the time.

Anyway, I went back.

21

I WENT back the next night, Friday, and the drill was the same. I let myself in just after eight. The fog had gone but the fire was still there and Mrs Macadam had left her farewell on the desk. *Dear Sir gone to my daughter back about eleven Sat. a.m. Yours respectfully Beatrice Macadam.*

That night I read through Volume II, blocked PRESS CUTTINGS 1919–1922 on the brown buckram spine. On the first page were cuttings from *The Times* and the *Cork Examiner* all dated neatly in ink along the newsprint edge. They were all reports of attacks in County Cork on the R.I.C. and I worked that out as Royal Irish Constabulary. In the next twenty pages there was more along the same monotonous, murderous lines, and then, deep in the 1919 record, was the first modest mention of the Baron's name, but he hadn't been a baron in those old times: he was just a by-line in a provincial English evening and it was a straightforward despatch from Cork covering a recent journey through the South, and I remembered the Baron's words from a week before: 'I first saw something of Waterman during the Irish troubles. I was a reporter then and he had gone over to the Irish side. . . .' Well, here was part of that acquaintance, but not much. Simple reportage with no mention of Waterman or any other Englishman, just a general lament for the desolation he had seen. And in the next four pages there were five similar pieces the Baron had written those many years before, all from the Southern half of Ireland.

From then on I examined the cuttings with all the care of a beachcomber looking for the ambergris, but there were no other cuttings in that volume. And by that time it was eleven o'clock, I was weary of Waterman and it was time to go.

Saturday evening, too, I went down and I wondered why I wasn't putting in overtime chits to Wensley, but it was warm in the Waterman flat and I was beginning to feel at home. I even looked for the note from Mrs Macadam and there it was: *Dear Sir gone to my daughter and do not expect to be back till Sunday tea-time. Respect. B. M.*

By eleven that night I was through Volume IV and into Volume V. The story hadn't changed: it was still brave Waterman against the wicked world, with the world still

winning in its carefree way, but I read on, making notes
of pages to return to, but they were as few and far apart as
summer days in England, and as far as I could see, life as a
revolutionary was much the same as life round any other
parish pump: pretty damn dull to the passer-by.

By midnight I could see that with one more hour I
would finish Volume V and I decided to take Mrs Waterman at her generous word and stay the night. I went out
into the kitchen, made myself some coffee and then went
back to Waterman and read until two, and by two I was
through with Waterman and his paste-up of his own dear
life, and I totted it up: fourteen hours of solid research.

Perhaps I should have sent a midnight wire to Wensley
that the student-biographer was still at work, but I had
nothing to show but a few scrawled notes and even those
meant nothing. But I was tired, too tired to try to be
funny, and I staggered into the prim spare room, un-
dressed and flopped into the clean cold sheets and slept.

22

SOME time later I came awake and listened to the key
in the door and the footsteps in the hall, and in the
drowning moments of waking I thought, *Dear old Ada
Burton, and the coffee won't be long*, and then I remembered
where I was and looked around and it was daylight of
sorts and I knew I was in the Waterman spare room and
Mrs Macadam had come back early.

I rolled over and took a cigarette from the packet I'd
left on the bedside table, lit up and looked out at Sunday
London and once again the world was as full of fog as a

scarf is full of wool, and I thought approvingly of my sound common sense in being thus recumbent in a narrow bed with my feet quite warm. And I watched my cigarette smoke curl to the ceiling and waited for Mrs Macadam to learn I was there and bring in a cuppa, and I was as comfortable as any bed-lover is likely to be at nearly ten o'clock in the morning with no more work until the afternoon.

Then I heard the footsteps in the corridor again and I yelled as politely as the well-behaved guest does yell, 'I stayed the night, Mrs Macadam! Shan't be long!' and the door was pushed open and it wasn't Macadam but a pale-faced, red-haired young woman in a dark blue suit. She was surprised and stepped back and then came in again but not very close in, and maybe the sight of my dark unshaven jowls and bare and solid torso was enough to keep any young woman fixed at the threshold and I said in speedy explanation, 'Good morning. Sorry to shout. I thought it was Mrs Macadam.'

'Who are you?' she said, and it was plain she didn't care for the puzzle I presented.

'You're probably Miss Miles,' I said. 'I've heard about you. I've even been waiting for you.'

'Who are you?' she said again, and maybe it was the morning, maybe it was the warm and comfortable bed, maybe it was the puzzled face before me, but all I said was, 'I'm a friend of Mrs Waterman's!' She said 'Oh!' and I could see my simple words had set her back, and then she said icily, 'I'm sorry to intrude like this. Could you tell me where Mrs Macadam is?'

'She's staying with her daughter Lil. She won't be back till tea-time,' I said, and even to myself I sounded like an old friend of the family, and I could see I had Miss Miles guessing, but she made a passing shot and said, 'Well, you'll want to get dressed,' but I had my story well set in my mind by then, and I said, with as much charm as my stubbled face could make, 'As a matter of fact I'm staying here a few days.'

'But you'll still want to get dressed?' she said, the words falling like little icicles.

'I can't at the moment. I'm not dressed for getting up,' I said and I liked the remark.

'I'll make some coffee,' she said with dignity, and went from the room and shut the door with a click as precise as the *No Sale* note of a new cash register.

Miss Miles is getting back into her secretarial stride, I thought as I lay there and finished my cigarette, and I wondered where she had been since Waterman had got himself killed. I could soon find out and I wondered if she came into my story or rather, Wensley's story. And where? She certainly had a place as someone to be seen at a later date, after I'd been through the Waterman archives, but now she was here she could help straightaway. Or would she? She plainly didn't like anyone around. Or maybe it was just my own sombre face that had upset her early-morning mien, and I was glad I'd related myself to old Mrs Waterman on such a firm and friendly basis. That would help, I thought. I got out of bed, washed and dressed, left half a crown for Macadam and then went out to meet Miss Miles.

Three large suitcases were set on the floor in the corridor and a camel-hair coat was thrown across a chair, with the morning's *Sunday Times* on top. I picked up the paper and went into the kitchen. Perhaps after coffee I might find a razor Waterman had left, but for now Miss Miles must take me as I was.

She was in the kitchen, watching the coffee in a Kond come to the boil, and I stood in the doorway and watched her at her chores. She was above middle height, almost tall, slim, compact and neat, in a blue tweed suit like those you see in the Dorville ads. Under the suit she wore a light blue shirt and the outfit set off her dark red hair and pale, pale skin. Her shoes were dark brown brogues and not too clean. Her features were good. A well-shaped nose above a good mouth, the lips maybe a shade too thin, and a small cleft pointed chin. Too pale, probably anæmic, I thought, but it was a face you would notice in a train or a bus. A sad, pre-Raphaelite face, I might have said if she'd found her way into *Objects and Subjects*. Then she turned from the stove and her look said clearly she would try to do her best, and I might have been deceived by her desire to dissemble if it hadn't been for her pale green eyes, as baleful as the eyes of a cat pipped on the post by a record-breaking mouse, and she said, 'It is rude to stare.'

'Not in my job.'

'And what is your job?'

'I'm a professional starer,' I said in truth, but she turned to the coffee and set the two large cups on a black lacquered tray and I noticed the time was ten-fifteen by the kitchen clock.

'White or black?' she asked.

I chose black.

She studied the coffee as it came from the Kond. 'Have you known Mrs Waterman long?' she asked, not looking up.

'Not long.'

'Did you know her son?'

'I saw him once or twice.'

'Recently?'

'Before your time.'

She turned and looked at me with a glint in her eyes, but I was just waiting for coffee, and she said, 'Why are you staying here?'

I thought it was time to call a halt to this questionnaire and to play my part, and I said, 'I don't quite understand. I am staying here as Mrs Waterman's guest. Are there any biscuits? Mrs Macadam had some rusks yesterday,' and I took the tray and crossed to the table and sat down. Even in a flat with central heating an old-fashioned kitchen is still my choice for an early morning bite. She followed me to the table and took the other wheelback chair, and I was glad to see she knew her way around and had the tin of biscuits with her.

So we sat down to our frugal breakfast and we probably looked more like a couple of welter-weights waiting for the bell than any young Darby and Joan, or even the secretary and would-be exhumer of a week-dead Red.

'Forgive me for my rudeness,' she said. 'It was all rather unexpected. I was surprised to find a stranger here. You haven't been here before, have you?'

'No, I've always been to Guildford,' I said, truthfully enough. 'Anyway it's understandable enough, coming into what is virtually your office and finding a stranger here. This is your office, I take it?'

'Most of the time,' she said—and then the front door bell rang and she shot up quickly out of the kitchen and into the hall. I took up the *Sunday Times* and looked for the headlines. Then I heard words and the tread of manly feet, and there at the kitchen door were two men in dark grey suits with felt hats held politely in their hands, but I had seen their counterparts before, and I knew them for what they were—stalwart members of His Majesty's Metropolitan Police, and they were young, upstanding characters, seemingly anxious to do their duty, and Miss Miles was saying in a voice as breathless as a sprinter's, 'This is the man, officers. I found him here when I got in. He has no right here.'

One of the policemen came into the kitchen. I put the paper down on the table and stood up. 'I don't understand,' I said, and even to me the words and the voice sounded far too thin.

'This young lady reported an intruder in this flat. That's all,' he said. 'Anything to say?'

'Quite a lot,' I said. 'There's been a mild misunderstanding. It can easily be explained.'

'Not at all!' Miss Miles interrupted. 'You've no right here.'

'We could ring Mrs Waterman,' I said.

'This is not her flat,' Miss Miles said blandly.

'Whose is it, then?' I asked.

She turned to the police. 'We can't go on like this, officers. The man is trying to bluff his way out of the whole thing. I returned from the Continent this morning. The flat has been empty and I found him there in bed. I rang you straightaway. There may be an explanation, but I think it had better be made elsewhere. I've no wish to press any charge, but I want him out of this flat.'

The police were getting puzzled and fidgety. Perhaps the situation wasn't routine even with a 'Q' car team, so I said, 'Surely the best idea would be to try and see the management even though it's Sunday. Maybe somebody down in the office can explain about the tenancy; then we can deal with the rest.'

'Seems fair enough,' said one of the men, probably a sergeant, I thought. 'I'll go down. Stay here, Frank.'

I went back to my rusks and my coffee and the *Sunday Times*. Miss Miles moved into the living-room and Frank stayed out in the hall. So I ate my rusk and tried to work this one out: why had Miss Miles dialled 999 as she plainly had? It had been easy enough while I'd been, O, so cosily dressing and telling myself how smart I'd been *vis-à-vis*

Miss Miles. And as I crunched into the rusk I tried to sort out the reasons that could have prompted Miss Miles to her gross unfriendly act.

I started with the charitable thought that maybe she did think I was a burglar. Not very likely, but possible. I hadn't given her my name and I'd certainly tried to be clever. *But I'm not the burglar type*, I told myself, and maybe a plaintive note was creeping in, for I suddenly stopped crunching and back came the memory of the face I'd just left in the mirror, and I rubbed my hand over my chin and it came to me I was dead right for the part. *But burglars don't stay the night*, I protested to myself, but again the still small voice piped up: who knows what the modern burglar with his newfangled ideas won't do next? He cooks himself a meal, he drinks a glass of wine, so why not stay the night? It's only one station further on.

I began to look my story more harshly in the eye. There might be moments of awkwardness, but the whole thing could be cleared up in half an hour, if not here, then round at the local police station, or even at Court House, but with those calming thoughts I suddenly got one that was not so calming. Maybe all Miss Miles wanted was me out of the flat, maybe just for half an hour or even for a short ten minutes, and then I knew I'd got to stay, but how if Miss Miles was firmly fixed on my ejection and the flat wasn't in the name of old Mrs Waterman and the manager wasn't on my side either?

The doorbell rang again. Then I heard words in the hall and a split-second later the two plain-clothes men were standing at the kitchen door and I knew it was thumbs down for me, and as the senior, the sergeant of my guess, came into the room he said quite firmly, 'I'm afraid I shall have to ask you to come with me. Have you an identity card?'

'Certainly not!' I said, and tried to stay my inevitable departure with the pathetic repetition: 'Why not ring Mrs Waterman at Guildford and check with her?'

'The flat used to be in the name of Waterman. A month ago it was transferred to Miles,' the sergeant said patiently, and my jaw went down like a brewer's trap-door, for, as I saw it, there was no way out of that, at least not here, and I took my overcoat and hat and went, and as we crossed the hall to the door Miss Miles was standing in the doorway of the library and her eyes were as cold and clear as the eyes of the cat that got the mouse after all. It was as simple and sidesplitting as all that.

I went down in the lift with the upstanding pair. A black car stood against the kerb, but no crowd, thank God and fog, I thought. Frank got in beside the driver. I got in the back with the other.

'D'you really want my identity card?' I asked as the clutch went in.

'It might help,' said the man beside me.

'It's not far,' I said, 'Lincoln's Inn Fields.'

'Lincoln's Inn Fields, Fred.'

'O.K., Len.'

'So it's Frank and Fred and Len,' I said.

'It's Frank and Fred and Len,' he agreed, in a voice as flat as a dud penny's fall.

We were at Lincoln's Inn Fields in less than five minutes, despite the fog.

'Come with me, Len,' I said.

'I'm coming, all right,' he said and followed me out of the car. Frank was already waiting on the pavement.

We went up the stairs and I let myself in. Mrs Burton was in the kitchen and she bustled out, holding a dish-cloth.

'Good morning, Mrs Burton,' I said, 'I've brought

some friends back. Shan't be a minute. Mrs Burton. Len. Frank.'

'Good morning,' she said, but it was plain she was on my side and she warily backed towards her stronghold in the kitchen.

I went into the bedroom. Len was at my side. He watched me dip into the recesses of the wardrobe and hunt for an ancient odd tweed jacket. I hauled it out and from the outside ticket pocket I took my identity card.

'Knew it was here,' I said. 'Took it on a trip to the Fleet up north last year.'

He took the card. He was as unsmiling as a statue in a park, looked around the bedroom and then the living-room with that keen sniffing look the efficient blood-hound affects.

The flat was tidy. I'll say that for Mrs Burton, but it lacked the luxury of Whitehall Mansions and I could see Len was already thinking I hadn't made such a bad exchange, redhead and all. But it was doubtless his job to think along these uncharitable lines, and I let him keep his thoughts.

'Let's go!' he said.

'I'll be back, Mrs Burton!' I called aloud. 'Half an hour, I'd say, wouldn't you, officer?' But he didn't answer.

'I'll 'ave some coffee ready, sir,' she called from the kitchen.

'For one,' I said.

'Suits me,' said the voice from the kitchen.

We went out and downstairs.

We went to Cannon Row, 'A' Division, but it was all Scotland Yard to me. There I listened to Len's improbable story as two other constables looked on and one made notes. Then the duty officer phoned Guildford and old Lavinia was there and, judging by the splutter from the phone after he'd told her the flat was in the name of Miles and not Waterman, she was anxious to be up and killing, but he seemed to pacify her, and then asked if she knew of me and apparently she said she did.

And all I could do was to sit looking on.

Then they tried Wensley at Dorset Court. He was away but the maid had another number and I heard the duty officer ask for a number on an exchange via Cheltenham, and while they were getting that number maybe they began to see the truth shining in my eyes, for one of them confessed he read my column and the other took him up and they began to criticise the items in Saturday's paper and to ask how I dug out the stuff, and I said, 'Mainly by sleeping in strange beds' and they thought that was funny.

Then Wensley came through on the trunk call and it seemed he must have described me accurately enough and even admitted I sometimes worked for him, for the cops began to smile. Then the duty officer said, 'I can give him a message, sir,' and he listened and then he turned to me and said, 'Mr Wensley says you're a credit to the paper, sir.'

'Please thank him on my behalf.'

He gave my message and then he grinned and said, 'All right, sir. Not quite regulations, but seems clear enough. No need to reverse the charges, I take it you won't be long?' He laughed again and beckoned me towards his desk, holding out the phone.

I said hullo.

'You seem to have balled things up pretty thoroughly,' Wensley's voice intoned.

'Appearances are often deceptive,' I said.

'I take it this is part of the Waterman story?'

'Only part of.'

'This seems a new line. How did it happen?'

And as my companions of the morning were standing around and it seemed a chance to explain again, I said in patient explanatory tones: 'The old lady said I could stay any time I worked late. Well, I worked late. His secretary girl came back from the Continent and didn't like the look of me. Apparently Waterman had switched the tenancy to her. Some bosses do that sort of thing. That's all.'

'What's her name?'

'Miss Miles.'

'She wanted you out?'

'So I gathered.'

'Had you found anything worth finding?'

'Nothing.'

'Will you be going back?'

'Probably.'

'Face like an old boot, I suppose?'

'Not so old and not such a boot,' I said gallantly.

'I'm coming up this afternoon. I'll come and bail you out.'

'Thanks a lot. I hope to be out before then.'

'I'd like to know a bit more about this Miles woman. Where's she been? How close was she to Waterman?'

'Our friendship was very brief,' I said.

He laughed. 'Well, take it easy. See you about five,' and he rang off and in less than ten minutes I was out, warmed by a cup of black tea from the station canteen, reunited with my identity card, a free man again, with grins and apologies all round.

They offered to take me back, and I took up the offer. So I went back in style and waved the boys good-bye and climbed to my eyrie, and all I wanted was a wash and a shave and a moment to rest.

23

BUT I didn't get my rest. Mrs Burton was there pottering about, her sketchy sabbatical dues long done, but this was a chance in a million and she was seizing it and she said, 'Coppers, wasn't they, sir?'

'Coppers, Mrs Burton.'

'Did they take you in, sir?'

'Just for a general check-over.'

Too ostentatiously she dusted the spotless table. 'Nothing in partic'lar, sir?'

'Nothing in particular, Mrs Burton. Drunk, disorderly, rape, the usual. No more. Can I have some coffee?'

'You're 'aving me on, sir. It's all 'ere, sir, just on the boil.'

It was certainly a morning of innocent drinking, so I had more coffee and, later, as I stared at the stubbled face to shave I could quite see the whole operation or most of it from the viewpoint of Miss Miles, but that bout of good-fellowship didn't last for long: I finished shaving in a fury and changed into another suit, went out into the living-room, finished my breakfast, said farewell to Burton and walked down to Kingsway, into the Strand and along to Whitehall, and the clock over Bravington's at Charing Cross told me I'd been awake for nearly two short hours.

24

FOG was moving in the streets, burning the eyes like foaming chloride, and the town was as dead as Nelson on his column.

I bought the morning papers and wandered across Trafalgar Square to what I hoped would be a second meeting with Miss Miles. And as I crossed the Square I felt the key of her flat in the pocket of my best grey suit and wondered whether that key was enough. It had let me in before, but now there would doubtless be a bolt, a catch and a lock, and with any one of those modest items my morning walk would be a walk in a fog and nothing more.

I tried to remember, but it was all too vague. I'm not the Boy Scout type. I never notice numbers of suspicious-looking cars, I never look at locks in the houses I stay in, and I knew I could peer into my black blank mind till dusk and still no image of that Whitehall door would glimmer back and I gave it up. My only hope was the mitred key.

The block was quiet and forsaken as I went in through the hall. The lift was empty and I let it stay that way and began the long climb to the fifth floor. The stairs were covered in a red-green Turkey carpet and that helped. Creaking stairs were no part of the prelude I wanted for my social call.

At the fifth and final floor I paused for a deep and needed breath and looked from the window, but only the fire-escape stared back. Fog moved around and within its old iron limbs like wisps of dank grey hair. Then I turned into the corridor and walked along to the flat.

I probably stood outside the door for three or four seconds but the seconds moved like hours, then I put the key in the lock and turned and the door opened as smoothly as any anticlimax, and I was inside the hall, and two seconds later, inside the library.

Miss Miles was standing by the writing-table and it looked as if she had been working hard while I'd been away, for the green steel filing-cabinet was open and the leather table-top was covered with papers. She showed no surprise as I came in and said my piece about happening to be passing.

'Then I'm afraid you'll have to leave again,' was all she said in a weary voice, as though I were a spoiled brat who must be taught a lesson and she reached for the phone, but I said quietly, 'Not again. It gets monotonous,' and her arm dropped heavily, almost in relief. Then she crossed to the fire and sat down in the armchair.

I was glad to see the fire going, but not so glad to see she'd already started burning the Waterman archives, and as I looked down at the charred papers she said, 'What is it you want?' in a tired flat voice.

'I told you. I'm a friend of Mrs Waterman's.'

'I know all Mrs Waterman's friends. She has three and they're all over eighty.'

'I'm eighty-three and feel eighty-four,' I said. 'Anyway, phone her.'

'I have,' she said. 'At least she phoned me. That's one reason I didn't bolt the door. I guessed you'd come back.'

'Then you know I'm telling the truth.'

'I know you're a liar!' she said in a sudden spurt of anger and got up suddenly and crossed towards the desk.

I crossed with her, but she was only after a cigarette from her bag, so I let her take it and even lit it and took one for myself. 'What are you after?' she asked, and it was plain she was nonplussed.

'Nothing much,' I said. 'In fact, it's all very simple, as I would have explained before if you hadn't been so keen on the police. Mrs Waterman has probably told you I'm writing a short Life of Waterman, that's all. You've kicked up a shindy about nothing at all.'

'Who are you writing it for?'

'A publisher.'

'Which publisher?'

'One of the few my agent likes.'

'Why pick on Waterman?'

'I should have thought that was fairly obvious,' I said. 'You were his secretary. You must have known he was quite an influence with some people. He set himself up as a public figure. He ought to be written about. That's all.'

'That's not all!' she said, flinging out the words. 'And you know it!'

'I'm just after a few facts,' I said.

'Facts for that beastly rotten newspaper of yours?'

I was back on my heels for a split-second, but then it came to me and I said, 'Mrs Waterman told you that, I suppose. Well, now you've got that off your chest, why not sit down and give me a few facts.'

'Facts!' she scoffed. 'I hate all you stand for. Now get out! Please!'

It was temper—temper all right. Her cigarette was going like Stephenson's Rocket on a gradient. She couldn't keep still. Two steps this way and two steps that across the Kelim carpet. She was at the limit of her nerves. *A few more questions*, I told myself, *and she'll crack like an old plate*. So I went on with a few more questions.

'I take it you were in Yugoslavia with Waterman.'

'I was,' she said.

'Why did you dial 999 this morning? A touch of hysteria?'

She slumped into Waterman's armchair, threw her cigarette in the fire and asked for another. I took out my case, gave her one and lit it.

'Not at all. When I came in here this morning I smelt stale cigarettes and then found the last volume of George's —Mr Waterman's—Press cuttings out on the desk. I wondered who'd been at them. Then I found you here. I didn't know you from Adam. I wanted time to think. I had to get rid of you. So I dialled 999. That's all.'

'Why couldn't you have asked me to go?'

'Because I knew you wouldn't. Two words with you told me that.'

She was right enough there, I thought, but I went on: 'Why didn't you lock the door on me again?'

'Because Mrs Waterman was angry and said you were her guest.'

'But the flat's in your name. You don't have to bother with her any more.'

'I know. I know,' she said wearily, 'but I don't want to face all that just yet, that's all.'

'What d'you mean by "all that"?'

'Nothing!'

'Why did you try to dial the police again when I came in just now?'

'Let me alone. Please. I was only trying to bluff. I wanted to be alone. I'm tired, tired, tired,' and she said the words as if they were small dull blows. Then suddenly tears came, one, two, three. I watched them as they moved down her cheek. She stared straight ahead as if she were weeping absent-mindedly, her thoughts far off. Then suddenly more tears came and her head drooped. I took the blue foulard from the outside pocket of my best grey suit and threw it in her lap, and as she groped for it I said, 'Take it easy.'

I wanted her to take it very easy, for I had a lot more questions, but I had most of the day before me and I thought she might as well build up now for the question-time ahead. So we were quiet for a while, and I crossed to the window but there was nothing to see. London was part of the fog. The city and the river were as still and distant as if they had never been, and I stood there going over the sad case of Miss Miles and perhaps the sadder case of George Weston Waterman, and when I turned round I said, 'Why don't you go and lie down for a while? You've obviously been under considerable strain.'

Her eyes went straight to the papers on the table and I said, 'I'll look after these,' but she sat on with a near-wild look in her pale green eyes.

'No you won't. You're not to. I have his instructions.'

'Maybe I can help,' I said.

'You!' she scoffed in a high-pitched voice, and then, as if resigned, tired beyond endurance, she said, 'I'm sorry, but there's so much that's private.'

'I shall know what is and what isn't,' I said, but she wasn't ready to let go yet, and she shook her head, and I could see I had need of a few more questions, but that was easy, for the first fine fervour of her would-be bluff had died and she sat there in the armchair as near all-in as an all-in wrestler.

I said, 'How long had you been with Waterman?'

For a moment the fire came back, and she said, 'Why do you ask so many questions? For your ghastly news-paper?'

I shook my head. 'Just interest,' and maybe that was the truth or maybe she was just too tired for she said, 'I've been here about four years.'

'After he came out of Wandsworth?'

She nodded. 'Soon after.'

'Your first job?' I went on and again she nodded and looked up, and something in her look, way back behind the eyes, brought a vague idea, as vague as a cloud, and I said, in a voice as quiet as I could make it, 'You came to know him *very* well?' and my *very* was the word in a million. I knew and she knew and she nodded, and her nod was limp, a sign to say there was no more fight, at least not yet, and she fingered the foulard kerchief and tears were near again, and suddenly she was no longer a young ex-mistress to a dead old man, but a young worn woman, out on her own with a new job to find, but maybe Waterman had also taken care of that and she would slog no more with her pencil and her notebook and her typewriter, but I could get around to that later.

For a while I had no more questions and I sat there looking at the rug and wondering how a citizen of sixty-six gets around to running a mistress some forty years his junior, and it seemed to me, in that contemplative moment, as it had seemed to me before, a performance to salute if not to applaud.

But *before* had always meant the same, the usual mint, familiar as pennies: fat old men with bursting bellies and sagging jowls, pie-eyed blondes, as innocent as gaolers and as hard as mahoe. And the exchanges had been made on a very strict basis of cash-and-collect. The popsy got her comforts, her mink and her shekels, and the old tycoon got a cosy companion made of little chips of granite.

But here was the mint with the coin somehow different, and I looked across at young Miss Miles and I thought again of her recent protector with the dry, professorial face I had seen on long-ago platforms and in latter-day photographs, and my thoughts were the speculations anyone sponsors in similar circumstances. I could see his point, but what had she been after? Well, I could try finding out, but not just then.

So I went on wondering, and I could see the young redhead meeting her boss the very first day. And maybe the spell was spun the moment she gave old Pitman's outlines to Waterman's words of woe, his message to the masses. Or maybe the sense of being at the centre of a new world in the making. Or maybe it was the usual mint with the usual milling: an old man's siege and a final giving-in.

I looked up and she was sitting back in the chair with her eyes closed and she looked near enough to the end of that morning's tether. So I got up and took her arm, and I could have put up a brass plate as consulting hypnotist the docile way she followed me into the main bedroom and flopped down on the double bed, and I pulled the patchwork quilt over her and said in my best tones, 'Take it easy for a bit,' and I wished Wensley had been around to see his columnist engaged on research.

Or did I? I wondered, as I went back into the library.

There, spread out on the writing-table, was a section of the Waterman record I hadn't seen. I went across to the open filing-cabinet and took out a folder and it was loaded with the originals and carbons of a long correspondence with a group of characters whose names began with N, and I turned over the sheets and some of the names were names I knew, and they were names well known on the farthest Left, but most I didn't know, for more than half were foreign, residents of Paris, Prague, Belgrade, Warsaw and a dozen other cities. I took the folder back to the armchair by the fire. The day was still young.

I must have spent nearly an hour going through the

files. Waterman had been quite a correspondent, a one-man intelligence unit, and here were the records: instructions given, information received, payments made and data noted. The files held the names of a multitude of citizens and much of their works: politicians, scientists, technicians, but mostly Party organizers of the workers of the world, and I could have sat there most of the day and a month ahead, learning enough about my fellows to fill a column every day in a leap year, but I was a superficial spy: I was just looking for exchanges between the Baron and Waterman. But the files on that account were blank.

I used another half-hour standing by the cabinet, going through another drawer stuffed full of negatives, photographs, drawings, notebooks, galley proofs and diaries, but as far as I was concerned it was a big double-blank all the way.

By then it was half-past one and I was hungry, and I thought I owed a guest's duties to Miss Miles and I went out and into the bedroom. She was sleeping soundly under the patchwork quilt and, looking down, I thought that Waterman's choice had been reasonable enough. Even the London fog, milling round the windows, couldn't dim the lustre of the dark red hair, and if the features had been just an old man's pleasure, well maybe I was old some years before my time. But this contemplation, I reminded myself, was no part of the morning's labour and I gently shook her shoulder, and as she came unwillingly awake I told her it was time for lunch, and I went out, before she was ready for another display of suspicion of my good intentions in the Waterman household. And anyway I was hungry.

I lit a cigarette and waited, and in less than ten minutes she came into the room. Rouge, powder and lipstick had helped and she looked ready for any battles ahead, but I said, 'Let's leave all this,' and without demur she nodded, and we left.

We went down in the lift and out into the fog and Whitehall and walked up through Trafalgar Square across Piccadilly Circus to the Café Royal. We did not talk and that suited me, for it was late and it was time I was beginning to compose my paragraphs for Monday's paper, and although dalliance with Miss Miles and the Waterman files had their manifold attractions, I kept to *Objects and Subjects*. They promised a more likely and regular income, and I began to write and rewrite the crossheads in my mind.

25

WE went up to the first-floor gallery and took a table for two, and late as it was the waiter let me order lunch, and as we waited for the two large Martinis Miss Miles smiled for the first time that day as she said, 'It's just as well Mrs Waterman told me something about you or I'd be sitting here with a complete stranger.'

'I tried to stay for breakfast,' I said, and after she'd smiled dutifully I asked about her own life. 'I know you were Waterman's secretary, but that's all.'

And as if she were waiting for the cue she said her piece in self-assured, staccato shots: 'Ruth Helen Miles. Spinster. Twenty-five. Secretary. Any other details?' and what might have been a few awkward moments of sparring and shadow-boxing faded away as she said, 'I must apologize for this morning. Finding you there was a shock, but I didn't mean to do anything as foolish as I did. Everything about the last fortnight has been awful. I suppose it all suddenly caught up with me and . . . oh, I don't know. Perhaps I lost my nerve or maybe I was over-tired. Anyway, I know I feel thoroughly ashamed of myself. Can you forgive me?'

'We're lunching together,' I said, and after some inconsequential chatter about her journey back by the overnight Dunkirk–Dover ferry, the state of the waves in the English Channel, the fog in London and other travellers' asides, I asked whether she had been with Waterman when he'd been killed, in another jeep or anything, but she said no, she'd stayed behind in Belgrade to type out the notes for his farewell speech. Then I asked whether she'd been having an interesting time till then.

She said 'Very!' with emphasis and began to talk about the Yugoslavian journey she had taken with Waterman, and to me it sounded like a saga of pointless purgatory with its junketings and jaunts, its tongue-twisting names of the proud politicos and its flood of figures on Tito's five-year plan, but her eyes lit up as she lived it all again, and I could see I was as far from understanding the unsullied subtleties of Left Wing politics as I was from following the late Professor Planck's additions to the Quantum Theory. So I let her talk and soon 'Waterman' became 'George' and I sat watching her come alive again, and in the recital her eyes held a far more civil glow than they had held for me that morning, but why not? I hadn't paid her, taught her, bossed her or slept with her as Waterman had doubtless done, and she still had her memories, so I waited for the minestrone, sipped my Martini and listened.

She talked quite fluently and it was doubtless a tale of a noble endeavour, and Tito came into it and his henchmen, too, Kardelj, Rankovic, Djilas and half a dozen other outlandish names that never found a place in my homely column, but to her they were plainly heroes of a Workers' War and a Movement of the Masses that couldn't be matched by Attlee and his minions in the septicæmic west, but I was host, the day was Sunday and I was hungry, so I let her talk, but twice she stopped. The first time she said, 'These things mean nothing to you,' and I said, 'Maybe, but go on. I'm a newspaper man. I'm always willing to learn,' and the second time she said, 'I'm talking too much,' and I said, 'That's all right. I won't give you away.'

'What do you mean?' she asked.

'Well, aren't you being very unfaithful to the Party, coming back so keen on Tito? It isn't toeing the Party line, is it?'

'I'm not a member of the Party,' she said.

'What are you, then? And what was Waterman?' I asked.

'That doesn't come into it at all. I'm merely telling you what I saw.'

'All right. All right,' I said. 'You're as sold on that old tough Tito as Zillyboy himself.'

'I'm *not* a member of the Party,' she said again.

'And Waterman?' I asked. 'You missed that out before.'

'George went out to see for himself,' she said. 'He wasn't a member of the Party either. He never saw eye-to-eye with Pollitt. And he wasn't as keen as I was on what he saw in Yugoslavia, but he was very impressed.'

Then the waiter reappeared with the soup and even some rolls, and for a while there was silence, apart from those decorous little decibels that even the most sophisticated soup-drinkers have never yet subdued.

I passed the time by sketching in my mind an outline for a portrait of my unexpected guest, but the first trial lines were inclined to be blurred. I hoped that lunch-time would bring some strength to my wavering draughts-manship. I started with the line that she had some sort of courage. She had called the police and that took resolve if nothing more. Then there was her liaison with Waterman, and if I judged aright, and Miss Miles had come from the middle-class background I'd judged she'd come from, then that affair had also taken courage.

But why courage? I asked myself. It could have been cowardice. Perhaps Waterman had offered her the easy way. And maybe she had taken it. I didn't know. I hadn't been around, and I could see my portrait blurring already, and she said with a smile, 'You're very serious suddenly. Have you run out of questions?' And with this skittish departure from our mood of the morning I put aside the sketch and returned to my well-established manner of friendly cross-examination, and I said, 'You won't be angry, then, if I ask a few more?'

She shook her head, watching me closely. 'Don't forget I've had a sleep and you've had a shave since this morning,' she said, 'but first let me ask you one. May I?'

This was a new mood and it had me guessing, but I nodded and she said, 'Why are you so interested in Waterman?'

'Any man with all that money and those odd politics would interest me,' I said.

'Did he have so much, then?' she asked and for a moment I thought she looked as if she didn't know.

'Enough,' I said. 'More than most other Reds, anyway. The articles he wrote didn't pay the rent.'

'Is that the only reason you're writing a book about him?'

'It's the best I can think of.'

'Why just that?'

'I want to know whether it was having all that money that made him a Red, and if it was, why he didn't give the stuff away.'

'Why do you think he didn't?' she asked, unmoved.

'I think he was the old-fashioned kind who just likes having his cake and eating it too,' I said.

'I know that's the cheap way it reads in your newspapers,' she said coolly.

But I'd had that before: you get used to it and I said, 'It's the world's cheap curiosity as well. Anyway, I'm the one with the questions. You've had your turn. Can I go on?'

She nodded, but our cuts from the Sunday joint came then, I seem to remember, and we were silent for a time as the waiter flapped around. I waited until he'd gone and even then I didn't ask a question but offered a remark, without premeditation of any kind at all, or so at least I tell myself. I said, 'Somehow, somewhere I've picked up the notion that your boss and my present boss were mixed up in some business or other some years ago. It's probably a pretty far-fetched notion, but I'd like to find out whether there's anything——'

'You must be mad!' she said, jamming her sentence into mine. I watched her as she spoke and the words sounded genuine, but I didn't know, and I said, 'You never heard anything of it, then?'

'Whenever George talked about any newspaper baron he got very angry. He hated them all and all they stood for.'

'Fifty-fifty,' I said. 'They weren't so keen on him and all he stood for,' and I wished the Baron had been standing by to hear this defence by one of his merry men, but Miss Miles brushed the remark aside and maybe her feminine curiosity was coming into play, for she said,

123

'Why do you want to know if they were mixed up, anyway?'

'Just interest,' I said.

She laughed shortly and scornfully.

'Knowledge for the sake of knowledge,' I went on patiently. 'I was interested in the study of history once. If they'd ever been linked up it would at least be an interesting historical fact. Don't you agree?'

'Perhaps, but George never mentioned it. Anyway, I told you, he hated everything to do with newspapers and Press lords.'

'Except the *Worker* and the *Herald* and the *Mirror* and the *Sunday Pic* and *Reynolds* and the boys who own those little properties that love the workers.'

'He had very little use for the *Herald* and none at all for the *Mirror* or the others,' she said with a smile.

I was surprised to see the smile. Miss Miles was certainly back in the ring again, I thought. She even had a sense of humour, but maybe I was the joke and not the *Herald* or the *Mirror*, but that would doubtless be made clearer as the meal went on, and the meal, I remember, went on with fewer questions than I'd originally planned, but I started again with one I'd had in my mind for an hour or more and I said, 'You were very attached to Waterman?'

And again she smiled and she said, 'Why not?' and I said limply, 'I gathered you were.'

'Of course I was,' she said. 'I suppose you had a father.'

'It was a legend in the family,' I said, and watched the smile still set in her pale, pale face. The questions were by no means going the way I'd meant them to go, so I tried the trick I had tried at Harolde Towers and I said, 'He was a father to you, then?'

'Amongst other things.'

Again I was countered and again she smiled and then she said, 'He was my employer. I was also his mistress if that is what you are trying to imply.'

Even if the data is what you seek, it sometimes comes in disconcerting ways, and I wondered how I phrased a reply to that modest statement, but you don't, you let it pass.

Miss Miles had certainly recovered from her morning doldrums.

'Why do you beat about the bush so? Not every young woman is so keen on men of her own age. I found George Waterman a very interesting man. The fact that he was a good deal older than I was didn't seem as important to me as it seems to you, that's all.'

'Isn't forty years more than a good deal older?' I said with malice aforethought, but she was unperturbed.

'Only for some women,' she said in a quiet voice that was plainly meant to correct my manners, my faulty knowledge of the feminine mind and my general boorish outlook, but you can get to a point where those considerations pass you by, and I said, 'Why didn't you marry him, then?'

'We didn't want to.'

'Why not? It seems logical for a bachelor and a spinster.'

'I said I didn't object to your asking questions. I didn't say I'd answer them,' she said easily, a lot more easily than I deserved, but I wanted to shake her out of her equability. She was far too serene for the purpose I had in mind, but it was plain I would get no farther, and I put those questions aside for another time and transferred my curiosity to more urgent items, and I asked what she'd been burning in the fireplace before my return and she said, 'Nothing very important. An exchange of compliments between

George and Marshal Tito, a lot of notes and correspondence about our trip, some other letters. Something your paper would have made into a lot of mischief—even though the Press lords now love Tito.'

'Shouldn't you have sent it all on to Party H.Q.?'

'I've told you: I'm not a member of the Party and George wasn't a member,' she said and this time she wasn't even emphatic, but as bland as a Hindu dancer. 'Many people made the mistake of thinking he was.'

'He used to be?'

She nodded, 'He was, but he left the Party after he came out of Wandsworth. I know because he had just decided to leave when I first went to work for him.'

'Word didn't get around,' I said.

'Why should it? It was a personal matter. When a man leaves the Conservative Party he doesn't have to announce it in the *London Gazette,* does he?'

I laughed. It was a good point, a dialectical bull's-eye, and she went on, 'Why are people so keen to know what Communists do all the time?'

'People feel safer that way,' I said. 'Even the average Socialist doesn't feel so nervous when a Communist isn't likely to be his boss next week.'

'Why be so scared of a political party with scarcely forty thousand members?'

'Whoever called Communism a political creed was a genius,' I said. 'Maybe it's a religion of sorts. Maybe it's a disease of sorts. Maybe something between the two. I'd like to know what it is that persuades one comrade to send another to the chopping-block if it suits the Party line. What is it?' But she evaded the debating point and said in a quiet, almost apologetic voice, 'I wouldn't know. I'm not a member of the Party either.'

'Why did Waterman quit?'

'He didn't quit. I don't like the word. Neither would he. He left. There were several reasons, all mainly personal.'

'He could never see eye to eye with anyone for very long,' I said, trying to prick her out of this sabbatarian calm, but she said, 'Yes, that's true. He always had a knack of falling out with anyone in time,' and I could see that I had been side-stepped again.

Then some *biscuits glacés* were brought to the table and we were quiet for a while, doubtless holding on to our teeth, for the *biscuits* were certainly *glacés*, I remember, an unsound selection for a cold and foggy day, but with the coffee we began to talk again.

The talk was far away from Waterman, the Baron or words for Wensley's chapter. We began to talk of Miss Ruth Miles and her early life, and the first leading questions she answered civilly enough, and then there was no need for questions: she talked as any woman talks about that old, old subject nearest and dearest to herself.

The story was simple enough. She had no tricks of narrative and she had no reservations, or so it seemed, and she enjoyed the telling and I enjoyed listening, even though I told myself fairly early on that a simple story told by a redhead is never as simple as all that.

She had been born, a farmer's daughter, somewhere in the West Country, near Devizes, as far as I remember, and she'd lived on the farm until she'd gone to boarding-school somewhere in Cheltenham. Then just before the war her father had died, and in the first month of the war her mother had remarried and gone to live in Cornwall with her new-found partner, and mother and daughter had begun to drift apart.

Ruth Miles was fifteen then and anxious to play her part in the war, but she was too young and she stayed on, fretting in the old-established boarding-school her mother found convenient and far enough away, but at the age of seventeen she'd escaped, come to London, taken a course in shorthand-typing and prepared herself seriously to join one of the Services. She'd joined the Wrens in 1942, but as a communications officer and not as a secretary. She had gone to India, to Delhi and then down south to Mountbatten's outfit in Kandy. Then she'd picked up a malarial bug of sorts and had been invalided out. She'd come back to England, taken a secretarial course and then had taken the Waterman job at the end of '45.

Waterman had just come out of Wandsworth where he'd been under 18B and apparently he had wanted to get quite a few reminiscences down in black-and-white. After a week or so at Guildford he had come refreshed to Town, keen to take up where he'd left off those years before. Some days, she said, he had dictated like a man possessed for five or six hours. It had been pretty heavy going, but she had stood up to it with no more than three or four shots at a nervous breakdown. Then Waterman had begun to calm down. They had become more friendly.

'What did he dictate?' I asked.

'His memoirs.'

'Where are they?'

'In the flat.'

'Wouldn't they save me a lot of work?'

'You'd find them prejudiced,' she said.

'I'd find them interesting.'

'I don't think so. They were the record of his mind, not his movements, but see them, by all means. They only cover the war years, anyway.'

I asked her to go on, but the rest I knew, she added simply, and that was all.

And I said thanks, it had been an interesting story, and

by then it was three o'clock and the waiter was a black in-human shadow fidgeting at the edge of the table, so I paid him for his tribulations. And as we went down by the wide staircase Miss Miles said she still had a few questions of her own to ask, and by that time we were doubtless in a mood for exchanges, for when she said, 'You write that *Objects and Subjects* column, don't you?' I nodded genially and waited for the rest, but there was no rest. 'What did you do before?' she asked.

'I was a student of history,' I made answer. 'I told you before.'

She laughed. 'I thought once a student always a student. Aren't you a student of history now?'

'Probably, maybe a different kind of history.'

'Your boss's kind, for instance?' she asked, but I shrugged the question off. That sort of query is too easy and the answer is anything anyone wants it to be and may-be she saw that, for she quickly asked another, asking how I got into the newspaper business, and I said, 'A man called Wensley took me in. He's my editor.'

By that time we were downstairs round by the cloak-room, and as I put in my numbered ticket and took my coat she asked how I had come to meet him.

'A charitable friend of mine sent me to see him two years before the war.'

'As a writer of fame or of promise?' she asked with a smile.

'As a down-and-out historian. I was broke. It was as simple as all that.'

We went out into Regent Street and the fog was lifting fast. She asked how I'd come to start my feature, but that was easy and I said, 'The way any feature starts on a newspaper. Because another newspaper starts it first. The *Express* had Driberg and his Hickey feature: *These Names*

Make News. Probably before your time.' She nodded. 'So the Baron thought we ought to have a Hickey feature. So we started *Objects and Subjects* and I happened to be hanging around after two or three others had made a flop at it. Wensley gave me the chance. That's all.'

'But somebody had to start Hickey,' Miss Miles protested, trying to get back to first principles.

'Maybe Chaucer,' I said. 'Maybe Defoe. Maybe Addison and Steele. Lots of Grub Street types have had a shot at gossip,' and my words were a stern reminder that my next day's stint was still to do, but Miss Miles was really interested, it seemed. 'What happened to your column during the war?' she asked.

'It died a week after Driberg's dried up.'

'And what happened to you?'

'I was in a prisoner's cage most of the time. Not Waterman's kind. A long way off.'

'You were a war correspondent, then?'

'No, just an ancient mariner who came to grief like the original one.'

We were half-way down Haymarket by that time. A taxi came. I hailed it and told the driver, 'Whitehall Mansions, then Fleet Street.'

In the taxi I said, 'I still want to carry on with my work on Waterman. Are you willing to let me carry on or do we have to fight about it?'

'I'm willing,' she said. 'For one thing I want to see how historians work. For another I don't believe your story.'

'Why not?'

'It's out of character.'

'So is your story about Waterman and you, but I believe it,' I said, and even in the gloom of the taxi I saw her blush for the first time, and she was left without an answer, and I said gently, not noticing, 'How much stuff will you burn this afternoon?'

'None if you wish,' she said.

'Why the turnabout?'

'Put it down to the deep sleep and the good lunch,' she said.

The taxi had stopped outside the tall, red-brick block of flats. 'I've been coming in at about seven or eight o'clock. Will that be all right for you?' I asked as I left.

'Of course. I may be in. I may not. I don't know yet, but everything will be there,' she said, and I left her standing on the kerb and the taxi went on towards Charing Cross, and as I travelled I puzzled over the moods of women, how they can be hysterical at twelve o'clock, bloody-minded at one o'clock, reasonable at two o'clock, demure at three o'clock. But all that was old stuff. I was one of a long line of puzzlers stretching back to Adam. So I left it and tried concentrating on *Objects and Subjects*.

26

I'D half-finished my paragraphs by half-past four and then the house phone rang and it was Wensley and he said, 'So you're back. Come on in and I'll saw the handcuffs off.'

So I took up my three typewritten quarto sheets and went on in. He was sprawled along the sofa, deep in the leather, and he waved me to an armchair and grinned as I sat down. 'Tell me the whole squalid story,' he said. 'Right from the time you found her in bed.'

An editor has to have his little jokes, I thought, but for the sake of the record I put him right, and he said, 'I'm sorry. I knew it was one or the other. I always get these things wrong. Well, she found you in bed. And then?'

He listened as he always listened, staring at the ceiling or the Persian rug, but never in the eyes of the teller of the tale, and at the end he said, 'So you've found nothing?'

'Only the Irish cuttings the Baron wrote in 1919.'

'Well, we more or less knew that.'

'We know the Baron said they met.'

'Same thing.'

'But this at least places the meeting in Southern Ireland, maybe the Cork area.'

'A bloody big area,' Wensley said, 'but I suppose it does that, if that's the only reference Waterman kept. But it doesn't take us very far. Found anything else?'

'Nothing.'

'Is it worth going on? Maybe there's nothing in it after all. Maybe it's all my eye.'

'I'll go on for a bit. I'll let you know soon enough if I think the whole thing's a frost. He's written his memoirs apparently, but only of his prison life.'

'What's the redhead like?'

'Quite nice-looking in a pallid sort of way.'

'Intelligent?'

'She thinks she is.'

'Always a help,' Wensley said. 'Would it speed things up if you got her into bed?'

'I'm too slow a worker,' I said. 'You've got one or two experts on your staff. Try them.'

He laughed. 'You underrate your personal magnetism. What's for *Objects and Subjects?*' And he pushed and pulled his great weight off the sofa, and I handed the sheets across to him and he stood by the desk reading them through, and as he handed them back he said in his quiet and casual way, 'Why that piece about the Regency house?'

'It's interesting.'

'How many of our readers know what a Regency house is? And how many of 'em care whether a Regency house stays up or gets pulled down, especially if nobody's living in it. Do you care?'

'Vaguely,' I said.

'Why not fervently?'

'I'm not the fervent type.'

'You ought to be a bit more fervent about some of these items you print. I'd drop the house if I were you. What else have you got?'

'I was going to run the rest on Regency architecture. Show what it was. How it looked. Why it's worth preserving occasionally.'

'Any pictures?'

'Four engravings. They'd make quite decent line blocks. I thought I'd make a box of 'em.'

'Sounds a good idea,' he said. 'I should get cracking or you'll be late.'

I went from the room. Dealing with Wensley was sometimes like dealing with a handful of water.

27

I WENT back in the evening.

Mrs Macadam met me in the hall and I could see she was in a conversational mood. 'I hear you've already met Miss Miles,' she said as I took off my overcoat. She followed me into the library, and as I took the chair by the desk she said her piece, 'Quite a commotion, I 'ear, sir. Miss Miles told me all about it. Police an' all.' I smiled at the memory and hoped my smile was not as frozen as it felt and I said, 'Yes, we met. Is Miss Miles in now?'

'No, sir. She went off this afternoon. She said she was going off to see a friend. She thought you'd be back. No 'ard feelings, I 'ope, sir. She's a nice girl really. I can quite see her point.'

So could I, I said, but I wasn't going to be let off as easily as that, for Mrs Macadam was beginning to enjoy herself, and to stay her words I asked a simple question, 'Did Miss Miles tell you the flat's all hers, too?'

She nodded violently. 'Bit of all right for 'er, wasn't it, sir? Bit of a shock for the old lady though. Wonder what she'll 'ave to say about it!' She stood with her hands crossed upon her apron. 'I was just going to 'ave a cuppa. I know the fog's gorn, but it stays in your throat. Shall I get one for you?' and she went from the room and I looked around, and to my surprise the papers on the desk were as I'd left them earlier in the day: neatly arranged and apparently untouched, and there, too, was a pile of typewritten quarto sheets, and on top a scribbled note: *The Memoirs I spoke about* and signed *Ruth Miles*.

I turned the chair round and sat staring into the fire

until Mrs Macadam came back with a tray. What I thought about I don't recall, but it was doubtless the events of the day; what I do recall is the half-bottle of Haig on the tray along with the silver teapot and I remember my words, 'Mrs Macadam, you're a genius,' and her reply, 'That's all right, sir. I'm getting to know your ways.' But she didn't know those ways well enough to leave me alone. Life in Whitehall Mansions had acquired a more lurid glow for Mrs Macadam during recent hours and she sat on and talked until half-past eight, but she went at last.

I crossed to the manuscript and took it up, but after half an hour I knew there was nothing there for me. It was high-pitched hysterical stuff, an old man's voice running in a groove, how he'd always been right and the world always wrong. Prison under 18B had blunted the edge of the once-keen knife-edge brain, and I put the sheets down and crossed to the steel filing-cabinets, pulled at the top sliding drawer and it slid smoothly out, and I was still a whit surprised.

I started on the files from letter A and it was quite a tale the folders told as I dawdled through the originals and carbons in Waterman's record of his relations with his comrades in the Western World.

It was a solid documentary on the movements of the Left in the post-war years. Arrangements for arrivals and plans for departures; records of meetings and decisions made; commissions for articles and rows about fees; news of strikes and results of lockouts; notes on enemies and more on comrades. They came from twenty cities, and to me it was a dismal record, but who was I to judge? *Objects and Subjects* would have been pretty thin entertainment for G. W. Waterman and any of his comrades.

And in all the sheets there was no reference to the

Baron, no cross reference, indirect reference, no word at all. He was too practical a citizen to figure in that odd record of chilly notes and chillier dreams, I told myself, but even as I said the silent words I knew I was wrong. There was nothing impractical about the ice-cold communicants whose schemes I had been reading: ten years before they had all been unknown miners and mechanics, professors and police, and now half of them were rulers of the world that stretched beyond the Elbe, and the others had their hopes and knew the way to work. They were practical all right.

Then Mrs Macadam came back. It was ten o'clock. She was going off to bed. Would I be staying? And I said, no, I'd be there about another half-hour and I'd let myself out. Good night, good night. And off she went.

I was tired and I sat on, staring into the fire, reviewing my fulsome day, and around half-past ten I heard the front door click and a minute later Miss Miles came in from the hall. She was in a blue woollen dress that added colour to her hair, and as she crossed the room she said, 'I wondered if you'd still be here! How goes the history scholar?'

'He's run down,' I said.

'Am I interrupting?'

'Yes, thank God,' I said and she smiled and sat down and I asked whether she'd had a pleasant outing.

'I went down to Guildford to see Mrs Waterman,' she said, carefully watching the effect her words might have.

'Quite a way for a turkish bath,' I said.

She was puzzled by my words, but not for long. 'Oh, you mean that dreadful fug she has in her room. George told me about it. It is rather overpowering, isn't it? But I didn't mind. There were several things I had to see her about and I thought the sooner I dealt with them the better. After all, I was the last English person to see her son alive.'

That visit had taken courage of a sort, I thought, and I asked how the old lady had behaved.

'Very reasonably, considering everything.'

'Such as?'

'Well, the flat . . . and things . . . and this morning.'

'Did you tell her you were letting me stay on working here?'

'It was one of the first things she asked about. She's expecting quite a book from you, by the way.'

'She'll even be proud of her son by the time I've finished with him,' I said, and then, remembering the status of my listener, I added with a split-second change of voice that rang as true as a cracked and rusty bell, 'You, too, of course.'

'Leave me out of it,' she said firmly. 'I don't even think there's going to be a book. Not even a pamphlet. I read your article, by the way. She had it down there.'

'Why don't you think there'll be a book?'

'Partly because I read the article, partly because I don't believe you. Show me any notes you've written this evening.'

'I'm just reading through stuff at this stage,' I said. 'I keep what I want in my head. I'll come back to it.'

She laughed. 'I always thought a notebook was important to the bona-fide student.'

'The modern method is to read first, atmosphere and all that,' I said, but she wasn't impressed.

So we left the subjects of Waterman, his mother, my projected book and methods of historical research, and about midnight I came to and realized we'd been talking about the world in general and nothing in particular for well over an hour, but it had been a comfortable hour and for the first time in a fortnight Wensley's chapter seemed to have its points.

But it was time to go, and I said good night, and as I pulled on my coat I said, 'All these records—I'm up to E and I got through L, M and N this morning—how is it they only date from 1945?'

'M.I.5 borrowed all the earlier records,' she said quietly and smilingly, and I said, 'You ought to bring them up to date, then, and send 'em these,' but she went on smiling with her own variation of the Mona Lisa smile.

And as I walked up Villiers Street and then along the Strand I found the smile puzzling and irritating; but it was late, it had been a long day and I was tired.

28

THE next evening, Monday, was much the same, but Mrs Macadam was out and so was Miss Miles. A fire was burning and I started again, taking out the files and reading my way through from F to H, and then I took another peek at some entries in the M file. There was still no mention of the Baron's name, but by then I'd given up hope and I was glad when Miss Miles came in about eleven and again we sat talking and I said, 'I've just been reading one or two things about you in the files.'

'Nothing to link *my* name with your boss's, I hope.'

'No, just one or two things to link your name with Waterman's. For instance, I know how much you earn. Seven pounds fifteen shillings a week.'

'I got that when I started,' she said. 'I've had two rises since.'

'It's probably still less than the rent of this flat,' I said. 'Will you have to take in lodgers?'

'Not just yet,' she said. 'I saw Mr Oliphant, the solicitor, today and he says there's no reason why I should give up this flat if I like it here. Apparently George left me some money.'

'So now you're a poor little rich girl to add to all your other troubles.'

'Well-to-do would probably be more accurate.'

'How does it feel?'

'I don't know yet. I haven't handled any gold. But perhaps you'll find some of the details under O—Oliphant. Oliphant and Parmiter.'

'I'll make a few notes for you,' I said.

'I keep what I want in my head,' she said. 'That's the modern way. Would you like some coffee?' and she went from the room without waiting for my answer, and I heard the clatter of cups as I went on reading through the I-J file and I went on reading until she came back with the tray.

'We're out of whisky. You finished it last night,' she said. 'I'm sorry. Mrs Macadam told me how to keep you happy. I've sent her off for a week, by the way. You'll have to drink this tonight.'

And as she poured she said, 'What sort of things are you looking for? Perhaps I can keep a look-out for you. I've got to go through lots of George's papers pretty soon. Tell me what you're looking for and I'll keep one eye open for you. Of course, I'm not a scholar but I *was* an efficient secretary, I believe.'

'I don't know,' I said, and for the moment I put aside my fanciful tale about writing Waterman's biography and said what was in my mind and that was puzzle enough, God knows. 'Probably nothing, but once upon

a time, somewhere, somehow, possibly in Ireland, my
boss and your boss met and as far as I can tell they didn't
take to each other. Maybe it was just that. I'm beginning
to think it was. It would explain most things. The Baron
wrote an obituary of Waterman for my feature. Perhaps
you've read it. . . .' She shook her head so I went on,
'Well, it doesn't matter. It was a flabby piece anybody
could have written and usually he writes well and to the
point. I got the impression he'd known Waterman long
ago and hated his guts. In fact, he said as much. Maybe
it was just a clash of temperament and stayed in the
Baron's mind. Maybe he hated Waterman and Waterman
never even knew.'

'It could be that way,' she said quietly. 'I hate Oliver
Lyttelton and Brendan Bracken and I've never met either
of them. But I know I hate them and all they stand for.'

'It's not the same thing,' I said patiently. 'Yours is like
hating oysters without trying 'em, but I got the impression this was bigger. And more personal, but maybe I was
wrong.'

'You're imagining things,' she said. 'You get into the
habit as a journalist. All the time I was here I never heard
George mention your boss's name once. And why are
you so keen to find out whether there was anything between them?'

'Historical research,' I said. 'Habit dies hard.'

'How will it help you?'

'It won't,' I said.

'Do you want to pin something on your ghastly
Baron?'

'I'm not the type,' I said. 'Let's drop the whole thing.'

So we let it drop, and we drifted into other subjects,
and again it was well after midnight before I left.

29

WELL, this is supposed to be a record of research and doubtless the recital of the days gets a bit monotonous, but there it is, it is part of the record, and the next day was Tuesday, March 29, and I went down to 527 Whitehall Mansions once again.

I was late that night. There was a lecture at the Royal Institution by a titled historian and Wensley thought he would be good for a note in *Objects and Subjects*, and by the time I'd phoned my piece to Court House for the second edition it was nearly ten, and I wondered whether it was too late to go on with my studies, but I went as I knew I'd go, and Miss Miles was in, sitting at the desk, poring over papers, and as I went into the room she said, 'The studious life is not for me. Where is the magic in it?'

'Magic for some; money for others,' I said, and I looked at her papers and then across to the wall above the left-hand side of the desk and a Sickert drawing had gone from the wall and the heavy steel door of a small wall-safe was standing open.

'How many of these have I missed?' I asked and she said gently, 'Only one more. This one wouldn't interest you, anyway. It's the safe with all the financial records,' and her smile was back again.

'All the money you get from Moscow?'

She shook her head. 'Worse than that. The money George got from his parents, mainly his mother.'

'Quite a sum my instinct tells me.'

'Mr Oliphant said it was when I saw him again this morning.'

'Did you get it all?'

'Most of it, I gather.'

'Is there anything there for me? Information, I mean.'

She smiled and waved her hand towards the safe. 'I don't think so. I still don't know what you think you're really looking for. But look if you like. I really opened it for you. I want you to see everything.'

I crossed to the wall and looked in the safe, a narrow steel Chubb, the size of a brick and a foot or so in depth. But it was full of bankers' envelopes, counterfoils and other sombre papers. I picked them out, one by one, but they weren't in my line and I put them back and went across to the armchair by the fire.

Miss Miles had watched my movements with a quizzical smile and, when I was comfortable, she asked whether I'd eaten and I said yes, so we settled on coffee again, and as she went out I thought again of Waterman and his place in the long, long line of revolutionaries who had damned the iniquities of dividends and somehow found space for them in their own fat passbooks.

They set upon the task of bringing down the ancient world, but while it lasted they would take their own plump share of unearned increment from the brave ex-ploited workers of that doomed, decaying world. They damned the land-owners, coal owners, steel-owners and the owners of anything larger than a cobbler's shop; and shareholders, stockholders, oppressors and misers were synonymous lice, but four times, twice, or once a year, when the dividend chits arrived, they were glad to know their own familiar world would not be sundered yet awhile. And off they went to another bout of planning, dreaming, word-spinning or fact-finding to up-end the world they knew. It was an old, old story and Water-man's passbook was not unique.

Morris and his happy band of Kelmscott craftsmen had printed books, made furniture, woven tapestries. And old-fashioned dividends had subsidized the lot.

And dividends had come in pretty useful to the Webbs in their snug Home Counties home as they wrote their many words for their blue-bound books.

And dividends had helped a hundred other revolutionaries. Dividends from the factories of the Midlands and the mines of the North. Good old-fashioned capitalistic dividends.

And even Shaw, the most verbose of revolutionaries, had lived to see his Shavian quips turn to Shavian groans as his royalties made investments and the investments made dividends and the dividends went to pay for the debts of the Government he had helped to bring alive.

And Waterman was another, one of the old long line, writing away in his high warm room. He had done his best to write the wicked world into a classless, profitless limbo, and dividends, too, had helped to keep him warm.

They were all the same: they all loved their passbooks: they were all keen on dividends: they all liked the look of the things that lucre bought—houses and friends, books and gardens, travel and food, freedom and leisure. Not one of them ever got around to giving it away in one great magnanimous sweep. Not one. That was no more than a sentimental gesture, they said. It made no contribution to the fundamental problem, they said. So they hung on to the dividends. It was as simple as all that.

I sat staring into the fire with these merry thoughts for a long enough minute, and then I reached across and picked up a blue-leather folder Miss Miles had been examining. I opened it out and it was Waterman's *Statement of Account* with Lloyds Bank, Whitehall Branch. Well, she'd said I could look, so I looked, and the sheets made plain the happy financial state of G. W. Waterman at his death, at least as far as his Current Account had been concerned, a safe enough guide, I always think.

Waterman had certainly held quite a sum on tap. The total in the BALANCE column in the final sheet he had filed a month before his death stood at £3,466 4s. 7d., and that seemed sum enough for any man or any man's legatees, and I wondered what investments in the solid, unimaginative financial structure of Britain had produced this sizeable total. Left Wing journals didn't pay that well.

The answer was plain enough in the entries in the RECEIPTS column and I recognized some of the old-fashioned gilt-edged names of British Industry: Thomas Tilling, Distillers, British American Tobacco and a few other reassuring titles, but by then I was tiring of this brief essay in High Finance and I closed the leather folder, put it back on the desk, and took up a long manilla envelope which was also there.

I opened out the envelope and took out a tight wad of dividend warrants ringed with a rubber band, and the records in the wad would have gladdened the heart of a broker: interest at the rate of 4% per annum on Debenture Stock in W. & A. Gilbey; interest on Stock in British Electricity 3% Guaranteed Stock 1968–1973; interest on Thomas Tilling's 5% Ordinary Stock; final dividend at 13% on Ordinary Stocks of J. & J. Colman; interest on Deferred Ordinary Stock in Spillers Limited. And the sums, less Income Tax at 9s. in the £, ranged from a pound or so to seventy or eighty and they went on and on, sheet after sheet of solid returns.

Waterman had certainly believed in the future of British enterprise. Or maybe he'd merely taken his mother's word for it. Or maybe just his broker's.

There was nothing there for me: it was just black-and-white proof of something I'd already guessed.

Then Miss Miles came back and I put the warrants back in the envelope and down on the desk. 'These should go to Waterman's accountant,' I said.

'Put all that nonsense back in the safe,' she commanded lightly. 'Mr Oliphant can deal with it. I want the desk,' and she made to put the black tray down. So I picked up the folder and the envelopes and took them across to the safe, and as I put them in I again turned over the items I had spurned before: cheque-book counterfoils, envelopes, lists of securities, receipts and bills. I opened one of the envelopes and it held about a dozen recent share warrants. Then another and that had more. Then another and that held maybe fifty half-sheets of copy paper, some white, some green, some yellow, neatly clipped together, and each with a typewritten note concerning the transfer of holdings from old Mrs Waterman to G. W. Waterman, and they included the well-known names of British Industry that gave him the dividends I'd seen recorded in his passbook and they covered quite a lot of years. Each was Waterman's copy of the share transfer that made him a richer Red, and it was plain to see that George had long been well and truly bolstered by his ever-loving mum, for they had started in 1903 when he must have been at Oxford and they went on until recent days.

I flipped through the notes, but my fitful zest was dying and I put them all back into the envelope and all the envelopes back into the safe and turned to take my coffee, and Miss Miles was still watching with an appreciative smile from the opposite chair.

'Nothing of interest?' she asked.

'Only money, money, money. Waterman was pretty business-like for a man who wanted to get rid of the stuff.'

'Doesn't money interest you, then?' she asked.

'I like it. Who doesn't? But I've never got worked up over the idea of having loads of it. Looking after it's the curse.'

'That's what frightens me,' she said.

'You'll learn,' I said, taking up my cup from the tray.

'Why are you so certain?' she asked, and I thought for a moment an edge was getting back to her voice.

'You're young enough,' I said, and I wondered why I was setting out to provoke, but she drank her coffee and didn't reply, and I crossed to the other armchair and suddenly I was tired, tired of Wensley, tired of Waterman, tired of the world maybe.

But gradually the mood went and I came alive again as any tired citizen is apt to come alive again if the coffee is black enough and the dispenser of coffee is as personable as Miss Miles in the neat black frock, black suède courts and jet ear-rings she was sporting that evening, and after a time I said, 'Where have you sent Mrs Macadam, by the way?'

'Off to daughter Lil for a week.'

'How do you get on with her?'

'Very well, I think. Otherwise she probably wouldn't talk so much.'

I was silent again and then I got up to take more coffee, and as I stood by the desk she said, 'Don't you think it's odd the way we sit here and talk?'

'Why odd?'

'Well, I started by trying to get you locked up and here we are like two old gossiping friends.'

'One old, one young,' I said, and maybe some poison in the blood had to come out, and I added, 'Didn't you do it before?' and she said quietly, 'Not very often. Not at all, really.'

'How *did* you spend your evenings, then?'

'I worked or I went back to my digs in Queen's Gate. Sometimes I stayed here. How did you spend yours?'

'I worked too,' I said.

'All the time?'

'Mostly. Sometimes I took women out. Sometimes I slept in an armchair at the club. Mainly I worked.'

'How many women?'

'Two or three.'

'What are they like?'

'Just women.'

'Where are they now?'

'In bed with their husbands, probably.'

'Oh!' she said and then laughed. 'What else did you do?'

'Worked,' I said. 'Just as I said. Worked.'

'Was work so important?'

'Not especially. It's a habit. Or a drug. I clear my copy by seven. Then I have dinner or go to a show. Wensley sometimes likes notes on how or why half-dressed film stars get torn to pieces at charity shows. I usually get back and write it up. Other times it's a lecture like tonight.'

'And what was it like tonight?'

'Too erudite and too depressing for my simple public. The break-up of the Western World. Just your line. I phoned a hundred words.'

'And now: are you going to do some more delving here?'

'No, I'm going to talk to you.'

'Wonderful!' she said as if she meant it, and then, 'What have we in common?'

'Waterman,' I said.

It was the wrong thing again and I knew it even as I said it, but maybe it was too smart to miss.

'Can't you think of anything else?' she said in a cold voice from a thousand miles away. 'Why can't you act like a reasonable human being? I know you think I interfered with your work coming back when I did, but try to forget it.'

'I'm sorry,' I said, grudgingly enough, 'but it happens to be true, all the same.'

'I know, I know, but please try to forget it.'

'Do *you* want to forget it?'

'Sometimes,' she said simply. 'Anyway, I don't want to be reminded the way you remind me. I was fond of George in a way you could never understand.'

'Why couldn't I?'

'You think it was money, but it wasn't. I might have married him in other circumstances. I don't know. But how would it have looked? You and your filthy newspapers would have got hold of it and what a Roman Holiday you'd have made of it. Rich Red, 65, weds secretary, 25. I know. I didn't want it that way. I probably didn't want it any way at all. But you wouldn't understand. . . .'

This was the first outburst since Sunday morning and it was a sudden bitter outburst, and I wondered what had caused it: somewhere, somehow, deep down, she was beginning to get twisted up about Waterman, herself, the money and the last few years, and maybe she had been getting twisted up from the day it had started.

Well, she had taken Waterman for her very own, with her eyes wide open, and while he'd been around she'd probably thought he wasn't so bad, maybe even the only boy in the world. Who was I to know, anyway? He had probably been kind. He had probably made endearing little jokes. He had probably remembered her birthdays. All in all, he had probably been a soft-hearted old thing, despite his brittle bones and acid pen. But now he was dead and all that was left was the blank bland look of the disbelieving world, a general distrust of that kind of affection, and it was getting her down. She had seen it in my eyes, she had seen it in Macadam's and maybe in old Oliphant's that very afternoon. He had doubtless been explanatory, kind and understanding, but however he had phrased it, the words still meant an old man's money for a young woman's love.

And I began to think of headlines the story might have made, and *would make* when some bright newsman saw the notice of the will at Somerset House. But it was time for me to say something and I said, 'You could have married secretly.'

'Secretly! With people like you running around.'

'I never run—only to the Baron's,' I pointed out.

She got up from the armchair to put her cup back on the table. 'I'm sorry,' she said. 'Sometimes your cold-blooded look does something to me and I have to let fly.'

So we discussed my cold-blooded look for a few minutes, and gradually she seemed to calm down. Then I asked where the other wall-safe was and what was in it, and she said, 'Won't you ever forget your work? It really is a drug. I don't know. I haven't had it open yet. Mr Oliphant is coming to look through the things here on Saturday morning. You'd better look before then if you want to. It's all strictly illegal, I suppose, but now you've started you'd better carry on and finish the job!'

'Not tonight,' I said. 'I'd better be going,' and she said, 'Will you be here tomorrow night?'

'I've got this dinner with the Baron.'

'Come along afterwards.'

'He starts late and ends late,' I said. 'But I'd better go through that safe before old Oliphant gets here. I'll have

Thursday and Friday for that,' and I went out into the hall and got my overcoat and came back and she was standing by the fireplace with her hands resting on the tall mantelshelf, looking down into the little flames, and I said good night, and she turned and said, 'Do come if you can. Please. If it's not too late. I'd like it,' and I said, 'I'll try,' and as I went down in the lift I thought, *This sort of thing will spoil me for the old-fashioned kind of research*, and I wondered what Wensley would have said, but I thought I knew the answer to that. 'It's your feature,' he would have said; but it was his chapter.

30

BY the time my Thursday's piece was done, Tuesday was already a far-off time.

I finished *Objects and Subjects* by five and took them in to Wensley. He read and said, 'They'll do!' and then sat back and looked at the diary on his desk. 'We've got this jamboree up in the park tonight, I see. I'll call for you about eight. We can go on up together.'

I walked back to Lincoln's Inn Fields, climbed the stairs to my rooms and began to get ready. The best part of getting ready was taking a hot bath, and as I lay in the bath I fell to brooding over the changes in my daily life since Wensley had given me his chapter to write. I sat at a dead man's desk in the evenings; I went carefully through the dead man's personal records; I had become friendly with the dead man's sorrowing mistress. Yet Waterman was still a man in a mist as far as I was concerned. But something attempted, something done, I told myself and thought I would let it go at that, and I rose regretfully to shave and put on my rusted dinner suit.

But Wensley didn't let it go at that, and in the car he said, 'I suppose you've dug up nothing that would enliven the proceedings tonight?'

'Nothing,' I said.

'I'll probably have to liven things up on my own account, then. Maybe there is nothing. You're sure you've been through everything?'

'Not everything yet, but quite a bit,' I said.

'Much more to do?'

'One more safe, and that's the lot.'

'How do you crack the safes?'

'A girl I know has the keys.'

'How is Miss Whatshername? More friendly?'

'Miss Miles is the name: she's slightly more friendly.'

'You say she's a good-looker.'

'She'll pass,' I said.

Wensley looked round in the dark car. 'Don't you ever get enthusiastic about anything?' he asked. 'How did Waterman get hold of her? Money again, I suppose. Take it easy, driver, this isn't a Monte Carlo Rally.'

'Yessir,' said the voice from the driver's seat.

Wensley went on: 'It looks as if I may have to skip that chapter, then. A pity. It fits in with what I've got in mind. I'm damn sure it fits in somewhere.'

He paused and we were both quiet in the humming car.

'Have you put this Miles woman to bed yet?' he asked slowly yet suddenly.

I shook my head. Wensley looked round in the darkness. 'I've told you before,' he said. 'You ought to be a bit more fervent about some of these jobs I give you. Maybe that's the trouble. Maybe that's why you're not getting the facts I'm after. When you were a sailor you did what your commander told you, didn't you? Then do what I tell you now. You might not think it, but I'm your commanding officer in this outfit. Put her to bed!' He shifted his great bulk from one cheek to the other, and, as the back axle took the strain, he finished his instructions: 'There's no place like a good double bed for getting the secrets of the mighty.'

'You must have had very little sleep in your time,' I said.

He chuckled. 'Cut out the funny stuff,' he said. 'It's an historical fact. Anyway, they're my instructions.'

'I'll bear them in mind.'

He chuckled again in the dark. 'Do! Well, here we are at this ramshackle bloody palace. I wonder what sort of circus he's put on tonight.'

The butler let us in and showed us through the high, domed, chequer-floored hall into the small withdrawing-room beyond, and as circuses go this one looked a very modest Barnum.

Not more than a dozen guests stood around, taking their ease and their drinks and watching the latest arrivals.

Against the dark red velvet curtains and under the blazing halo of the crystal chandelier, the men all looked like cut-out shapes in black-and-white card and the women like painted plastic dolls, and I wondered again, as I'd wondered before, how the legend got around that evening dress enhances the austere dignity of men and the natural beauty of women, but I got no chance to examine the query, for the Baron left a group of three or four men and came across the room.

He took Wensley's hand and gripped it tight. 'Glad to see you, David!' he said in a hearty voice, and nodded to me with a cut-off gesture like an expert's bid at an auction sale, and he took Wensley off and I was on my own.

I began to wonder whether the invitation I'd had those days before had been just a figment in my mind, but that sort of worry need only grow if the butler comes to throw you out, and I said to a tall, slim, self-assured blonde, with keen eyes and a forceful chin, standing by my side, 'Do you often come here?'

'My first time,' she said. Her voice was the voice of Manhattan, and she smiled and the smile was the smile of someone who knows the smile will work.

'Do you know everybody here?' I asked, and she said with the directness of her race, 'Not a soul. Tell me who they are!' and I thought of her so-called English cousins who would have hedged with, 'Well, not everybody. Let me see ...' but all the blonde said was, 'Who's the big stout man?'

So I began to give her the names and brief biographies fit to print concerning some of her fellow-guests, and I said, 'He's a financier and a partner in one of our oldest private banking houses,' and I told her the record that filled out the entry in the *Directory of Directors* and *The Stock Exchange Year-Book,* and the things that made his name respected in the financial columns of the daily Press, but I kept to myself the other words that could have filled out the portrait: how he sold oil-wells before he bought oil-wells, how he bought shadow factories with something less than shadowy money, and there he was, a billowing, bellowing bull of a man, still shining from his valet's shaving, still rosy from his foaming bath.

He was talking to a girl and I told the blonde from Manhattan his listener's name and the blonde said, 'Oh, I've heard of her, of course,' as who hadn't, for one month she was in New York en route to Nassau and another month she was in Paris en route to Cannes, and she would be photographed on board the *Q.M.* or stepping off

Pan-Am, a columnist's delight, a thin, dark, white-faced creature with hollow eyes looking like a young holey-boley woman in a faint decaying fresco in an old, old chapel, but after that the likeness went awry. And I remembered how she had wanted some of the Baron's millions, or maybe just one of them, and how for one night she'd forgotten her ancient name and her long, long line of proud progenitors and she'd held the Baron in her slim young arms, and that was all. There had been no millions, not even one of them, and word had got around as word always gets around, and inside a fortnight her whole small world, her very own set, knew she'd slept with the Baron, and in sleeping had slipped. And now she was one of the long, long list and knew she was, too, a loser like the rest of them, and here she was, back for dinner, and money did it, or at least the hope of it, but the blonde from Manhattan was looking and relishing: the name and the face and the prospect of facts that were somewhere in *Debrett.*

And across the room listening to the Baron and sizing up Wensley was a tall and languid citizen with a hangdog face, smooth grey hair and sad, entreating eyes, and the world and his wife knew him for an actor, a Man of the Theatre with an international name, and the blonde from Manhattan looked up as I mentioned his name and looked at the player and said, 'Of course. I've seen him in New York. Only on the stage, though. He was over last winter. He looks kinda different offstage. Isn't it cute what a toopay will do?' I looked across the room. He was beginning to talk, moving his hands in gentle flowing movements, but his soft brown eyes were gentle and aware, watchful of his listeners, watchful of the room. He was pleading for the world to listen to him, take him seriously. *Although I'm a queen,* he seemed to say, *I'm still a great figure in the Theatre. You must realize that!* I agreed, so I told the blonde of his recent triumphs as a stripling Spanish lover and as Zeno the Stoic. She smiled and nodded sagely, but I could see she'd had enough of fellow-guests, and soon I was listening to her auto-biography, a saga of yet another girl from the Middle West who had moved East to tackle the naked city on its very own terms. Well, she had made it and now she was staff writer for a New York daily and her subject was foreign affairs.

'Of course,' I heard her say through the haze and the murmur that was beginning to grow, 'I've been across before, but not since the war. I came here then. My Chief back home didn't want to let me go, but I had to get over here. You got kinda bitter being back home with all those four F guys sitting around and taking all the coins. So when I heard they had a place for a writer in Psychological Warfare and they put in a special application for me, I went in to see the Chief and I said, "Look, Chief, I gotta go . . ."' and the saga went on and on.

I listened to the drawling monotone and watched the movements of her cold and innocent blue eyes, her firm and thrusting chin, and I knew that her wartime, peace-time chiefs had never stood a chance: she had vitality, vivacity, pugnacity and a few other qualities spelled in various ways, and the lot added up to a total that made her kind the terror of the Eastern cities, but it was one woman's Declaration of Independence, and as such I saluted the performance, and, in the same instant, prayed God her seat was not near mine in the Baron's cunning table plan.

I looked around the room to see what other specimens the Baron had collected, and it was certainly a theatrical evening. Over by the window, near the Baron's group,

was a group of four: two young women and one younger
man, all lovers of the Theatre, all quite young and all up-
and-coming, and the fourth was a playwright not quite
so young but quite as serious, and I began to wonder
what had caused this new interest of the Baron's. It was
plainly his latest fad and for a few weeks Wensley would
have a series of notes and one would begin: *You neglect
the serious Theatre. Many thousands of people visit the
theatre each week. Not all go to see the Crazy Gang. Not
all of them read* The Times. *Why throw them away?* Or the
note might be more topical and more pointed and it
would run: *A serious notice of a play takes no more space
than the cheapjack notice you ran about* The Wild Duck
this morning. And the chits would not be for Wensley
alone. I should get my share all right: *You are neglecting
the younger stars in the Theatre. Some of your readers are
not yet eighty*, and so on and so on.

I looked around, wondering which young starlet the
Baron had his eye on, and I looked at the group of four
again, and either of the girls would have satisfied the
average old satyr and I left it to the evening and the
Baron to decide, and I went back to listening to the
blonde from Manhattan.

And as I listened, the latest First Lady of the Theatre
made her entrance and I thought, *the Baron's taking to the
stage in a very big way if he's brought this old dreadnought
in*, and I recalled how he had taken to the stage before,
but not on quite such a level: he had patronized blondes
in musicals and even brunettes in operettas, but not
Shakespeare and not these figures, but my speculations
died at the spectacle before me.

As the Dame of the Order of the British Empire had
come in, conversation had gone out, but she wasn't dis-
tressed by the sudden stillness: it was her due. *All the*

world's a stage, and I looked again at the imperious once-pretty head set on a treble chin and the dress of orange-red watered-silk flaming around her like a tent on fire, and I looked too at the deep V-neck slashed in her bodice by a couturier with a taste for the sabre. *She has no navel,* I thought, in a sacrilegious moment, *or there it would be before my eyes,* but she had stepped past me, just a step, just far enough for the Baron to cross the room to kiss her hand, and as she stood there, the ruined profile of her lovely face was a foot away and powder couldn't hide it, paint couldn't hide it, rouge couldn't hide it, although the lot had done their best.

Later, after she had sipped her sherry as if it were poison for little Juliet, dinner was announced and we all wandered across the hall into the large, french-windowed dining-room. The purple-and-white striped curtains were drawn, the black-and-gilt Regency chairs were set, the candles were burning steadily and the three blue-uniformed footmen were as stiff as an old Staffordshire group, and it seemed we were to be a cosy round-table party, fourteen in all. So we took our napkins, opened them out and sized up our neighbours from lowered eyes, and already I could see it was not my evening, for on my right was the girl from *Debrett* and on her right was the Baron. And on my left was the blonde from Manhattan and on her left the financial genius and I wished him well. And on the Baron's right was Dame Ruth, then came Wensley, and next to Wensley was one of the two young starlets, and as I looked across I wished I might change places. She was dressed in old-gold velvet with a topaz brooch at the high-collared neck and her features were as fine as a Chinese figurine's. With her corn-coloured hair, parted down the centre and plaited in a bun above the nape of her neck, she was as out of place as I would have been in a children's tea party. I looked from her to the Baron and wondered, and then I looked around for the other young hopeful and already she was talking to the playwright as if she had him in mind for her very next part. She was dark and vivacious, and her close-cropped curls in a Bubbles cut were near enough to brush his brow and her dark dark eyes and red full lips were almost his, she seemed to say, if it weren't for the crowd around and the dinner ahead. And the off-the-neck line of her bottle-green dress helped in the great illusion.

We began with real turtle soup, and I watched the Baron as I'd watched him before, and soon it came, the magic word that goes across the table and sets the guests moving in a murmur of dissent, polite dissent, but the game had begun as he said to the playwright, 'With all this talent from the Theatre here, John, you ought to be able to write a charade with a fine fat part for everyone. We could play it after dinner. I ought to have had your dinner served in the library so you could have had it ready in an hour's time.'

'Have you any part in mind for yourself, sir?'

'Something in the robber baron line would probably suit me,' the Baron said with a self-knowing chuckle, and we all laughed, deprecating the idea, noting each other's hypocrisy with watchful eyes, but Dame Ruth went further with, 'Nonsense! I shall see John writes you in as a patron of the arts. I intend you to be one before you die.'

'You've started too late,' said the Baron. 'Twenty years too late.'

That was how the modest debate on the best time to start in a career got started, and that helped the course along, and by that time the conversation was general and the Baron was satisfied. His words had done the trick and he sat back in his Regency carver and looked around and, in the intervals between spooning the soup, I also looked around, and already it was a merry table the Baron had made, but with so many shining lights from St Martin's Lane and Shaftesbury Avenue maybe it wasn't so difficult. Dame Ruth joined in, the playwright joined in, the Great Actor, too, and the young and sparkling brunette.

As far as my cursory inspection took me, only the fair young beauty next to Wensley seemed out of it, but he had her attention and he was talking very quietly in the strictly avuncular manner he reserved for the young and beautiful, and she was smiling and her smile was plainly not perfunctory. She was enjoying herself, and I noticed that once, as she chuckled, the Baron looked towards her and to Wensley, but she was away, a long way off, unaware of his glance, smiling at Wensley's worldly wisdom. But a minute later the Baron said, 'What do you think, Jean?' and she came back into the room with a start, but Wensley gently expanded the Baron's question and it was plain he had been listening to the table's conversation and talking, too. She gave him a grateful glance as she caught up with the subject and said quickly, 'I think as soon as possible, don't you? We have to be apprentices for such a long time, don't we?' and I thought, *Not so long if the Baron thinks what I think he thinks*, and that was plainly the thought of one or two others in the room, for the slim young aristocratic creature at mine and the Baron's side said icily, 'It depends on the career, don't you think? Some seem to need longer apprenticeships than others.'

'How long did yours need, Muriel?' the Baron asked, brutally enough, and the room went quiet.

'I never really found out. I had one or two false starts. Maybe I'm a late starter, anyway,' she answered calmly and easily.

By then the second course, *sole bonne femme* with mushroom sauce, was on the table, but conversation was still on careers, and Wensley said, 'You started pretty late yourself, didn't you, sir? I mean as far as newspaper-owning went.'

'Fairly late, I imagine,' the Baron said. He didn't seem enthusiastic and I wondered what Wensley was after by his gratuitous slap.

Then the blonde from Manhattan piped up. 'Didn't you have a Lord somebody or other over here who started buying newspapers when he was quite a kid?'

'We had Lord Northcliffe,' the Baron said. 'He was comparatively young.'

I liked the word 'comparatively' and so, it seemed, did Wensley, for he said, 'He was twenty-two when he started *Answers*,' as if he had been waiting for the question, and had brought his Northcliffe diary along with him.

'My!' said the blonde. 'He musta been kinda cute wearing diapers around the office.'

We all laughed but the Baron frowned. Conversation was moving on to a few other newspaper proprietors and that was never harmony to him, as I had noticed before.

'I suppose the three Berry brothers were still fairly young men when they really got going,' said the financier, 'and one couldn't call Max an old man when he came here from Canada. Surely the pace of the newspaper game demands comparative youth?'

'It's no more arduous than the Theatre,' Dame Ruth said forcefully, turning to the Baron.

'You must ask Mr Wensley,' the Baron said speciously. 'He is more actively a newspaper man than anybody here, and he also knows something about the Theatre.'

Actively nothing, I thought. *He sits in his room and he never stirs. He grows corns on his backside sitting in that swivel chair, and when he wants an errand done I go,* but I looked across and wondered how he would deal with the Baron's little nod in his direction.

'Nobody would believe me for a moment, sir, if I said I found the newspaper business wearing. I just don't look the part. Neither do you, Dame Ruth. You've enjoyed every minute of the Theatre. And if you were given your time over again you wouldn't have it any other way.'

Dame Ruth smiled graciously, and turned to the Baron. 'Would you have ordered your life differently?' she asked.

The table had divided by this time as a table of fourteen is apt to divide, and the playwright who had helped start the debate was holding forth to the other half of the table on Maugham's place as a playwright and he was giving him fair marks, but lopping off a number for cynicism and the Negational Approach to Life, and his listeners were nodding and doubtless getting a modest miasma of sour grapes in the process, and I turned again towards the Baron, and he was saying, 'Only here and there, the way most of us would have liked things a bit different here and there. Don't you agree?'

'Probably,' she said, 'but not too different.'

'Neither would you, sir,' said the smooth financier, 'once you'd got your foot inside the front door. You liked it from then on.'

'You're probably right,' the Baron said. 'But there's a lot in what Jean said just now. It takes a damn long time to get started. Too long. I think all those youngsters who go up to Oxford each year have a much easier time. They are heard about quite early on. They get listened to in the Union. They write. People of authority are watching them. All that makes it easier when they get out into the world.'

'Northcliffe thought that too,' Wensley said. 'Just a year at Oxford he said. He'd always wanted the poise he thought the place gave its lucky young people.'

'It only gave me debts!' the financier boomed and laughed. The Baron waited and then went on: 'I've never thought I missed anything by not going to Oxford. I was merely talking about the question of apprenticeship.'

Dame Ruth spoke up. 'How long do you reckon your own apprenticeship lasted?' she asked.

'How can one say? More years than I care to remember now,' the Baron said.

By that time the third course had been swiftly and silently placed before us.

'How did you really start, then?'

The Baron looked at his plate, looked around the table to see how his guests were enjoying their meal, and then he carefully cut across the breast of chicken and moved a roast potato to one side of his plate. 'I started as a journalist. I suppose that was an advantage in many ways. Most newspaper proprietors seem to come into the business as financiers. I often think that gives them a one-sided and sometimes too careful an approach to newspaper problems. They're more interested in dividends than news. I never had that fear.'

'But you must have had some ideas about finance,' the banker said. 'You have a duty to your stockholders. You don't build up a chain of newspapers any other way.'

'I learned,' the Baron said.

'Yes, but how did you really start?' Dame Ruth persisted. 'Thousands of journalists would like to own a newspaper. Only one in a million ever does.'

'As Wensley just said, I really started rather late,' the Baron said, settling himself for a few moments of reminiscence, and the roast chicken was forgotten as he stared back along the long road he had come. 'And, of course, I had my share of luck. I had been a newspaper man. I was in the old tradition of the special correspondent. I was war correspondent in the First World War, and by the time that was over I was into my thirties and no longer a young man as far as newspaper work is concerned, but I had no particular wish to change. In fact I was beginning to enjoy myself. I was becoming fairly well known as a special writer and I was being given some extremely interesting assignments. Northcliffe sent me to Archangel after the war; later I went to the Middle East for Reuters, then to Ireland during the Troubles. Then about nineteen-twenty or twenty-one, I suppose it was, I was offered an interest in a printing- and publishing-house. Not the usual sort of publishing—this house specialized in printing and distributing newspapers for owners and publishers with no plant of their own. There are a few printing-houses like that, as you may know. Why I was offered the job I can't think. Possibly the printers thought it would be useful to have a newspaper man on the board to talk to their newspaper clients. I don't know. I certainly saw things with a newspaper man's eyes, but it's a very different thing writing for a newspaper from publishing a newspaper. In order to be able to talk with some kind of authority, and probably to look after my own modest interests in a practical fashion, I found I was beginning to learn something about printing costs, newspaper distribution and all the mechanical side of the business.'

About six diners were listening to the Baron: the other half of the table were really getting down to the job of tearing Maugham to pieces. I could have sat on listening for an hour or so. Newspaper shop like any other shop is interesting if you're in it, and the Baron talked as well as most men do when they talk about the days *before* they were successes.

I looked across to Wensley, and he was listening, too, in an abstracted sort of way, like a schizo divided between his meal and his master, but he was certainly listening. I knew the signs and most were there. Then he looked up and across to me and his eyelid gave the lightest flicker, but it had gone as the Baron went on: 'There is a good deal more to running a newspaper than getting the news, as I need hardly tell you. Getting news had been my life until nineteen-twenty-one. After that I had several more things to worry about. Then, in the way these things occasionally happen, I was asked to join the board of one of the newspapers we printed—as production adviser. You know the newspaper: it's one of my own now. The rest of the story . . .'

But the rest of the story was fading as far as I was concerned. Somehow the words *nineteen-twenty-one* and *printing-house* were dancing a jig in my mind. First he'd said, 'nineteen-twenty or nineteen-twenty-one.' Then he'd been more explicit with 'nineteen-twenty-one.' Well, why not. No raconteur carries a ready-reckoner around with him, but somehow the words and the numerals swung around like numbers in a roulette wheel and I was foxed. And why 'printing-house'? To anyone in Court House it was always 'the printers' or 'the machine-room.' So I let it go. Or I thought I'd let it go.

But the numbers and the words were still there, twisting about, scratching at the enclosing mind. And there is no more peace, not until the maggot wins and works its way from out the claustrophobic brain. And so it was now, and there was no way I could let it out. At least, no way I knew.

I swam back unwillingly into the room, to the Baron, and he was answering the financier with some financial advice. 'Yes, I found out something about advertising. I had to. No man can run a newspaper without advertising. Yet advertising can't run a newspaper. I got to know the agency chiefs in my early days and I've always kept a careful eye on the balance between the news columns and advertisement revenue ever since: two single-column inches every day for a year will almost pay an editor's salary. No wonder I watch the advertising revenue!' and he laughed.

Dame Ruth said in the pause, 'Does that mean if Mr Wensley put in less news you could get more money?'

'For a time,' Wensley said.

'Oh, how wonderful! Just like me knocking out matinées and getting more money. Why do you print so much news, then, Mr Wensley?'

'Why, indeed?' echoed the banker. 'News of other people's misery. Private tragedies. That's Fleet Street, isn't it?'

'Only for a few of us,' Wensley said gently.

'But why do you do it, Mr Wensley?' Dame Ruth shrilled. 'It's terrible! Sex and crime! Aren't there any other subjects?'

'Several!' Wensley offered. 'Football pools. Horse-racing. Fashions. Film stars. Sex isn't everything.'

'Dreadful!' she said. 'What an estimate of human life!'

'Not an estimate, Dame Ruth. Exact mathematical knowledge.'

Dame Ruth shuddered. 'Awful,' she said.

'Not so fast,' Wensley said. 'You thoroughly enjoy

playing Lady Macbeth. Blood, blood and more blood. You love it. The audience loves it. They shudder, but they're safe. They're out of danger, looking on. It's not their blood. It's the same with my paper.'

'But I don't batten on somebody's private grief.'

'Neither do I,' Wensley said. 'Thousands of women are dying of cancer at this minute. Thousands more are being jilted. Private grief is everywhere at any time. But if a husband mercy-kills his bedridden wife, or a jealous woman kills the man who jilts her, it's no longer private grief. It gets a bit public and that's when we step in.'

'But you make it *so* public. You revel in it so. We don't do that.'

'The Theatre always seems to have its fair share of private grief being made public,' Wensley said. 'I've never yet seen anyone get up and walk out of the "Caprice" or the "Ivy" when somebody was telling the latest bit of theatrical bedroom scandal. Unfortunately, I can't indulge in this hole-in-the-corner stuff. I have to come out in the open and print my information. And take the consequences if I make a mistake.'

'You don't have to print everything.'

The table had become quiet: everyone seemed to be waiting on Wensley's slow and seasoned words, and he smiled as he went on: 'I don't print everything. No newspaper prints half of what it knows about anything or anyone. The English libel laws look after that.'

'But why do you have to badger people so? The wives of murdered men, the mothers of ruined girls?' Dame Ruth was plainly beginning to enjoy her part as defender of the nation's privacy.

'They can always slam the door in our faces. Some do. You don't hear about them. But not as many as you'd think. You'd be surprised, Dame Ruth, how many stricken people enjoy their grief and, in a dreary sort of way, get as big a kick out of the limelight as any actress. It's sad but it's true. It doesn't take a lot of money to persuade the wife of a murderer to put down her reminiscences about her throat-slitting spouse.'

'But it's dreadful. You could change all that. You have a duty towards the public.'

'Who said so?' growled the Baron, joining in. 'What duty have I got towards the public? None at all. You don't demand that owners of theatres put on Shakespeare and Ibsen and nothing else. You don't, do you? You don't attack every bedroom farce that comes on and runs for three years, do you? Is the average musical comedy your idea of a duty towards the public? Yet it's all Theatre. Why pick on me?'

'Is it so important to have an extra million or so readers, then?'

'Do you like playing to empty houses?'

The table tittered.

'But you don't have to print all these dreadful murder details,' Dame Ruth protested, turning to Wensley. Maybe she found him a more chivalrous debating opponent than the Baron, who growled on, grinding her opposition into dust.

'I don't have to,' Wensley said. 'But when there's a particularly repellent murder trial running, the circulation manager tells me we sell a hundred thousand extra copies. Every day.'

The Baron joined in again. 'Perhaps the public owes me a duty. Perhaps the public should get itself educated. When some of these Labour fellows have stopped chasing after titles and got the people educated, maybe that'll be the time to demand some reform in newspaper owners. When my certified net sales prove to me that crime and sex don't interest the public any more, I'll set about changing my newspapers.'

'And the editor?' asked the banker, smiling.

Wensley smiled, too, but the Baron didn't answer and Wensley turned to his partner. Then the playwright joined in, presumably having buried Mr Maugham and wishful to stake his claim on the side of the angels. 'It certainly sounds the easiest way of getting money I've ever heard about,' he said in the voice he doubtless kept for such asides. A sweet had come to the table, a rarefied lemon meringue with a sauce I couldn't put a name or flavour to, but the arrival of such sweetness didn't noticeably sweeten up the Baron.

'In my experience there's no easy way of making money. Certainly not in a newspaper. D'you find play-writing easy money?'

The playwright went back to his meringue. 'Far from it,' he stuttered. His last two plays had lasted six weeks apiece. He wanted discussion, not brutality, but the banker was made of sterner stuff.

'Well, maybe making money out of newspapers isn't easy. Personally, I always thought it was, but there are other ways.'

'What's your easy way, then?' growled the Baron.

'Well, floating a private company as a public company is not exactly difficult, once you've got past the Capital Issues Committee.'

'Maybe,' the Baron grudged. 'What's your way, David?'

'Only successful blackmail,' Wensley said.

'Mr Wensley!' said Dame Ruth, shocked and then interested. 'Is there such a thing?'

'Here and there, I imagine,' Wensley said.

'How awful! But the victims can always go to the police, surely? Isn't it all hushed up then? Mr X and all that.'

'Some things you don't take to the police,' Wensley said slowly, as slowly as a bishop intoning a prayer. 'Let me take the most extreme and improbable case that could possibly come to mind. Permit me to make it both improbable yet personal, if I may. May I?'

She nodded watchfully as Wensley began: 'Let us suppose you were to fall in love with a very young married man and he with you. Suppose he happened to be the commissionaire at your theatre,' he raised his hand to stay her words as she opened her mouth to protest. 'Supposing he were twenty-three years old, ill-educated, surpassingly handsome. Supposing—and here I scarcely need to suppose—he loved you passionately and you returned that passion—in a physical sense let us say. Supposing I were less scrupulous than I am and less well paid than I am by his Lordship. Supposing I were to come to you with a proof of the story I proposed to run in the following day's paper unless you bought my silence. Let us imagine all these things were true: would you go to the police?' Wensley rested his case and gave attention to his neglected meringue. The rest of us looked at Dame Ruth and it was plain she was no longer seated at a dining-table: she was in front of the footlights and we were all her audience, footmen too, and she said quietly, evenly, with her beautiful eyes half-closed, 'Mr Wensley, I should kill you.'

Wensley smiled and inclined his head. 'That would be one way out, of course, but supposing you were anxious to go on with your career. Life has given you a great deal, and presumably life would not have less to offer you in the circumstances I've outlined. What then? You must remember I said I would not publish your story—at a price! Not necessarily money,' he added with a sudden smile, and she smiled too.

'Mr Wensley, you are incorrigible,' she said. 'For the sake of the young lover you have presented me with I would have to pay the price.'

'Bravo, Ruth!' the playwright said softly across the room, and the tongues of the diners were in movement again.

The Baron turned to Wensley. 'You sound as if you've made a study of the subject, David.'

'Only in dreams, sir.'

'Any of your dreams ever come true?'

'Very rarely, sir. The last time was when I dreamed Tunney would beat Dempsey. Saw the whole thing. Even the Tunney knockdown' . . . and then the room was away on the subject of subjects, dreams, but I was out of it. I had a dream in my mind and the dream was a year and the year was nineteen-twenty-one. I remember nibbling at some luscious muscats from way down south, then I drank coffee, and I was silent, a poor partner for both my partners, but that seemed a matter of no moment, for the blonde had at last got the financier all to herself, and the rest of the table was recounting dreams, analysing dreams, believing dreams and scoffing at dreams, and some time later we stood up to let the ladies go and then the men were seated again and the port was going round and I was still a faraway listener, still fidgeting with nineteen-twenty-one like a stooge in a strong-room fumbling for the combination that will unlock the safe, open up the contents and make things smooth for evermore.

I came alive again and conversation had come back to newspapers, and the playwright was back in the ring again and he was saying: 'I wouldn't mind so much, but it's the way the popular Press glamourizes everything that makes them so second-rate. Every murdered woman is beautiful, every divorcee is attractive, and so on.'

'We're an escape,' Wensley said. 'We add a little colour to the dusty world. And as these planners and political pundits make life progressively drearier, so we'll get brighter. Maybe it's all part of the bankruptcy of our way of life, whether you call it democracy or capitalism.'

'If you're so convinced that capitalism's a bankrupt notion, David, why d'you work for me?' the Baron growled.

'I'm like one of those thousands with cancer I mentioned just now, sir. I know cancer is a disease. I know I've got it. But I still sometimes hope there's a cure for it. It's as simple as that.'

'Why don't you chuck it then and go out and help find the cure?'

'I'm not the medical type, sir. I get along with the disease.'

'Am I a disease, then?'

'We all are, sir. That's what I thought I made clear.'

'Know any exceptions?'

'Not to my two main diseases: money or power or both. Most men want money: it looks easier to get. After all, a railway porter sees four or five pounds in his pay envelope every week. He gets acquainted with the stuff. He thinks how nice to have forty or fifty of 'em. If he's ambitious, he looks around. But he's not so well acquainted with the intangibles of power. Maybe he's even a bit scared of the foreman. Or maybe he doesn't even want to be foreman himself. And power brings responsibility, and not many are keen to take on that.'

'Doesn't money carry responsibilities?' the financier asked.

'Not that you'd notice,' Wensley said, as slowly as ever, almost lazily now. 'Look at the characters who have it now: pool promoters, stockbrokers, wide boys. Besides, if you get interested in power, you more or less have to come out into the open with it. Real power, I mean. Power over men's ideas, their minds, not just power through their bank balances or threat of unemployment.'

'What's mine?' growled the Baron.

Everything had to come back to him. I suppose if a man spends all his days with everybody around bowing, scraping and lickspittling it finally gets him that way. He wants the whole wide world in relation to himself. Maybe we all do, but mainly in the privacy of the bedroom or the bathroom, not in public, not at the dinner table, and Wensley said, with a smile the Baron could take any way he liked, 'You're luckier than most, sir. You get it both ways: power through their minds, power through the pay packet.'

The financial brain joined in. 'I'd take that power-over-men stuff with a pinch of salt, Wensley, if I were a newspaper man. It didn't cut much ice with the electors last time. Aren't you overrating the influence of your papers?'

'I never overrate the influence of any paper I edit,' Wensley said. 'Certainly not as far as power over the public's concerned. It's not that sort of paper.'

'What sort of paper is it, then?' the Baron said. His voice was blurred, but it was always blurred by the time the port decanter had been on its travels a bit, but his eyes of Sheffield steel were far from blurred: they still looked fresh from the foundry.

'As I've said before, sir, I always view it as a daily news-magazine, with a bias towards entertainment.'

'A bloody funny idea of entertainment you have sometimes,' the banker said.

'Three and a quarter millions like it.'

'That's nothing to be particularly proud of,' the Baron

said. 'Numbers aren't the whole story. The *Mirror* sells five. Even the *Express* sells four.'

'Numbers aren't the whole story, as you say, sir,' Wensley said.

So it was on again. I had seen it before. Wensley goading the Baron and the Baron getting back, and soon it would come, the bitter words across the table, and I wondered what Wensley was after. He hadn't done yet. He said, 'But we seem to have drifted away from the argument, surely. We were discussing the nature of power. I was leading up to the simple question: who has the power today? The shop steward or the managing director?'

'We shan't know for another ten years,' the banker said simply. 'But money usually wins. It probably will again.'

'D'you think Harry Pollitt's studying banking in his spare time?' the playwright said as a slight relief to the tensions, and we laughed.

'Haven't heard of it,' the banker said as if that were the end of the subject.

'George Waterman was a typical revolutionary: he had a few ideas about finance,' Wensley said, and as he said the name I looked firmly and quickly at the glass of port I held in my hand.

'Don't talk such balls, Wensley,' the Baron said. 'Waterman knew as much about finance as I know about midwifery.'

'Surely he wrote fairly sensibly about the subject, sir,' Wensley said.

'*I* never read him,' the banker said.

'I doubt whether you read many books about finance, Harry,' the Baron said. 'You've learned by experience— mainly other people's.'

'Too damn true!' the banker roared, and his red face split like a sliced Dutch cheese.

The Baron leaned forward. 'I think I've told you before, Wensley, I knew Waterman. Better than most. What he knew about practical finance could have been written on a penny stamp, and a torn penny stamp at that.'

I still looked into the port and tried to look as if the name was almost strange to me.

'I know his political writings, nothing of his other writings,' Wensley said calmly.

'I thought you and your staff had been making a special study of the bastard? Well, take it from me, he didn't. And let's drop the subject of Waterman, once and for all. He was a mean-gutted rat, and if he's a measure of the coming revolutionary I'd say let 'em all come. Now let's join the ladies!'

We all scraped back our chairs on the Aubusson and stood up. The room seemed suddenly cold. We grouped before the door, making way for the Baron, following him out of the dining-room into the high-domed hall. We all stood about at the foot of the curving staircase. Wensley spoke in a whisper to the Baron and the Baron was genial again in his growling voice. 'Of course, David. I'll excuse you anything, but kill that Waterman subject stone dead. He does something to me. You too!' he added, turning to me, and then he began to climb the staircase, stone step by step, and Wensley and I stood back and watched him go. Then he suddenly stopped and called over the balustrade to Wensley, 'I'll phone you when I get the paper.'

He was the boss all right.

We asked for our coats, and a minute later a big fat flunkey brought them and ten seconds later we were outside. A westerly was beginning to blow. I looked at my watch and the luminous dial said ten-fifteen. An editorial car was there at the kerb and we got in and drove towards York Gate.

'You seemed anxious to rile him tonight,' I said, as we turned into Marylebone Road.

'I have to reassure myself that Waterman's not something just in *my* imagination.'

'And isn't he?' I asked.

'God knows,' Wensley said, 'but the Baron's fairly sensitive on the subject, wouldn't you say?'

'I'd say that,' I said, 'but you certainly seem set on proving it the hard way.'

'How would you prove it, then?'

'Me!' I said. 'I'll just listen to you.'

Wensley placed his great soft hand gently on my knee. 'There's no better way. Listen to me. Keep digging away at the Waterman grave, and keep that girl happy. Do anything. Be kind to her. Indulge her. Just for another week or so. Get her to bed. Do what I say. She worked for the old buzzard. She must know more than most. Coming back to the office?'

I shook my head. 'I've still got two more of those features for Johnson. Surely you remember. Part of the price I'm paying for your interest in Waterman.'

'He pays you well. Thirty-five guineas a feature, I heard.'

'I'd choose freedom every time,' I said. 'Why don't you let dead dogs lie?'

'That's a question only a philosopher could answer,' Wensley said. 'I'm not a philosopher. At least, not this evening. Driver, we'll go to Lincoln's Inn Fields first,' and five minutes later we were there and I said good night and Wensley waved his hand limply from within the car, and the car slurred away towards Carey Street.

I climbed up the unlit, uncarpeted stairs, past the black office doors, into my own cold rooms. I phoned the flat in Whitehall Mansions. Miss Miles answered and asked where I was.

'Home. Putting out the slippers.'

'You said you'd come down here,' she said.

'I said I'd try. It's late. Half-past ten.'

'That's not late for you and you know it.'

'I've been getting into bad habits recently,' I said. 'My bedtime's ten sharp,' but I needed no television to tell me there were no smiles at the other end of the line, and she said again, 'So you won't come down?'

'Not tonight,' I said. 'I've two articles to write. Perhaps I shall see you tomorrow?'

'Good night,' she said quietly, and the phone clicked, and any ideas I might have had for progress in the gentle art of badinage were at an end. And as I went across to the table and poured out Mrs Burton's black coffee from the thermos I wondered what it was that kept me from my friend Miss Miles, but answers to those questions begin to twist the moment the questions are silently asked, and anyway I was still tied up with another question: nineteen-twenty-one and a printing-house.

31

THE next evening, Friday, the first of April, as I see from the diary, I got down to Whitehall Mansions some time after nine, and as I went up in the lift I wondered whether Miss Miles might have entered into the spirit of the day and answered my boorish mood of the night before by locking me out again, but no, she was there, and coffee was waiting, also a brand-new bottle of Haig and the fire was glowing.

Miss Miles was darning stockings and I politely asked why, now she was so rich? but she replied by asking had I enjoyed the previous evening? and I said not much.

'Why not?'

'I had something on my mind.'

'Something important?'

'I can't sort it out. It may be a year or it may be a number. Anything.'

'Anything to do with George?'

'I don't know. If I knew I wouldn't have to worry, would I?'

She smiled and it was a friendly smile, and I wondered why I seemed determined to be a boor, this night and the night before, but all she said was, 'Go back in your mind.'

'I've been so far back there's no mind left.'

'Well, try to forget it. Isn't that usually the best way to remember something?'

'I've tried, but it's still there, just below the surface. You know the way these things are. At least the way the psycho-boys tell us they are.'

'What will you drink?' she asked gently, smilingly, as

if there might be a doubt. So I had my drink and we were silent for a while until she said, without a smile, 'It was kind of you to come down tonight.'

This was certainly turning the other cheek and somehow not like the Miss Miles I knew or thought I knew, and I said 'Kind!' in a dim echoing voice, and I outlined to myself a list of what she meant by being kind: a fire made of coal and not electricity; Haig whisky and not Mrs Ada Burton's black coffee; her red-headed self and not the empty rooms of Lincoln's Inn Fields. It seemed we were both kind, and after that interlude she said, 'What did they talk about last night?'

'Power. Politics. Money. The Baron. The Baron's newspapers. The things they usually talk about. Not much else.'

'What did *you* talk about?'

'I didn't. I listened.' Then I said, 'Waterman cropped up,' and watched the effect the words might have.

'That doesn't surprise me,' she said. 'Did they tear him to pieces?' and she was as serene as a profile on a Wedgwood plaque.

'The Baron tried.'

'But I thought you said he told you to forget him.'

'He did, but Wensley brought the subject up again.'

'Why?'

'I don't know. Perversity. Or some reason too damned odd to follow.'

'What did the Baron say to that?'

'Told us both to drop the subject.'

'And can't you? Surely George is dead enough—even for his worst enemy?' Her words were almost a plea.

'Not for Wensley apparently, and maybe not for the Baron. Are you absolutely certain you never heard Waterman mention the Baron's name?'

'Never!' she said and the word was final.

So we went back to talking about the others at the dinner until Big Ben gonged eleven. I finished my drink and stood up, and she said quickly, 'You're not going yet?' and I said, 'No, I just wanted to know where the second wall-safe was. I have a job to do, don't you remember?'

'Over there, behind that painting.'

I crossed to the wall and took down the Wadsworth nautical group and there was the safe, as shut as a cell, and Miss Miles got up from her armchair and crossed to the larger breakfront bookcase, opened a drawer and took out a bunch of keys.

'You're going to be very disappointed,' she said, smiling, yet turning the lock of the safe.

I took out a black cash-box. She took it from me and opened it with another key and I looked down at a few scraps of paper and a small notebook. I asked what they were but she smiled and walked back to her chair. 'You're the research student,' she said, so I picked up the notebook and turned the leaves and it was plainly a cash-book of sorts, and I looked more closely and the amounts were the same: £10. 10. 0, £10. 10. 0, £10. 10. 0, listed monotonously under the heading 'Salary,' and ditto, ditto, ditto, week after week, with the week-ending dates noted in the left-hand column.

'Your salary, I take it?' I said, and I turned to the back of the book. Starting there was a similar set of entries, but this time listed under the heading 'Wages' and the amount was £3. 10. 0 each week, and I said, 'It's funny. It takes a rich Communist to pay a salary to you and wages to Macadam.'

'Temper! temper!' she said, and she was laughing as if nothing was serious any more, and I put back the small cash-book and took up some sheets of paper, receipts from Hatchards for books bought, and more receipts this time for stationery, also from Hatchards, and others were for printing and all were recent and all had been paid, stamped and receipted.

'The methodical type,' I said.

'Mrs Hoster taught us that,' Miss Miles said and she was plainly enjoying herself and I let the forms drop back into the cash-box, and as they floated down, the numerals I'd been chasing through the maze of my mind floated fleetingly before me and then were gone, but they were nearer and homelier, and I stood there frowning, going back, going back. I crossed the room to the other wall and took down the Sickert drawing and asked for the key and Miss Miles came across and opened up.

I took the papers and envelopes in my hands and felt like a man en route for a bonfire. I took them across to the armchair, sat down and began to go through the items I had glanced through two nights before.

I turned over the papers yet again. The stubs of cheque-book counterfoils going back for years, the list of securities, the clipped receipts for ancient bills, but none went back to 1921. Then I took up the fat envelope with the typewritten sheets that went back to 1903 and recorded his gifts from mum, and as I slipped off the paper clip I thought, *well, if 1921 isn't mentioned here I'll call it a day*, but it was mentioned there. Three times. Along with the words 'printing' and 'publishing,' and somehow, when I saw the three half-sheets of yellow paper with the typed information I was not one whit surprised.

I turned the papers slowly over. The first was dated 14th May 1921, the next 22nd May 1921, the third 30th May 1921, and each recorded the transfer of shares in the Metropolitan Printing and Publishing Company Limited of 192 Fetter Lane, London, E.C.4, from Lavinia Adelaide Waterman to George Weston Waterman.

I took the three and closed the box, and when I looked around Miss Miles was studying the scene with amused and tolerant eyes and she said, 'Well?' and I said, 'These make a coincidence. Can I keep them for a few hours? I'll let you have them back tomorrow. No, I won't even do that. I'll just make a note of 'em.'

'What are they?'

'Notes of shares that old Lavinia gave to Waterman.'

'Why should they interest you?'

'I'm writing a book about Waterman. Remember?'

'But why do these particular sheets of paper interest you?'

'Maybe they explain how he could afford to be a Red. Somebody had to subsidize him.'

She was nettled. 'Strange as it may seem, I know scarcely anything about George's finances, and I don't know what you're after and I don't care.'

'It's a matter of research,' I said, as I took up a sheet of paper from the desk and began to copy the dates and details I wanted.

'Why don't you drop the whole thing?' she asked.

I didn't answer.

'Well, let's talk about something else at least. Please!' she begged.

So we talked about something else, but as I talked I wondered. Maybe I had seen the dates and the word 'printing' two nights before, but I hadn't noticed them. Yet somehow, somewhere, sometime, something *had* registered, and the papers in the safe under the Wadsworth painting had sent me back to the papers in the other safe. Something similar has happened to us all. Dozens of times. Doubtless it is all an oddity of the mind, a mental quirk, an association of ideas. How it happens and why it happens just that way we leave to the psychological pundits. They can delve that much deeper into our mangled minds or say they can and they surely have the word for it in their double-jointed jargon that quietens the sceptic and rakes in the guineas. So I left it and came back to the conversation.

We talked until nearly midnight and then I left. We were friends again. My behaviour of the previous evening had gone unmentioned. But my thoughts moved on from Miss Miles and her forgiving mood, and as I walked up Villiers Street I brooded over my next nervous step, and that I thought I knew.

32

AND that next step I took the very next morning, Saturday, at half-past ten.

You go in from the Strand into Bush House, the south-west wing. You cross the busy hall and go through an open door, under a legend lettered in gold-leaf caps:

COMPANIES SEARCH DEPARTMENT

If you've ever wished to check on your board of directors, where they live and how they divide the spoils of the business in which you play your indispensable part, that is where you go—or went.

You go into a wide, low-roofed room, and sitting around at a dozen long tables are other inquisitive citizens, all studying books they hope will bring them knowledge, of the firms they work for, deal with, or merely hope to liquidate.

It is not a quiet room. Too many people are interested in other people's money for the room ever to be all that quiet—even on Saturday mornings. And you help swell the general clatter. First you cross to the multigraphed Visible Index system and you hunt for the name of the company you propose to investigate. I knew the drill, for I had done it once before.

So I crossed to the index files and went along the rows of metal flaps set at eye level on a high bench and I looked down the flap marked MEM-MEZ and I looked for the Metropolitan Printing and Publishing Company Ltd, but it wasn't there. I looked again, but there was nothing between Metropolitan Plastic Ltd and Metropolitan Properties Ltd and it seemed I had drawn another blank.

I was surprised and disappointed. For quite a few hours I had lived with the name and it had seemed a name I had heard before. It had a good solid ring about it.

Well, it had probably gone broke, but there were other possibilities. A company gets absorbed, or changes its name, and, as I was in the one place in England which would hold the knowledge I wanted, I went across to the counter and filled in the name of the company on a pink form and paid my shilling search fee.

'This firm's not on the index,' I said. 'So I can't put a number on the form, but I'd like a search made all the same.'

'It often happens,' the clerk intoned without looking up. He called to another clerk and explained the problem.

'I'll have a look,' the second man said in a livelier voice and moved away.

'I'll come, too, if you don't mind,' I said. 'I'm a

newspaper man, I've never tried to trace a dead firm before. I'd like to see how it's done.'

'It's simple enough,' he said, and I followed him.

We went out into the hall, down into the basement, past the old air-raid shelters into a large room stacked with long box index files.

On a long bench against the near wall were four or five vast books. He took down one of the volumes, dropped it heavily on a trestle table and began to turn through the pages, and as he turned I lifted the title-page and read the notice: *Alphabetical Index of Companies* 15*th July* 1856– 30*th June* 1920. *The Companies Act* 1908–1917.

'If your firm still had that name in 1920 it'll be in here,' he said. 'Let's see. Here you are.' He looked along a printed line and noted a number.

'290902,' he said. 'Now we'll check.'

He crossed to one of the box files, pulled out a long drawer and flicked through the cards. He stopped at one, held back the rest and took it out.

'Three changes in the name in the last twenty-five years,' he said, looking down at the card. I looked too, and there scribbled on the dotted line in four different hands were:

Metropolitan Printing and Publishing Company Ltd. 1904.

Metropolitan and National Publishing Company Ltd. 1922.

National Publishing Company Ltd. 1930.

National Newspapers Ltd. 1934.

'Still 290902 you see,' he said with parental pride. 'A company keeps the same number here, however often it changes its name. We'll go up and you can send down for the file under this name and number.'

We went upstairs again and I filled in another form and

handed it to the gloomy clerk. In return I got a small bone counter numbered 28, as I clearly recall, and I sat down in one of the spindle-backed chairs and waited, and somehow I knew that what I waited for would only confirm what I already thought I knew.

Around me were my fellow-men, bent over books on the long oak tables, and they looked like a group of ardent, diligent students and maybe they were. And some perhaps were studying the finances of Lord Dudley, Lord McGowan, Lord Beaverbrook or any other nobleman with a taste for Big Business. And others were certainly looking into the affairs of the midget, crackpot, flyblown, jerrybuilt companies that are also there. All can be opened for a shilling apiece.

A Civil Service messenger broke these thoughts with a cry of 'Twenty-eight!' I raised my hand, gave up the bone counter, and the statutory records of National Newspapers Ltd were placed before me, and a minute later I was deep in the early history of the Baron's own company, my very own employers. But the Baron had no place in the pages I was looking at. He came later.

The Metropolitan Printing and Publishing Co. Ltd had been formed in 1867 with two directors, a subscribed paid-up capital of £100 and offices in Ludgate Hill. Waterman *père* made his first appearance in the record in 1892, and I wondered how or why a Birmingham ironfounder had taken over a small London jobbing house, but whatever the reason, from that time on the firm began to grow, and quickly, too, judging from the increased capital subscribed, but it stayed a private company. Then came pages of names and figures showing the growth of the firm: fresh capital, fresh directors, but I skipped most of that and turned to the records farther on, and some time in 1906 all old Waterman's shares were in the name of Lavinia Adelaide Waterman. He had died then, I guessed, and I skipped more pages and was face to face with the record for 1921. Some time in April 1921, Lavinia Adelaide Waterman had transferred her shares to George Weston Waterman. I knew that. I had the details in my pocket. Within a month Waterman had transferred them again. This time they went to the Baron, but he hadn't been a Baron then, and doubtless never would have been without those very same shares.

Well, there it was in black-and-white, and I went back, trying in my tyro's way to pick out the story in the interplay of figures, but it was no good. I haven't that sort of mind, but I had got my simple facts and that was all. The rest was High Finance to me. So I pocketed my useless notes and went.

I went out into the Strand and it was quite a puzzle that I took along. I walked down into Fleet Street and into El Vino's and sat away in a corner trying to sort it out with a large Martini.

The record was there for anyone who wanted it, there in Bush House, but nobody knew and nobody cared. And why should they?

To the secretary of the company and a few accountants the entries were doubtless just figures, as they would be for anyone without the same bee that had flitted so fretfully in Wensley's bonnet. And why should anyone worry? A man has to start somewhere, somehow, so why ask questions? He gets on in the world. And as he gets on fewer and fewer questions get asked.

No man's record is as clean as a brand-new plate and the Baron's might be cleaner than most, and why shouldn't a newspaper proprietor start his real career as a director of a middle-sized printing- and publishing-house? What more natural? Perhaps Waterman had needed a journalist's help in the family property. Perhaps he had wanted help quickly and had been prepared to pay. He had certainly got the shares quick and passed them on quick. It might look as if he'd got them especially for the Baron, but again, why not?

I finished my drink and went out into Fleet Street, across to Court House and up to my room, and although it was Saturday and Saturday is as dead as death itself in any daily newspaper office, I began absent-mindedly on the usual routine and looked through the mail before going up to the Foreign Room. Then I went along to Johnson's room. He was out, but his deputy was there and he had the proofs of the feature pages on his desk.

I looked through my article, put in two commas and then glanced over the rest of the page. Johnson had put me on page two along with a feature on 'Russia's Agents in China' and the weekly City piece, 'For the Small Investor.' Maybe that was what the Baron had been those years before, I thought, a small investor, and I went back to my room. As if in a dream I picked up the phone and asked for the Guildford number I knew by heart. Maybe old Lavinia might help. But I had no hopes.

When the call came I got past the maid in no time at all, and then the old lady was on the line, and after a brief exchange of compliments I asked whether I could come down that afternoon, there were one or two questions I needed to ask, and she said, 'By all means. I had really expected you to ring before,' and I wondered whether her voice held solicitude or rebuke: I could never sort out the subtleties of her rasping voice.

So I went down again to Guildford and met the stiff-necked, mob-capped maid again and was shown into the old stale room again. And the old lady was there like a Victorian relic out of Tussaud's and we had another of her sweltering tea hours, but by now I knew the rig of the day and for this visit I had doffed my waistcoat and left it in the office. We talked of this and that, and as we talked I wondered how I would introduce the subject of her sometime shares in the Metropolitan Printing and Publishing Co. Ltd that later had become the National group of newspapers, but I knew the moment would certainly come, and I gave my attention to her sharp and acid comments on the news of the day. She had views of her own. She was a thoroughgoing Tory but she had no use for Churchill. 'He was all right in a war. No one better, but he doesn't understand peace or men. He cannot understand that the poor live by their stomachs and not by his sort of rhetoric. He should step down and retire from politics. His kind went out with Palmerston. I know. My father knew Palmerston and used to tell me about him, but I'm wasting your time. How is your book on my son progressing?' Her harsh voice ground the question into the biscuit she nibbled.

'Slowly, I'm afraid,' I confessed.

'I am sorry you had that bother. It was all most understandable but vexing all the same.'

I agreed. Then she asked if Miss Miles was proving helpful.

'Most,' I said.

'My son found her extremely efficient, I believe.'

'So I've gathered,' I said.

'From your remarks on the telephone I imagine you have some questions to ask me,' she said at last.

'One or two,' I said.

She picked up her teacup and I said quickly, 'You very kindly gave me *carte blanche* with your son's papers. As I have been going through them it has become quite apparent that he was a very wealthy man.'

'His father was a very wealthy man. I told you that,' she said in peremptory interruption. 'I am a wealthy woman, although it is not the sort of thing one is supposed to let anyone know these days.'

'You weren't keen, I gathered, that your son, with his political views, should have this money?'

'Not at first,' she said slowly, 'but when he was twenty-two he came into certain trust funds, which made him independent, and later, after my husband died, it seemed only reasonable that he should have more from the estate.'

'You transferred certain shares to him from time to time, even up to recent times?'

'Yes,' she said grudgingly, and I could see she was beginning to stiffen and I knew the rest was a race against time, and I said, 'These questions may seem somewhat personal and irrelevant, but I must get this financial background straight if I am to get your son straight. It's important in any appraisal of his character and personality and his political career. I'm sure you see that.'

'I can see that, but I cannot see that the views you are likely to present, judging by these questions, are likely to be very detached.'

'You will see the typescript,' I said.

'Well, what other questions?' she asked.

'Did you know that your son in turn transferred certain of those shares to my employer?'

'Your employer. That man! Nonsense!' she said. I raised my hand and tried to look as pacific as the local curate.

'It's true. A long time ago, but true all the same. Almost thirty years ago, in fact. Perhaps you did not know or it has slipped your memory.'

'My memory is excellent,' she said sharply. 'In any

case, the shares belonged to George as soon as I passed them into his keeping. He could do what he liked with them.' And then suddenly, 'Which shares?'

I took out my scrap of paper and read out the details. 'I seem to remember something about them, but very vaguely,' she said. 'I remember that as one of my husband's companies but that is all.'

'You took over those shares in this firm from your husband?'

'They came to me as part of my husband's estate. He died in 1905,' she said gently. 'Forty-five years ago. Time goes so quickly.'

We were both silent until she said, as if musing, 'Judging by these dates you have just mentioned, they would have been the first shares I passed to George after he came back from Ireland and all that dreadful business there.'

'Which dreadful business?' I asked quickly, almost too quickly, for she stared at me as she said, 'The Black and Tan troubles, of course. Perhaps they were before your time.'

'I was nearly ten,' I said. She said she was sorry but I asked quickly whether she had known that Waterman had known my boss in Ireland.

'How could I have known?' she asked.

'Well, he was a reporter in those days, and he got to know your son during the Troubles.'

'Perhaps they became friendly,' the old lady said, almost hopefully.

'Perhaps,' I said, but she knew I believed in the possibility about as slightly as she did herself.

'Your son never talked about his time in Ireland?'

'Never,' she said.

'Did he spend much time here after he came back?'

'Not very much.'

'Did he have visitors?'

'Scarcely ever. He met them in London. He worked here, but not for long.'

There was nothing more for me and the tea dragged on and I asked a few questions that didn't mean a thing, and slowly tea and conversation petered out and at last I escaped.

I went out to the waiting taxi and breathed in the good fresh air. Then I sat back and relaxed all the way to the station, and I kept on relaxing in the train for I knew I had drawn another blank.

I had an item of information, an interesting item, but it seemed to stand on its own. I comforted myself with the fact that no item of information stands on its own: it is always part of a jig-saw puzzle; it always has been, ever since that great and sparkling day when the Spirit moved on the face of the waters and the Almighty saw the light that it was good and set about building this major jig-saw. But meantime, I thought, I needed a little light myself.

It was just after six when I got back to Waterloo, and, spurning the queue, walked out into the Waterloo Road and picked up a taxi as the non-queuer always does.

Well, it was still Saturday and a damn dull day to be in London and I wondered whether it was still worth while to go away, but instead I rang Miss Miles and she was in and I said, 'Let's have dinner' and, to what I tried to kid myself was my surprise, she agreed.

I called for her at eight and we walked up into Piccadilly Circus and along to the Écu de France and, later, over the chicken casserole, I said, 'Would it surprise you to know that Waterman started the Baron on his newspaper-owning career?'

'Nonsense!'

So I told her the story, and at the end of the brief account she was silent for several long seconds until I said, 'Does it surprise you?'

She nodded.

'Does it upset you?'

'Why should it?'

'I don't know. I thought it might.'

'I suppose it would make you happy if I said it did,' she said suddenly and bitterly.

'But why?' I asked. 'It would be natural enough. Waterman meant something to you. You hate all the Baron stands for. It might well upset you if you thought they'd had an understanding some years before.'

'They could never have had an understanding. Never!' she said vehemently.

'Maybe,' I said.

'Since I met you,' she said, after another long pause, 'my life has been more of a mess than ever.'

'Why pick on me?' I protested.

'Why not? You seem to do your best to make it more of a mess than it need be. You seem anxious to spoil whatever George meant to me, either as a friend or a teacher. . . .'

That was one way of putting it, I thought, or maybe two, but I said, 'I'm interested in any relationship there was between Waterman and the Baron. I told you that at the beginning and now it looks as if it's not just hot air. I just asked if my piece of information surprised you. It did. Then if it hurt you. Presumably it did.'

'I suppose so,' she said at last. 'I'm just being a fool.'

But was she? I sometimes wondered. And how upset had she been? And later that night, back in Lincoln's Inn Fields, I began to wonder, as anybody wonders at such a time, just what kind of relationship was building up between Miss Miles and myself. She wasn't my type, even if I had a type. And it wasn't only that. Her attitude was changing, and any man is a slow-witted moron who doesn't recognize the moment the mood begins to change. But it was nothing I wanted. I wanted no love from a stranger, and a rich, neurotic, red-headed young stranger at that. All I wanted was a little information. And a lot of peace. But, there it was. Maybe I was the tame psychiatrist. Maybe when she said, 'You despise me for having been Waterman's mistress, don't you?' I should have said 'Yes,' and it would have helped, but I had no convictions either way. People have their own ideas. Some like danger. Some like security. Some like them old. Some like them young. It takes all sorts to make a world. Someone had said that a long, long time ago. And I was prepared to let it stand.

But maybe I'm moving ahead, too far and too fast. All that falls into some sort of place some time later in the record.

33

THE next day was Sunday and I lunched in Soho and then went down to Court House, and soon after five o'clock I went into Wensley's room with *Objects and Subjects* and I seem to remember he massacred two subjects and no objects, and after that exercise in editorial discipline, I said, 'I suppose you knew the Baron originally got hold of this group through Waterman's shares?'

He sat up slowly and ponderously. 'Waterman's

shares! How the bloody hell should I know? That's the sort of stuff I asked you to find out. Come on, out with it.'

'You said you'd got the earlier part of the Baron's life lined up. Surely that's an important part . . .'

Wensley slumped again in his chair. He picked up a ruler and looked along the edge. 'You're the one who's writing the chapter on the Baron and Waterman. So quit being funny. How many editors in Fleet Street know the financial set-up of the papers they edit? Not one. Does Schofield know the Rothermere set-up? Or Christiansen the Beaver's? Be your age. They're editors, not accountants. How did Waterman have any part of this outfit, anyway? And how long ago?'

So I took the scrap of paper out of my pocket, handed it across and told my tale with the facts and figures I knew, the dates, and the changes in the history of the firm that was now all the Baron's, and Wensley sat and stared along the ruler at his brown brogue shoes and looked half-asleep, and at the end he said, 'How should I have known all that?'

'You could have wandered up to Bush House,' I said. 'You could have put some other spy on to it. Years ago.'

'I've been here twelve years, six of 'em war years,' he said. 'All this happened thirty years ago.'

'But it was still all there twelve years ago. First in Somerset House and now in Bush House.'

'All right!' he said. 'The triumph's all your very own—so is the chapter!'

'But it's still a blank,' I said. 'You'll have to ask the Baron himself how he got the shares. Old Mrs Waterman doesn't know. I've been down there again.'

'How is she?'

'We seem to be drifting apart.'

'Perhaps she thinks you're not so interested in her son any more.'

'I'm too damned interested in her son,' I said. 'More interested than I want to be.'

'Maybe it's time you dropped him,' Wensley said, putting down the ruler.

'Long past the time.'

'Does this secretary woman of Waterman's know about these?' he asked, picking up the sheet of paper again.

'I told her. She doesn't want to believe it.'

'The trouble is, it doesn't go far enough. You say nineteen-twenty-one was the date he mentioned the other night. I wasn't listening. I'd always dated his real climb to power a year or so later.'

'It was!' I said. 'He changed the company's name a year or so later.'

'Maybe,' Wensley said, but it was plain he was some way off in time and space. 'Thirty years ago,' he said, handing the paper back to me. 'That's a lot of years judged by anybody's standards. Even by Almighty God's occasionally, I dare say. Just after the Irish business.' He shifted his gaze to his shoe. 'You'd better advertise.'

'Advertise!' I said. 'What for? And why me?' Wensley ignored the protest. He was warming up to a theory I'd heard him on before, and he said, 'I believe in advertising, that's why. I'm a great believer in the personal column of *The Times*. So is any editor. We get three good news stories a week out of it. You know that. Advertise in *The Times*. Ask anyone who knew Waterman in Ireland to step forward. You could put a note in *The Times Literary Supplement*, too. Say you're writing the official life of Waterman. It's a thin chance, but it might work.'

'What about the Baron?' I said. 'He reads. Even *The Times.*'

'Afraid?' Wensley asked.

I waited until the joke was over and he smiled and said, 'Use your head. D'you think I want your name in this? Tell this secretary woman of Waterman's to put 'em in under her name or put 'em in and tell her later.'

He reached across, took a red-covered atlas from the book-rack on his desk and turned through the pages. 'While you're about it you might as well put the same ad in any of the Irish newspapers that cover the area. Most of Southern Ireland. You say his stories had a Cork deadline. All of them. Well, here it is: write it down: Dublin, Galway, Cork, Wexford. Maybe the whole of the Southern Irish Press. What sort of papers do they have? God only knows. I know the *Cork Examiner*, but find out and put it in the lot. Blanket the whole of the treacherous bloody island.'

'I had an Irish grandmother,' I said gently.

'You're lucky,' he said. 'Damn few Irishmen ever had. As far as I can see, most of 'em come fully grown and roaring drunk straight out of the stinking bogs of their rotting emerald isle.'

'They bother you,' I said.

'They're all right,' he said grandiloquently, forgiving and forgetting. 'Anyway, get this woman, whatshername? Miss Miles. Get her to do it. She ought to be proud to gather in the facts while Waterman's memory's green. In a month's time he'll be as dead as cold cod, tell her.'

'Shall I give her the message from you?'

'Use your own words for it. It'll come to the same thing.'

34

SO, later that evening, dining with Miss Miles in the Café Royal gallery, I used my own words for it, explaining the plan as if it were my own, and I asked whether she would do it and she said, 'I suppose so. I was shaken by what you said last night. I seem to have gone so far I might as well go the rest of the way. Besides, I'd like to know something about George's life in Ireland. He never talked about it.'

'Maybe you weren't alive at the time,' I said.

She laughed. 'You can't upset me that way any more. I'm immune from now on.'

Maybe surprise was clear on my face for she laughed aloud, and a bald and squat old Babbitt at the next table with a young woman certainly not his wife, looked around, quickly and guiltily. The evil that men do lives sometimes with them.

I wrote out the advertisement on the back of an old envelope and read it aloud to see whether it made sense, and the words were:

'GEORGE W. WATERMAN. Any first-hand information concerning the Irish experiences (1919–1920) of George Waterman, the English journalist, who was recently killed in Yugoslavia, will be gratefully received and acknowledged by his former secretary, Miss R. Miles, 527 Whitehall Mansions, S.W.1.

Will that do? It's better not to have a box number, I think.'

'Supposing Mrs Waterman sees it. She's pretty certain to.'

'Tell her you're doing it for me. I'll drop her a note. It won't appear for a week or so yet, but this can appear next week,' and I began to draft a letter to *The Times Literary Supplement* under the heading, GEORGE W. WATERMAN. *Sir, I am compiling biographical material concerning George Waterman, the political journalist, who was recently killed accidentally in Yugoslavia. Any information, photographs, newspaper cuttings and other relevant material will be gratefully received and acknowledged and returned after copies have been made. Yours, etc.*

'What about the Irish experiences?' she asked.

It had seemed too pointed, but I gave it another thought, and then I scribbled and read out the additional note: *'Any first-hand information concerning Waterman's experiences in Ireland during* 1919–20 *will be especially welcome.'*

'What do you expect to get out of this?' she asked.

'Probably nothing. Anyway, we shan't know for ten days at least. But Waterman knew a lot of people and some might come forward. You can interview them. You ought to have something to fill up your time. You can go down to the London offices of the Irish papers and put the same ad in. Repeat it three times in each paper. Weekly intervals.'

'Do they cost much?' she asked. 'I don't know much about these things.'

'About two bob a line, ten bob in *The Times*. You can charge it up to me.'

'I can charge it up to the estate. The petty cash account isn't closed yet,' she said with a smile.

She seemed to be changing. She even joked about things she hadn't thought funny before.

So I shared the joke and asked how Oliphant was behaving. 'I don't know really. He says the estate is larger than he thought and needs a lot of work. Anyway, I shall stay on at the flat for a time, that's certain.'

'My work's pretty well finished there,' I said.

'Is that a roundabout way of saying you're not coming there any more?'

'I shall want to pick up the answers to these advertisements and any replies to *The Times Lit Sup* letter.'

'Is that all?' she said quietly.

'Not quite all,' I said and I hoped the words would tide me over while we drank our coffee.

Soon afterwards I paid the bill and we walked out and across Piccadilly Circus, down Haymarket, and soon we were crossing Trafalgar Square, heading in the direction of Whitehall Mansions, and by that time we were discussing other things, maybe even the weather.

35

MONDAY, April 4, I stayed late at Court House, I remember, long after Miss Arnold had gone, my feet on the scratched mahogany desk and my mind a long way off in time and space.

I wondered how a seeker after truth would dip into Irish history and Irish geography in seeking two forgotten men; and I wondered who would have known them in those long-ago days. And where would I find these helpful characters even if they lived?

I sat on until eight o'clock chimed unevenly from several City churches, and later, much later, I was still at it, chain-smoking fit to start a fire and I took up a pad and scribbled: *Miss Arnold: Dig out some books from the*

London Library on the Irish troubles and the Sinn Fein movement.

And I went on wondering. Where and who?

Somewhere in the Southern Irish counties, Waterman and the Baron had possibly met those years before or so it seemed, and maybe someone knew. That gave me a simple matter of several thousand square miles to play around in, questioning the Slatterys and the O'Sweenys, the Megaws and the O'Ferralls. Perhaps I could narrow it down to the Cork area. Apart from the Baron's despatches, the other cuttings in Waterman's Irish records had been from *The Times* and the *Cork Examiner*. But could I? It was all as clear as a mud-spattered windscreen.

Wensley said *advertise*, but maybe there were other ways. If I'd had a few months in hand I could have started with the parish clerks, the librarians, the oldest inhabitants. But I hadn't. I could start in a modest way with the secretaries of the social clubs of Cork, the local secretaries of any Anglo-Irish Societies and half a dozen other institutions with staunch supporters over many years. Amongst them and their connections I might find a few entries for the title of Oldest Inhabitant, but even then he would probably be a score of years too old.

And what others?

Where else did old members of the Anglo-Irish community forgather? I wondered, for it was in such a group that I would get my gossiping start, if any.

So I went back to first principles and that took me back to clubs, and I scribbled another note: *Find out the names of the leading clubs in Cork, preferably Anglo-Irish, and the names of the secretaries.* And just to give Miss Arnold a really lively morning I added *golf clubs, sailing clubs, hunting clubs* and, as I scribbled, it came to me that the average hunt covered quite an area and I added: *Find out how many hunts there are in Southern Ireland, around the Cork area, how much territory they cover, the names and addresses of the masters and secretaries, preferably the secretaries. I think there's a book called Bailey's Hunting Directory, or there was. That might help.*

By that time it was well after half-past eight and I went from the office, along the quiet corridors to the lift and down into the courtway, and the fountains were still spraying within the forecourt, and in the darkness the few lighted windows were as bright as teeth in a darkie's face. I walked out into Fleet Street, waited for a taxi and wished Eire as distant as the stars. And Waterman. And as inaccessible.

By midday Tuesday I had the answers, a neat, typed list of names and addresses, and muttering *nothing venture, nothing gain,* I dictated a letter to go to all the club secretaries and here for the record is what Miss Arnold typed: *Dear Sir: We are proposing to publish in the near future a series of short articles on those Irish clubs which have links with England. In order to show the continuing vitality of these institutions we should like to arrange interviews with a few of your older members who might be willing to spare a little of their time for this purpose. I shall be in Southern Ireland during the next week or so and I do hope that you will be interested in the project. If so, perhaps you will be kind enough to reply to this office.*

'You sound very Anglo-Irish today,' Miss Arnold said.

'I had an Irish grandmother.'

'Could it also be a free trip to Ireland?' she asked.

'An unwilling one,' I said, and then: 'Another letter. This goes to the hunt secretaries you looked up. How many?'

'There's six in the area between Waterford and Kinsale

and as far north as Clonmel,' she said, looking at the list.

'Send them this,' I said, and here, from a carbon, are the words I sent: *Dear Sir: We are proposing to include in this newspaper a series of articles comparing hunting conditions in England today with conditions thirty or forty years ago. It has been suggested that we should enlarge the scope of the series to include certain Irish hunts. As I shall be in Southern Ireland during the next week or so I should be grateful if you would let me know the names of any of your older members who might be willing to spare some of their time and their reminiscences for the purposes of such a survey. They would be able to see a proof of any relevant article before publication. I do hope you will be able to help: if so perhaps you will be kind enough to reply to this office.*

I signed eleven letters later that afternoon. There would be more the following day, Miss Arnold said.

'It's an odd feature for you, isn't it?' she asked. She was curious as occasionally she was when life was dull.

'Hunting is a subject and my feature's called *Objects and Subjects*, if it's of any interest to you,' I said heavily.

'But hunting's not your subject. At least not fox-hunting. Anyway, I've got typist's cramp. It's tea-time. I'm off to Kardomah.'

'Don't come back!' I said. 'But first see if the editor's free.'

And half an hour later, after toothcombing *Objects and Subjects,* Wensley came back to the subject he wouldn't let go. Always he came back as if it were an afterthought, an oddment thrown out in the madness of the day, but he was watching all right, watching for the answer as he said, 'Did you put that ad in *The Times*?'

'I sent it down. It won't appear for a few days. There's a newsprint shortage even down there.'

'And write to the *T.L.S.*?'

'I roughed out a letter for Miss Miles. I imagine she's sent it down.'

'What will you do if nothing comes of either?' Wensley asked.

'Go back to being a simple old-fashioned columnist,' I said. 'With your permission, of course.'

'Please yourself,' Wensley answered as gently as a bishop bent on benediction. 'But I still say there's a story there. It's there and I want it. And I'll get it. But please yourself.'

'There's a story behind anything,' I said. 'Murder, divorce, even peculiar friendships. The story's there, but we don't always get it.'

'We don't always want it,' Wensley corrected slowly. 'When we do want it we usually get it. Don't we?'

'All right, but we don't always publish. Do we?'

'Who said I was going to publish what you're after?'

'I was just being logical,' I said.

'Ah!' he said with a long-drawn lazy breath. 'Publishing's another subject. Logic rarely comes into it. Other considerations creep in. Libel. Damages. Stuff like that. Especially in a newspaper. Never logic.'

'People's feelings?' I queried.

'It's been known,' he granted. 'Long ago. Before my time.'

We were quiet for a while. Again I asked just exactly why he wanted this particular story and patiently he explained: 'Because it ought to be interesting. Because we're warming up. Because we ought to see whether we can dig it out. And because you want to dig it out. Aren't those reasons enough?'

So it had become a technical query the way everything becomes a technical query in this day and age, the way the surgeon wants a cleaner scalpel-cut next time, the way the shipping man wants a swifter turn-round, the way the hangman doubtless wants a tighter noose. No rights and no wrongs, but just how something happens just that way. Never *why?* I suppose Wensley was right and I wanted the story—to see whether it had a beginning and an end.

But Wensley was going on: 'There's nothing much you can do till we see whether these ads bring home any bacon. You can make one or two enquiries into the financial structure of this outfit if you like, but you seem to have got most of that. Anyway, please yourself. I've got this bloody newspaper to edit. Your day's work is done. Mine's just beginning.'

So I went, and I went back to my room, and later I wrote a few words that had been milling around in my mind as I'd signed the letters.

The letters might help to fling a wider net, and the net couldn't be too wide, so I scribbled: *ENGLISHMEN. Anyone who has recollections concerning any Englishman who fought with the Irish Republican Army* 1919–1920 *in Southern Ireland is asked to communicate with 'Historian,' Box No. . . . Cork Examiner.*

I put the note in Miss Arnold's typewriter with instructions to send down to the *Cork Examiner* office in the morning, charge to petty cash. Then I went across to El Vino's. The phone took care of itself.

36

YOU go back in the mind, turning it out like an old wallet, seeking for the time before a certain time, and you say, *On that day something happened: what did I do the day before?* but the day before has gone and cannot return. You even go back through an old calendar as I do now, trying to peg a memory on the numerals: *That was Tuesday, April twelve, and that was the day the letter came. What happened the week before?*

There were the moments of walking and talking, eating and drinking, and the many small felicities, but they are gone now. Gone for good.

But I can go back to April twelve, for that was the day the letter came. Miss Miles phoned me early and Mrs Burton answered, and from the bathroom I heard her succinct phrase, 'I'll get 'im.'

'Your bait worked,' Miss Miles said. 'Even your Baron's nibbling.'

At first it was too obscure for that time in the morning, and I probably sounded dim and distant, and Miss Miles said, 'Your letter to the *T.L.S.* Don't you remember? There are four replies.'

I came suddenly awake and said I'd come down, straightaway after breakfast.

'Come to breakfast,' she said.

So I went to breakfast.

In her dark blue quilted dressing-gown, Miss Miles was well worth looking at, even at that hour.

'You look less like a revolutionary every time I see you,' I said.

'You haven't seen me for four days,' she said. She was gay and almost carefree, not the young woman I'd first met in the very same flat sixteen days before.

'I went away,' I said.

'Where?'

'To Brighton.'

'I like Brighton,' she said.

'I wanted to read and smoke three hundred cigarettes.'

'I like reading,' she said. 'Smoking too,' and she went from the dining-room.

'Who'd have thought he read the *T.L.S.*?' I called out.

'Lots of people do,' she said and came back with coffee, scrambled eggs and other items in a breakfast Mrs Burton had never even heard about.

'Not lots of Press lords,' I said as I took up the letters, four of them.

The top sheet was scribbled on a memo form from one of the Left Wing weeklies and the words were, *Dear Miss Miles: I knew George Waterman well during recent years, as you probably know, and although I always considered his political views too violent and extreme I should be glad to give you what modest help I can. I corresponded with him over several years, as did one or two of my colleagues here. He acted as special correspondent for this journal on several of his trips abroad. He was always a vivid writer. We were all saddened to hear of his death. You could go through the files here and I should be glad to help you in any way I can, although I don't think I can be of much use concerning any Irish experiences as he was an older man than myself and I didn't meet him until the early 'thirties and I never heard him discuss that period of his life. I believe we have met.*

I puzzled over the signature as I ate the scrambled eggs.

'He says he's met you. Assistant Editor. Remember him?'

She nodded.

'So that's it. He's probably more interested in your red hair than my Waterman story,' I said.

'He's not the type. He's sixty, at least. Please don't romanticise. Read your Baron's letter instead.'

I picked up the second letter, typed in a large roman face on an azure bond under the die-stamped Regent's Park address: *I was interested in your letter in The Times Literary Supplement. I had some acquaintance with G. W. Waterman at the time you mention, and I should be willing to give you what help I can in your project, but I cannot think that my recollections will be precise enough for your purpose. If you would care to ring this number my secretary can fix an appointment.*

I read the other two letters. One was from a firm of publishers. They had published three of Waterman's books during the past twenty years. They would be pleased to help in any way possible. And might they ask if Miss Miles had yet discussed the question of publication of her biography?

'Quick workers,' she said as I put the letter down.

'All very logical: what else would you expect a publisher to say?'

'Perhaps I ought to tell them I'm not writing the book,' she said.

The fourth note was written on the London School of Economics heading. The writer had corresponded with Waterman over a number of years. He would be interested to add a chapter concerning the basic soundness of Waterman's economic theories. Getting around to this simple proposition took a lot of words.

'A good bag for one morning,' I said. 'There's probably more to come.'

'Will you follow them all up?'

'Only the Baron's.'

'How?'

'Acknowledge the others. Say you'll get in touch with them later.'

'How will you follow up the Baron's letter?' she asked again. Suspiciously, I thought.

'By sending you along,' I said.

'By what?' she said in horror.

'You know you'd be interested to meet him. I don't say you want to, but most people would be interested, especially a member of the Party.'

'I've told you before,' she said firmly and patiently, 'I'm not a member of the Party.'

'I always forget. Would-be member then. Ring him this afternoon and go up there and see him. It's worth it just to see how the rich live. Not more than a dozen people live the way he lives. You're comfortable here, but it's middle-class stuff compared with the Baron's.'

'You're very funny,' she said.

I thought so too, and later, maybe years later, the words come back, the time of the day you said them, the feel of the room you said them in, and the words are no longer funny, not funny at all, but just words, as cold and wet as night on the dark mountain.

So sometime during that afternoon Miss Miles rang the Baron's house in the park and someone said she could come on the morrow, and that evening at the Écu de France she asked what her plan should be, and I said, 'No plan. Just go up there and listen. Once he's convinced you're not a suspicious character he'll do all the talking. He'll tell you damn all about Waterman, a hell of a lot about the Baron. Remember what you can. Make a few notes if you can. You know enough about Waterman to string him along.'

'Do I?' she said, and again there was that momentary chill, until she said, 'Suppose he asks about you: have I ever met you?'

I'd given some thought to that possibility and I said, 'No, say you'd heard from old Mrs Waterman that I'd called on her, but that's all. He knows that, anyway, but she says she's never met the Baron and she's probably right. There was no call for them to meet, anyway. Not even when he took a slice of her fortune.'

'How far am I supposed to have got with my biography?'

'Not very far. Just getting the notes together.'

'Why am I so interested in the Irish part of George's career?'

'Because it's the part that's hazy. Any number of citizens could tell you about Waterman's life here. At least a part of it. You could for one. But nobody seems to know anything about that Irish interlude. There aren't more than two dozen Irish stories in Waterman's Press-cutting books. And that's all. Yet he was there for two years.'

'What sort of information do you expect me to get?'

'I hadn't thought. I didn't even think he'd see the letter.'

'Why did you write to the *T.L.S.* then?'

'I was after somebody somewhere who might have known something.'

'It all seems rather hazy, doesn't it?'

'Research work is,' I said complacently. 'Then, sometimes, the pieces begin to fall into shape—if you're lucky. Just like any other jig-saw puzzle.'

'Will this fall into shape?'

'I don't know how lucky you're going to be,' I said.

37

TEN times during the hour between noon and one the next day, Wednesday, I reached for the telephone to ring Whitehall Mansions, to say, *Cut the whole thing out*, but I didn't ring, the way you don't ring, and then I had lunch with the art editor and then it was three o'clock and too late anyway.

Then, by the afternoon post, I got a first faint word out of Ireland, the first reply to the twenty-eight letters Miss Arnold had sent to Southern Irish club-land the week before. It was a spidery note under the heading of *The Cork and South of Ireland Literary and Debating Society*, and the note said only: *Dear Sir: I am secretary of the above Society. I do not think I can be of any great help to you but I have been a member of the Society for almost fifty years and I would willingly give you what help I can. Yours sincerely, C. M. Edwards.*

'The first bite,' Miss Arnold said bravely.

'An old club bore on the edge of the grave. Make a note of his name and forget him.'

'Some people are never satisfied,' she said. 'You said you expected none!'

I went on to finish *Objects and Subjects*, writing as usual with one eye fixed firmly on the clock and the other on the Great British Public that Wensley thought he knew, and my paragraphs held no reference to anything beyond the compass of a child in an infant school, nothing upstage, nothing intellectual, nothing middle-class or even middle-brow.

And by six o'clock Wensley had passed my column

and by six-forty-five it had been set and passed for press, and for me the day was done. They could plate the leader page and not replate again through all the night-long hours as far as I was concerned, and I left and went by taxi down to Whitehall Mansions. I gave the lift a miss and went up the stairs two at a time, but by the time I reached the fifth floor I wished I'd kept to the lift, and I waited until breath came back. Then, although I still had the keys, I rang, as was my gentlemanly habit, and Miss Miles opened the door.

'You're out of breath,' she said in too-great innocence. 'Have you been hurrying?'

We walked into the library. 'Of course I've been hurrying,' I puffed. 'How did you get on?'

'Reasonably enough in a strange sort of way.'

I crossed to the desk and splashed out a whisky and then some water. '*How* strange?' I asked and crossed to the other armchair.

'I was even offered a job.'

'As what?'

'A secretary, of course. What do you think?'

'Research student,' I offered, and she said 'Oh!' in a quiet deflated voice. She had expected something bitter, something harsh, but I was curious and asked how the rest of the interview went.

'I don't really know,' she said. 'He's strange, isn't he? Just like a great big witch doctor.'

'Skip the descriptive passages,' I said. 'Witch doctors talk. What did he say?'

She laughed. 'He didn't say much at all. In fact I've been sitting here trying to sort out what he did say.'

'All right. How did you start?'

'He started,' she said simply. 'He asked me why I was writing the book. I said because I'd known and admired

George—and I thought the book would interest a great number of people. He agreed. Then he asked how far I'd got and I said I'd just started. Then he asked a lot of other questions, some of them a bit technical. Had I written any other books? How many words? Was I including any photographs? Who was going to publish it? He just snapped out the questions and somehow I answered them. I suppose he was pumping me. I think I gave him sensible answers. I'm glad we'd had that letter from George's publisher. That seemed to impress him. Then he asked if I'd met Mrs Waterman. I said yes. Then suddenly he said had I met you?'

'And?'

'I'm afraid I lost my nerve then. I said no, why, who were you?'

'And?'

'Nothing. Nothing at all. He waved his hand and walked across to one of those great windows in his room. Then he came back and said, "One of my men. He wrote a piece about Waterman. I gather he got his material from Mrs Waterman. Did Mrs Waterman mention that she'd seen him?" I said no, she hadn't. He said, "Strange, isn't it? You'd think a mother would have mentioned any other people who'd been after details about her son, wouldn't you?" I said yes, it did seem strange. Was that right?'

'All right so far,' I said. 'When did *your* interviewing start?'

'I don't think it did,' she said, almost ruefully. 'I managed to ask him how he'd met George in Ireland. Straight out. I had to. It was the only way. We were getting nowhere as far as I was concerned. Or you.'

'Did he say?'

'Yes,' she said, opening out a shorthand notebook and

looking at a page. 'He said he was in Ireland as a journalist in 1919 and 1920, representing a group of North of England papers. He said he'd heard vague rumours in Cork that an Englishman was commanding a small group of irregulars in the areas around the city. It sounded an interesting story and he went off to try to contact the man.'

'Did he say "Englishman"?'

She looked at the page and read back the outline.

'Englishman,' she said. 'Why?'

'I only wondered,' I said. 'Go on.'

She began again: 'He said he found Waterman on the run and commanding about two or three dozen rebels. He lived with them for about a week and then moved on to cover another story in Limerick. Apparently a lot of reprisals were being carried out by British troops, reprisals for Sinn Fein attacks upon police and barracks. He said it was a vicious, dirty war.'

'Did he say anything more about Waterman?'

'Not much. He said George gave the impression of being a very competent field officer. He was living in appalling conditions in a barn in the Fermoy area, but shifting his headquarters from night to night. He trusted nobody apparently, least of all his Irish comrades. Strange, isn't it? I asked the Baron why he thought George did it and he said . . .' She turned over a page and began to read from her shorthand: 'Here it is: "I often asked myself the same thing. He didn't love the Irish. In some ways he hated them. He hated their romanticism, their sloth and their easy-going ways. He hated the British too. Perhaps not the British as people, but Britain as a symbol. And most of all I think he hated himself. Perhaps I'm wrong about that, but he certainly hated all things that just lived without plan, direction, order, whatever name you happen to give it. He had a cold-blooded passion for order. He thought he knew how other people ought to live and given half a chance he was determined to make them live that way. He thought he had the secret. That sort of thing doesn't go down well in England, less still in Ireland. I got the impression during the week I lived in his H.Q. that even his Irish rabble loathed him. Yet he was obviously a first-rate leader. In Russia he would have been a born commissar. He should have been a German or a Russian. Either place was his spiritual home if spiritual is the word. I don't think it is." '

I looked at Miss Miles as she turned over the page of her notebook. It was like listening to a report on a long-dead figure in a history book, some brash rebel like Wat Tyler, not one man's obituary of another man, read by the dead man's mistress. The situation doubtless had a sardonic side, but I was too interested in the words she was transcribing to pay much attention to that, and all I said was, 'Go on,' and maybe I said the words impatiently, for she looked up suddenly from the book. 'There wasn't much else,' she said. 'I asked him if he'd ever seen George again. He said, "No, why?" and I said I just wondered. "Only at one or two meetings in London," he said.'

'What sort of meetings? Did he say?'

She shook her head.

'What's your general view of him?' I asked.

Miss Miles thought for a long moment before she replied. 'I've never met anyone so utterly sure of himself.'

'Nobody's ever utterly sure of himself,' I said. 'Not even Napoleon or Northcliffe. Anyway, go on. I'm sorry.'

She went on. 'He'd never question any single thing he

says or does. He's just like someone who's found out every man's price—and every woman's. After a while you get used to it. You don't expect to hear truth: you just expect to hear what anything's worth.'

'Maybe you get that way when you're worth ten million!' I said.

'No man has the right to get that way. Or have ten millions,' she said, almost passionately.

'Let's keep to things as they are,' I said, and anyway, another question was in my mind and I said, 'I wonder whether Waterman used his own name in Ireland.'

'Why shouldn't he?'

'I only wondered. Some revolutionaries like changing their names. Lenin changed his. Stalin changed his. Maybe Pollitt was born Pecksniff. Who knows? Maybe Waterman got bitten the same way, too!'

'Nonsense. He would have told me.'

'You didn't know him at the time. You weren't even born. And he didn't tell you everything.'

She flung her head back, annoyed. 'Again that joke!' she said and we were quiet for a moment. And tense. Then she let it pass. 'I see what you're after. Just because the Baron said "Englishman" and not "Waterman." It's the sort of expression anyone might use.'

'Not the Baron,' I said. 'He uses words and he knows their meaning. Even in a penny paper. You say he used the word "Englishman." Later on he used the name "Waterman." Then there's the word "meetings." Maybe he meant meetings in a solicitor's office, maybe meetings at Conway Hall. Maybe he likes leaving things that way, just like that, absolutely correct. Maybe he enjoys the joke.'

She was silent.

'What about the real question I wanted answering?' I

said unkindly. 'How did the Baron get his big flat foot in the old-fashioned Waterman property?'

'I didn't even ask him,' she answered shortly. It seemed my humour was beginning to rankle.

We were both silent. I was still thinking of the word 'Englishman.' Miss Miles followed my thoughts.

'If you think there was anything in his use of the word "Englishman" how can we find out?' she asked penitently, just as if she wanted to show how good she was.

'You can phone,' I said casually.

'Phone! And ask him that?'

Her horror was a spur. 'Why not? It's only seven o'clock,' I said. 'He'll probably be there. If you get past the butler and the secretary and any of the footmen sloping around you can pop the question. Try it! He's three miles away. He can't bite.'

She crossed to the desk and asked the house exchange to get the number and she sat there at the table, waiting, looking down upon the great river. I sat watching her. She gave her name and asked for the Baron, and after the butler and the secretary she was through to the Baron, and I listened to the words: 'I do hope this isn't inconvenient. I came to see you this afternoon. I'm afraid there was one question I forgot to ask.'

Even from the armchair I could hear the words 'And what was that, Miss Miles?' within the earphone.

'Could you tell me whether George Waterman used his own name in Ireland?'

I had moved over to the desk and heard his voice, indistinct but understandable enough in the overflow of sound from the instrument, but there was silence for a couple of seconds. Then the voice growled out the words, 'He did not, as a matter of fact, Miss Miles. Why do you ask?'

She looked across at me with her hand over the mouth-piece. I mouthed, 'You just wondered,' but the mouthings were incomprehensible to her and she said, 'It occurred to me afterwards, arising out of what you said more than anything else. I was reading my notes. You said you had heard of an Englishman. You didn't use the name "Waterman" in that particular context.'

By this time I was sharing the earpiece.

'Your awareness does you credit, Miss Miles,' he said. 'I chose the word deliberately. Is the fact important for your book?'

'It could be,' Miss Miles answered as I scribbled *Ask the name* on a page of her shorthand notebook, and she was going on: 'It was an unusual episode in his life and I want to document it as fully and accurately as possible. I'm sure you see that. Do you remember the name by any chance?'

'I'm afraid not,' the Baron said shortly. There would be no more compliments or data that evening. That was plain even as he said, 'Is there anything else you wished to know?'

'Nothing else,' she said, thanking him, and he said he was glad to have been of help, but he didn't sound all that glad. The phone clicked back in the cradle and the room was quiet again.

'He didn't like that question,' Miss Miles said. She was trembling.

'Take it easy,' I said. 'Maybe you got him out of a hot bath.'

'It wasn't just that. He didn't like it. One can always tell.'

'What was the job he offered you?' I asked to change the subject and the atmosphere.

'Nothing really. He said if I needed a job now that George had died and while I was writing the book, he would find me one on one of his newspapers.'

'Which one?'

'He didn't say.'

'What did you say?'

'I said I'd like to bear it in mind.'

'Why?'

'I didn't know what your next set of instructions would be,' she replied demurely, too demurely, and I said, 'Thank you, Ruth. Let's go out and eat.'

And I noted well that I'd used the name *Ruth* at last as sometime I had to use it.

And later, after a time of talking, we went out and walked slowly up Whitehall, across Trafalgar Square into Piccadilly and along to the Coq d'Or. We were quiet, and it was another of our evenings beginning, but that evening was different. The story had moved on a bit. Not only the Baron's story and Wensley's story but maybe the story of Miss Ruth Miles and myself. There was a strangeness in the air. And even tenderness.

Well, any story has its asides, and I suppose this is as good a moment as any other for this particular aside. For the rest of that month, April, until I went to Ireland, I saw a lot of Ruth. Lunches and dinners and other odd occasions. Nine days, I see, turning through the diary which has no fulsome entries, but merely the faraway dates and times and names. Well, a brand-new world can get built up in less than nine days, even the world of many millions we think we live in, so why not a world between two people? And, looking back from here, I can see how in a tenuous and disbelieving way a brand-new world could have got built up between the two of us. Maybe it did, but I didn't know it then, and I may delude myself about it even now, and anyway it was a world I didn't want, or thought I didn't.

They were evenings of escape, I thought at the time, but perhaps I was wrong in that, too, and those evenings were reality or as near as we ever get to reality in this world. Perhaps the world of the Baron and Court House was the escape, the escape from reality, but I didn't ask the question, or at least I didn't take it very far. There is no answer, anyway.

So we dined and wined and walked and talked, and when I stopped to think, as occasionally I did, I thought upon the threadbare lines, *Well, it won't last. There's nothing here I really want. An old man's mistress. No thanks. Too much money and what happens next? The usual. And then? The usual again. It's fun but let's leave it at that.* And way back, back in the dark recesses of the mind, I suppose I knew I'd have to go to Ireland within a week or so and there could be a break then. No real trouble. Just a convenient break in time and space to give an alibi.

But now, looking back across the months, those nine days and nights seem a time of more than dining and wining and, in the one week-end, lunching too. There was the strangeness. And the tenderness sometimes.

38

BUT that, as I said, is an aside, and that night, Wednesday night, it had only just started. I could think of other things. I thought, for instance, of the ads in the Irish Press which were now as worthless as German marks. I had asked anybody who had known a Waterman to step forward, but apparently George Weston

Waterman had been known by any other name but his very own, and it seemed unlikely I should be getting any worth-while replies out of the depths of Eire.

I didn't, as it turned out. Not one. But that is part of the process of research, as any student knows. The expected had happened again, that was all.

I thought again of the years of research, sitting in libraries, walking along shelves, turning over a hundred thousand pages of a thousand books, the books in the Bodleian, the shelves in the B.M., the archives in the Record Office, and almost always the day's work done and no way farther on.

And I thought again of the Admiral who had briefly been my boss in the recent war and how he'd said again and again: 'Intelligence is only intelligence in so far as it's intelligent to dig and dig and go on digging. Intelligence isn't a matter of hunches.'

So I added up the facts I'd taken two long months to find, and as I wrote them down I could see they were as much like facts as skunk is like mink, but there they were for my masochistic pleasure. *But why suffer alone?* I thought, and the next evening, Thursday, I put them to Wensley, after a fighting session over *Objects and Subjects.*

'These are the alleged facts concerning the beautiful friendship between the Baron and Waterman,' I said, and I gave him the quarto sheet:

(1) The Baron met Waterman in Ireland.

(2) The initial meeting was at the Baron's instigation and request.

(3) The meetings were few and all took place within a week.

(4) The Baron did not like Waterman, although he respected him for his leadership and courage.

(5) After they both returned to England the Baron met Waterman again, 'once or twice.'

In addition to these statements concerning the acquaintanceship between the two men the following facts are known:

(a) In 1921, within a year of meeting Waterman, the Baron acquired a considerable interest in a Waterman family property, the Metropolitan Printing and Publishing Company Ltd, an established and well-organised periodical publishing- and printing-house.

(b) This interest came via Mrs Waterman via G. W. Waterman in a transfer of shares.

(c) By 1924 the Baron controlled this company.

(d) The Metropolitan Printing and Publishing Company Ltd was the basis for the Baron's expansion into the present National Newspapers Ltd.

Wensley read through the typed sheet. 'We know all this,' he said.

'Read through it again and see how much of it you knew two months ago.'

He scanned the sheet again. 'That's true,' he said. 'Maybe there's something in research after all.'

'Not enough,' I said. 'Even this recapitulation doesn't add up to much.'

'Can't you strike out on any new lines? What about those Irish personal ads?'

'Nothing doing,' I said. 'Waterman worked over there under another name.'

'Why didn't you put that in your notes?'

'I don't know the name.'

'How did you find it out, anyway?'

'Miss Miles got it from the Baron.'

'Did she now? How did she come to do that? What else did she find out?'

'He answered the letter in the *T.L.S.*'

Wensley sat back. He waved his tired arms towards the armchair. 'Sit down and tell me more. And why the bloody hell didn't you put that in the notes?'

So I sat down and told him more, and he listened to the end.

Then he said, 'It's interesting, but it doesn't take us much nearer, does it?' He went on, musing aloud, 'How many people would know the name he used in Ireland? The Baron probably knows, but damn few others. Maybe nobody. In that sort of ragged-arse warfare, nobody keeps any records. And it was all thirty years ago, and that's a lot of years, even by Irish standards.'

'I wonder if Gibbings knew. He wrote the obituary in *The Times*,' I said. 'I never got after him.'

'It didn't have anything that wasn't available to us,' Wensley said. He swung the revolving chair in a half-turn away from his desk and he looked like a blown-out prelate from the good old monastic days, pushing himself away from a banqueting table, loaded to the eyeballs with the good things of the world, and he pulled open the shallow drawer of the desk and took out a folder and from the folder a cutting. He read it through and passed it across to me: it was the obituary from *The Times*. I read it through again: there was no mention of Waterman's adventures in Ireland.

'We seem to have drawn a notable blank,' Wensley said. 'Yet the information on that sheet you've typed suggests there's something more, doesn't it?'

'It could,' I said.

'It does,' he said. 'And if we get enough bits they'll fit together all right. You've only got to find the odd pieces.'

'Or the glue,' I said.

'You're the glue,' he said genially. 'The Baron's got the other odd pieces. That's all.'

'Do I carry on?' I asked.

'Of course you carry on,' he said. 'I didn't reckon this job would be over in a month or two. I said I wanted this chapter finished before the Baron dies, that's all. He's fit enough, at the moment, but one of these nights some nineteen-year-old popsy will be a bit too lively for him and he'll burst like an old red paper bag.'

'Paper bags are brown,' I corrected.

'Red in this case,' he repeated gently. 'The same way I'll be an old purple bag by the time I'm his age. Anyway, there it is. You've got plenty of time. There'll only be seven chapters in the book and most of the others are done.'

'Who wrote the others?'

'Just a hack,' he said.

'Another hack?' I asked.

He laughed briefly. 'Almost funny but not quite. Most of the other stuff he wrote himself. Some of it comes from his speeches, some from his writings and the rest is in the record. Some items I've asked him to add himself. News bulletins and Press handouts. Here and abroad. You know the stuff. His early life: his life as a newspaper man: his other interests: who he married: where they lived: when she died: the usual stuff. Here and there an odd fact creeps in. And some I've done myself. I've made enquiries. In and around Manchester. In and around Fleet Street. And I've kept a pretty close tab on most of what he's said these last twenty years. And I've come to know him pretty well these last ten or twelve. And odd facts drop out when a man's in his cups. You ought to read it sometime.'

'When?'

'When it's finished.'

'And he never mentioned Waterman?' I said again.

'Only in those two wartime chits and the afternoon you went up to the park.'

'Was it the chits or the obit first made you curious?'

'All three,' Wensley said laconically. 'They were too widely spaced in time to be an odd moment's whim. Waterman was something serious in the Baron's life if he popped up at intervals over eight or nine years. That's the way I see it. D'you see it different?'

'Not so far,' I said.

39

THE next afternoon I rang Mountain at *The Times* again and said I was still interested in the Waterman obituary and in Gibbings who had written it. Did he remember? Vaguely, he said, but wasn't Waterman dead enough?

'That was my great hope,' I said, 'but can I see Gibbings? I'd take about five minutes of his time.'

Mountain said he would ring back, and half an hour later he rang to say Gibbings would be delighted to see me. 'Oddly enough he reads your column,' he added.

'Why so odd?' I asked.

'No reflection,' he said, 'but he's no chicken, and I always think your column's addressed to the younger generation. Perhaps I'm not as well-informed about Fleet Street goings-on as I ought to be.'

I thanked him and rang off with his academic laughter

croaking in my ears. I finished another paragraph for the younger generation and then went out and walked slowly down Fleet Street, through Blackfriars Lane and into Queen Victoria Street.

I went up the steps at the commissionaire's office, which looks more like a horse-box than the password office of a number-one newspaper, and asked for Mr Gibbings. The commissionaire rang for a messenger and I followed the boy through a corridor, up a flight of stairs, into a waiting-room like a small mausoleum. Ten minutes later Gibbings came in, and he was a fitting human figure for the room. I guessed his age at sixty-two or -three, but life in the purlieus of Printing House Square had given him that shrivelled look that comes to dons and clerics, and he might have been seventy, but I kept to my first rough estimate. He was tall and gawky, with a thin yellow face, dry grey hair, bushy black eyebrows, thin pink lips, a small pointed chin and grey old eyes. He poked his head forward like a born Paul Pry, put out his hand and said, 'Good afternoon. Won't you sit down? Mountain was tolerably hazy about your errand. I gathered it was something about Waterman and the notice I did.'

'Only one or two questions, if you don't mind,' I said. 'First, I wondered whether there was any particular reason why you never mentioned Waterman's sojourn in Ireland in your notice?'

He poked his head forward across the small table. 'I didn't, did I? Well, I'd heard rumours that he'd been there. I overwrote in any case, y'know. He wasn't really worth the space he got. We cut him to ribbons in the second edition. Somebody else died, I seem to remember. It didn't seem a very important phase. Didn't I mention it at all?'

I shook my head.

'Odd!' he said. 'But there's very little known about that side of his life, y'know.'

'Did you know him?'

'I was up at Oxford with him. I was at the House. He was at Balliol. Met him in the Union. Came up against him in one or two debates, y'know. He was older than most of us, but he was already beginning to get a bit of a firebrand. God knows why. He was as rich as Solomon. At least so rumour had it, but rumour usually quadruples or quarters anybody's income.'

'Did you see much of him afterwards?'

'Scarcely anything. I heard about him from time to time.'

'What persuaded you to do the obituary?'

'Money and books,' he said, jerking out the words as he jerked forward his head again. 'I've built up my modest library with the extraneous work I've done here. Obituaries. Reviews for the Lit Sup. Oddments. You could say money and books and one or two coincidences persuaded me to do that particular notice.'

'May I ask what the coincidences were?'

'Not even that really,' he said. 'Just the usual run of experience and one's contemporaries. I was a tutor for ten years after leaving Oxford. Trinity, Dublin. There's nothing Irish about me, but I got the job. I was there until the war. The first war,' he added, smiling. 'I was in the Irish Rifles. In 1918 I went back to Ireland. I stayed until the Troubles, but teaching bored me. Probably the war brought it to a head. I turned it in. The whole country was mad, too, y'know. I'd had enough. I came here then. Yes, actually here!' He laughed. 'But just before I left Ireland I heard a rumour that Waterman was operating with the rebels. Only a rumour, but I was interested enough to make one or two enquiries.' I didn't interrupt and Gibbings went on, poking his head across the table again, his grey eyes staring intently from under his bushy eyebrows. 'I had to go down to Cork to see a wartime friend of mine, Tom Lawrie. He'd been in the Irish Rifles with me. Then he'd become a captain in the Black and Tans. Lots of 'em did, y'know. He told me he was after an Englishman. They never got him.' He paused. Then, relishing the drama of the climax to his tale, he jerked out: 'They got poor Lawrie, though. Through the head. Two months later.'

'Did you ever find out whether the Englishman *was* Waterman?'

'Y'know, I never did,' he said, 'but I always had a sneaking feeling it must have been. Not that I've given it much thought since.'

'You didn't think it worth mentioning in your obituary notice?'

'Much too vague,' he said. 'Nothing much more than hearsay however you look at it. Probably persuaded myself about it.'

'How did your friend Lawrie refer to Waterman—if it was Waterman?'

Gibbings laughed. 'That bloody English renegade is all I remember,' he said. 'Lawrie didn't mince matters!'

'Nothing else?'

'Not that I remember.' He tilted back in his chair. His pale eyes gleamed with the memories of his younger man-hood. Then he came forward again. 'No, I'm afraid not. Not a thing.'

'Did you come across Waterman later?'

'Several times.'

'I'm sorry to be so persistent,' I said, 'but did you ever ask him whether he was the man?'

'I did, as a matter of fact. I once met him at a P.E.N. Congress in Vienna. Must have been about nineteen-thirty-two or -three. Galsworthy was king-pin that year. King-pen I suppose you'd call him. Excuse me.' He laughed at his pun. 'I got talking to Waterman. He was a bit of an oyster, y'know, till he got on a platform. I had to make all the running. I mentioned my Irish interlude and asked him whether he'd been the Englishman my friend Lawrie had been after. More or less told me to mind my own business. I didn't go on. I used to get odd bits of news of him in the office here. I deal with home news. I noticed one or two odd paragraphs when he was falling foul of officialdom. One does, y'know . . .'

There were more reminiscences, but none of use to me, and after a while I bade him farewell and went slowly back the way I had come, and it was another blank I had drawn to take along with me, and even the wayward sun of the April afternoon seemed dulled as I looked across to the old iron bridge that cuts the vista to St Paul's.

I walked slowly up Fleet Street, past the patient queues waiting for the buses to their far-flung dormitories, and turned into the courtway, and there were the fountains playing delicately against the red-brick background of the three Georgian houses the Baron let stay when he built his paper palace. Then I turned left and in through the great glass doors and across to the lifts.

40

THE following Monday I had a note from Gibbings: *Our conversation of Friday afternoon prompted me to look up some correspondence I had with Tom Lawrie at that time,* he wrote. *I am afraid I found little enough to be of help to you in the two or three letters I seem to have kept, mainly out of sentiment. There is just one reference to 'this bloody English renegade,' and that is all. The letter is dated 27 January 1920. There is no address but the letter seems to have been written from Fermoy which is, I seem to remember, somewhere near Cork. Neither is there any reference to any name for the renegade. It is strange how I had the belief that it was Waterman. I seem to remember that one or two of my contemporaries had the same idea. We shall probably never know. My personal belief, quite without evidence, it now appears, was that he was on the Irish side. He never denied it when I taxed him. On the other hand he never admitted it. Then again, it would still remain to be proved that he was this particular renegade. It all seems very difficult. There were others, as you probably know. Erskine Childers, the author of 'The Riddle of the Sands,' was one . . .*

The rest of the letter was a further apology and a polite farewell.

There were four more letters from Ireland in the post along with Gibbings' note and the usual puffs and proposals for *Objects and Subjects* from a collection of Press agents and P.R.O.s.

Three of the Irish letters were from hunt secretaries. All suggested I should get in touch with them after my arrival in Ireland; two gave me names of members who would be 'delighted' (in one letter) and 'prepared' (in the other) to help me in my quest for knowledge of the Irish hunting scene of yesteryear. I noted the names: one, a Commander Winter, R.N. (Rtd), and the other, a Miss Elizabeth Darbyshire. The fourth letter was from the secretary of an Anglo-Irish literary society who promised to help, but thought the most practical way for me to get the information I wanted would be for me to lecture to her Society on *Aspects of the Contemporary English Novel*, and could she book me for the evening of Saturday, the 30th inst or the 7th prox?

'The biter seems to have been bitten,' Miss Arnold said in pleasure.

'Have I ever shown myself a biter to you, Miss Arnold?' I asked. 'Write and say "No." '

The next morning there were more letters from Ireland, two from secretaries of Anglo-Irish societies (one archæological, the other historical), a third from the secretary of a Cork Anglo-Irish Social Club, another from a club in Waterford. All offered to help. I also had another invitation to lecture from a Poetry Society I hadn't written to.

'A busy busman's holiday seems to be brewing up,' Miss Arnold said, still game.

'Fame has its penalties,' I said. 'And your images are mixed.'

41

'I THINK I'll do an Irish column for a fortnight,' I said to Wensley that evening.

'It'd been in the back of my mind,' he said. 'I thought in about a month's time, but if you'd like to do it now, then do it now. When will you go?'

'Next week?'

'Sure you're ready for it yet?'

'If you mean: am I any farther on with Waterman, the answer's no. But there's no more I can do here. It's just a blank wall.'

'Ireland's another,' he said, and I smiled dutifully. He went on, 'Have you got anything to go on?'

'Nothing, apart from a place-name and the prospect of meeting a few of the oldest and crustiest Anglo-Irish inhabitants.'

'What's the place?'

'Fermoy.'

'Never heard of it. Well, have a decent holiday, then.'

'Not with six hundred words a day to file.'

'You knock 'em off in an hour.'

That sort of comment needed no reply, and anyway I had a more interesting thought: 'Presumably the Baron will read them.'

'Of course he'll read 'em. I'll let you know what he thinks.'

'He'll smell a rat.'

'He'll smell something. Maybe that's the best way. There's nothing much he can do about it. Only sit back and wait.'

'He's not the waiting type.'

'That's true,' Wensley said genially. 'We'll see. After all, we did an Irish column once or twice before the war. Before your time. I'll tell him it was my idea starting it again. It was always a very successful feature. Not with the Irish, of course, but they're a humourless bloody lot. The Baron was always keen on it. Maybe he'll be keen on it again.'

'I doubt it.'

'I doubt it, too,' Wensley said, 'but we'll see.'

I went back to my room. Miss Arnold had gone and, although the day's work was done and I had a social engagement of a sort, I sat at my desk and wondered.

I wondered what I would take to Ireland and it looked little enough. I had a dozen introductions and those might give me another two dozen, and it looked as if I should be able to meet all the oldest inhabitants I wanted to meet. And I had a place-name, Fermoy, and I had looked that up in an atlas and there it was, a small town twenty miles north-east of Cork, standing on the River Blackwater, and I made a picture of the town and as it turned out the picture wasn't so ill-drawn: a grey river, a grey bridge, green grass, the main hotel, a few pubs, and a wide cobbled square, the loungers and the rows of small neat houses. They were all there and not much else.

That was all I'd take, apart from books, a razor, a toothbrush, three shirts, a pair of pyjamas and a second pair of shoes.

I wondered again how I would begin. First, the hunt secretaries and their recommended contacts. Then the other secretaries. Then the old routine I had had before.

You land in a village or a town or a city and you want to know who knows most about the life that has been lived there in the past thirty years.

In a village it's easy. Someone will know and will tell you before the sun goes down on the day of your arrival.

In a town it's not so easy. You go to the Town Clerk, but he's sure to be new, and even if he's been there fifty years he's been dealing with the dead stock of the town— the sewage and the garbage, the new town baths or last year's audit—and he'll put you on to someone who will put you on to someone who will put you on to someone. So you go to the public library and you dig out the street directories of thirty years ago if they've been kept all that time, and you go down the streets and their residents and you compare them with the latest directory, and if that's not later than 1935 you're lucky, and you plough on and finally you have a street, a number and a name that match in both directories, and if you have a month with nothing to do, you dig out half a dozen names and you go round and knock on the door or stand by the counter and you pose a few questions, beginning, 'I understand you've been here over thirty years?' and the citizen puts his cupped hand to his ancient ear and says 'Eh?' and you know a month is not long enough by many weeks.

And in a city it's the same but worse.

So I knew I would be back to the time-tested, time-honoured, time-devouring way: asking and asking until I heard of someone who maybe knew someone who had once heard of someone, and it is certainly a method for the earnest and the patient research man. I'd had it all before and I knew.

But *where* and *who?*

Where was somewhere between Cork and Clonmel, running south to north, and anywhere between Bantry Bay and Waterford from west to east, and that was a simple matter of four or five thousand square miles, and that seemed quite an area in which to search for the memory of a man now dead, whose sometime name I did not even know.

And *who?* Well, I could start with the willing and unwilling secretaries, then the oldest inhabitants and anyone else who came along. I could dig far back in the Back Numbers Department of the *Cork Examiner* and dig out what I could from the record of the years. And that could be a week's work, too, but not for me. I hadn't the time or the beginnings of an inclination.

I tried to think up some other way of short-circuiting this ancient, worn routine, but streamlining hasn't yet hit the old-fashioned method of question and answer for the curious enquirer. *Well, it worked for Plato*, I told myself, *so it ought to be good enough for me.*

But it still looked a slogging prospect.

42

SO three days later, on the twenty-ninth of April, on Friday afternoon, around three-thirty, I took the tickets and my passport from Miss Arnold's reluctant grasp, listened to a few mothering words of admonition, told her to be ready at four every afternoon, kissed her plump cheek a fond farewell, took up my canvas bag and went. Down two floors to Wensley's room.

He was slumped in the big settee, smoking one of his Ankara specials. A haze hung in the room like a smog over a power-house, but he was staring through it at the opposite wall, and there, as I knew, was a framed colour collotype of a Royal Academician's portrait of the Baron as he'd looked in 1934. I looked, too, and Wensley said, 'A lot more jowl and a lot less hair, but it comes to us all. Maybe it's as well we don't all have these reminders of how we looked in our prime. Put your bag down.'

'He hasn't changed as much as some,' I said, trying to be fair.

'*I* wouldn't want to change, with all his millions and all his papers,' Wensley said. 'I wouldn't want the world to change either. But it does. Noticed?'

I crossed the room, took a cigarette from the jade box on the desk, and said I was going: any final instructions?

'Why final?' Wensley asked, and it was plain the afternoon before him was a leisurely prospect, and half an hour or so of hair-splitting might help to pass the time. 'While you work for me there'll always be instructions.'

I accepted the amendment and modified my phrase: 'Any local instructions, then?'

'None. Have a good time, that's all I ask. You won't finish the chapter, but do what you can. I suppose you'll be living on steaks and grills for the next ten days.'

I said I'd try.

'Any plans as far as the chapter's concerned?' he asked.

'A hazy idea. Nobody could call it a plan,' I said. 'I've had some more personal ads put in the *Cork Examiner*. I'm not hopeful, but anything twice.'

'Make the same request?'

'More general this time.'

'Not a chance,' he said.

'You're the one who believes in personal column ads,' I protested.

'Only in *The Times*!' he said. 'Anyway, I wish you luck. Try and avoid your usual entanglements.'

Again I said I'd try, and asked whether the Baron knew I was going.

'How could he?' Wensley said. 'The first mention of the trip will be tomorrow's paper. And live up to the build-up, too. It's terrific. Why d'you want to know, anyway?'

'I just wondered,' I said.

'Wondered what?'

'What he'll do when he does know.'

'What can he do? All he can do is sit in that bloody showplace in the park and tell himself you've gone for the benefit of his three million readers. Reader interest. That's what he'll call it. And that's all he can do. Just wait.'

'He's not the waiting type.'

'Well, *you* wait instead,' Wensley said, raising his bulk from the settee as if moved by a mighty and majestic impulse. 'What can he do, anyway? He can only sack you.'

'That's all,' I said.

Wensley waved his free left hand in a large disclaiming gesture. 'And what's that?' He looked at me. 'Scared?'

'I quite like working here. I've said it before. That's all.'

'While I work here, you'll probably work here, too,' he said. 'Anyway, you're a marketable commodity. You could walk straight off this rag right into the *Express*. You could take up where Driberg left off. You're too modest.'

'It never struck me that way.'

'Your paragraphs can be your alibi,' Wensley said. 'And see you keep 'em to food and the beauty of the women and the funny Irish sayings. Keep off that Georgian architecture stuff and not too much about the Abbey and the Gate.'

'*Some* people are interested in the Theatre.'

'*All* people are interested in food,' Wensley replied.
'*All* people are interested in women. You can mention
the Squares and the wrought-iron balconies and the
pretty fanlights. You can even write up Lord Longford
and his merry band of players. I'm no spoil-sport. But
keep a sense of proportion. Nobody ever does, once he
sets foot in that priest-ridden rat-hole. But try!' and he
ground out his stub in the ash-tray on his desk, and I
knew we were back again on one of his favoured hobby-
horses, but I had a plane to catch and, after a few minutes
more of this catch-as-catch-can conversation, I picked up
my bag again, said farewell, and went down by the lift,
through the glass doors, out into the courtway and into
Fleet Street.

Under the late spring sun, Fleet Street was its tawdry
worst: a crowded thoroughfare of crowded buildings,
crowded stragglers, crowded buses, and as I crossed by
Fetter Lane, a tall City cop was having trouble with a
brewer's dray with the reins in the hands of an aged
character who should by rights have been dozing out his
days in an olde-worlde almshouse, and behind him the
driver of an *Evening News* van was honking discreetly
to make known his wish to make his time to Euston or
King's Cross.

I got a taxi and sat back. For me the world I was
leaving was a world without enchantment, and as we
passed the Law Courts and then the shell of St Clement's
and took our place in the usual traffic jam at Wellington
Street, I wished I could have seen it all with the eyes
of Sir Philip Gibbs or one of those other rosy-eyed
romantics who found a magic in Fleet Street I never saw.
For me it would always be a street agaggle with scribes,
and above them, way above, bossing the scribes and the

shining machines, the executives with their advertising schedules, their circulation drives, their promotion stunts and their balance-sheet minds, the men who could make a modest hundred words mean a thousand shining shekels. But maybe it was merely a holiday I was needing.

By the time I reached the B.E.A. station in High Street, Kensington, my mood was changing. For one thing the place is all an air station needs to be: simple, lofty, clean; and, for another, Ruth was waiting inside. She was wearing a fawn woollen dress and her dark red hair was free of a hat, and I said gallantly enough, 'Tell me you're coming,' but she shook her head, saying, 'I thought I'd see you off. I know how you hate public farewells.'

'Or any other sort.'

We stood by the weighing machine and watched my canvas case make all of eight pounds thirteen ounces, and Ruth said, 'I really came to ask again whether your journey's really necessary?'

'Imperative,' I said.

'But why?'

'I've told you before. I have to earn a living and we're making my column an Irish feature for a week or so. That's all.'

'That's not the whole truth.'

'All right, it's not. I'm going to blow up the Dail.'

'And that's not funny.'

'All right, all right, so I'm not going to blow up the Dail, but I am going to write a column a day on the Irish and their captivating ways.'

She let the words stay and we walked the length and breadth of the station. Then we began to talk again but the words were stilted, a playing out of time, a lot of words we had used before, words ten million others have used before, and at the end, when the coach departure was called, we'd got no farther, made no plans, no new discoveries, and as the microphone spoke again I took her by the arms and kissed her. A brother-sister kiss it was meant to be, but by the time we stepped apart the brother-sister touch had gone for good and there we were. Different. Very different.

So we parted and the coach moved off, and sometime later I looked out and in a mild daze I could see we were moving through the lustreless streets of Shepherd's Bush.

One plane journey is much like another, I suppose, although the hop from Shannon to Gander doubtless has its strange and secret moments for each and every traveller, and two hours after taking off from Northolt, the Dakota was coming down out of a clear sky on to the landing-strip at Collinstown, an airport that looks like an airport, not like a corner of Siberia, and it was good to climb down from the plane and to be out and about in the cool soft air of County Dublin.

I had a room at the Gresham and there I stayed for more than a week and it all totted up to an excursion made for columnists, and every day the copy wrote itself, and every day, at four o'clock, I sat down and phoned and dictated to Miss Arnold, and the first day it was the journey and the food; the second day a visit to Trinity and the food; the third day it was Phœnix Park and the food; another day it was a visit to the Heraldic Museum, the only one in the world; another day it was a trip round the Guinness Brewery, the largest in the world, and another day it was the Dublin Zoo with its proclivity for breeding lions. And every day the food.

All the paragraphs and stories are in the Court House

files, and if you're the inquisitive sort, you can even read them there. You go down to Court House and ask for 'Back Numbers,' and the tall, one-armed commissionaire with the M.M. ribbon on his chest will take you to a small dark room on the second floor and leave you, and there are the big red volumes stacked along the shelves and there, if you're still the inquisitive sort, are the paragraphs and stories.

Yet maybe not quite all the stories.

43

THERE is no story there of why I didn't ring or write the flat in Whitehall Mansions, not even when I opened the telegram the next afternoon and read PLEASE PHONE TONIGHT PLEASE PLEASE RUTH.

Perhaps there is no story. At least no story to be re-told.

You look at the phone and you wait for it to ring and when it rings you don't answer. You let it ring until the last ring dies in a final fading tinkle and it doesn't ring again. You could pick up the phone and ask for the faraway number but you don't. Instead you get up from the armchair and cross to the table and you pour yourself another drink, splash in the soda, go back to the armchair and wait. And you think round the ravelled circle again and again for the thousandth time, maybe the millionth time.

Well, it all seems long ago now, in time and space, and I tell myself it would take ten bright psycho boys with ten pairs of shining tweezers to prise out the story and get it straight at this late stage, but it's a simpler tale than that. And I know it. And more old-fashioned.

And I tell myself the tale again as I told it to myself those many moons ago: *You kissed a young woman and you thought the kiss meant more than sleeping with any of a hundred women. Don't be such a bloody fool. Be your age. You were sixteen more than twenty years ago. Or is it the money you're after? Remember? The old man's money. Or have you really fallen for the old Red's red-headed piece? His popsy till a month ago. So you'll take over where he left off? And don't forget she wants marriage this time. She's been a mistress once too often. Is that what you're after too? Marriage? Again? On her money? Or his? Or yours?* And the questions and the images are there in smart array, and they go on and on with never the answer that you want, for there is no answer. You want your cake and you want to eat it too, but cake that simple isn't made. Not in this world.

And I looked at the phone but it didn't ring again. I could have asked for the faraway number but I never did. Instead I got up and stood myself another noggin, and another, and the kiss died with the soda in the glass, and maybe a world of dreams died in the silent phone.

44

ON Wednesday, after I'd dictated my copy to Miss Arnold, she said the editor wanted a word, the call was transferred, and Wensley's voice came through, somnolent as ever, and he said, 'Every meal a banquet, I suppose?'

'Exiles have to live,' I said.

'The Baron's interested in your trip,' he said. 'Wants to know how long you'll be away, and where else you're going?'

'I've booked to go south on Sunday.'

'Good. What's on tonight?'

'I'm off to the Gate.'

'You've covered the Gate once.'

'They've got a new show. First night.'

'What?'

'Molière's *Malade Imaginaire.*'

'Christ! You must be mad. How many of our readers understand French? Maybe a hundred thousand.'

'They may be interested in the actors.'

'Only if Longford's signed up Bob Hope.'

'Well, I'm going for my pleasure, not theirs.'

'Keep it that way then.'

And he hung up.

I lasted out a week and two days in Dublin town and the paragraphs went on writing themselves: a note about Lord Longford and his brave Gate players, notes about the Abbey, notes about the Liffey, notes about the Georgian architecture, notes about the pretty women and the gay and winsome colleens, notes about the Irish and all their pawky sayings, and every day, for full sadistic measure, I included the lunch-time menus for my readers' pleasure.

They were fulsome, solitary days, and up to a point I enjoyed the life an Irish columnist must lead, but maybe not on an Irish expense account. And beyond that point enjoyment faded when I thought of other things, but I had made my choice and I went on.

I went on through the days to the quiet Dublin Sabbath, as quiet as Sunday in Doncaster, and that morning

I paid my bill, took my canvas bag and walked down O'Connell Street towards the bridge. I found a taxi and told the driver the Station and I had plenty of time, but we drove along the quays as if he had a wager to win, but it was a clear, calm Irish morning and I let him run, and five minutes later the ticket collector was saying, 'The steel coach at the end for Cork, if you will,' and I walked to the far end of the platform, past the wooden coaches, and knew I was still in Ireland.

Travelling through the morning the knowledge stayed, for it was a greener land than England, the fields not so neat, but the land a lot less pocked by bricks and mortar. The restaurant car, too, with its ham and Irish salad, was away beyond the imaginative span of British Railways Executive.

I wrote my piece for my very own public: six hundred words on differences in railroad travelling in England and Ireland: a paragraph on the attentive Irish steward, a piece on two college girls from Montana giving Ireland three days out of a 17-day European itinerary, a piece on Irish ham, another on the shapeless Irish fields, another on station architecture and so the stint got done, and the paragraphs were all in favour of the Irish way of life and Wensley could brandish his 8B lead like a Saracen his scimitar. I was a full and genial man and Wensley was four hundred miles away.

After that I took out the map of Ireland the Tourist Bureau in O'Connell Street had given me, and the bunch of letters from the secretaries and the helpers and well-wishers, and the list of names and addresses they'd given me, and I began to pinpoint the place-names in the southern half of Ireland. At the end of an hour I had noted four names within a ten-mile radius of Cork, five more within twenty miles, and six others between twenty and forty.

Waterman was still going to keep me busy.

The train dragged into Cork just before four. My paragraphs were finished. All I needed was a wash, a phone and a bed. I went out into the station courtyard and asked a taximan the way to the hotel. 'Five minutes in my car. No more,' he said, so I got in the large Chrysler and went: we were there in under two.

There was half an hour's delay to London so I got my wash. Then I went down to the lounge and dozed until I was paged by a sleepy waitress and Miss Arnold was waiting on the line. I dictated my copy and she took it down, unhurried and unfussed, then she read it back and it was all there, as right as a comptometer with last week's wages.

'You seem to be having a riotous time,' she said.

'Mostly in trains. Is Wensley in?'

'Not yet. At least he hasn't phoned this room yet. Shall I put you through? Miss Munro's probably there,' but I said no. From the phone booth I could see two of the visitors drinking something cool and inviting and I went out and ordered myself a Pimm's, and when it came I took out the list I'd made in the train and examined the map and it seemed the nearest contact was a Miss Darbyshire of Mallow up in the north-west or a Commander Winter, R.N. (Rtd) of Crosshaven, down along the Bay.

Neither place looked very near-to-hand, but I had the evening before me, and the only alternative was Sunday evening in the giddy life of Cork. So I went across to the phone booth to see whether either of my prospects was in communication with the outside world. Miss Darbyshire wasn't, but the Commander was, and a minute later

I was introducing myself and asking myself out for the
evening and he seemed agreeable. Then I went back to
the lounge for another Pimm's.

Under the glass roof and the afternoon sun the room
was like a stoke-hole. But maybe that was the idea. I had
a third. Then I went up and slept.

45

I WOKE about seven and my mouth was like an old
sponge full of sand. I washed and went downstairs.
The place was still dead. I went out into the cool Irish
evening, and walked until I found a café, where I ordered
eggs and bacon. Afterwards I crossed to one of the taxi-
ranks lined with the high-powered American saloons
that stretch down any street of any size in Cork.

The first driver on the rank was a dark, round-faced,
unshaven character hunched over the wheel of a Buick.
He was wearing a cap and a cigarette drooped from his
lip. I said I'd like to go out to Crosshaven.

'Now that's a run I've been waiting for,' he said, and
he made to get out of his seat to let me in the back, but I
said I'd take the other front seat.

Well, it's a pleasant ten- or twelve-mile run for a
Sunday evening, going out by the road between the hills
at a steady forty-five, with the fleeting sight of Lough
Mahan, then out to Carrigaline and then along the
southern bank of the Owenboy River, with the sight of
the Harbour at the bends.

'You're from the other island?' my driver said, breaking
the silence, and I nodded.

'How do they take the state o' things in this island?' he said.

'They don't worry overmuch,' I said. 'Their own has its awkward moments.'

'I guess so,' he said grudgingly. 'Will ye be staying out at Crosshaven: or will ye be wanting me to wait a while?'

'Probably wait. I'm going to Commander Winter's house. River Lodge. Know it?'

'No, but that's no matter.'

I wondered what his age could be. About forty, I judged and thought him worth a shot. 'Were you around here in the Trouble?' I asked.

'Indeed I was,' he said.

'Actively?'

'Faith, I was a boy then,' he said. 'Fifteen or sixteen. I ran messages. No more than that.'

I knew I could make my questions as direct as I liked. It was a faint hope, but never say die. 'Ever run a message for an Englishman?' I asked.

He looked round. 'For an *Englishman*!' he echoed in disbelief. 'It's a joke you're after. I ran messages enough against 'em and round 'em. Never *for* 'em. I'm an Irishman, as my father was and my son is.'

'I heard there were Englishmen who fought with the Irish,' I said.

'It's a fine thing there were such men,' he said. 'I would I had met one to shake him by the hand.'

We both laughed. I lit a cigarette and put it in his mouth. We were quiet until we came to Crosshaven, a village above the river, overlooking Cobh Harbour. The villagers were taking their Sabbatarian ease, some sitting along the wall above the river, others standing talking. I asked an old man in a stiff serge suit where Commander Winter might live, and he told us in topographical detail.

We backed up a narrow steep lane, swung round and drove inland. River Lodge lay between the river and the sea, and by asking twice more we found it, a small pink two-storied brick and slate house at the end of a wooded drive, with a lawn set around the house as if three ancient gardeners had spent all their days to make the turf the greenest and closest in the island.

I got down from the car and went to the door under the prim white portico. A small man, small as a jockey, white-haired, red-faced, came from an inner room into the small hall. He was like a puppet made for *Punch*: a minute creature with blazing blue eyes, hooked nose, thin lips, sharp chin. I had seen the type before, as what sailor hasn't?

'Commander Winter?' I asked.

'Good evening to you,' he said, and bowed gravely. He was five-foot-two but he bowed like a seven-foot duke.

He brushed aside the letter of introduction I offered him. 'Jennings told me,' he said. 'I almost said "warned me," but that's not quite fair, is it? Come in.'

I mumbled the usual things about not disturbing him, but he brushed the words away. 'Go on now. My wife and I will be glad to hear an Englishman's voice. Come inside. What about your driver?'

'I've arranged for him to wait.'

'Then he may have a drink at the back.'

We went through the hall to a small room on the right. An old lady sat sewing in an armchair by a smoking wood fire. She put down her sewing as we went in and made as if to get up. She was obviously in pain and the Commander bade her keep her seat and introduced us, and in two minutes I was in another armchair, with a tumbler of Irish whiskey in one hand and a cigarette in the other.

Then my host went from the room and I looked around, and it was more like sitting in a corner of the Antique Dealers' Fair than a small living-room in the south of County Cork, for even my tyro's eye could see that most of the mahogany in the room had a longer history than the average family tree.

I began to talk to my hostess of the beauties of County Cork.

'I don't get around much now,' she said after I'd spoken of the journey down. 'I have what they call arthritis. It is a silly and inconvenient ailment.'

She seemed more regretful of the inconvenience than anything else; she was as cheerful as a minstrel, talking away until the Commander bustled back. 'Now fire off your questions,' he barked, genially enough. 'One at a time, mark you. I'm not one of those city slickers you're probably used to.'

So for ten minutes I fired my questions, and they were two, and the first was, 'When did you first come here, sir?' and the second was, 'How does hunting today compare with hunting thirty or forty years ago?'

Over the first reply he took three minutes, over the second nearer ten, and I sat and drank his Irish whiskey and listened to his monologue: how the great days of hunting had been long before the First World War, and he gave me his views, a few anecdotes, a few apologies for his verbosity and no information I wanted.

So I moved the conversation round to the Trouble, and that was easy enough for he had mentioned it himself. It had upset his hunting for a while, and, anyway, that subject is in Ireland what the weather is in England, and once again I sat back after I'd said the words, 'You were here in the Trouble then, sir?'

'Only at the end. I was in the Navy until after the end

of the first war. Then I was axed as so many of us were, but I was more fortunate than most of my term. My family has been in these parts for generations and this house was mine. So we came back here to farm. It is small but enough. It's difficult to imagine all that was nearly thirty years ago.'

I wondered how old he was. Near enough to seventy. He had retired as Commander, probably Acting Captain, and who would grumble at his present life? A bit far from El Vino's, I thought, but we are all creatures of habit, and, in time, even that need be but a memory, and then I asked whether he had ever heard of any Englishmen who had fought with the rebels?

He thought for a long moment, his brow creased in the effort. Then he said the words that had been there all the time, but it was plain he didn't like bringing the English into such a dastardly business. 'Unfortunately there were several throughout the country. Erskine Childers was the most notorious, of course. One of their leading gunmen was another. Chap called Burgess, I believe. Even got himself a Gaelic name of sorts. Bruga or something. Then there was Johnson. Odd as it sounds now, he became Secretary of the Irish Labour Party. He had been an English commercial traveller. Something like that. How it all comes back.'

'Did any Englishman fight for the rebels round here?' He shook his head.

'There was that awful man, that sergeant or whatever he was,' his wife said.

'So there was!' he said. 'Cobb. Of course!' He was forgetful of myself, back in the past again. 'Cobb was an ex-sergeant from the British army who'd taken an Irish wife. He hated the British, I believe, for some ill he reckoned they'd done him about a pension in the early part of the war. So he came to Ireland to his wife's people. Almost from the time of the Easter Week Rising he was a trouble-maker. That was in 1916, as you probably remember.'

'I was six at the time,' I said.

He laughed. 'Forgive me. It's so near to me. I am apt to forget it's not so to others, but it was rather an unnerving time for those who were left here.'

By 'those' I gathered he meant the Anglo-Irish.

'What happened to Cobb?' I asked.

'Disappeared. Rumour had it he was killed in a reprisal raid by the R.I.C. up in the Fermoy area.'

'And his wife?'

He looked at me closely as if suddenly getting a drift of my questioning.

'I was an historian before I became a newspaper man,' I said in explanation. 'Somebody asked me to do an odd bit of research while I was over here on this hunting feature. That's why I probably seem to be very interested in trying to trace any record of an Englishman.'

'I wish I could help you,' he said. 'I only know of Cobb and little enough of him, or his wife, but maybe I'm not the best man for the job. Perhaps there are others you could ask.'

'Such as?'

He opened his hands and let them drop. 'This country has changed so much. The people who might have helped—the English—they've mostly gone. Others have come, but they're not quite the same. Mostly taxdodgers.' He spoke sadly as if lamenting a departed golden era.

I made one last shot. 'You never heard of anyone named Waterman, or an Englishman who had been known as Waterman?'

He shook his head. 'Never,' he said. 'What kind of man was he?'

'A scholar, a communist, rather a ruthless sort of fellow. So it's said, anyway.'

'So many of them were that,' Mrs Winter said sadly. 'Both sides, I'm afraid.'

'Not that communist fellow who died a few weeks back?' the Commander said suddenly.

'The same.'

'Surely I read about him in *The Times*? One begins to read the obituaries rather carefully when you're my age,' he added, almost in apology. 'He fought with the rebels here? I don't remember reading anything about that.'

'You didn't,' I said. 'It was only a rumour.'

From that we drifted into more talk about Cork, the Catholics, Ireland, Costello, the Dail and England, especially England, and I sat listening, drinking his whiskey, looking out through the tall windows to the lawn and the meadow beyond. The small sturdy Kerry cattle were chewing the cud within the shelter of the white ring fence, and it was a rare and peaceful background, an odd one for Waterman to have brought me to.

And when I left, about half an hour later, the Commander walked with me, round to the courtyard at the back of the house, and there was the Buick with the driver asleep, hunched along his seat. I nudged him awake as I thanked my host for his kindness. Then I asked my question again: could he think of any other citizen of Cork or dweller in County Cork to whom I might apply for information?

'Nobody, I'm afraid,' he said, and he said the words as if in apology for some inadequacy as host.

'Will you let me know if you think of anyone?'

'Of course. I will walk with you to the gate. Your driver can follow.'

We turned from the open door of the car and walked back, past the house, down and along the narrow gravelled drive and behind us I heard the powerful car start and then move away from the courtyard, following us down along the uneven, curving track to the white iron gate at the drive's end. The car braked heavily behind us. The Commander opened the gate. I shook hands and walked to the car. Dusk was on the meadow, the parkland and the lawn. I got in the car and we moved through the gateway and out to the road. I looked back. The house was a hazy pink shape in the dusk. I remembered I'd left no telephone number, but let it slide. There was nothing there for me.

We began to pick up speed. I asked the driver whether he'd ever heard the name of Cobb around those parts. He thought before answering, 'There's no one of that name I know at all, but I could be asking my friends.'

It didn't matter, I said, and we fell to talking about the countryside we were speeding through.

At the hotel I asked his name. 'Daniel Ferriter,' he said, and I told him I would want him for journeyings on the following afternoon.

'That's a bargain then, sir,' he said. 'And will I be asking after this Cobb fellow?'

'Ask by all means,' I said, 'but you'll have no luck.'

He touched his cap and went with a smile.

46

I SPENT the next morning in the offices of the *Cork Examiner* in Patrick Street. For four long hours I was deep in back numbers of that cosy old journal, moving slowly through 1919 and 1920. Six hundred newspapers is quite a lot of newspapers and the work was slow and unrewarding. There was a good deal about England and the English but nothing I could see concerning any Englishman in Southern Ireland, and all I came away with were three more names to add to my list of names to track down, but what a hope of finding them, thirty years later! And I knew my morning had been a blank to add to all the other blanks. It was a bare black cribbage board I had won for myself.

After a meal I went back to the hotel and up to my room and took out the list of names, and listed the order I would go a-visiting. Then I computed the mileage for that afternoon and it was somewhere near a hundred. I wondered what the roads were like: rough here and there, I guessed, but those worries were Daniel Ferriter's and not for me.

Meanwhile I had my own modest worries and the foremost was my copy, and I thought I would make it a busman's holiday and write up my visit to the *Cork Examiner*, so I sat down and in half an hour I had done my piece, and it had its share of topography, journalism, Irish history and the venomous nature of that dolorous war.

Then I went down and phoned Miss Arnold, two hours earlier than usual, but the perfect secretary was there.

By then it was three o'clock, Ferriter had arrived and we went.

47

THERE'S no need to go through the list. In four days I travelled six hundred and seventy miles, saw twenty-four residents of Ireland and got nowhere.

There was Miss Elizabeth Darbyshire, a tough old whip of a woman, sixty or maybe sixty-five, grey-haired, jut-chinned, who lived in a large, grey, stone formal house on a hill, all alone if you call five servants and two grooms all alone, and she came out on the steps and towered over me, and, despite my letter of introduction from the local hunt secretary, it was clear she had no time for me or for my errand of enquiry. Sport had never been better, she said. No difference between now and thirty years ago. People made the sport and people hadn't changed. And it would stay that way, so long as farmers kept their fields free from wire and the Irish railways didn't get nearer her country than twenty miles off, and when I got around to 'The Trouble,' she said that had been politicians' business, not a woman's. She'd lived in this house all alone through the Terror. ('The Terror!' she echoed and laughed as if it had been a picnic and no Irish rebels had swung on a gallows and no Black and Tan had died in the night.) Nobody had bothered her, despite her English forebears, and she took me round the stables and there was her long life's labour of love: eight chestnut hunters and each a king, or so my unhorsy eyes persuaded me. Then she gave me coffee in the faded yellow morning-room above the lawns. I was a newspaper man, a Grub Street hack, to be humoured and got rid of, swiftly and certainly. And I was.

There was the sixty-year-old village shopkeeper, Mr MacCarthy Edwards, who was also a poet and a writer of local dialect stories and honorary secretary of the literary and debating society in Cork. Every Thursday, come winter storm and summer sun, he cycled fifteen miles to Cork and fifteen back, through the steep roads under the hills, to listen and to lecture. But even Mr Edwards, for whom the words *Fleet Street* were a peal of beautiful bells, could give no news of Waterman, and I left him behind the counter of his hardware store and went back to the Buick.

And in between were more than twenty others: all to be found, questioned and blarneyed along, even the citizen who lived on the ground floor of a Victorian villa in Blarney itself, a retired English Civil Servant who had come south in 1922 after the Treaty. Fear of Sinn Fein lived with him still, but his only daughter had married an Irish farmer between Blarney and Cork and he had settled there to be near her, he said. But the name of Waterman meant nothing to him.

They were all beautiful, beautiful blanks, including the afternoon we spent in and around Fermoy where I questioned another dozen: a constable, a publican, three farmers and half a dozen others who had known the Trouble but had never heard of Waterman. Or said they hadn't. Or of any other Englishman.

And soon right to the last, right to Mrs Vincent Meadows, widow of Captain Vincent Meadows, M.C., an English regular killed at Loos in 1916. She was living out the long hapless years of her pension in a three-room cottage overlooking Tramore Bay away in County Waterford. She had spent her brief honeymoon there in 1913, she said, and then went on to say how she loathed her neighbours, their Catholicism, their narrow slothful ways, and it was hatred dreadful to see, but maybe she liked her soul-eating life.

We sat over tea and buns and she talked of the Catholics and the Catholics and the Catholics, and twenty full minutes had gone before I began to pop my questions about the Trouble and Waterman, but it was no good: there had been no rebels for her, only Catholics, and that was the end.

I went out to the lane to the Buick and to Ferriter and said 'Cork.'

We were silent all the way.

By then it was Thursday and I went back and phoned my copy and then sat in the lounge, called for a drink and longed for Friday, for every Friday at six o'clock in the afternoon, by the grace of God and the City of Cork Steam Packet Company, the boat returns to Fishguard. *The Innisfallen Way* some romantic railway publicist has named the boat, and for me it was a way back to a gentler round than bumping my head on the roof of Ferriter's Buick as we roamed around the southern sector of the Emerald Isle.

But the mind doesn't stay that way. You are seasick and you vow no ship will ever carry you again, but one day ashore and you are ready for the Main again, and I sat in the hotel lounge and looked through my list again, even looking for a chance for further research, but by then I was beginning to know I'd spent a week on one of the wilder Irish goose chases: all my geese were as useless as those that lie on the poultryman's slab: from gallant Commander Winter, R.N. (Rtd) to shrivelled Mrs Meadows. But I ticked their names to see what I had missed or whether one had given me the prospect of a lead. But not one. Not even old Winter, who had said he'd phone if he remembered anyone, and he plainly hadn't, but I remembered I hadn't left him my address or my number, so he was scarcely to blame.

Well, the diligent research student checks and re-checks and I went out from the lounge and across to the phone booth and asked for his number. He came through with his brittle quarterdeck voice. I introduced myself again, but he cut me short with a kindly 'Of course,' and before I could say what I wanted he was saying if it wasn't too dull a prospect would I care to come out again, they didn't often see an Englishman straight from London? And remembering the pink house and maybe the Irish whiskey, I said yes.

'Splendid!' he said, his pukka manner back again. 'Come to dinner,' but I dodged that and we settled on coffee at eight-thirty. Then I rang Ferriter's garage and left a message for him to pick me up at eight.

I went back to the armchair in the lounge and moved to take out my list again for a final check, but it wasn't there. So, still hunting in my pockets, I went back to the phone booth, but a big red-necked citizen in a brown suit with his back towards the outer world filled most of the booth, so I waited, still searching, and of course the list was stuffed in my trouser pocket along with a handkerchief and a pencil. I smiled the way you always smile in those moments of milder lunacy, the self-deprecating yet self-indulgent smile, and I looked to see whether the fellow at the phone had noticed, but he still showed his back. Then he turned and I was smiling foolishly into the unsmiling blank brown eyes of a middle-aged man in a too-square-shouldered, dark brown suit. He stared through me as he would through a plate-glass window and turned again to the phone as if a call had just come through.

I stood there for a moment, for I had seen the face before. Sometime, somewhere.

He was a tall, thick-set, powerful-looking man, with thinning, brilliantined hair, a bulbous nose and a shining sweaty face, and eyes like muddy puddles.

You see a face and it will not let you go. It isn't important to remember, it doesn't mean a thing, but you think you won't do another worth-while thing until you've placed and labelled it. You don't even need a name for the face, you'll settle for where you saw it, and you go back in your mind, looking for the photograph of the face in the crowd, the face at the opposite table, the face in the phone box. And until you've placed the face in time and space, drink gets drunk more slowly and food gets left on the plate. So I went back to the chair in the lounge and waited for the brown-suited, shining, flaccid man to reappear, but he didn't. I hadn't seen him in the lounge before and I didn't again. Maybe he was just an old phone-booth addict, I told myself, and tried to leave it at that, but it was no good. The face was there, wedged in my mind for keeps, and I packed up and went up to wash.

Going down to dinner I stopped at the reception office, and on the counter, in front of the sliding window, was the Visitors' Book, open and free to see, and I went back slowly over the half-dozen names of the guests who'd registered during the past week, and somehow when I came to the name I wasn't surprised, for the line read:

Thomas Cobb. English. London, N.W.1.

He'd arrived on Monday, the second of May, the day after myself.

I went in to dinner and I said *coincidence*, always a word worth carrying around for such a circumstance, but somehow I knew the word didn't quite fit.

48

AFTER dinner, Ferriter drove me out to Crosshaven and it was another quiet evening of anecdote and whiskey in the small pink house, and we talked of Ireland, England and occasionally the world beyond, but not much.

The Winters lived in the past, but it had been a lively past, and I was glad to sit and listen. And although she was an invalid, Mrs Winter by no means languished in the bath-chair: she could talk of Miss Elizabeth Bowen as well as the Misses Somerville and Ross, and she was keen for any modest news of literary London that I might have. So we talked and drank and it was a warming last evening to have in County Cork, and not until some time after ten did the subject of Waterman come up again, and Winter introduced the subject.

I had to explain at length what manner of man Waterman had been, and it was plain that the idea of any Englishman who could be a traitor to his race fascinated him. Maybe that was why he'd remembered Childers, Burgess and the English commercial traveller, for he said, 'According to you, this fellow Waterman, an educated chap, actually fought against the English?'

I nodded. I suppose it is a tough image for an R.N. commander to face, but he did his best.

'Quite a number of people do from time to time,' I said. 'You mentioned some last time I was here and there was Joyce in the recent war. And a dozen others.'

'I know, I know,' Winter said, 'but Joyce was a ghastly misfit. He'd probably had his backside kicked by every

Tom, Dick and Harry and had to get his revenge. But what went on in Waterman's mind?'

'He was just a good Marxist and thought the world was more important than England. That's all,' I said.

'Maybe it is,' the Commander said, 'but that doesn't mean you've got to kill off all the English, does it?'

'Some people think it would make it easier,' I said. 'We've upset one or two other world-planning ideas. Philip of Spain came before Napoleon and Napoleon came before Hitler. Word gets around.'

He laughed shortly. 'You make it sound almost logical for Waterman! You don't hold any brief for him?'

'Maybe he was sincere. Maybe he was just in training for the bigger war ahead,' I said. 'Maybe he was just a crank. To my mind, any man who wants to run the minds of his fellow-men is a crank and ought to be smothered at the very first signs.'

'Don't forget Doctor Ford this time, Ralph,' Mrs Winter said quickly. She turned to me. 'I said to Ralph after you'd gone last time . . .'

Winter took over the explanation. 'Ford's a crank if you like. Mad as a hatter. Clever though. Doctor of Medicine and Doctor of Divinity. I sometimes used to think he was after having too much cleverness, but that was all long ago. Years since I've seen him. He must be nearly eighty.'

I probably looked puzzled, for Winter said, 'It was just that my wife thought there was a slight chance he'd be useful to you. I'd have phoned you but it all seemed rather far-fetched, and, like a fool, I didn't take your number.'

I tut-tutted vaguely and asked what Ford did.

'Nothing much, I gather. My wife thought he might be vaguely useful. During the Trouble he got about between both sides.'

'How?'

'Oh, lots of odd characters flitted between the lines. There weren't even any lines. And Ford was a jolly good doctor and doctors of any kind were damned scarce at that time. For years Ford's had a bee in his bonnet about the Irish and the English. Thinks he's got a God-given mission to bring the two races together under the Established Church. He was a Protestant minister in Cork at one time, by the way.'

'As well as a doctor?'

'He practised as a Reverend first.'

'What do the local Irish think about him?'

'They love him,' Mrs Winter said quietly.

'I'm sure they do,' Winter echoed. 'There's nothing they love so much as an honest-to-God crank. And he's a first-rate doctor. At least he was ten years ago. Half the time he worked for nothing. He's got absolutely everything to commend himself to the natives of this island.'

Maybe I looked unhopeful, for he said again, 'My wife thought maybe he might help in some way. Apparently he was trying to reconcile the Irish and the English all through the Trouble. Thought he had the answer. As I said, he was such a crank and such a good doctor he had the run of both sides. So I've heard, anyway. Martha thought he might have met your Waterman fellow.'

'He might,' I said. 'He seems worth trying, anyway,' and I asked where he lived.

'Somewhere down by the quays. Anybody knows,' Mrs Winter said.

'I wouldn't be so sure,' Winter put in. 'He must be eighty gone and we haven't seen him for over ten years. After all, we forgot him in all our talk last Sunday. Nobody's mentioned him for years. He may be dead.'

'That's true,' his wife admitted, almost sadly, I thought.

'You liked him?' I asked.

'I did, rather,' she said. 'I never knew him at all well, but he always seemed such a good man, almost a saint, and the Irish recognize that sort of thing. I suppose what Ralph says is right. People do change and he would be very old. We're all old out here.'

She talked for a while about Ford, and it was plain she didn't know much about him; her words were mainly hearsay. She hadn't seen him much herself. And how could the Reverend Ford, a fully-fledged crackpot saint, have got around in the Anglo-Irish society of County Cork?

I asked whether Ford was still connected with any church in Cork.

'I can't answer for now,' the Commander said, 'but he was many years ago. His father—Ford's father, that is—was an English horse-breeder. Started off with a good deal of land that had been in the family since Cromwellian times. Just like my own family. It shrank as that sort of land does. His son—the Ford we're talking about —trained as a doctor at Trinity. Got jilted, so it's said, the way it's always said. Turned to religion, evangelical Low Church and all that, and decided to take Holy Orders. So the story goes, anyway. I believe he studied at Oxford. Or Cambridge. I forget which. Then he came back here, God knows why.' The Commander was slipping into clipped sentences, once more a nautical man speaking of the oddities of landlubbers. 'Practised as a sort of combined priest and doctor. I suppose it isn't strange, really. The two jobs go together logically enough. He was in great demand amongst the poor. He was in the South African show as a medico and went off again in the first war. He's an odd bird, but he does a great deal of good down there. Did, anyway,' and he pointed towards the window, towards Cork. 'I haven't seen him, as I said, for years. I'm not much help, I'm afraid. But try him. As my wife says, he may be useful.'

'Maybe he's dead, as you said.'

'I shouldn't think so. We'd have heard. Might have moved away, of course, but I doubt it.'

From Ford we drifted into talk about religion, the way the Protestant authorities had been to blame for submitting to the Catholics, but it was a tale I'd heard before and I let it drift, then came the long tale of the Irish churches and the dominance of the Irish priesthood, but it was a subject I was weak on, and I would rather have returned to discussion of Miss Bowen's worth as a writer on which I had some further thoughts, but they were both away on their favourite plaint. I was beginning to envy Ferriter his two long hours of blissful sleep, so I waited for a pause, then rose to go and went, out into the night, and once more the Commander walked down to the gate with me as if he couldn't bear to let an English visitor go. Before I climbed into the car I asked the Commander whether he had any more data on the man Cobb he'd spoken about on my previous visit, but he hadn't. So I bade him good night, climbed into the car and, despite Ferriter's driving, slept all the way back to Cork.

At the hotel I asked Ferriter whether he'd ever heard of Doctor Ford, but he shook his head.

'Two Fords I know,' he said, 'but neither is a doctor.'

'Is one a clergyman?' I asked.

'Never one,' he said.

I laughed and told him I'd ring him in the morning if I wanted him, but I'd certainly want him at four o'clock for Penrose Quay.

49

FERRITER might not know the Reverend Ford, but others did, and after breakfast on the following morning, and after packing my canvas bag, I went down to the hall and began to ask. The waitresses didn't know of him, but the old doorkeeper did. 'But it is Doctor Ford he is called to his face, sir,' he added. 'An old man who sleeps on a sack of straw, and that all through the winter, I have been told. I have not met him, but faith, everybody in Cork knows of Doctor Ford.'

'Not everybody,' I said. 'My taxi-driver had never heard of him, neither had the girls in the dining-room.'

'They leave their brains by the roadside or to drown in the kitchen sink,' he said, and went on to tell me the way to Kerry Quay Hill where the doctor lived.

So I went down to the quays to find Kerry Quay Hill, past the hopeless old men who stand by the quayside walls and make big talk, past the toothless old crones with wide black shawls drawn tight over their shapeless dresses and their bare white legs jammed into busted shoes.

And wherever you look is a tall church spire and a snotty-nosed unkempt kid.

On Kerry Quay Hill I began to ask again, and at the first house a blowsy young black-haired slut told me it was in number thirty-seven I should find the doctor, so I climbed the hillside street, away from the quay, and looked along the doors of the narrow Victorian houses, and in the bright sun of the morning they were a row of small brick boxes, grim, grey, dingily unloved, copies of a hundred thousand others in Runcorn, Widnes and Camden Town.

There was nothing to put 37 apart from its neighbours, not even an old brass plate, but I let the knocker drop dully on the dark green door. A boy and a girl, about six or seven, prised open the next front door. Their faces were almost clean. I said 'Good morning' and they shot back into the shelter of the passage and quietly shut the door.

I knocked at the door again, perhaps out of nervousness, *but why nervousness?* I ask now and the answer doesn't come.

The door opened and a plump, plain, white-haired old thing stood there, and maybe she was a bit crotchety on her legs, for she held to the door as I asked whether the Reverend Ford was in.

'The doctor is out now, but you may come in,' she said in a lilting voice nowhere near as old as herself. 'You are early, but come in.'

'Early?' I queried.

'Patients don't come until midday. It's the rule, but come in,' and she held the door more widely open and I went in and stood waiting for her to lead the way, wherever the way should be.

She opened a door to my right and I walked in. The room was as sparely furnished as a monastery cell, apart from the books along the walls.

'The doctor will not be long and will you excuse me, I am cooking?' the old lady said.

'Of course, of course,' I muttered and then was alone.

The room was as musty as a warehouse. I crossed the bare boards and put back the window latch. The heavy net curtains began to stir after a long deep sleep. *Not a fresh air crank, at least,* I thought, *although rumour says he sleeps on straw.*

The house was a box and the room was a box, ten feet square, pierced four sides by window, fireplace and two doors. Where the walls weren't pierced were books to the ceiling. On the floor was a tattered old rug. In the middle of the room was a small round table. On the table were some copies of the *Cork Examiner*, *The Lancet* and a few old copies of *Punch*. Eight old ladder-backed chairs with tatty rush seats stood in front of the bookshelves and that was all. Maybe the room wasn't as stark as I'd first thought, no room with that many books ever is, but it wasn't the average doctor's ante-room.

I crossed to the door in the wall opposite the window and tried the handle, but the door was locked. Then I turned to the books and looked along the titles and it was plain that few of the doctor's patients would have found them worth borrowing: they were mainly medical volumes with a bias towards cardiography as far as I could judge, and in the lower shelves stood two long rows of bound volumes of *The Lancet* back to 1890. I crossed to a side wall and there I judged were five or six hundred theological volumes, mostly bound in black or dark blue cloth.

I tried to place the man such a room might fit, a room Gandhi might have furnished for his followers if he'd been interested in medicine and the historical Jesus. It was certainly no room for anyone fresh from the fleshpots of Fleet Street, but I was there and the visit might be worth a paragraph. So I took down *Doctrinal Aspects of the Gospels* and settled down to an interlude of theological browsing.

The world outside was quiet. Occasionally a car climbed the hill with a harsh homing of gears. Or a child shouted, but no more. I sat in the sunlight shafting through the curtains and tried to read the unaccustomed prose.

I suppose I'd been there about half an hour and had mastered a few modest *minutiæ* concerning the Gospel according to St Mark, when the front door opened and closed and steps shuffled along the passage. There was a murmur of voices, another door opened and shut, and the shuffle crossed the floor of the adjacent room.

I got up and put the book on the table and waited for the inner door to open, for I was keen to meet the Reverend Doctor Ford.

You picture your imminent visitor, guest or host, and your picture is always wrong, and what I'd pictured was a tall, bent, once-fine-figure-of-a-saint with iron-grey hair and the wan remains of a chiselled profile, or, as a comely alternative, a blue-eyed, bearded martyr. But what opened the door was a withered old man with a high, bald, waxen pate, hooded eyes, sunken cheeks and no chin at all, and as I got up from the slatted chair the hooded eyelids rose in enquiry and I was looking into pale brown eyes as ancient and serene as a year-old child's.

I said I was sorry to butt in, but the old man raised his thin hand calmly, glanced at the book on the table and said, 'Not at all. I am glad you were able to sit here for a while. What can I do for you?'

His voice was as tired and quiet as the ebb on a far shore, Irish with an overtone of England, a voice from a never-never land, and I introduced myself, and said Commander Winter had suggested I should come to see him.

By then we were in the back room and it was a still smaller room, maybe ten by eight, furnished with a plain deal desk and two more slatted chairs and more books in the spaces left by two doors and a small window, well above eye level.

The old man crossed to a chair behind the desk and gravely pointed to another. I started straightway on my tale. 'I went to Commander Winter concerning a feature about foxhunting for the paper I represent. From that subject we began to talk about the "Trouble." I told Commander Winter I was anxious to trace any information concerning an Englishman named Waterman who is believed to have fought with the rebels.'

'Who believes?' he asked quietly.

'His mother for one,' I said. 'Myself for another.'

He looked at me and through me. The hoods came down again and he began to talk as if he were reciting a speech he had memorized.

'I was here in the Trouble. Not all the time. I had been away in France and I came back here and it was a terrible world to come back to. All the people I had loved, Catholic and Protestant, Irish and English, were put against each other. I did what I could, but nobody would listen. I am an old man now and perhaps I talk too much about the things that mean much to me. Here, in Cork, things were as terrible as anywhere in Ireland. As you probably know, much of the city was burned in 1919 and 1920, and the fighting was bitter as a crazy house.'

I sat on listening. I had nothing to do but listen until the patients came, but the old man, with his eyes half-closed, was going on: 'On the way to Fermoy, twenty miles from here, you will still see burnt-out houses by the roadside. In Fermoy itself you can still see the black shell of the barracks above the town.' 'I've seen it,' I said, but my interruption made no difference. The doctor still went on: 'I did all I could to make them see that no good comes out of such things. There is nothing to put the

English and the Irish apart. Religion should not put them apart, but it does. Politics should not put them apart. Yet I saw Irishmen killed and Englishmen killed. And there was no need for such bitterness.'

'Were many killed in these parts?' I asked, trying to bring him down to facts.

'A great number,' he said.

'Are there many still alive who took part?'

'A number,' he said.

'Where do I find them?'

'You could go out to ask but you would never learn anything from them, not in a year of Sundays. You look and sound like an Englishman.'

'I know,' I said. 'I've met it already and, anyway, I can't spare the time.'

'Who is it that you want to meet?'

'Anybody who met the Englishman I spoke about—Waterman,' I said.

'I saw only the Englishmen who died at the hands of the rebels.'

I was puzzled and silent. He opened his eyes and gazed gently across the desk. 'I buried them,' he said in explanation.

'Were there many, then?'

'A hundred and fifty perhaps in the two years. Not many, judged by other wars, perhaps, but civil war is always worse. The ambushes and pitched battles were fought in fury. And afterwards, men, prisoners were shot in cold blood.'

He let his hands fall apart, sadly, almost supplicating. 'Why not let all these things rest? They were evil and they are gone. No good ever comes of resurrecting evil.'

'That is your view,' I said, 'and I respect it. Other people have other views.'

He placed his hands on the table, palms upwards, thin, twisted, knotted hands, and he let them lie there, and it was plain the interview was at an end. I had touched him on the raw somewhere and I knew I'd better go, so I got up from the chair and said I was sorry to have taken up his time.

He shuffled with me to the door and let me out, and as he let me out he rested his cramped old hand on my coat sleeve. 'Let all these things rest, my son,' he said. 'Shakespeare was right. The evil that men do lives after them. And those were evil things.'

The sun slanted on the street and the doctor's ancient skull, dust danced within the shafts like powdered brass, but by the time I'd got around to that pretty picture I was striding downhill, back to my well-worn position of full stop.

I walked down the grey hillside terrace, down to the quays, and I leaned against the river wall and watched cattle going on board a coastal steamer, but I cannot recall the colour of the cattle or how many: I was reviewing only the dead ends of my quest.

I was depressed and in depression you take it out of someone: there is always a scapegoat: it is never Number One, and I leaned against the parapet and gradually I began to blame poor old Doctor Ford for my unprofitable trip to his God-forsaken city, and I began to blame his blarney, his love for his fellows, his blameless ways and the way he'd dodged my questions, and in a mood nine parts fury and one part boredom, I suddenly turned and stumped uphill again, the way I'd come, and I let the heavy black knocker fall on the green door again.

The old woman came to the door, but this time I asked for the doctor and I went in and into the waiting-room, and in two minutes I was in the stark consulting-room again.

Ford was still sitting at the desk and he looked as if he had been sitting there for half a century, and would still be there for a century to come, and I said, 'I'm desperately sorry to burst in again like this, Doctor Ford, but I'm going back to England again and there were one or two questions I forgot to ask. I wondered whether I might bother you again.'

He moved his hand gently towards the other chair.

We were quiet for a long moment. I watched his brown eyes, now open and calmly regarding me. I said, 'When I asked you about Waterman you didn't give me an answer. Neither did you when I said his mother believed he'd fought in these parts. Nor when I asked whether it would be possible to meet anyone who might have known him. You sidestepped that by telling me of the Englishmen you buried. I've no right to badger you, but I can at least ask you why you dodged the questions?'

He stared at me for a long time, two seconds, four seconds, ten seconds. Does one ever know? Anyway, it was quite a time, and then he got up from his chair, slowly and stiffly like an old, old mechanical doll, and he turned to the shelves behind him and took down one of a row of tall ledgers.

'There are no secrets in my house,' he said, 'but sometimes there is silence when I think silence is wise. Come round here, my son.'

He sat down in his chair and began to turn over the pages of the book and it was a ledger all right, but a ledger-cum-diary and there was the life of the Reverend Ford in page after page of copperplate script across the blue-and-pink-ruled lines. And as he turned the pages I could see, pasted amongst the script, an occasional photograph and sometimes a drawing, and it was plain the drawings were of medical interest, outline drawings of torsos and limbs, like those you can see in this week's *Lancet* or *B.M.J.* He began to turn the pages more slowly and then he came to a double-spread, all photographs, and I looked down on two full-plate shots of a group of soldiers at rest, then I looked again and it was plain they were at a very long rest. They were dead.

'An ambush?' I asked.

'I wish it had been,' he said, and he sat back and I stepped back to my chair. 'Those men were captured and shot in cold blood after a so-called trial lasting ten minutes, no more.'

'It's the same in any war,' I said.

'Not always,' Ford said. 'Not quite. This was not an isolated occasion. You can count twelve bodies in those photographs. There were other, similar occasions. These men were Englishmen, tried and ordered to be shot by an Englishman.'

'Waterman?' I asked.

'I do not know. An Englishman, it is true, but I never heard him given any name, although I went amongst both sides.'

'How did you know he was an Englishman?'

'Many of us knew. He was always called the Englishman or Mann or the Duke.'

'How were you able to take these photographs?'

'I am a doctor,' he said simply. 'I was usually left alone with them. Few men are interested in dead enemies.'

'Why haven't I heard of this Englishman during my week here? I've asked thirty people a thousand questions.'

'Only the Irish would know. Men before your time. I imagine you have spoken to such as the Winters. The Anglo-Irish community.'

'I spoke to several Irish in Fermoy.'

'They would be silent about this thing now,' he said. 'Even if they knew. And most of them never knew.'

'Did any journalist ever come to these parts in the fighting?'

'Occasionally,' he said.

'Did you ever meet any?'

'Occasionally,' he said again, and I knew he wanted the questions to stop.

'Did anybody ever know you had taken these photographs?'

The brown eyes looked up from the photographs. 'Certain of the Irish, but it is strange you should ask that. An English journalist borrowed the negatives of another group after a similar barbarity. He said he would do what I had had in my own mind to do: write to the loved ones of these youths, for most of them were no more than that.'

'How would he have known their names?'

'We all knew their names,' he said simply, 'when we buried them. They carried identity discs around their wrists or their necks.'

'You never got the negatives back?'

He shook his head. He turned over the pages and stopped. 'Those are all the photographs,' he said. 'This was the last of the killings. A month later the Treaty was signed.'

We talked awhile, but my mind was too full of shapes that might or might not make a pattern and I forget now what we said. At the end I asked whether I might borrow the photographs, but I knew his answer before I made my request. 'No. No. All this is dead. I should not have brought it alive again today. Forget all these things, my son. They are a record of evil. I am foolish to have brought them out.'

'Did you ever hear of an Englishman called Cobb?' I asked at the end.

He repeated the name but it meant nothing, and then as if from a great distance I heard the dull thud of the knocker on the front door and I knew it was nearly midday and the patients were beginning to arrive, and, anyway, I knew my time with the Reverend Doctor Ford was up, and I bade him farewell again, and again he shuffled after me into the passage.

The plain old housekeeper was at the door, letting in an old couple, the woman dressed in black, a short, white-faced woman with a shawl round her head, leading a rheumy old man by the hand as if he were a three-year-old instead of nearer eighty-three. And in that passage-way, five of us made quite a crowd and suddenly I wanted to be out of it, away from all the Irish double-talk, poverty and sloth, the land of tomorrow and the land of the dead. And I said quickly, 'Good-bye, Doctor, many thanks,' and I squeezed through the crowd, out through the open door and into Kerry Quay Hill and I went downhill at quite a pace.

I looked back to the house but the door had closed. Higher up the hill a big American car moved away from the kerb, and as it gathered speed and passed me I could see it was a Chevrolet taxi, and inside, next to the driver, was a man in a brown suit, red-faced and doubtless sweating hard in the midday sun, and I had no need to look again to know it was Mr Cobb from London Town, and again I said to myself the word *coincidence* and even the silent word had a hollow ring.

I had lunch at the hotel and went up to get my canvas bag. Then, as it was only three o'clock, I went down to the hall and put through a personal call to Wensley. He was through in ten minutes. I said I was coming back that afternoon and would be in the office Sunday, maybe Saturday.

'Any luck?' he asked.

'Nothing much,' I said. 'At least nothing I could put on paper.'

'Don't put it on paper then. Talk about it. Now's as good a time as any.'

'Not yet,' I said. 'A lot of guesswork. It hangs together in the mind, but I've no proof. Nothing.'

'Write it down. Things get clearer that way sometimes.'

I said I'd try.

'Try! Do it! And that's an order. I want that chapter before that old bastard dies.'

'Another twenty years,' I said.

'I'm not so sure,' he said, and I could imagine him waving his arm, gently and forlornly. 'I'm not so sure,' he said again. 'How well did you know that Waterman woman, by the way?'

'So-so,' I said. 'Why?' but he didn't reply and in the silence I said 'Why?' again, and even to me it sounded an odd repetition.

'I just wondered,' Wensley said. 'I should've thought she'd have been worth quite a bit of information.'

'Dead loss,' I said.

'I told you before. You should have slept with her. That's the way to get information from a girl like that. You say you didn't. Why not?'

'A simple and old-fashioned reason you wouldn't understand,' I said. 'I just didn't get around to it.'

'It's old-fashioned all right,' Wensley said from far away, and then he went on with the sudden word, 'Look! I've done a lot for you here,' and his voice was almost paternal. 'Is it so much to ask? Sleep with her. As soon as you get back. Believe me, it's the only way with that bird.'

'How do you know?' I said. 'You haven't met her.'

'She dined at the house in the park last Tuesday. I was up there, too. You've got to hand it to him. He must have coined that phrase about attack-the-best-method-of-defence. He introduced her to me. Explained she was Waterman's official biographer.'

'What did you make of her?' I asked, and I hoped my voice was as casual as a phone could make a voice.

Wensley waited for a second. If he hadn't been an editor he could have been an actor, maybe even a very good one. 'A good-looker. I'll give you that. But Christ, what a neurotic!'

'Is that why I'm supposed to sleep with her?'

'Partly,' he said. 'Sex is a great healer.'

'Not for anything I'm suffering from,' I said, and I hoped the casual note still held my voice.

'Who's talking about you? Why d'you think she went up there?'

'Maybe she likes him?'

'Likes him, hell. She hates his guts. I watched her. I'm a great woman-watcher.'

'Why did he ask her, then? You tell me.'

'That's easy enough. You sent her up there in the first place. Maybe he knows that. Maybe he doesn't. You think he doesn't. You think he thinks it was her idea. Either way he wants to know how much she knows. You said he left the door half open, offered her a job and all that. It's all part of the same scheme. He's keeping a watchful fatherly eye on her, that's all. But why did she go up there? You ought to know. If you don't know you ought to find out.'

'That's where sex-the-great-healer comes in, I suppose?'

'Is it such a price to pay?' Wensley said, still pleading like papa.

'I don't know,' I said. 'No price has been mentioned.'

'You're wasting *my time* and the Baron's *money*!' Wensley said suddenly. 'See you Sunday!' and he hung up.

Well, I had a lot to think about, but I had no time for thinking, so I went back to the lounge and then across to RECEPTION and paid my bill. I also asked the cashier whether Mr Cobb had checked out.

'Half an hour ago,' she said.

I took up my bag and went out to the steps. Ferriter was waiting there, a cigarette drooping from his thick, unshaven mouth. I was silent all the way to the quay. Other thoughts were beginning to take over.

You live your own life the way you want to live it, or think you do, and part of the process is expecting the rest of the world to stay the way you want it to stay, but it doesn't. I'd expected Ruth to stay in Whitehall Mansions. Every evening? I couldn't say. Or had I? Maybe I expected nothing. Certainly not a visit to the Baron.

The afternoon sun and the slow passage down the Bay were oppressive, and I could not stay in the lounge or in my cabin. The moving ship was a prison to the mind. All my thoughts were a long way off.

50

SOMEONE knocks on the door and you stumble awake and a steward comes in and puts down a tray, and gradually thought comes back, *Fishguard and nearly four o'clock in the morning*, and you pull yourself out of the bunk and begin to shave and dress, jerkily, like a character in an old-time flick, and you pack and totter on deck, go through the Customs, come out on the platform and the world is cold clammy flannel.

You walk along the platform, buy some papers and look for an empty carriage, but the train is a row of cold coaches, cold lights and cold faces at the windows. You try to stamp a semblance of blood into your toes, a semblance of warmth into your heart, but the time isn't right, neither is the heart, but you find a coach, put your bag on the rack and sit back, hidden in your coat, and maybe, if your luck is in that day, you sleep again.

And later, hours later, the train jangles into movement, breakfast is called and the world begins to have a more rubious glow. For a moment you can even bear to look out on the huddled Pembrokeshire smallholdings. Gradually you come alive. But only gradually.

So I came alive and followed the steward along the corridor and into the nearly empty restaurant car, past the steward's 'First-class? Straight through, sir,' and then I saw Cobb.

He was alone at a table for two and reading the *Mirror*. I sat down in the opposite seat. He looked up quickly, took up his cup, drank, and went back to the news. The steward leaned over my shoulder, saying, 'Aren't you first-class, sir?' but I said, 'I'll sit here,' and then to Cobb, 'Extraordinary the way we keep bumping into each other.'

He looked up again and it was still a big, red sweating face, even in the chill May morning with the coach just beginning to thaw.

'Is it?' he said. 'I hadn't noticed it meself,' and he flapped the paper open to the inside spread.

'But isn't your name Cobb?' I persisted.

'It is,' he said from behind the paper.

'Don't you remember? We met by the phone booth at the hotel in Cork and I thought we passed each other yesterday on Kerry Quay Hill.'

He put the *Mirror* down. 'You must be making a mistake. I don't know you and I don't know Kerry Quay Hill.'

Then he took the *Mirror* up again.

I mumbled an apology but he didn't answer.

Well, I hadn't got very far with Cobb, I told myself as I got up and walked along to the farther coach, and maybe he was right, maybe he didn't know me from Adam. Where had I seen his face before then, long before Ireland? But the query had no answer, at least not then. I ordered kippers and took up *The Times*.

The train was twenty minutes late into Paddington. I was first off and waited at the barrier for Cobb. He marched along the platform like an overblown sergeant, stiff back, head erect. No glance. No word. I went across to the phone booths and dialled Court House. Miss Arnold was in as I'd expected her to be. She hoped I'd had a pleasant holiday, but I brushed all that aside and asked what news and was Wensley in?

'Why should he be?' she said. 'It's Saturday. But I'll

try.' She tried the house phone while I waited, but there was no reply.

I lunched in the Great Western Hotel, but the room held too many travellers, the plaice held too many bones and my head held too many thoughts. I came out into a bright May day, got a taxi in Praed Street and told the driver Court House, but half-way down Marylebone Road I told him Whitehall Mansions instead.

I sat back in the taxi and wondered why I'd changed my mind, but the reason was there, plain enough and simple enough, and I tried to think of other things, but I was back in London, back from the never-never land, and London now seemed linked with Ruth. The thoughts I'd taken away and carried around for two long weeks had gone for good. I would let things work out the way things always work out. Life would come my way. I'd been too much alone. Things weren't as high-pitched as I'd made them out to be. I'd had too many noggins in the Gresham. I'd had too many since. Now it was all going to be different, the way things are when a man makes his peace, his own particular compromise. Ruth would understand.

Well, those thoughts can carry you along for quite a while, even as far as Charing Cross, and by then I was excited, or almost so, and I paid off the taxi, swung out my canvas bag and went quickly into the hall and along to the lift as if I were starting all over again, right from the beginning. I remember the lift seemed slower even than usual.

I rang but nobody answered. So I put politeness aside, took out the key and let myself into the flat. It had the smell of Mrs Macadam's soap and furniture polish. The living-room, the desk and papers were as neat as a grenadier's kit. A fire was laid in the grate. I went from room to room. Everything was ready for anyone or no one. It was all very neat, but homecomings can be that much too neat.

I scribbled a note, making a date for dinner, signing with my initials in a heart entwined with a hammer and sickle, which I thought was funny. But the humour had a hopeless touch about it, and I knew it, but wouldn't face it. I left my canvas bag, went down in the lift, and walked towards Villiers Street.

At Charing Cross I bought a *Standard*, but there was no news; they were leading with a half-dead UNO story. No one had died, no one was news.

I walked slowly along the Strand with the Saturday crowds, and it was a relaxing spell with only a few dozen buses to dodge and a few thousand citizens to mill against, but finally I was there, or almost there, and I crossed Fleet Street and turned in by the courtway and there was the palace the Baron built out of a few primeval forests.

Miss Arnold was still at lunch and I began to type my copy for Monday's paper. Most of it was the journey: a paragraph about the voyage down the Lee: another about the last meal on board: another about Fishguard Harbour in the very early morning: others about the return to the grime of London: and finally a few reflections on the Irish. You know the sort of stuff. Perhaps you even read it.

Miss Arnold came in about three and I gave her the nylons that were her due. She made her cooing noises, but I cut her short: I wanted the Court House gossip, but it seemed there was none worth having, or none she'd heard, and I said, 'Why are you in today, anyway?'

'You said you'd be back,' she said demurely.

'Well, now let's leave. There's my copy. You can type it tomorrow.'

So we went. I left her by the bus stop and walked along to Chancery Lane, then into Carey Street.

Lincoln's Inn Fields was just the same, and why shouldn't it be? But always the egotistical traveller expects the familiar world to change in his eventful absence, I told myself, as I climbed the bare flights of stairs to my top-floor fastness.

There was a note from Mrs Burton. I'd had no visitors, it seemed: *there have been some phone calls and a lot of letters what I have put on the table with last weeks bill for services rendered thanking you Sir.*

I began to sort the mail: there were letters and cards, but, looking back, I remember no letters, no cards, invitations, no requests, nothing, before I came to the registered envelope. And I recognised the writing. Too slowly I slit the envelope and took out the manilla foolscap folder with the note clipped to the outside cover, and the note was for me and it began with my initial. No *Dear*. No *Darling*. And then the words:

By now I realize what an utter fool I've been. Suddenly at the air station I thought everything would be all right. I didn't begin to doubt until Sunday. Then like a fool I sent that wire. I even phoned the hotel to know if you had booked in. Then I phoned again that night and the next night. And when you didn't phone I knew.

I suppose I knew before, but I persuaded myself otherwise. I suppose it's not your fault. I can't blame you. I dreamed there could be a different life for me if you were part of it. But you weren't looking for anybody, certainly nobody like me, and how you've shown it!

I can see now—only too well—how you didn't want me. You just wanted me for one thing. Not even the usual thing. Just the papers about George and your filthy Baron. Well, I had them all the time as I think you knew

I had them. I could see it in your eyes every time you looked at me. I didn't know at first what you were after. I didn't find the papers until the Wednesday after that first Sunday. I knew from George there was something special I had to find and burn or do what I liked with. But I didn't find them at first. When I did I knew they were what you were after even though I never really read the papers until last night.

Then like a fool I fell for you. I suppose I thought you had the strength I wanted, the strength I never had, but when I begged for help you treated me like a fourteen-year-old schoolgirl who'd had a crush on an old man. I suppose you could never forgive me for having been George's mistress. You said it once—an old man's friend—and you smiled. I never denied it. I knew nothing about life then when I met him. He was kind. But why go on, why should I try to explain now? It's just that I thought things had changed, but I see now. You just wanted the papers and you didn't want me. That's all it adds up to, I suppose. Well, here they are. Do what you like with them. I should have destroyed them, but I don't care now. They'll bring you no peace. They're as rotten as anything I've ever read of in this rotten world. All I hope is that they bring you some of the unhappiness you've brought me.

There was more besides, but it was just the same thing in other words, some hysterical, some sane, the words that have been used in bitterness and gall a million times before, words without end, at least until the world itself ends.

I turned to the file and for the next two hours I was lost in a story I had never thought to see in old-fashioned black-and-white. Part of it I knew. Part of it I'd guessed at, but the rest had been a blank. Even after my morning in the old Cork doctor's surgery there were still blanks, although not so many, but here it was, all of it. Or almost all. Typescript, letters, statutory declarations, enclosures, footnotes, negatives, photographs, captions, covering notes and anything else that was necessary to the job the writer had in mind, and it was quite a piece of research and worth a doctorate from any University Senate, and I went through the contents slowly, turning over the papers, so neatly stabbed and stapled in the left-hand margins.

The first paper was a half-sheet of grey-tinted writing bond die-stamped with old Lavinia's Guildford address, and there in Waterman's script, which I knew by now, were the laconic words: *The following documents were handed to me on the 15th June 1921, in return for 1500 £1 shares in the Metropolitan Printing and Publishing Co. Ltd.*

That was all.

The next entry was a letter typed on two sides of a small sheet of paper from an address in Gordon Square and dated 13th April 1921 and these were the words:

Dear Waterman: You may remember that as special correspondent for various English newspapers, I interviewed you twice in your headquarters near Fermoy while I was in Ireland last year. Arising out of those interviews which were not published at the time, and further enquiries which I need not enlarge upon here, I have today discussed with the editor of the London Daily Mail *(who has since seen Lord Northcliffe) the question of publication of three articles concerning your operations in Southern Ireland. These articles are likely to cause a considerable public outcry as you will see from a glance at the enclosed carbon copy of the first article. The proposed headline (which, I may say, has been discussed and approved) is perhaps somewhat sensational but the articles themselves, although coloured by one or two journalistic phrases, nevertheless present a sober account of what I believe to have been your career in Ireland.*

Publication of these articles would not be likely unless the facts of my story were utterly irrefutable. Of that I am sure you are aware. Yet because I have steadfastly tried to keep to a code of responsibility throughout my journalistic career I propose, somewhat unusually perhaps (even quixotically some might say), to give you the chance to read, in advance, the attack I propose to make upon you in the Daily Mail *next week.*

If you think I have been unfair I shall be prepared to hear your side, but I must inform you, on the highest legal authority, that on the facts contained in my two succeeding articles (which I do not *propose to show you) you will have to leave the country or stand trial for treason.*

I enclose the first article. You will doubtless be aware of the conclusive nature of the evidence in my possession by which I have been enabled to make certain statements in this and the two succeeding articles.

Nevertheless, as I have said, I will willingly hear your story before publication, and would be prepared to publish a fourth article concerning your own version of these events, but that is doubtless a remote possibility.

A note to the above will find me.

The letter was signed by the Baron. He'd carried an old-fashioned plebeian English name then, not a new-fashioned English title. Underneath this letter was a typescript, double-spaced on thin foolscap paper, with a heading in caps: AN ENGLISHMAN WHO DESERVES TO BE HANGED. Then followed the story:

This is the story of George Weston Waterman, a man who calls himself an Englishman, a man who deserves to be hanged.

It is the story of a man who was reared in luxury and ease, a man born to wealth and security, who somehow got twisted on his growth to so-called manhood, so twisted that he could send his fellow-countrymen to death with less compunction than he would have killed a fly.

Let me tell the story of this man.

George Weston Waterman was born in 1883 in the Midlands, the son of a wealthy industrialist. He did not go to school: he was a weakly youth, with poor eyesight and indifferent health. So he stayed at home under the care of a succession of tutors.

In 1902 Waterman entered as a commoner at Balliol College, Oxford. There he read Classics and became a prominent speaker in the undergraduate debates in the Oxford Union. He began to show revolutionary tendencies and a gift for wild invective.

After leaving Oxford, Waterman travelled a great deal in Eastern Europe. He mixed with Russian and other exiles, men of similar outlook to himself, in Switzerland and the South of France. He also wrote many pamphlets, which he had printed at his own expense, calling upon his fellow-revolutionaries to overthrow the existing order.

These things might have been dismissed as the outpourings of an unbalanced and youthful political theorist, and indeed, little attention was paid to Waterman or his pamphlets until the outbreak of war. Then, however, his activities took a more sinister turn, for, although he called himself a pacifist and conscientious objector, he also called upon the workers of England to join in subversive activities to sabotage the country's war effort.

Despite the overwhelming case against him, Waterman was lightly dealt with. He was confined to prison and left to cool his heels with other extreme Left-Wing politicians with more venom in their minds than patriotism.

Immediately after his release from prison at the beginning of 1919 Waterman went to Ireland. There, under the *nom de guerre* of James Mitchell, he quickly joined the Sinn Fein organization and within a few months was enabled, by means known only to himself, to take over command of a group of Irish rebels operating in the South, mainly in County Cork, although their guerilla activities ranged through several counties. He again changed his name, this time to John Mann, although he was more usually known as 'The Englishman' or 'The Duke.'

Assault and robbery, cattle-driving and train-wrecking were part and parcel of his terrorizing tactics. Extreme violence was used mainly against the members of the Royal Irish Constabulary, then against harmless members of the community and against any who spoke for sanity in the conduct of Anglo-Irish affairs. In all this barbaric waste of men and the morale of a nation, Waterman was a known but inconspicuous leader.

His real chance, however, came with the reorganization of the R.I.C. under Sir Nevil Macready in July 1920, the strengthening of the army of the Crown and the introduction of the auxiliary police (known to history as the 'Black and Tans') under Major-General Sir Henry Tudor.

As if these British appointments were a direct and personal affront, Waterman immediately began a campaign which was not equalled throughout the length and breadth of that terror-ridden island. Working anonymously, yet through a network of spies and informers, Waterman increased the scale of his sabotage and murderous guerilla activities and, in addition, was able to ambush, almost at will, members of the police and army throughout the whole of that quarter of Ireland. These are perhaps evils inseparable from civil war, part of the normal practice of warfare, but in Waterman's case this viciousness took a sadistic and inhuman form which must prove incomprehensible to all Englishmen.

This traitor, this so-called son of England, gave to himself the power of life and death over all English prisoners. In the course of several months of careful enquiry I have been able to piece together Waterman's activities, and to prove beyond all possibility of doubt that he gave special orders that all Englishmen were to be brought before him and tried as soon after capture as possible, with himself as the sole prosecutor and judge. Like a man demoniacally possessed he would arraign a dozen captured Englishmen, and in the course of half an hour summarily accuse, sentence and condemn them. There was no appeal. In all cases the men were shot immediately after the inevitable verdict of guilty. Waterman personally supervised the carrying out of his own death sentences.

In my enquiries I have been able to account for Waterman's direct personal responsibility for the deaths of upwards of seventy Englishmen during the past two years. The identities of most of these men are known, and despite the fact that publication of these names will bring pain to many parents and wives in this country, this newspaper believes that such publication is the only course by which one of the most infamous traitors in our history must be brought to justice.

This typescript was followed by two others, one headed A CHALLENGE FROM THE DEAD, the other A MURDERER AT LARGE.

The second article in the projected series of three was a record of deaths and dates, as carefully documented as a register in Somerset House, and it was plain that the Baron had put in a lot of research work in Ireland, and in England, for his CHALLENGE FROM THE DEAD. The list was boring, but it was full and factual, and some of the names carried asterisks and the words *photograph attached*. Then came a batch of small snapshots, all different shapes, like a miscellany from many family albums. Then came duplicates of the prints I had seen in Doctor Ford's decrepit surgery, the same flat attitudes of soldiers caught in death, but these were different, each lifeless image carried a lettered label and I read the labels: PRIVATE P. J. Moss, PRIVATE R. Johnson, CORPORAL M. Pike and so on written above the bodies. Then came a batch of photographs of identity discs and the names were repeated: PRIVATE P. J. Moss, PRIVATE R. Johnson and so on across a monotonous row.

The photographs plainly recorded the deaths of three groups of men shot at different times within a period of two months in 1919. Photographs, names and details concerning twenty-eight soldiers were included in the file.

They made a bulky inset, the large full-plate prints in large white captioned envelopes, the negatives in large manilla envelopes.

Then came the third article, A MURDERER AT LARGE, and this was a challenge to the Law Lords and the House of Commons, and it was all strong stuff beginning:

Yesterday I gave details of some of England's young men murdered by George Weston Waterman, an English Bolshevist, now residing near Guildford in Surrey, a man who should be brought to trial at the earliest possible moment for one of the oldest, foulest and bloodiest crimes—Treason. Today I challenge Waterman to reply to these grave charges. But I know he will not because he cannot. . . .

The article went on, and beneath the rodomontade was a careful building-up of a case that no man so accused could leave to die as a newspaper stunt. The accusations were too bold, the implications too plain for evasion or dissembling. This was a case to be refuted immediately or the accused stood condemned in silence.

Then came another inset, a Statutory Declaration made before one Richard Powell, Commissioner for Oaths:

I, Sergeant Charles John Cobb, formerly of the Royal Kentish Regiment and latterly of the Irish Republican Army, and now residing at 136 Jubilee Crescent, Camden Town, London, N.W.1, do solemnly and sincerely declare as follows:

1. I served in Ireland from July 1917 until November 1920 and during all that time was a member of the Sinn Fein organization, and that from 1919 I was under the command of Commandant G. W. Waterman (known as James Mitchell and also as John Mann) in charge of a detachment of the Irish Republican Army.

2. I finally left the I.R.A. after violent disagreements with Commandant Waterman concerning the conduct of local irregular military activities, in particular the treatment of English prisoners-of-war.

3. These disagreements were concerned with the following incidents:

   (a) An ambush and capture on the 12th May 1919 at the Roth Grange Cross Roads near Fermoy of a detachment of 8 members of the auxiliary police and their summary trial and execution on that day under the orders of Commandant Waterman.

   (b) The capture on 15th August 1919 at Protestant Hill, County Cork, of 7 English members of the Auxiliary Police and their summary trial and execution under the orders of Commandant Waterman on that day.

   (c) The ambush and capture on the 3rd November 1919 at the Derry Hill Headquarters of the Auxiliary Police, County Cork, of 3 English members of the force and their summary trial and execution under the orders of Commandant Waterman on that day.

And so the list went on through (d), (e), (f), (g), seven specified instances of Waterman at work in the wilds of Southern Ireland during 1919 and 1920, and even in those plain black-and-white legalisms it became a monotonous record of a maniac at work. Then at the end was Cobb's final piece.

AND I make this solemn declaration conscientiously believing the same to be true and by virtue of the provisions of the Statutory Declarations Act 1835.

   DECLARED at 177 Doughty Street, London, W.C.1 in the County of London this 4 day of March 1921.

Before me, Richard Bathurst Powell, COMMISSIONER FOR OATHS.

Well, Cobb had been sewn up, too, before the letter

had gone to Waterman. The Baron had worked carefully and cunningly those years before.

I read through to the bitter end and some of it I read again for I wished to have as much in my mind as memory would hold. Then I re-read Waterman's laconic note. Well, he had been outwitted and he had bought the tale at the specified price. The Baron had done a thorough job, a thesis fit to earn a Ph.D., but blackmail sometimes carries other honours and awards and he had gone for those instead.

I closed the file but opened it again to take out Ruth's letter. This I pocketed. This I still have. Then I picked up the envelope again and checked the date. It had been franked and registered the previous day by afternoon post from Dover.

I sat in the armchair for ten more minutes and wondered what step next. I had been given a chapter to write, and here were the facts for the writing of the chapter. Then I did the thing the research man always does. I made a few notes and then took out the portable I kept in Lincoln's Inn Fields and made rough copies of the main items in the Waterman file. I almost wondered why I took the trouble. But force of habit dies hard. Then I got up and crossed to the phone and dialled Court House.

I asked the operator what address the editor had left for week-end panics and he said, 'No out-of-London address, sir. Just the usual, apparently.'

So I phoned him at Dorset Court and the maid answered. Yes, Mr Wensley was at home, what name? and Wensley said immediately from his own extension: 'The traveller returned from the Emerald Isle? Where are you?'

'At home,' I said.

'Come on up,' he said, and it was the office over again and I took the file I'd had from Miss Miles and I went on up: out into Lincoln's Inn Fields, then into Kingsway to find a taxi, and ten minutes later I was crossing the soft pile-carpeted hall of Dorset Court to the lifts, and I went up to the top floor to the Wensleys' penthouse flat.

Wensley came to the door and he was dressed for relaxation: dark blue slacks, blue angora waistcoat, cream shirt and moccasin shoes.

'Why aren't you in the country?' I asked, for he had a cottage somewhere near Newbury.

'I'm going down later. My wife's at a dog show near Reading: showing two of her flyblown pedigree corgis. What the hell's that file you're hugging like a man from a Ministry?'

'It's your chapter,' I said, letting the file drop on a painted console in the hall.

He took it up. 'Let's go in,' he said.

We went into the large lounge, as Mrs Wensley doubtless called it, all in the very best taste, nothing extravagant and nothing to remember: settees and armchairs upholstered in green tweed; draped glazed floral chintz at the windows; a sycamore modernistic sofa table, a few flower paintings in an eighteenth-century French manner, a lot of tinted mirror, flowers in amber-coloured vases.

Wensley moved his arm in a limp embracing curve. 'My wife fancies herself as an interior decorator,' he said. 'I prefer the office myself. Make yourself comfortable, if you can. When d'you write it?'

'I didn't. Waterman and the Baron wrote it between them.'

'Sounds like a game of consequences. Let's see.'

We sat down in armchairs on opposite sides of the electric fire. The room was warm, too warm. Wensley opened the file and began to read slowly through the first entry, Waterman's simple note of introduction, then the letter to Waterman, then the articles, then the photographs. He turned over the papers and the photographs in the slow-swift abstracted manner of someone who has spent a lifetime appraising the worth of a story, the value of a photograph.

I watched him for a while and then got up and went across to the tall windows, opened the steel casements and went out on to the balcony. The view was worth the rent.

London sprawled away to the south, the west and the east: a daze of chimneys, roofs and spires. And below the chimneys, the roofs and the spires were a few million citizens, shopping, sightseeing, sleeping, and maybe even gardening, and I stayed there trying to sort out why I was there, too, but there was no answer to that and I wondered where Ruth was at that moment, and why a Dover postmark?

Gone away. That was all and that was enough. I wondered whether that was best, but I didn't know the answer to that one either. Best for whom? Best for what? And why best, anyway? Bleakness and blankness were beginning to freeze the mind. My mind at that. But behind me, in the big low armchair, Wensley slowly turned the pages of the file, and I stayed where I was and looked.

At last, an hour later, maybe not so long, he closed the file. I heard the plop as the board cover closed and I went in. He said, 'This is a book not a chapter.'

'Value for money,' I said. 'Do I have to write a book now? God forbid.'

'This'll do,' he said. 'This is all I wanted from you, anyway.'

'That's all,' I said.

He smiled. 'How d'you get this?' he asked.

'Mainly by not sleeping with Miss Miles.'

'Every man his own line. So long as it gets results.'

'What will you do with it now?' I asked.

'Nothing *now*. This is for posterity. As journalists we're too much concerned with *now*. This is where I become a man of letters. Drink to my career as a littérateur. Over in the cabinet there. Give me one while you're there. How did you like Ireland?'

'How did the Baron?'

'He liked it. A lot of reader-interest, he said. Especially that stuff about food. Irritates people. We had quite a lot of letters. You know the line. Why can't we do it here? Why must we go on with bulk-buying?'

'Any letters about Georgian architecture?' I asked, giving him his drink.

'None.'

'What will you do with that?' I asked, pointing to the file.

'Keep it.'

'How long?'

'Till I give it to the British Museum. Why did your girl friend cough it up?'

'That's not part of the story,' I said.

Wensley took a deep gulp of his Johnny Walker.

'I think there's another character after this chapter,' I said.

Wensley looked up. 'D'you mean the Baron or the old lady?'

'Both, maybe, but I mean one Cobb. A Cobb is mentioned in the file and a Cobb followed me around in Cork. At least I think he did.'

Wensley laughed. 'It's logical enough,' he said. 'I noticed the name in the file. Cobb's been the Baron's valet and odd-job man for years. A red-faced, bull-necked character?'

'That's the chap,' I said.

But all Wensley said was, 'It all fits together.'

'I thought I'd seen the face before,' I said, 'but I didn't remember where. I still don't.'

'He was hovering around the night we went to dinner. He saw us off the premises when we left early. God knows where the butler was. Remember now?'

In a swift, fading moment I placed the big fat flunkey in his black coat and round, red, shining face as he'd loomed over me as I'd taken my coat, and the front door opening and the wind beginning to howl outside in the park. I remembered all right now.

'How was it I never heard his name?' I asked.

'Be your age,' Wensley said. 'Why should you? You've been to the house three times in four years. You just remembered a glimpse of a face. D'you know the name of the Baron's current popsy?'

'No,' I said.

'Yet it's all round the town. And you call yourself a gossip writer.'

'Journalist,' I corrected.

'Words!' Wensley said, dismissing them all.

'Well, how does it all fit together?' I said. 'You're the Sherlock Holmes today.'

'The Baron bought up Cobb about the time he settled with Waterman. The dates say that. He needed him. He'd probably seen him in Ireland, marked him down as a possible help, and squared him in London. Cobb probably doesn't even know to this day why the Baron was so good to him all those years ago. Probably doesn't even know the journalist who befriended him was the man behind that statutory declaration in the file. Maybe he did. Maybe he didn't. It could easily have been fixed by a snide solicitor without Cobb ever seeing the Baron or knowing he was behind it. Then later, maybe a couple of years later, he went to work for the Baron. And the Baron's had an eye on him ever since. He likes having an eye on people. Have you checked with your Waterman woman why he had her up there to dinner?'

'Not yet,' I said. 'Anyway, why send Cobb to look after me?'

'Why not?' Wensley said. 'It's logical enough. Maybe he thought he'd keep an eye on you, too. It all fits together. When a man begins to get as jittery as the Baron probably is, he's apt to do obvious, simple things. He's apt to use what's near to hand. Cobb's probably loyal enough in his own solid way. He's doubtless got the average sergeant's share of animal cunning. He knows the Cork area. He was unknown to you. Maybe the Baron even put the fear of God in him. Probably told him a journalist was on to his, Cobb's, own early days. It's a wonder you're back so safe in wind and limb. Cobb's a big chap, as I remember him.'

'How often have you met him?'

'Often enough,' Wensley said. 'When I've been haled to the presence in the South of France, or down in Wiltshire. I was amused to read these details of his early life in this,' and he tapped the file.

'You didn't mention it,' I said.

'The chapter's finished as far as you're concerned. You don't want to clutter up your mind with these things. Do you?'

We were silent for a while.

'And now what?' I asked.

'Cobb's probably in Wiltshire by now. Reporting,' Wensley said.

'And then?'

'Nothing.'

'Something,' I said. 'For one thing he'll tell the Baron I met old Dr. Ford.'

'Who's he?'

'The old crank in Cork the Baron got those photographs from.'

'And you met him? Tell me more.'

So I told the tale of Ford, and under the cool appraising eyes of Wensley it sounded a fine old saga from the never-never land. 'So there it is,' I ended. 'I learned a lot that's in that file from old Ford. And I could guess the rest. Maybe Cobb doesn't know who I called on, but it would have been easy enough to find out. Maybe he doesn't know who Ford is, but he must have come across him thirty years ago. The Baron will know all right.'

Wensley considered the low line of whisky in his glass. 'So now the old bastard knows you may know quite a bit, but he doesn't know you've any proof. How could he?'

'He might think I've dug something out of Ford.'

'Only words.'

'Maybe the photographs,' I said.

'It makes it more interesting,' Wensley said, 'but this is the only thing that really matters,' and he tapped the file, and again he turned through the pages and the insets, studying the photographs, holding the negatives against the light. Then he lumbered up from his chair. 'I'd better be getting down to Berkshire,' he said. 'I said I'd be there for supper. Why don't you come down? There's a spare room.'

I had something to do, I said.

He took up the file and went from the room. 'Say good-bye to this,' he said.

'For now or for ever?'

'For ever,' he said. 'It goes into the Wensley family vault along with a few other unrecorded items.'

'I wonder why Waterman kept it?' I asked as Wensley came back empty-handed.

'He bought it,' Wensley said laconically. 'I suppose he thought he might as well keep it. People keep the things they buy. Noticed? Even after they're no longer useful. Maybe he bought that secretary woman of his. He kept her, didn't he?'

The words and the thoughts stayed with me all the evening. And the thoughts were there when I let myself into the flat in Whitehall Mansions again that night, switched on the lights, went into the living-room and saw my so-funny note of the morning still lying on the desk. And the joke by then was as empty as the flat itself, and I took it up and screwed it into kindling for the fireplace, and then went along the corridor into the room that Ruth had made her own, but the room was as neat as a room in a nursing-home waiting for a patient, and the wardrobe was as bare. She had gone all right.

And later, much later, I took up my canvas bag and went, and as I walked back along the Embankment, up through Arundel Street, and crossed by St Clement's, my mood was a text-book case for manics, the classic anticlimax, the first fine careless flatness after the job is done. And what a job at that!

And as I walked through Kingsway and passed two constables in the black shadows of the Stoll I thought of the job itself, and even in the pellucid light of the moon I couldn't make it more than a few odd scraps of knowledge, part of a mosaic of two men's lives, and even those odd scraps I hadn't collected myself and never would have collected if they hadn't fallen plumb into my lap.

And I thought of the other partners in the deal. Waterman in his distant grave. The Baron on his Wiltshire farm. Wensley in his Berkshire cottage.

And Ruth where?

Wensley had got what he wanted, as he doubtless always got what he wanted. The Baron was where he'd been for nigh on thirty flourishing years, peaceful and prosperous, with his papers and his profits. And Waterman . . . he didn't care any more.

That left Ruth and me. Perhaps we hadn't even stood a chance. The shades of Waterman, then Wensley, then the Baron had seen to that. I wondered where she might have gone. A Dover postmark might mean anything. There were places enough. Even back to Tito and his merry men. I could follow her, of course. But where and how? I wasn't the Errol Flynn type. For one thing I had a newspaper column to fill every weekday morning.

51

THE next day was Sunday, the day of rest, so I rested, and after I'd phoned Whitehall Mansions half a dozen times with no result, I went out and lunched and got down to Court House some time after three o'clock. As soon as I reached my room I could sniff the smell of panic and Miss Arnold said, 'The editor's been ringing.'

'Often?'

'Twice in ten minutes.'

'A rise!' I said. 'I thought that Irish stuff was good, too, didn't you?' but she didn't answer and I dialled the house phone, and Wensley's voice said, 'Come on in. The Baron's upstairs and he wants to see us both.'

'The Baron! Sunday!' I said.

'Cut out the commentary and come on in.'

So I went on in, down two flights, and Wensley was standing by his desk, waiting, and he said, 'Queer, that old bastard here on a Sunday. Hasn't happened in years. There's probably something in what you said yesterday. Sunday visits always spell trouble, God rot his soul. Well, we'll see.' His voice was as quiet as a man's in prayer.

I thought it was queer, too, but I stayed quiet as my views weren't in demand, and we went out and along to the lift and up to the twelfth floor and there were some more swing doors and just there, athwart the corridor, a cubicle with two commissionaires inside, and one, a tall, thin citizen with a long grey face, stepped out and said, 'Good afternoon, sir,' and he turned and led on as if he'd been expecting us.

Up there even the corridors changed. They were wider and higher and panelled in British Honduras mahogany, or so the legend said, and the carpets were deeper, like clouds sprung on clouds, and then the commissionaire stopped and I came out of my cloudy daze and we were in Miss Wilson's room and she stepped from behind her streamlined desk with its three white phones, said, 'Oh yes, Mr Wensley,' and came round the desk, round the dictaphone, round the armchair, across to the other door, and I wondered why she was working Sunday. Everybody was too damned energetic.

She was tall and dark with a face and a figure like all the faces and figures you see in *Vogue* or *Harper's*: fine bones, fine legs and a fine thin mouth that comes from years of saying 'No.' She probably had a home, maybe she even had a husband, even children, but you forgot those things when you met Miss Wilson. You thought only how well she guarded the Baron within, but that day she had other orders and she opened the door and showed us in. Straight in.

Well, it was quite a room. I always thought the Baron had read somewhere how Northcliffe said, 'Big rooms, big ideas,' for the room stretched away like a cantilevered railway station on a new electric line, and there, at the far end, was the Baron and he had risen from his desk and he was smiling in a genial gruesome way, and he said, 'Glad to see you both. Sit down and I'll tell you what's on my mind.'

So we sat, and those chairs, too, were big, too big, too deep and too soft, just like the chairs in the house in the park, and you went down and down, and maybe that was the idea, for when you were all at peace, or near enough, the Baron was there above you, perched comfortably at his desk a foot or so above your topmost eye level. I wouldn't know. I've never been a Baron with a handful of newspapers and a staff to keep in order. So I sat there and looked him over and he was much the same as I'd seen him at the dinner six weeks before. His jowls were as heavy, his head was as bald and his eyes were as cold.

I looked around as we took our cigarettes and the room was unchanged from the year before when I'd been here last: the massive walnut bookcases and the monumental globe, the great span of windows and the table spread with papers, and, dominating all, the big desk before us with the Baron in command. And behind him, through one of the windows, seeming just next door, was the dome of St Paul's, and from here you could begin to see something of the picture Wren had in mind before a few local landlords had begun to take a hand, but the Baron had started and he had started on me with a fixed cold look but some reassuring words.

'I liked your Irish feature,' he said quietly. 'It had a lot of reader-interest. The stories were about people, real people, and, of course, they interested people. Don't you agree, Wensley?'

'I do indeed, sir,' Wensley said.

'There's too little of that sort of reporting these days,' the Baron went on, and it was plain he was in a mood to talk. 'Journalists seem too anxious to tell us about themselves, too dull to tell us about other people. Yet when somebody comes along and writes real stories about real people they wonder why their own stories are so dull. . . .'

I sat and listened and wondered what was coming, and I thought, *This line leads to nothing worth having that I know*, but he was saying, 'We have too little of that lively writing in the Group as a whole, and . . .'—here he looked at me again—'. . . I've been wondering how we can use your obvious talent to its best advantage.'

I sat looking on and I could have been a visitor and not the man in question, so coldly did the words come. Probably I blushed dutifully, and I glanced at Wensley.

He was seated in the dark red leather armchair looking like a Michelin tyre as dressed by Savile Row, and he was smiling thinly as if he knew what was coming and would appreciate it when it came, and then the Baron was taking up the story again and he said, 'I've been perturbed by the quality of the copy we're getting from America,' and as he said 'America' I could see the plan, as simple and neat as a blueprint for a villa, and it was a natural, and I looked at Wensley but he was just sitting and watching the Baron, and the Baron was saying, 'Foster is good, but I've come to the conclusion he isn't good enough.

There's this vast continent and you for one, Wensley, aren't getting more than two American stories a day out of him.'

'Not from Foster,' Wensley said. 'I do from the agencies.'

The Baron nodded. 'Yes, but it's the personal note the agencies lack, and it's the personal note Foster lacks. Perhaps he's not enough of an egoist. Iddon's worth a good deal to the *Mail*. Cooke's the best reading in the *Guardian*. D'you read him regularly?'

'Every morning, sir.'

'What did you think of that baseball feature yesterday?'

Here it comes, I thought, but I needn't have bothered, for Wensley said, 'Personally, I thought he was rather hard on Di Maggio, sir,' and they both smiled like two fat killer cats on a narrow, narrow fence.

'Well, you see what I'm driving at,' the Baron said. 'I want that kind of personal reporting for my newspapers. We can use it throughout the Group.' He turned to me: 'How does the idea appeal to you? Of course you would have a roving commission. You wouldn't be expected to sit in New York. In fact, I'd insist that you didn't. I want someone to get up and get around that continent. Foster's too comfortably married. That's been his trouble all along. What do you say?'

I said it sounded like an interesting venture. The Baron turned to Wensley and asked what he thought of the idea.

'Fine idea for the Group, sir, but who am I to put on to *Objects and Subjects*?'

'Find someone. You're good at that sort of thing. A shake-up does us all good from time to time. There's many things to work out, but it's been in my mind for some time.'

I sat thinking of New York, wondering whether I'd like it as a place to work in, and I didn't take to the idea. I'd been to New York twice before, once in peace-time, once in the war. New York's not America, I told myself, but it's quite a goodly part of it, and I remembered no place like Lincoln's Inn Fields, not even Washington Square, but the Baron would get his way. He wasn't the editor, but he held the tricks and the money-bags, and who was I but a hired hack, and he could buy them anywhere? and suddenly I wondered whether Ruth would like New York, especially in one of those damned, stifling, dreadful summers, but those were day dreams all right.

The Baron had risen from his chair behind the great dark desk, and he was saying, 'That's fine, then. I'm glad you see it that way. I thought you would. You'll make your arrangements with Wensley and the Foreign Department, but I'd like you there within the next few weeks. By the end of the month. That will give you almost three weeks.'

We all stood up but the Baron put up the flat of his hand to Wensley. 'No, stay on, David,' he said. 'I've one or two things I want to talk over. This and some others,' and he came round the desk, shook me by the hand and led the way across the deep pile to the door, and he opened the door, and as he opened it, he said, loud enough for Wensley to hear, 'By the way, I had a note from your friend Miss Miles yesterday. I gather she sent you some papers which should have come to me. Let me have them back as soon as you can, will you?' and his voice was as curt as any order ever was.

Some things you remember all your life, and maybe even after. The words and the tone and the way your heart stops, and the way cold air begins to stir within the room, and the long, long silence of the second after the words. And I clearly remember the way the furniture stood around the room as if it had stood that way for a thousand years and I'd seen it every day, just that way, in all that time. You remember your thoughts, too, or maybe the way you stopped having any thoughts. I remembered the words I had read in Ruth's letter: *I hope they bring you some of the unhappiness you've brought me.* Well, she had started off all right if this was the beginning and not the end already.

I looked into the outer office and Miss Wilson was there, sitting at her desk like a well-chiselled Sphinx, and I looked back to the office I was still inside and there was Wensley, still in his armchair, carefully considering the ceiling and drawing on one of his Ankara specials, and even as I looked he glanced over his shoulder at the pair of us, and I said, 'I don't quite understand, sir.'

'I think you do,' the Baron said. 'Miss Miles wrote to me on Friday evening saying she'd sent you certain papers written by me some years ago. As they were my property, I should like them back. I don't even know why she sent them to you. That is all. I should like them back this afternoon.'

Well, it was the millionaire newspaper owner talking to his hack all right. His voice had the clipped, authentic note, and I wondered what the answer was. Maybe no answer but just get out and think it over, and smile a bent smile at Ruth's rich revenge, but from his armchair Wensley spoke and his voice was as quiet as a curate's talking to his dean. 'I'm afraid that's not possible, sir,' he said.

The Baron swung round and for the first time he moved that much too quickly for a man that much sure of himself, and he barked, 'What do you mean, not possible?'

'I mean they're in my possession,' Wensley said.

The Baron closed the door and I watched Miss Wilson as the door shut her away, and then the three of us were alone in the big quiet office again, and the Baron walked slowly back to his desk and I watched him, and I looked past him, through the window he walked towards, and St Paul's looked very near.

He sat down and picked up a heavy silver paper-knife and he began to trace a lost, wandering shape on the tooled leather top. I could see. I was the only one standing. Wensley was still deep in the armchair, still enjoying his cigarette.

And the room had the homely, cosy touch of a morgue.

'Perhaps you'll explain, Wensley,' the Baron said. 'So far, I confess, it all eludes me.'

Wensley shifted his great bulk from one cheek to the other and sighed gently as if the effort hurt, even in that chair, and then he said, all in his own good time, 'It's really as simple as I said just now, sir. I've got the papers I think you're discussing.'

'You've got papers that belong to me!' the Baron said, and then he laughed shortly. 'Well, if they're the same papers Miss Miles wrote to me about, you can return them. It makes no difference who has them so long as I get them back this afternoon.'

'They're locked up, sir, and I thought I'd keep them that way,' Wensley said.

'With what idea?'

'No particular idea.'

'You don't deny that these papers are my property?'

'I'm afraid I do, sir. You sold them to Waterman. Waterman gave them to Miss Miles. Miss Miles passed them on. Now I've got them. Willingly given. No coercion. I think that gives me a clear case for possession.'

The Baron had listened as the words ticked off, and he let them pass, even that word 'sold,' which stung into the room like an asp.

I watched them both from where I stood. The Baron's face wasn't as red as it had been a quarter of an hour before. Wensley's face was paler, too, a shade more the colour of linen, a shade less the colour of lard, but that was all. They had both forgotten me and I wondered which of them would remember first, but I need not have bothered with this egotistical thought: they had a game of their own to play and it was well into its stride as the Baron said again, but in a quieter voice, 'What exactly have you in mind, Wensley?'

Wensley said, 'I should say you know exactly what I have in mind.'

'If you're after what I think you're after, blackmail's the only word I know for it,' the Baron said.

'It's as good as any other,' Wensley said, unmoved.

'And what makes you think you can get away with it?' the Baron barked.

'Just one thing,' Wensley said. 'There's a telephone on your desk. Dial 999.'

Perhaps the Baron was an actor. I suppose any man in business for millions has his histrionic moments. Or maybe he was gambler enough to know the game was showing signs of running against him and it was time to play another line. Whatever it was, the old high note came back again and he said in a voice like a rising wind, 'Don't talk to me like that, Wensley. Remember who you are and where you are. And remember it's a dangerous bloody game you're trying to play. It's brought down bigger men than you. And tougher. And that goes for the pair of you.'

But Wensley didn't answer.

And it was plain the Baron had expected an answer. And when it didn't come he was at sea for a moment, but not a long moment, and his voice went quickly on, 'You needn't think I haven't known your game these last few weeks.' He swung round on me. 'First, that old Mrs Waterman line. Then your Irish jaunt. Then this Miss Miles mystery. But it won't work!' His voice was rising fast as he turned back on Wensley. 'It won't work! Get that? You must think I'm a bloody fool. By God, I'll break the pair of you like a pair of bloody match-boxes.' Maybe he had got the line he wanted, for he came to his climax like a tornado from the South, and he yelled, 'Now, get out! And I want your resignation by the morning, Wensley.' He looked across to me again. 'Yours, too. Both of you, you cheapjack bloody pair. No, goddamit, I'll have them now. This afternoon before you leave the building. Sewell will see you in the morning to settle your contracts.'

The room was quiet the way the world is quiet after the thunderclap dies and it was quiet for a long second or maybe two. Then Wensley said, 'I don't think so, and I'll tell you why. A: I'm not the resigning sort. B: You don't stand a dog's chance, and I'll tell you why.'

He lifted his spreading shape from out of the chair and he lifted it the way you'd lift a wet sack with grappling irons, and then he sat up on the broad arm of the chair, took his cigarette-case from his inside pocket, took out another Ankara special, lit and watched as the smoke came about him like a plume from a power-house stack. And both his listeners watched.

And we both listened as he began in a voice like a tired

old college lecturer's: 'Listen! And I'll tell you precisely why you don't stand a dog's chance. Go back thirty years. Thirty years ago you got Waterman where you wanted him. He'd come back to this country from a brave career in Ireland. You knew how brave and so did he. But no one else did. And he didn't know you knew. So he came back. He was going to start a new life. He had it all taped. He wanted to stay on in this country. He thought he had work to do—like a lot of other Reds. He thought this place was made for him after his training in Ireland and what had been happening in Russia. Like a lot of other people, he thought the English revolution was just around the corner. Maybe he saw himself as the English Lenin. Maybe a lot of things. Then suddenly he found you were the nigger in the woodpile. He'd kept pretty quiet, but not quiet enough. And when you put your piece to him he saw it the way you wanted him to see it. As you saw it. You could have got him run out of this country. Maybe even got him hanged. I don't know. You thought so, and he thought so, too. You built up a pretty foolproof case, and with Carson and Birkenhead on your side—and you could probably have roped 'em in on a case like that—you could have smashed him like . . . like a match-box. Yes, match-box will do.'

The Baron was sitting back in his chair. He had put the paper-knife down by now and his hands were resting on the top of the desk, bent like an old man's hands in cramp, and then the fingers unhinged and they moved stiffly to the edge of the desk, and began to grip the moulding tight, and he was staring at Wensley like a man who stares at the teller of a tale that will not let the listener go, and his pale eyes were as hard and fixed and cold as a pair of grey or blue glass marbles. I couldn't say which. But Wensley was going on, and it was a tale he was plainly enjoying: 'So you dropped a note to Waterman. Remember? The thirteenth of April, nineteen hundred and twenty-one. Then Waterman really knew you held the cards. You fixed your price and he bought it. He was buying time. He needed time. He wanted to stay in this country. Maybe he thought he'd be the Big White Chief within ten years. Maybe he thought it was cheap at the price. So you moved in on the Waterman properties, or, at least, the one you had your eye on.'

Some of it was bluff, but how much? Not a thimbleful as I saw it. The tale was there: bits in Bush House, bits in old Ford's bleak surgery, and all that really mattered in the Waterman file. Even the odd bits and pieces that weren't recorded there were plain between the double-spaced typewritten lines, and Wensley's eyes were sharp enough to read the simple invisible words, and now they came out, bold and black as his own black 8B lead.

'Well, the rest was up to you. The Metropolitan Printing Company gave you what you wanted and it was quite a property. You did the rest. You did a good job— by Fleet Street standards. But like a tomfool murderer who will go back to spy the spot again, you went back to Waterman. Not while he lived but when he was dead. You wrote the piece the day he died. It was a natural thing to do, but it was an odd thing to do. So I asked myself "Why?" You get into the habit of asking why in my job. And I smelt a story. I'd smelt it twice before when you put stops on wartime Waterman pieces. Remember? Well, you know the rest. . . .'

It was a sudden end to a story that had promised to be a long, long tale, and the silence was like the silence in the great sky when the engine of the plane cuts out, and in the hush the Baron reached across and took a cigarette out of the chased silver box, and, as he lit and snapped his

Ronson shut, he said, 'Well, what do you propose to do? There's damn little you can do about it, even if your story's true.'

'There's plenty I can do about it,' Wensley said, 'and you know it. There's a dozen M.P.s who wouldn't say "No" to the papers in the case. Just to keep around. There's a couple of sixpenny weeklies. There's two or three dailies and maybe one or two Sundays. And I could even write the tale myself. You'll need a definitive biography one day. Say two years after you're dead. And I'm the one with the story. The only one.'

'Who's to say it's true?'

'It's true all right,' Wensley said. 'Otherwise you wouldn't have sent Cobb after it.'

'That bloody fool!' the Baron said, but his voice was quiet, the voice of a man who wants to be reasonable, who doesn't want a coarse, unholy scene, the voice of the man who wants to get things straight, and it was a small voice, coming from a tight, thin-lipped mouth, and it was as pitiful and sad as the last hiss of any snake, and Wensley said, 'So you see, there's plenty I can do, and you know it. I'll talk about that, and some other things,' and he turned to me and said, 'Your copy will be late,' and he waved his hand limply towards the door, and maybe I muttered agreement, and maybe I didn't, but what I didn't say was my copy for Monday was ready. I went.

I went down to the seventh floor to my pigeon coop, and Miss Arnold was there and she said, 'Your copy will be running late if you're not careful.'

'So everyone's keen on telling me,' I said, and I pulled the typescript towards me.

And two hours later when the house phone went and

the voice said, 'Come on in!' I went on in, down two flights, and Wensley had a proof of the leader page on the desk and he was going through *Objects and Subjects* with his 8B lead, and he said, 'This Irish interlude must have upset you. You're three inches over.'

'I can cut,' I said.

'I've done it,' he said, and then, 'Sit down.'

I crossed to the settee and sat down, and he said, 'How will you like the States?'

'So I'm still going?'

'Why not?'

'I thought you might have other ideas.'

'Why should I?'

'No reason. Just an odd thought. One can't help having them sometimes.'

He watched me for a long slow minute.

'There's no alternative, then?' I said at last, to break the silence.

'Should there be?' he asked. 'What would you suggest?'

'I quite like it here,' I said, and even to me the words sounded like a gramophone needle in the same old groove.

'Look!' he said suddenly as if he'd decided to cut short the cat-and-mouse game. 'From tomorrow morning— in fact, from an hour ago—I'm Managing Director and Editor-in-Chief of this outfit. The whole bloody Group!' He waved his arm loosely and forlornly before him, but loose as it was it took in the room, the building and everything in sight, and forlorn as it was, it took in me, too, and I said the obvious thing, the simple, worn, old-fashioned word, 'Congratulations!'

'Don't be funny,' he said, 'but now ask yourself why there's no alternative. Hanging around here you might get ideas. You've heard a lot. You know a lot. Maybe you've even learned a lot.'

'I don't think I'd be much good at it,' I said.

'People learn,' he said. 'Fast. Especially after watching other people. As I see it, you'd be better off three thousand miles away. And I'd sleep safer.'

'You'd sleep safe through anything!' I said, and perhaps my voice was as bitter as the thought, but all he said was, 'That's the way I like it.'

'And if I don't,' I said.

'You'll resign.'

'You mean the sack.'

'Harsh words,' he said, 'unnecessarily harsh. I should ask you to resign. There'd be a handsome sum for breaking your contract. The usual Fleet Street gag. How long have you got to run?'

'About two years,' I said.

'You'd be sitting pretty,' Wensley said. 'Two years' money as a lump sum. No income tax. Loss of earnings and all that. Think it over. You'll never have a better chance to get hold of some capital. You'll never save that much. You could rest for a bit. Travel a bit. Then get another job. Think about it.'

'Till when?'

'Till tomorrow morning.'

'You're very generous,' I said.

He smiled the tired smile and again we were silent until I said, 'Have you thought? I might have taken copies of the stuff I gave you.'

'You'd be a mug if you hadn't,' he said.

I laughed. 'I didn't do it thoroughly enough.'

'People learn,' he said. 'You'll do better next time.' He was interested for a moment, almost the technical adviser on the finer aspects of the art.

'As a matter of interest,' I said, 'what about the Baron?'

'It's all very simple and logical,' he explained. 'He'll take more time off as Chairman. I'll do more work. After all, he's getting on. He sees that. He ought to take more time off.'

'He's lucky to have you around,' I said, but Wensley wouldn't bite.

'He sees that, too,' was all he said.

'And the new editor here?'

'A man who will listen to me.'

'And the new man for *Objects and Subjects?*'

'Another man who will listen to me,' he said, the tired smile back again.

'You seem to have worked out the pattern,' I said.

He lumbered up from the chair like an elephant rising from the sawdust ring, and I knew the interview was getting near the end. 'So-so,' he said. 'It was a logical step. For me and the Baron. This job had its limitations. Any editor's has. Managing Director's the only job worth having in an outfit like this. And Editor-in-Chief. Both. With a share of the stock, of course. There's more scope that way. More security.'

'More money,' I said.

'It comes with the job,' he said simply, and then almost as an afterthought which wasn't quite an afterthought, he asked, 'Now what about you? Have you thought it over?'

'I've got till tomorrow morning,' I said. 'Remember?'

'I'd almost forgotten,' he said. 'It's a long time. I was too generous. I've got decisions to make. One or two depend on your decision. Staff. Salaries. Stuff like that.'

'Your job must be very interesting,' I said.

'It will be,' he said, and I knew the day was done.

Well, a story begins any time, any place you want it to begin, and maybe it ends that way too, and maybe my story ended there, in Wensley's room, that Sunday evening, or maybe later that Sunday night when I let myself into the empty Whitehall flat again and it was still an empty flat, as I knew it would be, no note, no clothes, no bags, nothing; or maybe the following day when Oliphant said he had no news and no forwarding address; or maybe ten days later when I went aboard the Pan-Am Constellation, first stop Shannon, then Gander, then New York; or maybe in New York itself and the States beyond, grinding out new angles on the New World news.

Or maybe it really ended ten months later, a year ago, that day I'd finished with the air-mail edition of the London *Times* and glanced as usual down the personal ads and saw, away to the left in the *Marriages* column, the words in five-point type that bawled out loud like poster type, the words I came to know like a player in Rep: GIORGIADES: MILES. On March 25th at St Paul's Church, Athens, Georgios Ioannis Giorgiades and Ruth Helen Miles.

Well, it had been a long journey for Ruth, from White-hall Mansions to a church in Athens, and I wondered how she'd made the trip and whether Georgios was young or old, rich or poor, thin or fat, Left or Right, and I wondered where they'd met, and a hundred other things.

Well, hers had been a long, long journey and mine had been a longer journey still: from Court House, Fleet Street, to 48th and Lexington, New York. Just two journeys among a million others that hadn't ended in lovers' meetings.

I sat on wondering for quite a while, but rented offices

on the seventeenth floor of a New York daily's office-block aren't the best background for such fanciful moments and after a time I gave it up. There was no answer, anyway. And there were cables to send.

But a man can have his thoughts.